Dolores Stewart Riccio

The Divine Circle of

LADIES
PLAYING
WITH FIRE

The 5th Cass Shipton Adventure

ISBN: 1-4392-3686-0
ISBN-13: 9781439236864

Visit www.anhonorablerun.com to order additional copies.

For Anna Morin,
a very special sister...

And with loving thanks to my husband Rick
for giving his support, enthusiasm, and inspiration to all my works

A NOTE TO THE READER

This is a work of fiction. The characters, dialogue, events, businesses, love affairs, criminal activities, herbal remedies, love potions, and magic spells have been created from my imagination. Menus and recipes, however, may have been taken from actual kitchens, probably my own. Plymouth, Massachusetts, is real place, but some of the streets and locales in the *Circle* books are my inventions. Greenpeace, too, is a true crusading organization, but any misadventures here described are fictional.

In a series like this, families keep growing, changing, and becoming more complicated with time, so that even the author has to keep copious notes. For my fifth *Circle* book, therefore, I'm including a cast of primary characters and their families—to be consulted when confusion reigns. It will be found at the back of this book.

— *DSR*

PROLOGUE

A hooded figure slipped silently out of the dark pines and dashed toward the burning stable where horses were screaming in terror. Firefighters, who had just roared into the stable's driveway and were jumping off their trucks, shouted at him but he paid no attention. He ran swiftly and surely, never hesitating even when the heat and acrid odor of the fire hit him in the face. As he sprinted forward, he stripped off his jacket and grabbed one of the halters hanging outside the barn door. With the aid of the halter and the jacket as a blindfold, he pulled the first horse he encountered, a trumpeting stallion, out of the stable door to safety. Someone grabbed the horse and led it into a fenced paddock, and the man darted back into the stable. Three times he entered the burning building until the roof collapsed on the remaining animals. When the shrieks and the stench of burning flesh had subsided, Fire Chief Mick Finn wanted to thank the hero who'd rescued three of the eighteen horses being boarded at the stable, but the man had disappeared into the woods from which he'd come.

None of the firefighters, not even Finn, had got a close look at the man, whose features were obscured with a balaclava. Onlookers described the rescuer as being of medium height and build. One woman among the flock of spectators claimed to have seen a man with a similar gait and bearing somewhere in town. She couldn't recollect precisely where, however; he had something to do with medicine or art supplies—or maybe it was books, she said.

Pilgrim Times.   January 13.

ARSON RULED OUT IN DEADLY STABLE BLAZE.   A fire that killed fifteen horses at Fresh Meadow Farm in Plymouth, most of them boarded by various local owners, appears accidental. Preliminary findings show last week's fire could have been sparked by an electrical malfunction or spontaneous combustion in wood shavings, a common bedding in horse stalls, said Ed Dulinski, deputy commissioner of the state Department of Housing, Buildings, and Construction. No evidence was found of the use of an accelerant. Captain Mick Finn of the Plymouth Fire Department, however, has expressed dissatisfaction with the deputy commissioner's findings and declares the investigation to be ongoing.

Owners of Fresh Meadow Farm Richard and Susan Churchill were at Jordan Hospital where Richard is recuperating from hip surgery when the fire occurred. They, too, expressed doubt about Dulinski's report. A recent inspection found Fresh Meadow's electrical system up to code. Richard Churchill noted that wood chips were among the few items not burned to ashes in the ruins. But Dulinski said, "They're not going to be totally consumed. Fire burns upward and outward. My heart goes out to the Churchills. I hope they recover from this tragic loss."

Twelve horses perished in the stable on Fresh Meadow Road, three escaped but had to be euthanized because of their injuries, and three were rescued from the conflagration and are in good condition.

I believe in the practice and philosophy of what we have agreed to call magic...in the visions of truth in the depth of the mind when the eyes are closed...that the borders of our minds are ever shifting, and that many minds can flow into one another...and that our memories are part of one great memory, the memory of Nature herself.

– W. B. Yeats
Ideas of Good and Evil

ESBAT OF THE WOLF MOON
CHAPTER ONE

Some say the world will end in fire,
Some say ice.
From what I've tasted of desire,
I hold with those who favor fire.

— Robert Frost

"So, do *you* believe in reincarnation?" I asked my friend and mentor Fiona Ritchie. I'd come to consult her at the Black Hill Branch Library, a cozy bungalow furnished with warm aged oak, where she was sole librarian on the three days a week it was open. As usual, the few patrons had cleared out early; we had the place, to ourselves except for her Persian cat, Omar Khayyám, who was draped across the top of a bookcase, studying the scene through slitted copper-colored eyes.

"In a manner of speaking, I do. But not in the simplistic *I-was-Cleopatra* way. To me, it's more like tuning in to a sympathetic vibration among all the storied lives of the past. Time being eternally present, as the old masters taught and the new physics confirms." Her wise gray eyes studied me over half-tracks perched on her nose. She was calm and focused; there was only one pencil stuck in her coronet of braids. On days of supreme stress (and we'd had a few of those) as many as three pencils and a crochet needle might wind up in her carroty-gray hair. "Why don't you ask me your real question, Cass. What's on your mind, my dear?"

"Dreams. Nightmares, really," I said as she poured hot, spicy ginger tea into thistle-painted mugs. The many silver bangles on her plump arms jingled softly. "In the dreams I've been having lately, sometimes I find myself trapped in a burning building, a huge empty place like an abandoned factory. Other times I'm tied to a tree. Fire is inching across the clearing, igniting fallen pine needles and creeping toward my legs. A cloud of acrid smoke is choking me. I feel the terrible heat, smell the pine sap. I struggle and scream but I can't free myself and no one comes to help me." I shuddered as the aura of the nightmare smothered me again in clouds of fear. "I suppose I ought to take this as a particularly vivid clairvoyant dream not a personal threat, but it feels personal. I began to wonder...if in some past life in Europe maybe... well, you know."

"You wonder if you were burned as a witch," Fiona said calmly. "Just because we've chosen to form a Wiccan circle in this life doesn't mean we followed the same path in an earlier existence, if any. You may very well have been a Buddhist monk or a Jesuit priest. Although I have to admit I find the notion of a Jesuit Cass difficult to imagine." Chuckling in that deep infectious way that I could never resist joining with a nervous giggle of my own, she opened a tartan tin and offered me a homemade shortbread cookie.

This was the moment for which Omar had been waiting. He sprang down from his watching place and landed smack in the middle of Fiona's desk causing her PC to buzz in an agitated manner and her Tiffany dragonfly lamp to wobble dangerously. I steadied the lamp. Fiona lifted Omar off the desk and dropped him into her ample lap. "Does Mommy's little precious want a piece of shortbread?"

Before Omar could profit from his feline acrobatics, however, he found himself unceremoniously dumped on the floor as Fiona and I sprang up from our chairs and ran to the windows, galvanized into action by the escalating shriek of Plymouth's fire alarm.

"I think we can take this," Fiona said, "as a little Cosmic nudge. We know you're subject to clairvoyant visions. We're sitting here talking about your recent fiery nightmares, and now the fire alarm goes off. Ergo: you're onto something, Cass."

"Where is it? Where is it?" I was saying. "Oh sweet Goddess, I hope they save the animals."

"What animals?"

"I don't know. It was just a flash. Went by too fast." People who think a clairvoyant episode is easy to interpret have never had to tangle with the mishmash of insight, intuition, vision, and nausea that I do when the insight strikes.

Immediately Fiona was on the phone calling the firehouse, where she has special influence due to Mick Finn, the Fire Chief, being so sweet on her. "Hi. Fiona Ritchie here at the library. Heard the alarm and got worried Sounded *real* close. Oh, yes? Oh, really? Okay. Thanks a lot, you've set my mind to rest—just that old warehouse. Who owns the eyesore, anyway? Well, it must be part of the town records— I'll look it up. Thanks anyway." She put down the receiver. "It's not too terrible, Cass—no animals, no people, and no stock to speak of—this time"

We sipped and nibbled thoughtfully for a few moments. "Animals in danger, hmmm," Fiona said. "Can you say, at least, whether this is a past or future event?"

"Ah, Fiona, that eternal present you were talking about—that's clairvoyant time. So...not a clue."

Fiona was already turning to her computer and keying a search subject into Google. A minute later she exclaimed, "Oh, look at this item, Cass. *Pilgrim Times*. Just a few days ago, on the 13th, you remember—there was a stable fire at Fresh Meadow Farm. Maybe that's what your visioning is all about. Mick's so frustrated that he hasn't found any evidence of arson, poor baby. But you ought to consult Heather. She'll know all about it."

"Yes, of course I remember that Fresh Meadow fire." Staring at the desk lamp I felt myself slipping into an all-too-familiar fugue state. Certainty came over me. "But I'm sensing another event. I know it's the future. And I see a shadowy figure. There's an impression of evil. It's arson, for sure." I was half-aware that my voice had taken on a dreamy tone.

"Very good, Cass." Fiona nodded approval. "Keep probing until you get a clearer picture. Maybe this coming disaster is preventable."

Our circle of five, after all, has been in the unofficial business of bringing evil-doers to justice for a few years now. A little sleuthing, a little spell-work, a lot of luck, and we had ourselves a pretty effective (if unorthodox) crime-busting unit. "I'll check, but you know Heather. If I suggest some pervert is going to harm animals, she'll be up in her widow's walk room making black candles again."

ରେ

"If I could have zeroed in on the wicked monster who set that fire, I would personally hex him into the next century and beyond!" Heather Devlin (nee Morgan) balled up my computer copy of the *Pilgrim Times* article into a missile and fired it at the waste basket. Her hazel eyes flashed dangerously.

"Banish that hex from your thoughts," I advised. "You know that it will only return threefold to haunt you. Maybe the fire fiend's own evil karma will follow him into his future lives."

"Maybe I could help him to depart this life a little sooner," she declared, giving the wastebasket a vicious kick for good measure with her faux alligator boots. Cruelty to animals tends to bring out Heather's most vengeful impulses. We were in her office at Animal Lovers, the pet sanctuary she supports with her substantial trust income. As a Morgan whose ancestors made a fortune in the China trade, Heather enjoys near royalty status in Plymouth, which has often proved useful in our past escapades.

"Arson is Mick Finn's idea based on no evidence, as far as I can find out," I said. "Dulinski believes it was accidental, but Finn's claiming it's a suspicious fire and calling for the State Fire Marshal to investigate. These guys are specially trained detectives. So really we can release our concerns into their capable hands," I added, hoping to bring a calming influence to bear before Heather started up with the candles and curses. Truth to tell, though, I knew right then that the investigators would find little or no evidence of this clever arsonist.

My sure knowing, when it comes, often appears like
a minute film, flickering pictures in my mind's eye, the
invisible clairvoyant eye in the middle of my forehead, the
sixth chakra. Sometimes just a quick image that flashes and
fades in an instant. As we were talking, I had "seen" a man's
gloved hand pushing together wood chips, pouring a liquid
over the pile, taking a lighter out of his pocket, flicking it
into flame. I had "heard" a horse whinnying, striking his
hooves against the stall door as the vision faded.

"*Earth to Cass, Earth to Cass,*" I heard Heather saying.
"What's wrong with your eyes? Going into one of your
creative comas again?"

I didn't speak for a moment as the old nausea gripped me.
Breathe in, breathe out... slowly the feeling passed. "Yeah," I
said. "Now don't go off the deep end, but I know Mick Finn
is right. There is a devil setting fires in Plymouth. More than
that, I've seen an event in the future in which other animals
may be involved."

She grabbed her camouflage cell phone out of the safari
vest she was wearing. "I'll call Mick Finn right now."

"What are you going to tell him? That my eyes rolled back
in my head and I spoke some arsonist's name in tongues."

Heather stopped punching numbers but she was still
holding the cell. "Actually your eyes *did* roll back a little.
You know that I'm against capital punishment, but in this
case I could make an exception." I was glad to see she aborted
the first call and punched in number one. That would be her
husband Dick Devlin, the holistic vet—a marriage made in
heaven. "Cass has that stable fire at Fresh Meadow wrapped,"
she said by way of greeting. "Oh, sorry, honey—you're doing
what? Gee, that's tough. Yes, Cass says it was no accident.

And worse, she's sensing some future tragedy also involving animals. So, you know, the circle is going to have to get into this."

"Esbat," I said. Full moon, January 25. Esbat of the Wolf Moon.

∾

"I'm giving up cooking for good," Phillipa said, banging her favorite wooden spoon on the saucepan in which she was gently cooking lemon curd for tarts. The spoon was worn thin as a clam shell. The tarts were laid out on a rack on her immense marble table, each perfect in color, form, and texture. Not for nothing was her cable cooking show called *Kitchen Magic*.

"You're kidding." I certainly hoped that she was.

"Oh, I won't quit whipping up pastries and whatnot," she admitted, realizing what she was indeed doing at that very moment. "I'm giving up *writing cookbooks*. I'm giving up the show. I'm going to concentrate on my poetry from now on."

"Ow, not the show! My only claim to fame is that I know someone with a TV show!"

"Ha ha. Your claim to fame, dear Cass, is inveigling the circle into criminal investigations and embarrassing my beloved."

The slight conflict to which Phillipa alluded was that Stone Stern, her husband, a detective with the Plymouth County State Police Unit in Middleboro, often finds himself investigating the same cases in which we five also are taking a lively interest. And sometimes in our messing about, we get to a solution first. But Stone is a gentlemanly sort and has got used to me. To us. The circle.

"Anyway, that's what Raoul says."

"Raoul who? Says what?" I asked.

"Hasn't Fiona told you that she's started a poets' group at the Black Hill branch? The Erato Poetry Club. Raoul's the guy we elected to be president. He's the only one who's had a book published. *We Drowned at Dawn*. Raoul Lazaro. Cuban refugee."

"And the only man in the group?"

"Well, yes. You know how women are."

"Yeah. But you go right ahead and pander to the male ego. So what exactly did this Raoul say?"

I realized right then it has been years since I'd seen Phillipa blush, which she was doing right that moment. The color had a softening affect on her high cheekbones. Phillipa has the kind of severe but alluring features that distinguish some fashion models. On a routine police call to investigate a shot fired through Heather's front window, Detective Stern had been smitten the moment he saw Phillipa smile. She leaned forward now so that the raven wings of her hair covered the telltale flush of heat. "He said that I need to give myself completely. You know, *to poetry*."

"Sure he did. Has Stone met Raoul yet?"

"Oh, give me a break. It's not a *thing*. It's an aesthetic friendship."

"It's not a *fling*, you mean. Sure I believe you. Got a bridge, maybe the Bourne, you want to sell me now?"

Phillipa was gently stirring the lemon curd to cool it faster so that she could fill the tart shells. It always amazed me to see the patience she lavished on pastries, considering her edgy nature. "Cass, I'm simply sick and tired of being a culinary artist. Talk about ephemeral. People polish off your work of art in a few minutes, and then what have you got? A rapidly fading memory. But poetry now...a great poem might live for a thousand years."

"We never know what may be remembered—or forgotten—about our lives."

"Oh, don't go all karmic on me. Cappuccino?"

"I thought you'd never ask. Listen, Phil, would you have a look at the tarot for me? I'm sensing something terrible. No details yet, but it's arson and there are animals involved. Again."

"Oh, shit! I hate that. Zelda? Zelda!" Phillipa began to obsess over her own black cat, a waif once rescued from a dumpster who was now the best-fed fat cat in Plymouth or maybe the world. Zelda glided suavely in from the living room and jumped onto the marble table. She was swiftly but gently removed, however, before one tart shell could be assaulted. "Have you *seen* whodunit?" Zelda's mommy asked me.

"Just a gloved hand—and a lighter—starting that stable fire at Fresh Meadow Farm. And the next one, I'm feeling *that* in the pit of my stomach. Not a vision, though."

Phillipa reached for the red silk bag that protected her Ryder deck from bad vibes. A rough piece of sodalite to enhance psychic awareness fell out with the cards. "Let's see what we can see, then." Zelda jumped into her lap and settled down purring. Phillipa scratched the cat's silky tummy absently. "We'll have to put a stop to this sick bastard, that's for sure."

Not surprisingly, the reading was entirely wands and swords. Action and menace. Especially menacing was the card that depicts a heart with the three swords stuck through it. Phillipa calls it the Heartbreak Special. Phillipa is a whiz at the tarot, especially when she's not so much looking at the cards as seeing through them.

∽

"Mick Finn is beside himself," Deidre said, sticking a needle firmly into the poppet she was making. (Into the seam not the heart. We work on the white side.) Deidre is our mistress of craft, amulets, and poppets. Her husband Will Ryan, recently promoted to Deputy Fire Chief, is another direct pipeline to the firehouse.

"Sort of a doppleganger," I commented, stirring whiskey into my weak tea, anything to give it a flavor. Fortunately, Deidre usually offers "a drop of the Irish" to accompany her insipid brew.

"Well, *both of him,* then, are convinced that he's dealing with arson of the worst sort, because only a real nutcase sets fire to a building with live animals in it. If it was arson, of course. Dulinski says no. Hard to prove without finding one of the usual accelerants. But they don't always, that's what I hear. Anyway, what I've been dying to tell you is that now that I have Bettikins, *I can go back to work, hooray!*"

Betti Kinsey is Deidre's au pair who appeared out of nowhere in answer, we're convinced, to a "call" from the circle. As it happened, she bore an uncanny resemblance to one of the magical dolls Deidre had been creating—the one named Bettikins. Some would dismiss this as a coincidence, but we Wiccans know better. This is the way the Universe of Infinite Solutions should work, and does—if you succeed in tuning into its energy.

"Wonderful! Back to the vitamin shoppe at the mall?"

"Naw, that management gig was scooped up by someone else as soon as I left. I haven't decided yet. Maybe I'll open my own doll shop and keep the internet business, too."

"You're going out to work just as Phil is quitting the cooking business."

"For what?"

"For poetry. Urged on by Raoul, president of the Erato Poetry Club."

"Uh-oh," said Deidre. We might have had more to say about Raoul but just then the Ryan bunch trooped into the house from the backyard. With Jenny, Will Jr., Bobby, the two toy poodles Salty and Peppy, and Bettikins merrily stamping off snow and giggling and/or barking, suddenly the neat yellow kitchen seemed more like a crowded school bus. I thought I would get out of there before Baby Anne woke up from her nap to add her own share of noise to the melee. I have three children myself, but they're grown now, and I like it that way.

"So happy for you. I'm sure a doll store at Massasoit Mall will be a big success. Gotta go now. My two fellas are waiting for me. What are you going to call it?" I shouted over the merry din.

"Spells 'R Us?"

"You're kidding."

"Yes. I'm going to name it Deidre's Faeryland, same as my internet shop.

"Yeah, well take it easy on the anatomically correct dollies this time. At least avoid unfavorable publicity until you get well established."

"Don't be so quick to banish them to the back room, like the so-called adult videos at Pryde's Video Place." Deidre's baby blue eyes were twinkling and a dimple flickered in her cheek. I didn't have to be clairvoyant to know that she would welcome any publicity, even if it were adverse. "Besides, I've a dynamite idea for using toddler dolls with the correct waterworks for toilet training. I'm calling my little guy Tommy Tinkle. Comes with his own doll-size training potty and instructional pop-up book. And Tillie Tinkle, too, of course. What do you think?"

Well, it could have been worse. What if she decided to open a daycare establishment where sooner or later she would be suspected of teaching Satanic doctrine to the little darlings—and of other evil doings. So many people still confuse modern Wiccans with Satan's mythical minions.

"See you at the Esbat," I said as I made my escape from the Ryan bedlam.

CHAPTER TWO

That orbed maiden with white fire laden,
Whom mortals call the moon.

– Percy Bysshe Shelley

Alas, only my dogs awaited me at home—Scruffy and his offspring Raffles. My husband, Joe Ulysses, is a ship's engineer for Greenpeace, meaning he does anything and everything needed to keep his ship in good order. Right now he was on the northwest coast of Sumatra where a Greenpeace crew was helping Medecins Sans Frontieres to bring supplies to areas devastated by the Indian Ocean Earthquake. Not the usual Greenpeace mission—it's not an aid organization—but the *Rainbow Warrior* was in the region. The ship with its crew of nineteen was able to reach remote areas with needed relief, so it had been enlisted into the rescue effort.

Occasionally Joe could steal a little time on the ship's computer to send an email, and sometimes he called, but mostly I had to muddle through on faith. We'd been married for two years, but I wouldn't want to add up the number of days we'd actually spent together. Much as I admired the quixotic adventures of Greenpeace, I longed for the time when Joe's compact muscular body with its steady warmth and its sensuous scent of sun-warm herbs would be in my bed again. With all these separations, however, every moment together still had the aura of a honeymoon.

As soon as I opened the kitchen door, Scruffy bolted onto the porch and out the pet door into the snow. Raffles, the gawky half-grown spit-and-image of Scruffy, dashed after his sire but was not quite quick enough. The adolescent pup sat down on his rump and looked back at me with innocent confusion as if he had never seen a pet door before. Okay, I opened it for him. A doorman for dogs, that's me.

Scruffy was dancing around in the icy yard where my perennial herb gardens were sleeping under the white comforter of snow. *Ow, ow, wow...it's cold out here. My pee is freezing on the tree. Why can't I have indoor accommodations?*

"Because you're not a namby-pamby toy dog," I explained. "Run around for a minute, you couch potato. Exercise the pup. Get the blood circulating. Work up an appetite for din-din."

That mangy mutt—who needs him? Why don't you just bundle him back to the blonde bitch.

Raffles' mama, Honeycomb, a registered therapy dog who belonged to Heather, had been scheduled to breed with another prize golden retriever before being spayed. Heather and I were still blaming one another (and Dick was blaming us both) for the royal miscalculation that had allowed Scruffy to get there first and sire a litter of cute but mixed breed pups. After their birth, the previously playful Honeycomb had taken to giving Scruffy a curled lip and barely audible growl that signified a canine cold shoulder. Since Heather had insisted that I make a home for one or more of the unplanned litter, I had chosen the irresistible Scruffy-look-alike. Scruffy Sr. was not amused.

"You'd miss Raffles, and you know it. He's good company when I have to be away. Dogs prefer to live in packs, all the experts say so. "

Having piddled awkwardly in the general direction of a bush, with half a squat and half a leg lift, Raffles was now gleefully nosing the fluffy snow, tossing it up into the air and biting the refreshing iciness as it fell back on his snout. Scruffy stared at him incredulously.

Yeah, sure, Toots. We had it pretty good here, when it was just you and me. First you bring home that furry-faced guy and now this dumbledog.

"If I didn't know that you're a secure, mature character, I'd think you're a wee bit jealous of that adorable pup."

Well, sure I talk to the dog, and I believe I hear him talking to me, whether in my head or in actuality, I couldn't say without getting into a long dissertation about the nature of reality. Suffice to say what every dog lover knows: *if we listen, they will talk.*

Scruffy started to stalk off with injured dignity, but just then a bold squirrel sneaking up on a bird feeder caught his eye, and the chase was on. Raffles wobbled after, merrily following in the paternal paw prints.

༺❦༻

With Scruffy and Raffles as my early warning system, I didn't need that tremulous knock on my back door to tell me that I had a visitor, and the visitor was a stranger.

"Hi, Ms. Shipton? I'm Sylvie. I need help, and I hear you're the person to see, being a witch and all."

A flash of *deja vu* zoomed across my consciousness. In just this way had I met the irrepressible Freddie who later became my daughter-in-law. Well, I'd had only one son to donate to the distressed maidens of the world—so what else could happen?

The willowy young woman leaning against the doorframe looked as if she'd been blown there by a gust of wind off the Atlantic. Her long light brown hair seemed to have silvery-green highlights; it swirled around the shoulders of her flimsy jacket (trimmed with what I hoped wasn't kitten fur). Instantly I was caught and held by her wild green eyes Not dark hazel-green like mine, but the pure clear green of a mossy pool.

"Wiccan, Sylvie. I belong to a Wiccan study group, sort of like a book club"—my regular low-profile reply to doorstep gambits like this one, just in case this undernourished gal was on an evangelistic witch hunt. "...but I don't know how that will help you. May I ask who suggested you contact me?"

"Mrs. Peacedale over at Gethsemane. She said you'd be the local expert in automatic writing, possession, and weird stuff like that."

Patty Peacedale, the minister's wife, bless her heart, often consulted me on parish problems since I was safely outside the church grapevine. Okay. I was fond of Patty and so would take a chance on Sylvie. "Well, then, come on in, dear, and I'll make some nice hot tea. Looks to me as if you could do with a warm-up. Then you can tell me more about your, eh, troublesome phenomena."

After several warning *woofs* through the half-opened door, Scruffy was checking out the suspicious fur around the stranger's coat hem. *Ick. She smells like a pile of dead leaves. Why don't you sweep her back out the door?* Raffles was nuzzling the half-tied green sneakers, pulling experimentally on one of the lacings.

"Scruffy and his son Raffles," I introduced my two nosy mutts. "I apologize for Scruffy's excessive interest in your coat. Might be the fur. Some foreign makers trim garments with kitten fur."

Yeah, some long dead hairball for sure.   No one I knew, though.

"Oh, no. I'm sure it's faux fur, Ms. Shipton. I'm very careful about being kind to animals and all. Nice doggie, nice doggie." Sylvie sat gingerly on the edge of a kitchen chair and looked around. I looked around with her, sensing her apprehension, seeing the place through her fearful eyes. Jars of anonymous leafy stuff, bundles of dried sweet basil, oregano, sage, and lavender hanging from the wooden beams, fresh pots of rosemary, mint, and parsley burgeoning on the kitchen windowsill, kettle steaming, fat bayberry candle burning on the table,—could be worse, meaning more witchy. .

"So," I said, spooning one of my new tea blends into the pot—I call it Peaceful Heart—and pouring in near-boiling filtered water, "what's all this about automatic writing?" I set the table with two bone china mugs, lemon, honey, and a plate of Joe Froggers, chewy molasses cookies of old New England.

"It's this weird thing that keeps happening to me. Sometimes when I have a pen in my hand and get distracted—you know how that can happen. Maybe there's a noise or you lose your train of thought, whatever. Anyway, so maybe I'm writing a shopping list or something and I get diverted for a moment—the pen will start writing all by itself. Too fast for me to follow. Right off the paper, too. It's scary, like I'm possessed, you know what I'm saying? Really bizarre. Drives my boyfriend nuts."

Deliberately, I laid my hand over hers where it was resting on the table. Physical contact often tells me much more than I want to know, but right now I was following a hunch. Yes, a moment after I touched Sylvie's cold white hand I saw and almost felt the cruel stinging slap against the side of her head, delivered by an irate boyfriend whose macho aura came right through to me. Well, we'd have to get rid of *that* bozo. In some white magic way, of course. Maybe a humming spell. I drew my hand away and poured the tea. The scent of mint, chamomile, cardamom, and whatever else I'd added to the mix in an inspired moment, wafted into the air—aromatherapy for the soul.

"Smells funny," said Sylvie as she lifted the mug toward her fine thin nose.

"It's herb tea, dear. Try stirring in a little honey and a slice of lemon. And have a cookie with it."

Sylvie put the mug back down on the table, the tea untasted. "Want to see?"

"Sure," I said.

She began rummaging around in the woven bag she'd hung on the back of her chair and came up with a Sharpie. "Damn! I thought I brought my notebook."

I got up, rummaged though my kitchen desk, and grabbed an order form for *Cassandra Shipton, Earthlore Herbal Preparations and Cruelty-free Cosmetics.* Ripping off a few pages, I turned them to the blank side and handed them to Sylvie.

She began to write her name over and over in a fair round hand, like a kindergarten teacher's: *Sylvia E. Waldes. Sylvia E. Waldes. Sylvia E. Waldes.*

"What's the E stand for?" I asked.

She looked up, startled out of some private reverie. "Oh. Elana. My grandmother on my mother's side. My father's mother was Sylvia."

Out of the corner of my eye, I could see that her hand was still writing, was in fact writing faster and faster, covering the back of the order slip and onto my kitchen table. Keeping our eye contact, I shoved another page under her flying pen. "That's a lovely combination of names."

"English. German. Romani. I know I don't look Romani. I take after my dad's family there, though I always wished I had my mom's gypsy coloring." Sylvie looked down as if suddenly becoming aware of what her hand was doing. Yet it was she who had suggested this demonstration. Bigot that I am, the word "gypsy" made me wonder if this was some kind of psychic scam.

"Where is your family now? Are they local?" I don't know what I was picturing. Covered wagons and golden earrings in Jenkins Park?

"Dad's gone. Mom's dead of cancer," she said flatly, offering no further explanation.

"So, you live in Plymouth then?" I pried carefully around this closed shell.

"Uh-huh."

"And you—what?—go to school? work here in town?"

"Yeah. I work at Finch's Floribunda in Plymouth Center. Got that small apartment above the shop. Me and my cat

Misty. That's short for Mistletoe." She pushed over the pages to me. There was a gap where the words had gone on writing themselves on my kitchen table. The handwriting was bold, strongly slanted, with high pointed capitals and sweeping downstrokes, completely different from that chaste gentle *Sylvia E. Waldes.*

I read the script, in which the letters were all run together, with difficulty, mouthing the words as you might a poem, but not saying them aloud. *"I am dance of fire I am transforming force I am winged phoenix I am blaze of death I destroy and renew I am..."*

Here there was a break in the script until it continued on the second sheet of paper. *"...my trust my mission my faith I take unto myself the unclean and make them pure and true again..."*

Great Goddess! Was I sitting here calmly having tea with another firebug like the one who'd destroyed the Fresh Meadow stable?

Something of this horrifying thought must have shown in my face, because Sylvie said, "It's not me, Ms. Shipton. It's not me writing whatever it says. That's what I don't understand. That's why I came to you."

I couldn't stifle the deep sigh that came right from my third chakra. *Okay, I believe her. I'm in it now.*

"Call me Cass, please. Do you know what's written on these pages, Sylvie?" *And on my kitchen table, too,* I was thinking. I'd have to decipher the rest of the message before I attacked the table with my orange peel polish.

"It's about fire. That's all I know. But I could feel a sort of heat when I was writing, as if my hand were being singed. I had to keep writing faster because of the burning. I know that sounds crazy. Should I read it now, do you think?"

I passed her the pages, curious to know what her reaction would be.

"Oh, golly," Sylvie said, wrinkling her high narrow brow. "Some nutcase. Am I like, *The Three Faces of Eve?*" She drank deeply of her now cold cup of tea.

"No, because you don't change personalities and become, say, Syl, Jill, and Bill. This is definitely automatic writing. Multiple personalities are a whole other thing. The writing is a paranormal manifestation, though. I hope that doesn't alarm you." I refilled her mug as if to press calmness upon her.

But Sylvie gazed at me serenely, her green eyes fringed with barely brown lashes, seemingly unmoved by my diagnosis. Without exactly looking, she reached out and tapped lightly on the kitchen table with her knuckles. That was a gesture I'd seen before. My Druid friend Meave knocked on wood from time to time to summon the tree spirits.

"What shall I do, then?"

"It depends. Do you want this manifestation to cease? It would be difficult, but it could be done. Or do you want to keep on channeling this fire-obsessed personality and perhaps solve some mysteries connected to him, if there are any? Or would you rather change channels and hope for a nobler or at least more sensible entity to speak through your writings? That's what is supposed to happen to automatic writers."

"Golly," she said, still rapping on the table from time to time. "So you think I might actually, like, help to stop this person, if he's real? Fire is such a horrid hurtful thing."

Of course it is, I thought. *Wood is her talisman, her charm. Fire is her enemy.* I touched her hand again, to reassure, and to be sure. "Now, Sylvie, there's a young man in the picture, right?"

Her pale cheeks flushed ashes-of-roses, and I could read her thought, *Yikes, she* is *a witch!* Looking at me apprehensively, she said, "Not any more. We were living together, but I left him for good when I took the job at Floribunda. Nick doesn't even know where I am."

"Good," I said. I was still reading her hand. "Because he hurt you, and Misty, too, didn't he?"

"But how...did you know, Mrs. Shipton?"

"Cass. Call me Cass. Because, Sylvie, similar to your talent for automatic writing, I have the talent of clairvoyance, which means clear seeing. Also like you, my talent isn't always convenient or easy. But I've learned to live with it, and so will you."

After we'd made an appointment to confer again about the girl's automatic writing—actually, I wanted to delve into the subject with Fiona, the better to guide the girl wisely—Sylvie left and I called Patty.

"Hell-o! Patty Peacedale here," was the musical response from the parsonage.

"Hi. It's Cass. Sylvie Waldes just left here, and I wanted to ask you what you know about her before I get into this too deeply."

"Oh, she's a *lovely* girl. Lutheran, you know, but *lovely*." Patty's husband Wyn is the minister of the nearby Presbyterian Church, The Garden of Gethsemane. "Being worked to death by those Finches over at the flower shop. Minimum wages, of course—they have to pay *that* much. But then they take most of it back in rent for that pernicious little apartment. Well, I'm working on Wyn to do *something* supportive. Why can't we build a really nice Christian hostel for young ladies, I asked him. Well, not just Christians. For *any* girl who needs a *homey* home away from home. And he said he would broach the idea to the Craig Foundation. So I said to him, let's not beat around the burning bush, Wyn—you *are* the Craig Foundation."

"How did you happen to meet Sylvie and learn about her problem?" I asked, hoping to get Patty back on track.

"Oh yes. Let me see. I met Sylvie at this ecumenical *do*—the Season of Light and Love Carnival and Craft Show. She was working at the Protestant Posies booth—that girl has *such* a green thumb. Anyway, we got to talking about *euphorbia millii splendens* and *maranta*."

"Crown of Thorns and Prayer Plant," I murmured.

"Yes, indeed, and apparently I should really be allowing the soil in my maranta to dry out completely between waterings in winter. But you must be familiar with all that, dear, aren't you?"

As Patty knows, not only did I major in plant science at the University of Rhode Island, I'm descended from a long line of herbalists on the Shipton side.

"So you got off plants and onto the paranormal...how?"

"When she heard I'm a minister's wife, she was suddenly desperate to talk about the funny writing thing she does, and right away I thought of you. And I felt you wouldn't mind if I sent Sylvie along. You've helped so many young people, I just think you have a touch of the Mother Teresa about you!"

This was a notion of Patty's that I would have to nip in the bud. But for now, I couldn't bring myself to Bonsai her enthusiasm.

"I'll see what I can do, Patty," I promised. "And I'll probably be bringing her to meet the circle. At our January moon get-together."

"Oh, capital!" caroled Patty. "Say a prayer for me, too."

"Okay. Anything special?"

"No, no, dear, I'm just fine. But you can never have too much of a good thing, I always say."

That's what I loved about Patty—her faith was big enough to include everyone, including Wiccans around the corner who were celebrating the full moon Esbat.

CHAPTER THREE

Nymph, in thy orisons
Be all my sins remembered.

—William Shakespeare

"In automatic writing, a person channels the higher self or some spiritual guide," said Fiona firmly. "Not the local pyromaniac."

Fiona knows everything (Phillipa always says that Fiona should be bound in volumes) and is the official "finder" of our Wiccan circle. Not only does she amass tons of trivia in the ordinary course of her profession, but she's also a reference goddess who understands exactly how and where to locate information that is not currently stored in her head.

Some of that information might be found spilling out of the curious green reticule from which she is never parted, crammed as it is with esoteric pamphlets as well as butterscotch candies and childcare supplies. Since taking on the custody of her grandniece Laura Belle, Fiona has reluctantly given up carrying the pistol left to her by her late husband, *we hope*— we never really know what she'll pull out of that bulging tote bag. Many times in the past, Phillipa has tried to impress on

Fiona that cayenne pepper spray makes a good substitute for an unregistered Colt forty-five.

"Maybe it's just a case of crossed wires—you know, like when you pick up someone's cell phone conversation by mistake. And I never said he was local," I declared. "But I have a strong feeling he's very much of this time and place."

"Well, anytime you have a strong feeling, Cass, it has to be respected, I'll give you that. But what about this girl, this Sylvie whom you say is channeling a pyromaniac person? What was your impression of her?" Fiona heaved herself out of her reading chair and made her way to the little kitchen in her fishnet-draped cottage in Plymouth center. As she lifted the kettle off a burner, Omar sidled between her ankles, trying (and failing) to look famished.

I hesitated, letting visions form into words, which they are sometimes reluctant to do. "What can you tell me about dryads?" I asked through the open kitchen door.

"Woodland nymph. Tree spirit."

"There's more than a hint of the dryad about Sylvie."

"Well, my dear, there's her name for one thing.

"Oh, yes, Sylvia...Sylvan you mean."

"And Waldes. That's German for forest." Fiona laid the tea tray on the much-scarred cherry coffee table, and we waited for the lapsang souchon to steep. "And her middle name, Elana, didn't you say?"

"Yes."

"The meaning of Elana is a tree."

"Well, that's wildly coincidental. So, what else, Fiona?"

Fiona searched the memory banks of her mind. "A true dryad will be nearly invisible when standing among trees.

And she's self-healing—a neat trick, eh? Her anathema, of course, is fire. Fits, doesn't it?"

I could feel the chill of things to come walking down my back like an ice-footed lizard.

"But let's keep one foot in reality here...this is a girl not a sprite. It's just that..." I was at a loss for words

"It's her aura, you mean. Something of the dryad in her aura?"

"Yes, that's it. Although I have to confess that I can't see auras."

"No clairvoyant is perfect. Since the girl's been sent to you for counseling, you may as well bring he to the Esbat of the Wolf Moon and we'll all have a look at her."

"Okay. Good idea." I had already planned to do just that, hoping Sylvie was made of sterner stuff than the wan maiden she looked to be and could take our raucous five in stride.

A van stopped outside and honked lightly. Fiona rushed to the door to retrieve Laura Belle fresh from nursery school. She helped the four-year-old peel off the many layers of winter life-support clothing in which she'd been swathed. The little girl smiled her rose-petal smile and hugged her great aunt. Over Fiona's shoulder, Laura Belle's eyes were the color of morning glories at dawn.

"Tea, Fifi," she said. Laura Belle was not one to waste words. In fact, she rarely spoke. Fiona fixed her a cup of Cambric Tea well sweetened with honey. Conversation now centered on the little girl and the nursery school where Fiona hoped she would become more social and voluble. We said no more about dryads that day, and with what happened later that week—another arson!—I forgot to worry how Sylvie would fare at the Esbat ritual.

∾

In January, tourist attractions in Plymouth are mostly closed up tight, including Soule's Grist Mill. Although it's still a working mill in a limited way, activities grind to a halt from December through February. The sprawling gray clapboard building housed a waterwheel-driven mill that still produced cornmeal and rye flour the way it did in 1680. The mill suffered some fire damage in 1842 but was rebuilt after the Civil War by new owners, John and Emily Fletcher, and the business has remained in the Fletcher family until the present day (still known as Soule's, or sometimes Olde Soule's, since property names rarely change in Plymouth.) Nowadays, most of the mill's revenues came not from the sale of its specialty flours but from the tourist trade and the gift shop where one could purchase Olde Soule mugs and commemorative plates, flour sack aprons, natural grain cookbooks, a cardboard grist mill for the kids to put together, and so forth.

When the mill burned for the second time two days before our Esbat, it was clearly a case of arson, there being no wood chips to blame. A trace of accelerant was found under the wooden stairs to the office. No human was in the mill at the time, but two Manx cats, excellent mousers belonging to the owner, Buddy Fletcher, perished in the conflagration. Heather was fit to be tied.

"Couldn't that bastard have left the door open so the cats could escape?" she cried. Her tall graceful figure paced back and forth in my living room, the long bronze braid swinging angrily over the creamy Irish sweater and Harris tweed slacks. You have to have a really neat seat to wear that outfit and not look baggy. Heather looked terrific.

"Don't forget that families of plump innocent mice also fried in the fire." Perched on the windowseat, Phillipa was attired for this event in her signature black, turtleneck and wool pants, the scarlet silk tarot bag dangling from her waist. We were celebrating the January Esbat in the oil-heated comfort of my place, a cozy Cape Cod house of the saltbox style that I'd inherited from Grandma Shipton. It had the advantage of overlooking the Atlantic where later that evening we would view the rise of the full moon over the ocean from my architecturally-incorrect back porch.

Our guest Sylvie Waldes huddled in a wing chair near the blazing fireplace, looking nervously from witch to witch, proving again the power of generations of negative press. *She must be chilled right through*, I thought, studying her thin sage-colored skirt and sweater. Plastered against her legs, Raffles was doing his best to keep the new girl warm and get some pats in the bargain. Disdaining such overt maneuvers, Scruffy plopped down in the middle of the braided rug where everyone would have to walk around him. *Someone ought to teach that putty pup some canine reserve.*

"You have to admit that he has excellent people skills," I said.

"Who? The arsonist?" Deidre said pertly from the other fireplace-flanking chair.

"She's talking to Scruffy," Fiona explained. In her coat sweater of many colors and gaily striped skirt, the reticule propped beside her, she occupied most of the sofa.

"Our very own Dr. Doolittle," Phillipa added, humming a few bars of "talk to the animals."

"Have you told everyone about your decision to abandon your cooking career, Phil? Encouraged by Raoul, of course." I calculated that would put my friend in the hot seat for a bit.

Phillipa was equal to the challenge. "Yes, and I've packed away all my *Kitchen Magic* reference and videos. Even my precious notes for future shows. I feel there's no going back now," she said smugly.

"You're responsible for this," I said to Fiona. "You started that poetry club with Raoul and the desperate housewives. Let it be on your conscience."

"My conscience is pure as the driven you-know-what," said Fiona. "I follow the forgive-yourself-as-you-go spiritual path, which if you did, too, you'd be a lot less critical."

"Wow!" said Deidre. "Great notion. But I think it would be good if we ceased chatting about our personal stuff now and gave Sylvie some help with the problem she's brought to us this Esbat. Automatic writing, is it, Sylvie?"

"Yes, but it's funny," whispered Sylvie. "I don't feel right after. I think it's like being possessed, so what I'd like is if you ladies would exorcise the demon that's using my Sharpie."

Fiona, of course, was drawing an applicable pamphlet out of her reticule. It was titled *Exorcism—Twelve Steps to a Demon-free You*.

"I don't see this as a case of possession," I said firmly. Sometimes my friends tend to move too fast—*hex in haste, repent in leisure.* "I think it's a form of clairvoyance, the written equivalent of my visions. Sylvie, do you think you could give us a demonstration?"

"All right, I'll try. Or rather*, not try*, that's how it happens." Sylvie coiled closer to herself in the wing chair, curved like an ivy vine. "Where?"

"Here's okay, I think. What you need is a table." I took a wooden tray table from the stack reserved for dinners in front of television and set it up in front of Sylvie. Having learned from the first demonstration, I brought a legal-size pad of paper from my office. I brought a pen, too, but Sylvie reached in her Floribunda tote for the favorite Sharpie. That might be important, I thought. A touchstone of sorts. She gripped the pen in the fist of her left hand. I made a mental note to check if that was her "automatic" hand. Had she written left-handed before and I never noticed? *Sinister. Gauche* So many negatives are associated with lefties. Was her normal dominant hand the right or the left?

Poising the pen over the pad, she looked around the room shyly. We were all watching her too keenly.

"Say, Cass, you are keeping an eye on the time, aren't you? You'll want to cast our circle before the full moon rises," Phillipa said.

But Fiona was beginning to speak at the same time. "Have you ever been to an Esbat, Sylvie? It's January, so we call this the Esbat of the Wolf Moon. I hope that's not scary. From time before time, country people, called *pagans* in Latin, have held ceremonies to celebrate the changing seasons and the full moons. *We are one with the Earth, Mother Earth, we are one....*" and more in that vein. Fiona's voice, always low and musical, had taken on a hypnotic rhythm. Sylvie was listening in a dazed way when her hand began to move, writing words of which she seemed unaware on the page.

"Winters are always wolfish to me," Sylvie was saying. "I can feel the cold tearing at me. I guess that's fanciful, but there it is." Her hand had speeded up, had in fact reached the end of the long page, and I hastily turned it for her to the next page. I noticed that the beginning of the page looked like an exercise in Palmer Penmanship, rows of circular shapes and slanted verticals that continued for several lines before the words began to appear with no spaces between them. The same bold, angular handwriting as before, letters so large that it took only a few words to fill up the space. Finally, the girl sighed deeply and the pen dropped from her fingers.

"Come, Sylvie, you'd better have a sip of this," I said, pouring a splash of brandy for the pale young woman who was now leaning back against the wing chair with her eyes closed. She opened them when I handed the glass to her. "What does it say this time?"

"*Fire fire fire fire,*" I read slowly, having to separate the run-on words from each other. "*First element first power Earth was born in fire a burning star Earth will end in fire so it is written so it will be done I am the angel of God's fire the angel of renewal I shall cleanse the Cities of the Plain according to His will I shall destroy the demons the whores the witches...*".

"Un-oh," said Phillipa.

I looked around at the intent and horrified faces of our circle. "This is much too negative to continue reading now," I decided. As the Esbat was being held at my house this month, I was priestess of the event. *So must it be.* I turned over the pages. "Suffice to say, psychotic ramblings."

Sylvie, sipping her brandy, made a face, and looked dismayed.

"Not your fault, dear," Fiona said hurriedly, reaching over to pat the girl's knee. "You are channeling someone entirely foreign to you. That can be very disturbing, I know. But now you are to let go, *let go.* Here, shake your hands as I am doing to rid yourself of this negative influence." The silver bangles jangled shrilly as Fiona stood and shook out her hands over my braided rug. Obediently, Sylvie put down the glass and followed suit. They danced around the dog for a few minutes, shaking their hands high and low. Then Fiona took a small Navaho bag of corn pollen out of her reticule and scattered a few pinches around Sylvie.

Scruffy stood up, gazed at us with an insulted expression, and stalked off to my bedroom. *Those crazy broads are at it again. There's no peace around here for us noble canines when this pack gets to yowling.* Yipping worriedly, Raffles trotted after him. I took the opportunity to shut the door on them both. Scruffy had already hopped up on my white chenille bedspread and was signaling *sotto voce* to Raffles to stay off. I made a mental note to cover that bedspread with an old quilt next time.

"Now, you do this shaking thing, dear, every time you feel that negative presence take over your hands," Fiona was saying when I got back to the living room. "And it wouldn't hurt to dust your shoes with ground clove, as well. Just lightly on the soles for protection. You don't want to go around leaving brown footprints." She laughed merrily and plumped back down on the couch. "But if what you really want to do is to prevent the phenomenon from happening until a time and place of your own choosing, you will have to be more mindful, less open to fugue states. Here..." She drew out a glossy little book from her reticule and handed it to Sylvie.

"Seven Highly Effective Ways to Mindfulness," Sylvie read the title aloud in a bemused manner. If ever a girl needed mindfulness training, Sylvie was it.

"Good thought, Fiona," I said.

It was turning out to be a most intense evening. I would have to get us back to the essence of the Wolf Moon, which is devoted to change and independence, as well as to protection and healing. Well, *protection* made sense, as Fiona had noted, what with this danger hovering over us psychically and physically. Tonight I would emphasize protection.

When the moon rose in its full majesty over the waves, we bundled up in sweaters and went out to the porch. I cast our circle there, we moved into the space between worlds where all things are possible—the plane of magic. We drew Sylvie into our midst, and the threatening aura that her writings had induced seemed to dissipate like the sulfurous odor of a lit match soon fades in a fresh breeze.

After our invocations, when I'd entered into that slightly tranced state in which the goddess of a thousand names may be invoked, I drew down the moon into our circle. *Artemis, Astarte, Aphrodite, Isis, Sophia, Hecate, Diana, Brigit, Gaia...* Each of us feeling a spark of that divine heritage. We held hands and passed the energy of our wishes for change, protection, and healing from one to the other until the spirit moved so swiftly and strongly it could no longer be contained. At a signal from me, we cast out hands upward to release our wishes into the cosmos. A collective sigh rose from our hearts.

I turned to see how Sylvie was reacting to all this. She was blue-lipped, shivering, and smiling. "What a ride—my mother would have loved that," she said.

"Sylvie's mother was Romani," I explained to the others. "Come on, let's get warm." After I opened the circle, we hurried into the living room for the merry "cakes-and-ale" conclusion of our Esbat. Heather had brought bottles of a delectable cabernet sauvignon, quite able to stand up to the January chill, and Phillipa unveiled something she called an Eight Treasures Chocolate Cake, laden with plump dried fruits and drenched in liqueur.

"Ah, to appreciate the richness of life —that's the proper response to winter," Fiona declared, brandishing a fork in midair to stress her point. "Now in the matter of our young guest here. Perhaps Heather will introduce her to the Kellihers, what do you think?"

Heather, perched on the arm of the sofa, smiled at the thought. "What could be more perfect?"

And it did seem like a good idea at the time. But deep down, I felt a twinge, not so much a feeling of misgiving as an intuition that fate (or the Goddess) was moving us along a preordained path. That's the twinge to which I should always listen.

Sylvie's apartment was practically in Plymouth center and very near Fiona's cottage, so Fiona was elected to drive the girl home. After they left, Heather said, "That went well, I thought. The girl is picking up on our arsonist, I would guess, but not enough specifics to nail him. Which I would dearly love to do before another animal is harmed."

"What made Fiona hone in on the Kellihers, I wonder?" Phillipa paused in the act of putting on her boots.

"We think there's something of the dryad about Sylvie. *Dryad, meet the Druids,*" I said. Our friends the Kellihers are authors of the book *Living the Druid Life*, text by Brian, drawings by Maeve.

"Let's drink to all woodland creatures," Deidre said. "And to quenching that fire fiend. Just think of the danger to everyone, including my Will and all the other firefighters."

Heather opened another bottle and refilled our glasses—a task she was born for—and we toasted all of that and more. "Quench is the perfect word, Deidre," she said thoughtfully. "I'm thinking along the lines of a water spell. What do you say?"

"Without Fiona?" I asked nervously. "Without a book
of shadows or a proper recipe?" With her unerring eye for
authentic reference material, it was Fiona who had found a
dark, moldering *Book of Shadows* in a box of donations for
library sale, and later purchased at a yard sale *Hazel's Household
Recipes*, a 19th century compendium of arcane recipes for
useful stews, soaps, salves, and spells. These two moldering
books had been our dependable source for magic, given that
we had come from no tradition at all but our own studies. A
self-professed, self-initiated circle of novice witches can get
themselves into such a metaphysical muddle if they are not
very precise and careful.

"This can't wait," Heather averred. "And besides, a simple
little water spell. What can go wrong?"

So before Heather, Phillipa, and Deidre went home that
night, we improvised a ritual involving a doll, a candle, a
book of matches, and a galvanized tin watering can full of
sanctified water. Phillipa said a quick rhyme (a traditional
assist to magic). I remembered later that the chant went
something like *All tinder drench, all fires squelch, his spirit
singe, his evil quench, all fears go hence.* But Phillipa claimed
she couldn't remember a word.

We put the bucket out on my porch and forgot about it.
At the same time, I brought indoors the pitcher of Moon Tea
I'd set out there—just like Sun Tea, only brewed by the light
of the full moon. It was nicely chilled and subtly spiced; we
all tried a sip, but we Esbat celebrants proved to be more in a
mood for wine that evening.

CHAPTER FOUR

Love is ever the beginning of Knowledge
as fire is of light.

–Thomas Carlyle

Moon Tea is as delicate as an unspoken wish. When Joe came home, we shared its subtle taste, and I thought no more about our arsonist for several idyllic days. Despite the icy winter rain that had fallen continually since the night of the Wolf Moon, we were warmed and brightened by our own inner fire.

Aegean blue eyes, the strong Greek profile with neat beard, bronze skin, and deep sexy voice—his rich presence was always more powerful and passionate than my imaginings. It seemed as if he filled everything—my rooms, my body, my spirit, my life—to its fullest capacity. This time, however, he brought no exotic presents, but instead a pervasive sadness at the tragic scenes he had witnessed as the Rainbow Warrior carried supplies to devastated villages. Although he talked little about those horrors, in the way of clairvoyants, I sensed far too much.

To dispel the lingering aura of *welttraurigkeit*—world sadness—I regaled him with tales of Sylvie showing up on my doorstep and her adventures in automatic writing. "Only instead of channeling a noble spirit from the past, she finds herself lending her left hand to some arsonist nutcase who may be responsible for recent local fires. Do you remember my telling you about the Fresh Meadow stable fire?"

"So I suppose there's not a chance of dissuading you from getting into mischief, maybe danger, over this arsonist skulking around Plymouth?" Joe said, filling two pressed glass tumblers with a robust Merlot. A familiar warning, loving but resigned; both of us seem to have been born with the Crazy Crusader gene. Maybe that's why we were *simpatico* from the first moment we met. That was the night a Greenpeace crew had joined Heather's rally to save endangered eagles in Jenkins Park—and a whole other magic had begun for me. I was thinking of our first encounter while I admired the muscular chest his open shirt revealed, the gold cross he always wore, as I wore my silver pentagram.

We had gone to bed early, but after some breathlessly satisfying lovemaking and a short drowse, found ourselves to be ravenous. Now we were in the kitchen working on roast lamb sandwiches, with two eager dogs watching our every move and bite.

Smells nice and fatty. Some of that lamb sure would make my coat shine, Toots.

"Only if you roll in it," I said.

"Roll in what?" Joe looked momentarily confused.

"I was talking to Scruffy. He claims that a hunk of lamb will improve the condition of his fur." I gave the two dogs my steeliest alpha dog stare. "You guys go lie down now and wait until we're through. You know the drill."

With a snort of canine grumpiness, Scruffy threw himself down on his kitchen bed. Following awkwardly, Raffles was nosed over to the far edge.

"I don't see how a little informal investigation could put me in danger," I lied. "After all, I won't be alone. This is really a circle project. Especially with the worry about animals at risk—you know Heather."

"The idea that your friends in the circle are involved is what worries me most," Joe said.

"Try to think of it as a sort of environmental safety campaign—which you could join, while you're home. However long that may be."

"Sweetheart, I have no idea." Joe went right to the heart of my central question. "As I told you already, I have been absolutely promised three weeks leave before the next assignment, maybe as much as six."

"Ha ha," I said. "So...are you game for stirring up a few answers in the ashes?"

"Isn't that why the law has arson investigators?"

"Sure, they'll find the evidence, but do you seriously think they're going to find the arsonist himself?"

"I will certainly want to be involved in whatever you're up to now," Joe said. "Although I was planning to resurface your kitchen counters this week."

Good Goddess! I've always prayed that Joe's do-it-yourself enthusiasms would not reach into my kitchen. Although I have a workroom in the cellar where jars of herbs and bottles of essential oils fill the shelves that once had held my grandma's home-canned vegetables and preserves, the kitchen is the heart of my herbal laboratory. Anything to delay that turmoil. "What's wrong with the counters?" I demanded.

"They're okay—badly stained with your herb trade, but okay. I was just thinking of how functional and durable granite would be."

"Granite? In an antique New England saltbox kitchen with exposed beams?"

"Sure, sweetheart. You'll love it. But if we're going to be tooling around town after some firebug, I might not have time to get the job done this tour."

"Yeah," I said. *Ceres save me.* "So, let's go back to bed and talk this over." I got up to stash the dishes in the sink.

"Talking is one option," Joe said, smoothing his hands over my hips and pressing against me. "And by the way, why are that doll and candle frozen in your watering can out on the porch? Upside-down, too."

"Oh, dear...did I leave my watering can out there?"

"*Jesu Christos*, sweetheart. I hope there are no pins in that doll."

"We don't do voo-doo," I said in a tone of injured dignity. Moving away from Joe's importunate hands, I drew myself up into a full glamour. Fiona would have been proud of my using her mesmerizing technique for giving oneself a queenly presence—a handy method of diverting discomforting questions.

"I've never thought you did," Joe said, eyeing me affectionately. "And I think I know you pretty well by now."

"Better than anyone," I murmured, resting my head on his shoulder.

He pulled me close, and I felt that melting sensation in my second chakra. "You do have those occasional flashes of insight and intuition," he continued reflectively. "Very impressive they are, too. And you celebrate holidays according to some ancient astrological calendar. But that's just the same as agricultural societies do all over the world, each in its own way. Then there are all those goddesses, but we Greeks are right at home with goddesses. Still, you're not really into the eye-of-newt thing, right?"

"Right. Maybe a few hairs from a shedding wolf now and again, a pinch of a victim's grave dust, but it goes no farther than that. I'm not even sure I know what a newt is exactly."

"It's a salamander, sweetheart. Small, slender, brightly colored. Lives on land mostly, except for the breeding season, when it becomes aquatic."

"Is that some course they teach you at Greenpeace? Weird Animals of the World 101?"

"Greenpeace has been an education, that's for sure. Take the Patagonian toothfish, for instance..."

"No, thanks. Saving that little bugger has kept you on the other side of the globe too many times."

"I'm here right now."

"Good point. Let's go to bed."

The dogs got some delectable lamb scraps, while we snuck away to the bedroom and quietly shut the door on them. By now, Scruffy was so used to this maneuver, he hardly said a cross word. As a wild east wind slapped sheets of rain against the windows, I felt uneasy about the unleashed powers swirling about us and grateful for Joe's warm, protective embrace.

CHAPTER FIVE

...to stand with our Secret mocking itself
And hiding itself among flowers and mandolins...

–Edgar Lee Masters

Nick Deere brought his Harley to a gravel-splattering stop in front of Pryde's Video Place near Plymouth center. Jumping nimbly off the motorcycle, he entered the store, where he found Lucius Pryde unpacking adult videos for the back room.

Being a hunting buddy of Deere's father, who owned the Erin Go Bragh Pub in neighboring Kingston, Luke welcomed the young man, whose worn leather jacket and deceptively slight build hid a steel-muscled body like a jockey's or a bicycle racer's. He was a dead ringer for his dad, with slick dark hair and hard brown eyes that brought the term Black Irish to mind, which Luke had too much good sense ever to say aloud to the Deeres.

Nick stayed to share a beer while he pumped Luke for information. He was looking for a girl, a remark that would have made Luke snicker if he hadn't correctly read the icy warning in Nick's eyes. Tough as the Prydes were, they all shared an innate sense of trouble. They tended to avoid any danger that their coping skills of mere bravado and cunning might not be able to avert. And Nick, leaning his chair against the wall and smiling thinly, exuded the quiet menace of a curled cobra.

Lucius Pryde swore he didn't know anything about the young woman Deere described, although flickering in the back of his mind was the image of someone who had taken a job recently with a cousin-in-law, Marigold Finch. Yes, maybe. Knowledge was money in the bank, however—not to be squandered without adequate return. Lucius did not amend his original statement. *Maybe later*, Lucius thought. After he got rid of his guest, he'd stroll over to Marigold's and have a look at the gal who'd escaped Nick Deere. She must be some plucky bitch.

⁓

At Imbolc—a.k.a. Groundhog Day, Candlemas, St. Blaise's Day—we celebrate the first stirrings of spring, which if they cannot be felt at the beginning of February, at least may be hoped for. The unceasing rains and ice storms of January had gradually, almost reluctantly eased to a cold heavy mist.

"I've never seen so much drenching rain," Phillipa complained.

"Drenching, yes. I think I'll get rid of that watering can on my porch. Do you imagine? No, that would be just too smug…"

"*Yes*, I do imagine that in an effort to quench the arsonist, we may have helped to drench the entire South Shore as well.

I feel like the Sorcerer's Apprentice, don't you? Let's never do a spell without Fiona's imprimatur again."

"Right," I agreed. "But let's never tell her about the one we did do, either."

"It's a pact," Phillipa swore. "You have to admit, though, there haven't been any suspicious fires recently."

"Who could light a match in this downpour?"

༄

Celebrating the bare anticipation of spring, Heather improvised a dinner party to take place immediately after the circle's private Imbolc ritual at her house. From her seagoing forebears, Heather was heir to a Federalist mansion near Harlows Landing. The house has an authentic widow's walk and acres of wooded land. The three-car garage built in the twenties had been converted into dog kennels, because there are never less and sometimes more than a half dozen canine companions in residence, including Raffles' mama Honeycomb. If Heather found herself keeping more than the legal limit of dogs allowed to one household without a kennel license, Heather had a cousin at City Hall who fixed things for her.

The Kellihers, close neighbors of the Devlins, were invited to join the party, so it seemed to be an entirely natural time to introduce Sylvie to our Druid friends. Brian and Maeve brought with them a house guest, Pieter Brand, a fellow artist whose frozen plumbing had driven him out temporarily from the derelict Craig place, a Victorian monstrosity which he had bought and was restoring.

"Talk about 'handyman's special,'" Maeve said. "Not only did the place suffer decades of neglect, the roof was stoved in by a catalpa tree during that heavy snowstorm last year. I'm so relieved that Pieter is rescuing that fine old home."

"I remember what an old wreck it was," Heather said with a broad wink at me. Heather, Fiona, and I had been involved in an investigation on the Craig property, after its owner, Lydia Craig, had been poisoned at a church function, so we knew the place informally (truth be told, we'd broken in). Ms. Craig's will had ordered that all her real estate holdings be sold; the Presbyterian minister, Reverend Peacedale, had been the principal inheritor of her considerable fortune.

"Pieter and I met *ages ago* at the Museum School." Maeve put her hand through Brand's arm and drew him closer. "Architectural drawing classes. Then I married Brian, and Pieter went on to join a Boston architectural firm. What was the name of that stodgy company, dear? You're among friends here, Pete. Tell them about the scandal."

"Better forgotten," Brand growled, but it was clear to me that he was spellbound by Maeve and would do whatever pleased her. "Some old fogey in the firm accused me of plagiarizing, although my work had moved so far ahead it bore no relationship to his. But the firm supported the senior guy, so I had to leave. Classic case of 'when one door closes, another opens,' though. I was so down in the dumps about my employment prospects, I started doodling around with drawings for a children's book instead."

That "doodling around," I knew from Maeve, had become *The Dragon of Utrecht*, based on a Dutch folktale. With its marvelously sculptured drawings and mysterious story, Brand's book became that season's surprise success, winning the Newbury Award. The royalties had enabled him to purchase the Craig property.

"Pieter won't talk about the book he's writing *now*," Maeve said. "It seems he's superstitious about siphoning off his energy, or some such rot." She beamed fondly at her friend who grinned back at her.

"The second book is always traumatic.And it's entirely possible to talk a project to death," Phillipa agreed. "Better to let repression fuel expression, I say."

Brand turned the grin her way. His pale blue eyes were unreadable behind the old-fashioned dark-framed glasses with thick lenses that dominated his pale, square face. His hair was so blond as to be nearly white. I squashed a maternal impulse to check that he used sunscreen with that vulnerable fair skin.

Nothing vulnerable about his handshake, though. When we'd been introduced, I'd been taken aback by the fierce passion that burned through his fingers. It was elemental, obsessive, and somehow shocking. Now while I studied him as he sat arm in arm with Maeve, the image of that dragon of his flashed through my mind, but somehow it was more a dinosaur. Passion direct from the old reptilian brain that coils within us all.*Maybe it's just the artist thing*, I told myself. *Is Maeve having a bit of a flirt with this guy?* Although slowed by her walker, and sometimes confined to a wheelchair, Maeve, with her wild cloud of dark hair, pain-haunted eyes, and the sweetness that radiated from her inner being, was a fascinatingly beautiful woman. She certainly had her husband Brian completely enraptured.

It must have seemed a glittering social event to Sylvie. Her face wore the apprehensive, sad look of one who had often tried to please and always failed. Wearing leaf-green slacks and a matching sweater, she leaned against the Victorian red wall of Heather's parlor as if trying to hold it in place.

Fiona bent her head and whispered to me, "When we go into the conservatory for dinner, notice how the girl's form will seem to disappear among the potted trees."

"Well, naturally," I muttered back. "She always dresses like M'lady Greensleeves."

"Just watch," Fiona insisted before Deidre got my other ear.

"I wonder if we couldn't stir something up for Pieter and Sylvie," Deidre murmured.

"Can you never let people enjoy single blessedness?" I asked my mischievous friend.

"It's Imbolc, Cass. Feast of fertility and so forth. Time to breed new ideas. And I'll thank you to remember that I am more than a little responsible for *that* love match," Deidre replied, nodding toward Phillipa and Stone who were sharing an intimate smile and clinking glasses.

"Ah, the wine flows abundantly, the sun grows in strength, and Valentine's Day is on the way," I said. *So what if Deidre brings a little romance into Sylvie's young life?* I thought, as I took an appreciative sip. Heather's wines were always exceptional, and she kept busy refilling glasses. I examined an emptied bottle. *Chateau de la Gardine Chateauneuf de Pape, Blanc.* Any name that long and that French was sure to be a cut above my favorite serviceable Chardonnay.

Our host Dick, a big warm teddy-bear of a guy with bushy hair and a hearty laugh, was passing frosty bottles of an obscure micro-brew to Will and Joe. Joe had taken out his pocket notebook and was showing something in it to the other two men.

"I fear that may be a remodeling plan for my kitchen," I murmured to Deidre. "I just know Joe has no intention of merely replacing the countertops. He's thinking more in terms of Extreme Makeover."

"Is that one of your clairvoyant flashes? A vision of your kitchen all glossy and upscale in the pages of *Architectural Digest* perhaps?" Deidre's dimple flashed.

"Not exactly. I happened to find several do-it-yourself pamphlets from Home Warehouse on that workbench he's constructed in my garage. Well, I suppose it's *our* garage now. One of them advertised multi-paned glass cabinet doors and, *Ceres save us,* another one illustrated Pergo laminate flooring."

"You'll love the Pergo. It's indestructible, even with four kids and two dogs," Deidre reassured me. "Oh, goodie. I think dinner's ready."

What was wrong, I wondered, *with suitably seasoned (like for about a hundred years) and attractively distressed (some might say scarred and burned) wide pine planks?*

In the conservatory, the Devlins' houseman, Captain Jack, a retired seaman, served up a feast of whole baked, stuffed salmon, garlic-mashed potatoes, and spinach and shrimp salad, accompanied by baskets of his flaky, golden biscuits. This was the room where the smaller dogs usually flopped down on folded blankets for the night, but on this occasion all canines were relegated to the kennels, and the Death-Valley array of chew bones had been swept away. A long plank table had been set up, covered with creamy linen and set with Limoge in a spring floral pattern. Since Imbolc was a Feast of Candles and Heather's craft was candle-making, the room shimmered with her handiworks from tall and elegant to fat and evocative. In the glow of all those candles, the many potted trees that surrounded us threw long shadows on the white walls and floor-to-ceiling windows.

"Where's Sylvie?" I asked as we took our places around the table.

Fiona positively cackled. "Take a closer look, dear."

I couldn't see her anywhere.

"Where's Sylvie?" Deidre echoed. I suspected she was commencing her usual matchmaking maneuvers.

"Here I am, Dee," Sylvie said, stepping out, it seemed, from a potted palm.

"Oh, good, dear. You know, I didn't even see you there. Now why don't you take this chair here beside me," Deidre said, moving over so that the girl would be placed between herself and Pieter. She leaned over Sylvie to speak to the fair young man, who gazed at her through his thick glasses with a faintly alarmed expression. "Pete dear, our friend Sylvie works at the Finch Flower Shop, Floribunda. Besides having an amazing green thumb, she dabbles in automatic writing, which is how we all got acquainted with one another."

"So many unusual talents in one place. Is it something in the Plymouth air?" Pieter's smile was pleasant but, I fancied, a bit skeptical. "Maeve, as you know, is an expert in ancient Druid lore and its application to modern life—an interesting notion. You should get her to tell you about the Mist of Invisibility sometime. And she assures me that every one of you has a gift like that. Now who is the one who reads tarot?"

"That would be Phillipa Stern, the dark-haired gal at the end of the table who looks like a proper witch," Deidre said impishly. "Heather creates magical candles, as you see around you—and they *do* evoke an atmosphere, don't they? Fiona is our finder, and I myself make amulets and poppets." She turned to the girl listening intently. "Sylvie, why don't you tell Pieter all about your automatic writing. Did you know, Pete, that Samuel Coleridge wrote his most famous poem, *Kubla Khan*, in a trance? Unfortunately, he was interrupted by a visitor knocking at the door—a person from Porlock, I believe—and he was never was able to finish the work."

Pieter laughed. "I think I'm out of my depth here—a mere artist. Sylvie—you have a lovely name. Perhaps you can show me how to channel my next book through automatic writing? With me, you know, the art comes first—the images in my brain that flow easily through my fingers—then as an afterthought, I write a story to hold them together."

"There's automatic drawing as well as automatic writing." Fiona pawed through the reticule leaning against her chair. "Oh, drat it, I must have left that pamphlet at home somewhere. *Drawing in the De Vinci Mode.*"

Sylvie, I noted, was gazing at Pieter like a mesmerized rabbit. *Anxiety or admiration?*

"Brand," said Fiona thoughtfully. "Now that's Dutch for fire, isn't it? Sylvie, on the other hand, has a triple-tree name."

"What about Deidre?" asked her doting husband Will, who was slightly flushed with a largess of micro-beers.

"An Irish heroine whose name, alas, means sorrowful," Fiona said.

"Hey, that's not like my darlin' Dee at all," Will declared. "Except the heroine part fits okay. She's a terror, all right."

"Oh, Will," Deidre said. "You make me sound so bossy."

"What is this, Fiona," Phillipa asked sharply from her end of the table. "Entomology parlor games?"

Undeterred, Fiona continued, "Did you know that Stone is English and simply means stone?"

"Forthright parents who valued silent strength," Stone said. "The Sterns may be traced back to a long line of British bankers and physicians. Not a copper among them."

"And Phillipa is a lover of horses. Have you ever done any riding, Phil? A terrible shame about those poor horses at Fresh Meadow Farm, wasn't it?"

"Oh, how I wish you hadn't brought that up, Fiona" I whispered.

"That man should be shot to death by a firing squad on the town green," Heather declared, brandishing her glass to the detriment of the table linens. Then seeming to recollect that she was surrounded by guests, she added, "after a fair trial, of course."

Leaning over slightly, I could overhear that Pieter was continuing to talk soothingly to Sylvie about automatic writing. Motion had returned to her form and color to her face. Maybe Deidre was on to something, after all. And what could be a neater way to get rid of the abusive boyfriend than to replace him with a new love interest? *Everyday magic.*

Maeve, who was seated on Pieter's other side, at the table's foot where there was room for her walker, interrupted the tête-à-tête to draw out Sylvie about her job and the apartment over the flower shop. "Are you happy there, Sylvie? Is there someplace else you'd rather be working?"

Flushed with all this attention, Sylvie smiled shyly. "Oh, yes. What I'd really like to do is work for some environmental concern, like Save the Wolves or the Whales or the Rain Forests—but I have no idea how to go about finding that kind of job."

"You could be a Greenpeace volunteer," Joe suggested. "Of course, if you insist on being paid a *salary*..."

Heather looked at Dick meaningfully. It took him only a few moments to get the message. "Sylvie!" he boomed. "Ignore that wily Greenpeace recruiter! I know just the place for you. Plymouth Nature Conservancy will be looking for secretary and Gal Friday in the spring, or maybe even sooner. I'll give someone a call. That is, trusting you can use a word processor and all that."

"Oh, yes, I took Microsoft and keyboarding in high school, and after I graduated, two years at the Botch Business School in town, the Administrative Assistant curriculum. But then, they couldn't seem to place me in a job as they promised. You are all so kind to me," Sylvie enthused, clasping her hands together against her chest like a true Victorian damsel. *She's rather a pretty girl*, I noticed suddenly, *when she smiles and there's pink in her cheeks.* I had an urge to hum *Jeanne with the light brown hair borne like a vapor on the summer* air. That was the thing about Sylvie, I realized right then. She seemed to belong to an earlier, gentler lifetime.

"I wonder if we keep meeting the same people, life after life," I mused quietly to Fiona.

"Our spiritual family," she replied, then she chuckled in that merry way of hers. *"When shall we five meet again, in thunder, lightning, or in rain?"*

"Not just the circle. Sylvie, for instance. Sometimes people simply show up and demand a place in one's life."

"I think that happens to you oftener than to most," Fiona murmured. Then we turned our attention back to the general discussion of Sylvie's future.

"She'll need a place to live, then," Phillipa pointed out as she took another spoonful of the salmon stuffing, no doubt to analyze its ingredients with her educated palate. Far be it from Phillipa to actually request the recipe from Captain Jack. She took that last taste just in time, too, because the houseman began clearing the table. There being no dogs present, the captain's parrot Ishmael was riding on his shoulder, kibitzing.

"*Place to live, place to live,*" Ish said with a mocking lilt.

"Brian and I may be able to help there," Maeve said. "We'll talk about this again, Sylvie. You must come over to our place for tea. I hope you like cats."

"Oh, of course. I have a kitty of my own," Sylvie said.

"We have thirteen. At least I think it's still thirteen, my lucky number. Good, then," Maeve said. "I'll call you at the Floribunda, if I may."

"Oh dear, I'm not allowed personal calls," Sylvie said.

"Don't worry your pretty head about that. I promise you that when I call, no one will hear our conversation"

"All right...how do you work that?" Pieter was intrigued.

"Don't ask," Brian said. "It's a Druid thing, and you know how they are about secrets."

Maeve smiled and looked down at her hands.

"No, not exactly." Pieter assumed a skeptical expression.

"Right. What they keep secret is never revealed, don't you know? That's why their history is so sketchy. What you read was largely invented by their enemies, the Romans."

"That so?" Pieter said in a challenging tone. "Perhaps it wasn't true, then, that the Druids burned people and animals alive in a giant wicker basket?"

I didn't care for the turn this conversation was taking, but fortunately, just then, Captain Jack brought in pots of delicious boiled coffee and several dried apple pies, causing Pieter to exclaim that he hadn't had a proper cup of boiled coffee since he last visited his mother in Holland.

Overall, it was a very lively dinner party, and I said as much to Joe on the way home. But why did I have this lingering frisson of worry?

"Because you're you. Cassandra," Joe said. "Speaking of the meaning of names, did you know that Cassandra is Greek—a Trojan princess with the gift of prophecy?"

"Yes, poor blind girl. No one believed her. But I'm not sure about what Joseph means."

"It's Hebrew. *God shall increase.*"

"Sounds good, but increase what?"

I felt him grinning in the darkness of the car. "Whatever one wishes to increase, sweetheart."

CHAPTER SIX

Deep in the human heart
The fire of justice burns...

—William L. Wallace

For the sake of my peace of mind and the serenity of my kitchen workspace, I welcomed any project that would distract Joe from his home improvement schemes. Designed to divert as well as inform, a visit to the site of the stable fire would do very nicely. Many days had passed, so I had no idea what this would actually accomplish; perhaps I'd gather a few impressions. Worth a try!

Riding royally in the back seat of my new Jeep Liberty, the two dogs gazed out their respective windows. As we whizzed by pedestrian dogs, Scruffy was disdainful, Ruffles wagging his entire body enthusiastically. But they both became suddenly subdued when we reached Fresh Meadow Farm. Who can tell what animals sense?

A bulldozer was at work leveling the dirt over what I knew to be, from the newspaper accounts, a mass grave that held carcasses of the horses who'd perished in the blaze. Soon grass would be covering the scarred earth, as it had so many battlefields. Two teen-aged girls were watching this grim restoration. One of them was wiping away tears with the sleeve of her parka. In her other hand, she held a new halter and lead shank, pretty colors, teal and purple. The other girl fastened a wreath to the paddock fence. Other mementoes were already hanging there: flowers, balloons, poems, and photographs.

Raffles howled mournfully.

Scruffy nosed my ear. *The kid is right. This is not a good place, Toots. Let's high-tail it out of here.*

"We won't be long," I reassured him, jumping out from the driver's side and quickly closing the door on the two nervous canines. Joe joined me and I took his arm as we walked casually around the misshapen, blackened remains of the burned building. It looked like the petrified ribs of some giant prehistoric animal. All the worse by contrast, since an L-shaped extension from the stable appeared to be unharmed.

A woman came out from the sprawling white farmhouse with green shutters, stood on the front porch, and yelled at us. "Hey, you two! Get away from there. I can't have this continual gawking. Are you reporters, or just plain ghouls?"

"Let's go, Cass." Joe tugged at my arm, prepared to flee back to the car. "It's not right to be intruding on this woman's troubles."

Instead of running, however, I attempted to summon a reassuring glamour. "Hi, there. We're not here to gawk, honest. We're from the Animal Lovers Association—you know, the animal rescue facility near Plymouth Center? Heather Devlin, the manager, asked me to stop over to see if there's anything she can do, and also if we might speak with the investigator on the case?"

"What the Christ for? Haven't I had enough trouble from him? " the woman asked. Obviously there must be glitches in my reassuring glamour.

"Hi," I said again. "You must be Sarah Churchill, then. I'm Cass Shipton."

"Cass Shipton the witch?" Implacable Sarah Churchill looked as if she'd been cut from the same bolt of cloth as Heather, tall and athletic, with shining hair pulled back in a simple pony tail.

"I wouldn't put it just that way," I said. "We like to say Wiccan."

"Just a minute here," Joe said, bristling now in my defense.

"Calm down, Joe. I can handle this," I whispered, not at all as confident as my glamour would suggest.

"Witch...Wiccan, I couldn't care less. Are you the one who caught that serial killer a few years back? And then the deadly angel nurse?"

"Eh...I guess the *Pilgrim Times* may have mentioned my name in connection with those incidents, yes. Actually, it was Plymouth County law-enforcement officers who deserved all the credit."

Sarah Churchill put one fist on her hip and glared at me imperiously. "You go, girl. Do your worst, or your best, to hex and curse that monster, may he burn in hell."

Wow! Banish that thought! was my quick reaction. "Thoughts are things," as my grandma always said. Of course I would like to see this arsonist caught, but not with curses.

Sarah Churchill gestured toward the wing of the building still standing. "You're in luck, then, if you want to talk to that sonofabitch insurance investigator. He's still poking

around, in the tack room today. There's a fire wall kept the
tack room and office from going up with the rest. Go have a
look, if you like. Maybe you can find an answer, because I'll
tell you right now, it wasn't any goddamn wood chips. And
our electrical system was in A-1 shape. Just had it inspected.
But that bastard would sure love to blame us for something
so's he can deny our claim."

From the house, a voice called to the Churchill woman,
and she turned on her heel and hurried back inside.

"You handled that very well, I thought. And I see a lot
of angry confrontations." Joe said. "You didn't tell me that
Animal Lovers had taken an interest."

"Didn't I? Let's go see that guy in the tack room before
she changes her mind," I said.

We found the tall gaunt investigator leaning over the
Churchill's office desk shuffling through correspondence. His
navy blue jacket was emblazoned with *IAAI* in white letters.
I spoke to his back: "Hi. I'm Cassandra Shipton, and this is
my husband Joe Ulysses,"

From the way he jumped to face us, it was apparent that
we'd startled him. Dark circles under his protruding eyes
gave him an owlish expression. *Sinus problems and hyperthyroid*,
I thought.

"Who? Who?" he hooted, holding his clipboard up like
a shield.

I repeated the introduction again, and added, "Heather
Devlin from the Animal Lovers Association asked us to touch
base with you and ask if there's anything AL can do to assist
in your investigation." I made a mental note to catch up with
Heather real soon and fill her in on these spur-of-the-moment

inventions. "The association has a canine named Trilby who's a registered accelerant detector."

I became aware that Joe was looking at me incredulously. "You mean that old bloodhound?" he asked. Very gently, I stepped on his boot. If he was going to sleuth with me, he'd have to learn not to ask questions at delicate moments. I value honesty as much as the next witch, but there are times when pure truth is too lofty a concept for the world of the mundane.

The office reeked of disaster. As the investigator pulled himself together and handed me his card, I wondered how long I could endure the stench of burned wood and Goddess knows what else.

"Oliver Keen, International Association of Arson Investigators," he said. "You have a CADA dog in Plymouth? First I've heard of it, then."

"Oh, well...I'm sure you have everything well in hand, Mr. Keen, without the services of an accelerant sniffer. Besides, according to Ed Dulinski, this fire was accidental."

"It's accidental when I say it's accidental," Keen retorted huffily. Clearly, he was not pleased to have Dulinski center-stage, getting himself quoted in the *Pilgrim Times* et cetera. "We have to look into everything, Missus. Like how hot and fast the fire moved, the pattern of burning, the demeanor and whereabouts of the owners. A state arson team has been down here, and they're far from satisfied, too, I can tell you that. There's a long way to go yet before we'll be paying out on this baby."

I was glad I wasn't Sarah Churchill with a husband recovering from surgery, a stable in ruins, a mass grave outside the window, and this mordant fellow sniffing around Fresh Meadow Farm's business records.

"An experienced investigator like you must have seen enough incidents of this nature to have a pretty clear idea of what's suspicious and what's not." Joe said—conversational tone, *mano a mano*. "Have you found any hard evidence of arson?"

The guy narrowed his eyes and stuck out his chin. "There's more to this one than meets the eye," he said in the pompous tone of a small town official setting the public straight. "True, the electrical system *had* just passed inspection, so we rule out the usual faulty wiring. True, hay was not stored in the stable, and no cigarette butts have been found. True, the wood chips were not entirely consumed, which messes up Dulinski's theory. True, I haven't found any traces of accelerant—yet. *But* the way this one went up, *boom, boom, boom* makes the case smell to high heaven. By the time the smoke alarms sounded, this place was a goner. In my experience, the speed of the fire is a very relevant factor." As he made each point, Keen tapped his pen meaningfully on his clipboard. "Shouldn't say this but, *the owners are up to their eyebrows in debt.*"

I was amazed at the torrent of information Joe had got out of Keen. "Don't you need a search warrant to look at the Churchill accounts?" I asked. The investigator's obvious intent to deny all claims was making me testy.

"True, unless the owners tell me *go ahead and have a look*, which they did, Missus."

I began to feel slightly faint. The stink of burned stable was overwhelming me. As I felt my knees fold, I managed to slump into the visitor's chair beside the desk.

The office faded away from my consciousness, and I found myself in a stand of pine. It was night, but in the light from buildings beyond the woods, I could see a man crouched down behind dense low branches observing the farm house and L-shaped stable that lay in the clearing. He was wearing some kind of a hooded head covering. He put his right hand in his pocket and took out a lighter, which he used to light a cigarette. Although I couldn't see his face, I could smell the burning tobacco.

A workman in overalls moved across the courtyard carrying what looked like an armful of halters. After he hung them on a hook by the stable door, he got into a pick-up truck and drove away. A horse whinnied in the stable. Then the compound fell into silence except for a fresh quick wind whistling through leafless branches.

Again, the hooded man took a lighter out of his pocket. He flicked it several times, observing its small responsive flame, then put it back. When he rose to his feet, my whole being felt prickled with icy fear. Somehow, just looking at the set of his shoulders and the clench of his fists, I could read his intentions. He pinched the glowing end of his cigarette with two fingers, dropped it, and stamped it into the earth with his boot. I could feel his irresistible need for release, quite sexual—the release that he could find only in a raging fire. I wanted to scream, but no sound came out of my mouth. I wanted to follow this man, to stop him, to tackle him if I had to, but as in a dream, I moved with the slowness of someone wading in mud.

Sensing what was to come, I watched in horror as the man slipped around the buildings, moving from one concealing shadow to another, until he reached the stable door. Then he was inside, a few horses whinnied restlessly at the intrusion of a stranger. In what seemed like only a few moments later, the man was outside again, running back toward me. The hood he was wearing covered everything except his eyes. He turned back toward the stable, crouched down as he had before, and waited.

Suddenly, an intense flame flashed up one wall of the stable. I heard one horse scream, then another—sounds I never want to hear again.

Cold water on my face. I became aware that someone was bathing my face with a wet paper towel. "Cass, sweetheart. What a scare! You must have fainted. Are you feeling better now?" Joe was murmuring in my ear, patting my wrists. "Here let me help you up now—you can lean on me. Need to get you outdoors away from these poisonous fumes. Keen, open that damned door!"

I was nauseated, of course, but quite lucid. Tempted as I was to play Victorian fainting female and whisper, *Where am I? Undo my stays*—it was so delightful to be fussed over—I stood up on my own two feet readily enough. "Mr. Keen, if I were you, I'd take a breather myself before you collapse like me—these fumes won't do your sinus condition any favor."

A look of surprise emphasized the owlish cast of his features. Probably wondered how I knew something that was as plain to me as the nose on his face.

Although my voice was somewhat weak, and I was tremendously tired, I continued to rattle on. "I feel you're perfectly right that this fire was set, *but not by the Churchills.* You're just wasting your valuable time examining their books. I believe you ought to be looking for a serial arsonist, and you'll want to stop him very soon, or your company and others are going to be paying out big bucks." Maybe I could convince Keen to cut short his ravaging of the Churchill business records.

"Who? Who?" Keen was repeating his owl imitation as we left the office.

"Thanks, darling. I think we can go now," I said to Joe.

Joe insisted in supporting me to the Jeep. "I'm driving you right home so that you can put your feet up and rest. That was a vision, then," he said, tucking me into the passenger seat with a disapproving look. "You've got to be more careful, sweetheart. What if I weren't there to grab you?"

"Did I fall?"

"No, but you might have if a chair hadn't happened to be right there. Are you all right now? Any more feelings of faintness?"

Scruffy was nosing my neck in a worried fashion. *Hey, Toots. Didn't I tell you not to go in there?"*

It's so embarrassing when your dog says *I told you so.*

"Okay, everyone. I'm fine now. Just the usual psychic hangover, which will pass very soon." There's no way to describe the weirdness of a genuine vision, that sliding step out the door of one dimension and into another. This one seemed to have left me with a talking jag, and I rattled on as Joe drove. "I saw him, you know, the man who torched Fresh Meadow. And I think it was the same man who was called a hero later—the guy who came out of the woods to rescue some of the horses, but no one knew who he was. Mick Finn said he wore a balaclava, as I recall. That's him, the depraved bastard. And I know he left a cigarette butt where he was hiding in the woods. Trouble is, I think he stamped it into the ground. It would be hell to find. "

"You're getting yourself all worked up again. Try to stay calm, sweetheart. Were you able to see any part of his face?"

"No, dammit," I admitted woefully. "Just his eyes, and it was too dark to get a good look at those. I just got an idea of his general build, and his walk. *Oh!*"

"*Oh,* what?"

"I just realized that he was wearing rather odd boots."

"How do you mean, unusual?"

"Clear plastic. I think I may have seen something like those boots before, though."

"Disposable boots, you mean?" Joe guessed.

"Yeah. I think I've seen a box of them at the Wee Angels Animal Hospital."

"Vets use them. Farmers, too, sometimes, and chemical workers," Joe said. "Would make a lot of sense to pull on a pair of disposables if you were going to sneak around a stable. Afterwards, you could just ditch them someplace. Clever guy."

I thought about the little quenching spell we'd dreamed up after the Esbat of the Wolf Moon. Creating a ceremony with all its sensual trappings is a wonderful assist to focusing one's mind on spiritual intentions. So the quenching might actually help to put out the madman's future fires, but we could never really predict how a spell would work. Sometimes the Universe of Infinite Solutions seems to take our amateur efforts too literally, or perhaps is showing a sense of humor in the way it fulfills our wishes. I mean, who knew that the houseman of Heather's dreams would arrive with a pesky parrot? Right now, however, I thought I had a better idea of the way we should move against this hooded monster, more along the lines of a mirror spell. Let its magic reflect back upon the arsonist his own evil nature. Short-cut karma.

"Not clever enough," I said.

Later I called Phil. "Tell Stone that the Fresh Meadow arsonist and the hero who rescued the horses must be the same guy—at least they were both wearing a balaclava. And the guy left a cigarette butt in the woods near the farm. I have a pretty good idea where it is, but the guy stamped it into the ground quite thoroughly. Wearing plastic disposable boots. Rather like looking for a needle in the you-know....but maybe Fiona could dowse around there for the butt. He would like to collect it for evidence, wouldn't he? I wouldn't dare look for it by myself in case that would be polluting something."

"DNA, for instance," Phil said. "You're sounding ditzy, so I'm assuming you've had a vision. It's really up to Mick Finn and the State Fire Marshal's team to investigate this case, but I suppose Finn wouldn't mind a helping hand—where he knows Stone and all. Anyway, I'll ask Stone if he wants to have a go. I'll have to tell him this is one of your psychic flashes, I suppose?"

" 'Fraid so. Joe and I went over to Fresh Meadow today and talked to the insurance investigator, Oliver Keen. I guess the fumes got to me. Well, really it was the whole atmosphere. Some girls were hanging around the burial site with such tragic expressions, mourning their horses and pinning up little mementoes. And the terror of those burning animals seemed to linger in the air. Ugh. Horrid."

"And you went there...*why?*"

"What can I say...I just feel I'm being drawn into this investigation by forces I don't yet understand. We all are. So I might as well get out and nose around."

"I would call that a neat rationalization, if it were rational. Okay. I've got a strong fear of this arsonist myself. Who knows where all this will end if we don't do what we can."

"In our own quiet ladylike way," I agreed.

CHAPTER SEVEN

I am here a Poet, that doth drink of life
As lesser men drink wine.

–Ezra Pound

Lounging in his favorite maroon leather armchair in front of the gas fireplace in his apartment, Raoul Lazaro was composing a poem.

As phrases flickered though his mind, he hand-lettered them beautifully on a pad of white unlined paper, first in Spanish and then in English, a system that had always pleased Frances his late benefactor who had been fluent in both languages. Sometimes she even made suggestions on nuances of translation. Well, she was gone now. Only her legacies and her protégées remained to memorialize her. Raoul smiled. Women were so easy to please. He'd grown up in a house surrounded by women, his mother and the girls. He shuddered, remembering their cloying adoration of the pretty, velvet-eyed boy he had been, the embraces and pinches. Even worse was the grabby old official his mother had taken up with when Raoul was twelve.

Still he'd learned all the tricks. Even in Cuba as a young man, so many women—secretaries, governesses, even housecleaners—had been a fountain of valuable information. And it hadn't taken him long to trade their confidences for cash.

Las cenizas de su sonrisa, sus huesos blancos, he wrote. *The ashes of your smile, your white bones.*

〰

"Stone claims he absolutely *has* to work tonight, so I've decided *you* can go with me to hear Raoul read from his latest book *We Drowned at Dawn.*" Phillipa's crisp voice brooked no refusal. "It's at the Black Hill branch. Fiona will be there, but Goddess knows who else. Poetry readings don't seem to be a big draw these days. Do you think Joe would come with you?"

"Joe reads Homer in the original Greek. I don't know that he'd be up for a lesser odyssey. Why don't you call Patty Peacedale? She'll go anywhere that's not a parish committee meeting, poor lady. But to tell you the truth, I'm feeling a bit washed out myself since I got back from Fresh Meadow Farm."

"Patty's already a member of the Erato Poetry Club, didn't you know that? Writes inspirational verses for funerals and divorce mediations. Getting out of yourself for an evening is just what you need, girlfriend. I'll pick you up at 7:15, so *be ready.*" And she hung up before I could protest further.

Phillipa and I often travel together since we live close by with just the width of Jenkins Park between us, a stretch of woodland we had a hand in saving from developers a few years ago. Now it's home to a nesting pair of American Bald

Eagles and also is officially classified as a wetlands, manmade due to some earlier careless sand removal. What could be better than living beside a park? I rejoice in retaining our rural pleasures, such as contemplative walks in the woods, my foraging trips for wild herbs and bayberries, and the occasional Beltane romp with Joe, weather permitting.

Whenever Phillipa decides to enlist my aid, her persuasive energy always manages to pluck me out of whatever I'm doing, and I suspect I do the same to her. There would be no escaping Raoul Lazaro and his exodus from Cuba, rhymed or unrhymed. Perhaps it would be a good thing to meet this poet who had persuaded Phillipa to give up her cooking career. Obviously Raoul was a force to be reckoned with.

The Black Hill branch library is a cozy place, a former bungalow now belonging to the Women's Cooperative for Folk Arts, which still has a quilting room in the basement. I never imagined we'd find it crowded with poetry lovers—most of them females in the same general age range as ourselves. Much as I would like to believe these gals were united in their urge to enjoy some mid-winter culture, once I caught sight of Raoul Lazaro holding forth amid a group of poetry devotees, I had to attribute the turn-out to his smoldering good looks and burning gaze.

"Shades of Antonio Bandaras," I muttered to Fiona. She was wearing her royal blue velvet dress, draped with silver moon and pentagram necklaces, and she'd tied a silver bow to the handle of her green reticule. When she turned her head toward the poet, I removed the one pencil still lodged in her coronet of braids.

"He does have a certain charisma," Fiona admitted. "And he's a terrific reader. Black Hill hasn't had much attention

lately. Sometimes I've wondered if library patrons even know
that we're here, the way they all go traipsing over to the main
library. So I thought I'd give our branch a little boost by
establishing it as a poetry center. And Raoul has been the
answer to a librarian's prayer."

"*Erato* Poetry Club? In Plymouth?"

"A perfectly respectable Greek muse of lyric and erotic
poetry. I was going to call it Sappho, but that might have led
to misinterpretation. Better to steer clear..."

"You're not worried that Lazaro may turn Phil's head?"

"Phil is far too sharp and sensible for that sort of thing,"
Fiona declared. "And devoted to Stone."

"Obviously you don't remember the disasters of her dating
days. She even placed a genteel ad in the *Globe* personals.
And what a bunch of losers that turned up! She could have
been a chapter in the book *When Bad Men Happen to Good
Women*. Deidre had to take the matter in hand and conjure
up the perfect guy for Phil out of the blue, so to speak." As I
looked across the room, I could see that Phillipa was listening
to Raoul with the same rapt attention formerly devoted to
bringing off a perfect custard sauce.

"*When Bad Men?* Is that a real book? I never heard of
it. Well, good for Deidre, I say. Stone is Phil's perfect
complement, sent to her directly from the Cosmos. He's
tolerant, gentlemanly, intelligent, and a great cook himself,
so they have that in common, too, only he's relegated to
Sous Chef in Phil's kitchen. So come on now, Cass—you're
getting to be as dour and doomful as a Scot. Find a seat while
I introduce Raoul to the audience. A decent-size gathering,
too." And she sallied forth, in full glamour, beaming with
satisfaction.

All I could find was a round one-step stool of the kind libraries favor. It was wedged between the fiction stacks, Q through R, which meant I only got to see the top of Lazaro's dark smooth hair. But he projected his lines like an actor, so I could hear every consonant of both the Spanish and English versions. The one about learning of his mother's death in Cuba while he was in a detention camp in Miami brought some audible sobs. "And she will rise, *mi madre del ángel*, on wings of mourning into *mañana.*"

Following the reading, Raoul signed slim volumes of *We Drowned at Dawn* for a number of adoring fans. A black and red line sketch of the poet was emblazoned across the white dust jacket cover, and on the back cover there was a full-page photograph of Lazaro leaning against a stone wall, cigarette dangling from his mouth, as if about to be shot by a firing squad, sans blindfold. With the sun or smoke from the cigarette narrowing his eyes, he managed to look at once pained, fragile, sensitive, and tall. A trick of focus; Raoul was not as tall as Phillipa, who kept slouching at the knees whenever she stood next to him.

I went in search of the refreshment table, where I found Patty Peacedale had just finished setting out goodies with a practiced hand. After we'd greeted one another, I said, "I had no idea you were a poet, Patty. You're full of surprises."

"Oh, I've always had an interest in poetry, ever since high school, even after I met Wyn, got engaged, and all." Patty settled herself behind the coffee urn. "It's such a solace, scribbling away in the odd moments between committee meetings. Wyn finds my Eternal Life poems quite useful in his funeral services, and I've done some work with couples, too, using my Heavenly Union poems. I believe I may have written over eight hundred poems now. Perhaps you'd like to read them sometime? I love sharing..."

I swallowed my alarm, struggling for a change of subject. "So...Patty...are all the members of the Erato Poetry Club here tonight? How many altogether?"

"Nine, counting Fiona, who oversees, you know, rather than actually writing anything. Oh, Cass, you want to join us? That would be so super!"

"Not unless I'm overcome with the sudden urge to write poems. I'm just curious. Could you point them out to me?"

"You're got some kind of bee in your pointed hat, Cass— I know you. Well, let's see—over at the signing table, the woman manning the cash box, that's Sister Mary Vincent. Roman Catholic nun in plain clothes. Devoted to Gerard Manley Hopkins and sprung rhythm, whatever that is. The girl next to her, the one unpacking more books, that's Cissy Ponder. Unitarian. Writes free verse—naturally. You know those Unitarians! And Marigold Finch the one who's rearranging Raoul's display —Marigold owns the Floribunda Flower Shop. You'd be surprised to read her poems—wow, are they hot! Belongs to our congregation, donates the occasional flower display when she overstocks. Two others are downstairs bringing up more bottles of white wine from the Folk Arts refrigerator. Harriet Hubble Hastie and Deanine Philbin-Dorrance. I always think three names sound more poetic, don't you? Harriet belongs to Gethesmane, too, and bakes the loveliest oatmeal-apricot bars. I quite lost my taste for brownies after the poisonings last year, didn't you? Deanine claims she's a card-carrying Agnostic, but her husband Don Dorrence is a Baptist and believes there is Power in the Blood. He's no poet, however—goes bowling on Erato nights. Phillipa, of course, so exciting to have a real Wiccan, and our dashing president, Raoul Lazaro, who claims no religion because of Castro but really anyone can tell from his eyes that he's Catholic. And little old me, Presbyterian Poetess for spiritual occasions."

I was beginning to feel a bit dazed by this fulsome litany. Mercifully, I could turn my attention to the wine and cheese—so necessary to any literary event. I was swigging down a fairly decent if cheap Chilean Merlot when Phillipa found me and dragged me away to meet the poet. "Didn't I tell you? Magnificent, isn't he?" My friend was breathless and glowing with a pale fever—not a good sign.

"Ah, Cassandra, the prophetess—I've heard so much about you," Raoul said.

"And I about you," *ad nauseum.* I held out my hand, if only to get the vibes.

Taking Raoul's hand was like falling into an endless well, a black hole. So dark that I could read nothing but a kind of whirling, sucking center. But one thing I could feel instantly: this man was an energy vampire, one of those people who live on the life force of others. And something else. Not *deja vu* but *absolute recognition.* I dropped his fingers, afraid he'd steal my breath away.

I moved into a shadowy place in the stacks, D through F, the better to watch Lazaro pull others into his vortex. Cissy Ponder went into "faint and fail" mode when he leaned over her and murmured a few words in her ear. Marigold, although made of tough Finch stuff, seemed literally to melt when he stroked her arm. One by one, the Erato poets flew toward the charismatic Lazaro like moths to a candleflame. Even Sister Mary Vincent blushed, clutched her rosary, and forced her gaze down to her sensible black shoes. Deanine and Harriet, like true handmaidens, brought wine and choice edibles and were rewarded with a searing smile. Didn't Lazaro's *harem affect* put Phillipa off? What had become of her usually reliable bullshit-detector?

Before we left that evening, I got Fiona aside. "Do me a favor, my fact-finding friend," I begged. "Is there any way you can check into Lazaro's past? His immigration status? I'm sensing we don't know the whole story. His family history, especially what happened to his parents. Political involvements. Anything. I can hardly ask Stone."

"Cass...Raoul is the centerpiece of my Black Hill renewal program," Fiona protested. But her gray eyes looked at me shrewdly over her half-tracks, and she made no further objection. "Got the whim-whams, did you?"

"It's like I've met this guy before. In another life. Not the best of my lives, either."

CHAPTER EIGHT

Time past and time future
What might have been and what has been
Point to one end, which is always present.

–T. S. Eliot

After Will and Joe got the last shelf and counter in place for *Deidre's Faeryland*, we took a break from setting up shop and went for "coffee and" at Sweet Buns, also in Massasoit Mall. I ordered a double cappuccino, Joe wanted plain black American coffee, Will went with Classic Coke, and Deidre asked for fruit almond tea, one of the more insipid herb concoctions. All four of us, however, got a house specialty, the Colossal Cinnamon Explosion Frosted Pecan Bun, a guaranteed thousand-calorie treat with plenty of artery-clogging sat-fat. But truly delicious, and we all savored the delectable sweet roll silently for several minutes.

When we got to the finger-licking stage, Deidre sighed. "I'll probably work it off this afternoon, getting my stock shelved. Will, tell Cass and Joe what you told me."

In Will Ryan, you could still see remnants of the handsome red-haired captain of the basketball team he had once been, but the hair had faded and thinned, the lithe frame thickened, and a florid, squeezed look had overtaken his face. His good-natured grin was still pure high school champ, yet when his face was in repose, it looked empty of thought and desire, even dully depressed. He obviously adored Deidre, who at half his size, was quicker, smarter, and more decisive. Energy burned so high in Deidre that she could accomplish wonders in a fraction of the time it would take anyone else. In her rare moments of quiet reflection, though, small lines of dissatisfaction pinched her mouth.

I wished I could help, but I was very careful (we all were) not to make intrusive wishes for one another. Whatever we asked for ourselves or another had to be open-ended so that the Universe of Infinite Solutions could work its often surprising magic. Perhaps I said silently, *May Dee's life blossom anew with love and fulfillment.* Later, even that careful wording brought me a twinge of guilt.

Sometimes I felt like the only person on a crowded river raft who could "see" around the next bend where white water was raging and cascading over the falls. *Danger ahead* surfaced in my consciousness like a mild electric shock. As I looked across the booth at my diminutive blonde friend and her big husband, I was aware of that little jolt now. Taking a deep breath, I pushed away the negative thought and tuned into what Will was saying.

"...and Finn says he'd sure like to have a chat with that guy who ran into the stable to save the horses at Fresh Meadow. Finn says that the true firebug will lurk around the scene of his crime just because he gets off on fires. Finn says he hasn't been able to find out one damned thing about the so-called hero's identity, which is odd in a small town like Plymouth where someone always knows something about anybody."

"I think Finn is right," I said.

"In that case," Joe said, "he'll show up again, the next time he needs a fire fix."

"What a terrifying thought," Deidre said.

"We've got to find out who he is, that's all," I said.

"That's all?" Joe scoffed.

I ignored him (well, not completely, being warmly aware of his thigh chummy against mine under the table of the small booth.) "Dee, if you're not too tired when you finish for the day, come around to Heather's after dinner. We've a few things to discuss."

"Discuss what? Some Oprah book?" Will asked. "You gals ought to try Clive Cussler. Now there's an author you can get your teeth into."

"It's not my book club, hon," Deidre said, her dimple twinkling. "It's our craft circle this time. What are we making tonight, Cass?"

"We're decorating a mirror," I said. "Reflecting back, you know, *whatever*. Maybe you have something in your workroom?" True enough, our project would be a shield and reflector to bounce evil-doings back to the doer.

Deidre had tried several times to explain the circle to Will but he persisted in the image with which he was most comfortable—*Girls Night Out*.

"Don't give it another thought. I know just what we need," promised our mistress of poppets, amulets, and other magical handicrafts.

Joe looked at Will, looked at Deidre, looked at me. "Women's Mysteries, is it? No men allowed?"

"If you remember your Roman history," I said, "the Mysteries were always off-limits to guys and therefore the subject of male erotic fantasies. Clodius Pulcher disguised himself as a woman just to get into the Bona Dea festival at Caesar's house and find out what the matrons were up to. When he was discovered, it was a great scandal with incendiary repercussions. Clodius was prosecuted for sacrilege, and Caesar divorced Pompeia. Bona Dea was their May Day thing. "

"*Bona Dea.* Good Goddess," Deidre mused. "Wish I could have been there."

"Maybe you were," I said. "In one of your past lives. Would you want to have been a Roman matron?"

"When I think about a past life, I most often see myself sitting in the solar of a drafty castle working on a wonderful tapestry. How about you, hon?" She patted her husband's hand and looked up at him playfully.

Will surprised her. "I wouldn't mind being a gladiator," he said. "Those guys were like rock stars." He grinned, grooving on the imagined applause and attention. "The glory days don't last long, though."

"I must have been a hedge witch," I said.

"You still are," Deidre said.

Ignoring the interruption, I continued my train of thought. "The village herb gatherer, healer, midwife, and all-around Dr. Phil. Maybe in Germany. Isn't it interesting how we can all come up with an answer to the question, *If you had a past life, who were you?*"

I looked at Joe, who had a faraway gleam in his eye, just the way he often did when it was a long time between assignments. *Cabin fever.* "The captain of a sea-going vessel, of course. One that was carrying ivory, gold, amphors of wine. Mycenaean."

"Perfect," I said.

By the time we went back to work in *Faeryland*, which was scheduled to open its doors on Valentine's Day, we were high on the boundless possibilities of time and an overload of sugar. While Will and Joe cleaned the floor of carpentry debris, Deidre and I stocked shelves with her prolific family of magical dolls, delicate fairies, troll guardians, and kindly brownies. The accurately endowed teaching dolls named Tommy Tinkle and Tillie Tinkle had their own special shelf and accouterments.

The centerpiece of the store was a cottage housing a dear little family of woodland "brownie" elves with all their miniature belongings—shoemaking tools, sewing baskets, and cast-iron cooking pots in the kitchen fireplace. The beds upstairs sported feather pillows, gaily colored quilts, and miniature chamber pots underneath. Outside the little house, there were tiny chickens, pigs, sheep, a cow, and a brown-spotted dog. A thimble-sized mailbox near the front gate held several tiny Valentines.

It was all I could do not to stay and play, but we'd promised Scruffy and Raffles a good run before dinner. The beach was still too cold, but there were plenty of sheltered paths in Jenkins Park.

☙

We met in Heather's Victorian living room, distributing ourselves on comfortably cushioned love seats and fainting couches, avoiding the antique side chairs for fear of shattering them when we plumped down. A tray of after-dinner liqueurs and cookies was set up on the sideboard, at odds with the blue enamel pot of Captain Jack's boiled coffee, for which he had provided shipworthy mugs. A cheerful fire was falling into glowing embers in the fireplace. Over the blackened remnants of logs, I laid the dried sage branches I'd brought. They fired up in a brief blaze, a fragrance meant to inspire us with Wiccan wisdom. Or at least, to help us avoid foolhardiness.

"Talk about *Lifestyles of the Witch and Famous*," Phillipa murmured as she gazed at the collection of jade objects d'art on the marble mantelpiece, which rivaled some of those found in the Boston Museum of Fine Arts.

"Loot brought back from the Orient by my ancestral benefactor." Heather swept into the room wearing a plum-colored velvet tunic that perfectly set off her slim, athletic figure. "Jade is the stone of fidelity, peace, harmony, and tranquility. In Asia it's prized for soothing the emotions and promoting good health. Great-great grandfather Morgan, that shrewd old Yankee, knew a good thing when he bargained for those pieces and brought them home for his collection. Perhaps to encourage his wife to remain true while abandoned at home during those long sea voyages. What can I pour for you? Fiona? Drambuie?"

"Thank you, dear." Fiona held up the glass to admire the warm amber color of one of her favorite potions. "I wonder if you gals realize that in Pieter Brand's book, *The Dragon of Utrecht*, the fire-breather is foiled by a brave young lad who holds up a mirror to reflect the dragon's blast of heat upon himself. So one would conclude, Brand is both conversant with and susceptible to a wee spell of mirror magic. Just in case, he's the one."

"I'd forgotten that," Heather said. A little scowl of concern wrinkled her brow. "But Pieter...no, it's not him.

It couldn't be. He's my neighbor, for Goddess' sake. If it's a new man in town, my money would be on.... Well, we'll see, won't we?" She pressed her lips together and continued to pour our various libations.

"Raoul was *so* pleased to meet you at last," Phillipa said to me, apparently oblivious to the direction of Heather's suspicions. "Isn't he amazing?"

"I was truly amazed at the turn-out," I confessed, accepting a mug of the captain's coffee, a real brain booster, and choosing an oatmeal crunchie to go with it. "And Raoul himself is quite devastating, as I believe you have noticed."

Phillipa's expression had a cat-in-the-cream quality that I found worrisome, but the moment for a sisterly warning passed in a flurry of exclamations when Deidre revealed the mirror she'd brought for our spell. *Where does she find the energy?* I wondered for the umpteenth time. If I'd dragged home from setting up a new shop to cope with a family of hungry nestlings, I'd be ready for nothing but a hot herbal bath and a soothing CD. Well, maybe a relaxing backrub, too, and whatever came of it afterwards. But Deidre was bright-eyed and dimpled, sipping Bailey's Irish Cream, her usual perky self. The round black mirror she unveiled, traditionally used for scrying, was believed to open the portal into another dimension. To tell the truth, I'd never dared to look into a real black mirror like this one, because I get enough dizzying visions on my own. But now I gazed at it sideways and squinting, like someone taking a quick peek at the dangerous eclipse of the sun. Deidre had decorated the frame with runes of protection, justice, and strength: Algiz, Sowelu, and Eihwaz.

"Don't look in it, girls!" Fiona echoed my own reservations in her commanding glamour voice. "This is for *himself* to look in and see his own fiery impulses turned against him."

Heather said, "Eh, Fiona...what about the little matter of our not knowing who he is?"

"That's okay, here's what we'll say," Phillipa improvised. *"Gaze inside this mirror dark, you who light the evil spark, the harm you do will thrice return--it's yourself whom you will burn."*

"Gee, strong stuff, Phil," Deidre said, reaching over to polish a bit of lint off her mirror without exactly focusing on it.

"It can't be too strong to suit me," Heather declared. "Fiona?"

"We're within the 'harm none' rule. If this bugger never lights another match, he'll be safe as houses."

"Good enough for me," I said, but Fiona wasn't waiting. She'd already begun the chant. Deidre laid the mirror face down on an antique game table, and we held hands around it, joining in, picking up the beat a little faster with every repetition until it rang into the corners of the room and sang out into the pitch black February night beyond the windows. When one of the smaller canines lounging in the conservatory began to howl, we sensed it was time; we threw hands upward, offering our spell to the transforming universe.

I thought my ears were still ringing. But as the truth dawned on me, I could see the same recognition in everyone else's face. Far, far in the distance, somewhere in Plymouth, a fire alarm was sounding. The dog who had begun to howl kept on, and others joined her call, feeling their wolfish roots in the wild music of mayhem.

CHAPTER NINE

The day of fire is coming, the thrush
will fly ablaze like a little sky rocket...

–Anne Sexton

The Shawmutt Dog Pound is not a nice place for a dog to end up, whether strayed from or dumped by its former human companions. It's as unlike the Morgan Animal Lovers Shelter in Plymouth as it's possible to be. At Shawmutt, a canine has only a few days to be claimed or adopted before the fatal injection, and those few days are spent in a no-frills pen of unrelieved gloom amid noxious odors of defecation, disinfectant, and depression.

But at Heather's place, a canine could find sanctuary for as long as necessary to locate a suitable new home or simply live out its golden years in comfort and dignity. The accommodations are spacious, gracious, and climate-controlled. Classical music is piped in, and there are plenty of tennis balls and squeaky toys. Volunteers walk the dogs daily, and there's a play yard where sociable dogs can bat around beach balls under the supervision of a canine physical trainer. A luxurious Kitty Kastle on the premises is equipped with plush hidey-holes, a large screened-in porch, Audubon videos, and a quarantine ward for the infectious. Dedicated holistic veterinarian care is provided by Heather's husband Dick Devlin. Clearly, if you're a furry creature fallen on hard times, you could do a lot worse than land on AL's doorstep.

As unattractive an alternative as it is, however, the Shawmutt Dog Pound does offer one last fighting chance to an abandoned dog. At least it did until that evil soul who was currently haunting Plymouth consumed even that slim hope by setting a fire that raged through the building on the evening we created our mirror spell. When the fire threatened nearby government buildings, firefighters from Plymouth and several neighboring towns responded.

Joe, who'd been helping Will to construct yet another cabinet for dolls at Deidre's shop that evening (anything to keep him out of *my* kitchen!) hitched a ride to the scene. It was, he said later, an overwhelming horror show. The fire had started in back of the building, a tall spume of fire shooting from refuse barrels and immediately leaping onto the roof. Fortunately, a janitor on his way home from the government offices had spotted the conflagration and called 911 on his cell.

When the trucks arrived, it was still possible to rescue some of the frantic animals toward the front of the pound. Some firefighters and volunteers (Joe included) simply concentrated on opening cages and letting the dogs run, which they needed no urging to do, unlike horses. Soon thirty or forty dogs were dashing madly around in the darkness of nearby fields. A number of injured dogs were carried out from the back cages, but many others perished in the blaze when it became impossible to enter the building again.

Dick Devlin was called and broke all speed records with his Wee Angels Rescue Wagon. At first, when he saw what awaited him, the big man broke down and cried, but shortly afterwards went to work with cool efficiency. Dick's associate Maury Levin triaged the injured animals, while Dick and a Marshfield vet administered what first aid they could. Some of the more seriously injured victims were euthanasized on the site.

Somewhere between shots and salves, Dick called Heather. "There's a whole passel of survivors running around here in a frantic state," he told his wife, who for once was listening intently instead of screaming at the plight of animals in peril. "Got any room for them at AL?"

"I'll make room," she replied with grim resolve. "How will you transport them?"

"Joe's here, and he's volunteered to drive the wagon, but I'll need him to transfer the injured to the hospital. That friend of the Kellihers, Brand, was driving by. He's offered his SUV. Is Cass there with the Jeep? We could use her help. And Deidre—she has the Voyager."

"Deidre had to rush home as soon as Will got the call. Their new nanny Kinsey is visiting her brother in Wareham for the weekend, so someone had to stay with the kids—but Cass is on the way to help you," Heather promised my services.

I grabbed my coat and keys, glad to assist with the homeless canines. Soon these survivors would be lucking out at Animal Lovers where no one would ever bump them out of this world to make room for new residents.

When I got there, Joe had already loaded the Wee Angels Rescue Wagon to full capacity and was revving up to depart.

We waved in passing, and I recruited Pieter Brand to give me a hand rounding up strays. We managed to induce three anxious dogs milling about to hop into the back of the Jeep.

I noticed Brand was not wearing a coat, only a heavy turtle-neck sweater, one sleeve tattered and turned up, the arm lightly bandaged. "What wrong with your arm?" I asked.

"I don't know how it happened." Brand grimaced. "Burning wood seemed to come out of nowhere. Devlin fixed me up, though."

"You're burned?"

"It's not too bad," Brand said. "Come on, let's get those two mutts lurking over there behind the fire truck."

"Okay." As we moved gingerly toward the skittish dogs, I saw Mick Finn putting an Irish Setter into the back seat of his red Chief's car. In the midst of all this noisy chaos, he seemed to be crooning in the dog's ear. *Good*, I thought, *that's one animal who's found a happy ending.* I was right about that. Fiona told me later that Mick Finn had adopted a survivor of Shawmutt and named her Flame.

A young woman dog officer inveigled three more desperate doggies into my Jeep. Eight was just about my capacity, with two in the front seat stepping all over each other and me. I lost no time in racing my mob of mutts over to Animal Lovers so that I could make a second trip. Heather and her sanctuary managers, Grace Hulke and Fred Crippen, were on hand, with several volunteers hastily summoned. They waited right at the door ready to take the dogs off my hands and escort them to kennels. Goddess only knows where Heather would find enough room, but I had faith that she would manage even if half of them ended up at her house.

When I got back to Shawmutt to transport the next batch of stragglers, the first sight that greeted me was Dick, Maury, and several firefighters huddled over an object on the ground. Running over to see who was injured, I prayed it wouldn't be Joe who could act really crazy when there was danger involved.

It was Will Ryan. A couple of his crew had gathered around, and Maury was administering CPR.

"What happened?" I gasped. How much tragedy could one night hold? Will was another foolhardy soul who would dash into danger without a thought for himself. I'd seen him tumble off an electric pole when he rescued Fiona's uncooperative cat Omar and, another time, get mauled by two hysterical Spanish women while trying to turn on a sprinkler system.

"Thought it was smoke-inhalation, but Devlin says it might be a heart attack," one fireman said. "We just gave the paramedics a shout."

Even as the fireman spoke, the paramedics were running from Plymouth Fire Department's rescue vehicle (parked up near the main road "in case" of just such an incident) to load Will onto a stretcher. I dashed after them, but one of the paramedics closed the door in my face. When the truck didn't leave immediately, I assumed they were working on Will right there, trying to bring him back to consciousness.

I wanted desperately to know if this truly was a heart attack or only smoke inhalation, but since no one was going to tell me anything, I occupied myself in punching in Phillipa's number. By the time she answered, the Fire Department's rescue vehicle was screaming its way to Jordan Hospital. Having left Heather's place right after I ran out the door, Phillipa was at home listening to reports of the fire on Stone's police radio.

"Phil, get yourself over to Dee's place on the double," I ordered. "In about one minute, she's going to get a call from Mick Finn or me, whoever gets through first, that Will's collapsed at the scene and is on his way to the hospital. She'll need someone to cope with the kids until Betti gets back. I'm still rounding up stray dogs to bring to AL."

"Don't worry about a thing—I'm on my way! But *Sweet Isis*, what a disaster this night has been! What happened to Will?

"Not sure. It might be smoke inhalation, but Dick thinks it could be a heart attack. Will was unconscious when I saw him. I don't know if the paramedics revived him or not. They'll be at the hospital by now. I'll get in touch later— right now I've got to call Dee."

"Of course. Are you going to the hospital?"

"As soon as I'm sure we've taken care of things here. Oh, when you get to Dee's, you'd better call Fiona, too. Just let her know what's happened."

Next, I called Deidre, apparently before Mick Finn had, because she answered with her normal cheeriness, "Hi, Cass— what's up now?"

I told her. She shrieked in anguish, ending in a kind of bubbling sob. I reassured her that Will was getting the best of care and maybe it was only smoke inhalation that had knocked him out. Phillipa would be there in about five minutes to sit with the kids, I said, and I begged Deidre to drive with extreme care. "While you're waiting for Phil, maybe you'll want to give Will's Mom a call, then collect whatever you need to take with you. I'll see you later at the hospital. I'm sending out all my best prayers and wishes—everyone is."

"I can't believe this," Deidre cried out. Abruptly she hung up, and I didn't talk to her again until past midnight, when Joe and I finally got through rounding up and transporting critters from the former dog pound to Heather's shelter. I had really wanted to run to Deidre right away but felt committed to the task at hand. I learned later, though, that Fiona had been with Dee at the hospital the whole time. She'd moved like the wind to pack up Laura Belle and dash over to Deidre's, where she left the little girl in Phillipa's care.

"Kids and pets are *not* my scene," Phillipa had often declared, but in fact she managed very well whenever she was pressed into service. By the time we all got back to Deidre's house, she was whipping up some kind of from-scratch apple-stuffed pancakes for the millions, with Salty and Peppy lying at hopeful attention at her feet so that she was forced to step over them with every move. I marveled that she'd found the makings in Deidre's convenience food-stocked pantry.

Joe more or less carried an exhausted Deidre upstairs, while I fixed her a cup of tea laced with Irish whiskey. "She's completely wiped out," he whispered to me as we passed each other in the bedroom doorway.

"Dr. Blitz's diagnosis was rather vague, I thought, didn't you?"

"Some kind of heart rhythm thing," Joe whispered. "I've seen this before. They'll do a battery of tests, and they still won't be able to predict...well. Like Elvis, you know. Nice little family—what a Goddamn shame."

With my heart sinking down to my moccasins, I brought in the tea and sat with Deidre until she fell into a restless doze.

"I'll stay the rest of the night and tomorrow," Phillipa said, pouring coffee all around for Fiona, Joe, and me in Deidre's sun-yellow kitchen. Caffeine was just what I needed, and I was pretty sure it wouldn't keep me awake for a moment once I got home to bed. "At least until M & Ms gets here." The Ryan kids' grandma, Mary Margaret Ryan, had been located at the Mohegan Sun on a gambling outing with her blue-haired cronies.

"Dr. Blitz mumbled something about arrhythmia and fibrillation," I said, gloomily tasting one of those delectable apple concoctions. No matter how badly I feel, I can always eat—a mixed blessing. It keeps up my strength but I miss out on the natural diet plan that depression offers.

Fiona looked up at me sharply over her half-tracks. "Did he say what kind of fibrillation. Atrial, maybe?"

"He didn't," Joe said. "But it must have been serious to knock Will out that way. Lucky thing the fire department's got that defibrillator in the rescue vehicle. I talked to one of the paramedics who brought Will in, and he said that equipment is brand new, the first time they've had to use it. You know, earlier in the evening, while we were working on that cabinet, suddenly Will collapsed into a chair, and when I looked at him closer, I saw that his color had gone ashen. Said it was nothing, just tired out."

"We'll pray over this," Fiona said, with a glance at Joe. "Later. After you girls get some sleep."

Phillipa was back at the stove, flipping and talking over her shoulder. "I tried to get Raoul, hoping to cancel tonight's club meeting since Fiona and I would probably be knocked out. It was the strangest thing, and I've been worried about him ever since. He said he'd driven down to Brant Rock in Marshfield—for poetic inspiration, you know—and he'd encountered a strange light, like a Will-o'-the-Wisp, in the dunes. He tried to take hold of it, he said, and it burned his face and hands. Isn't that a weird experience?"

Fiona and I exchanged covert glances. Hecate, goddess of witchcraft and queen of the night, has a luminous quality and sometimes appears as Will-o'-the-Wisp.

"Weird indeed,' I agreed.

"Not at all," Fiona said, bypassing the Hecate lore, perhaps to mollify Phillipa. "A phenomenon of decaying marsh grass in Marshfield has a certain appropriateness about it. All you need is a spark from hydrogen phosphide, and *voila!*"

"In February? Maybe it was, like, a UFO thing—you know, similar to alien abduction or crop circles. I guess in Marshfield that would be *sea grass circle*, though, wouldn't it?" I said.

"Classically, it's known as *ignis fatuus*, foolish fire," Fiona continued without really considering my alien theory.

"I suppose you have a pamphlet on that?"

Fiona looked at her green reticule regretfully. "Oh, drat. I think I left that one at home."

I lapsed into a brooding silence, sipping Phillipa's excellent coffee and thinking of our mirror spell. How quickly do spells take affect, if they are going to? And what about Pieter Brand's burned arm?

I felt my suspicions zeroing in reluctantly on two suspects while I hoped I was wrong on both counts. How much more acceptable it would be if the arsonist turned out to be someone we didn't know or, at least, none of us liked much.

⌖

By late morning the next day, I was back at the hospital with Deidre, along with Joe and Fiona. Father Dan Lyons from St. Peter's making his rounds was unsure how to proceed with the uncertainty of Will's diagnosis. But when Will had a second attack, lost consciousness, and had to be revived again with a defibrillator, Father Lyons administered the last rites.

Wyn and Patty Peacedale came by to offer their prayers and help, along with Sister Mary Vincent from the Erato Poetry Club. That morning she'd given Lazaro a ride to Emergency to have his strange sunburn (or whatever) checked out, and while she was there, she'd heard about Will. She and Will were distant cousins, the nun explained. This "small world syndrome" is not as weird as it sounds; in Plymouth, "six degrees of separation" are reduced to no more than three. Sister Mary Vincent said she'd stay to say a rosary for Will, and Deidre, looking like a bedraggled elf, hugged her gratefully. Meanwhile, firefighters cluttered up the halls in shifts offering awkward comfort.

Sister Mary Vincent, Deidre, Joe, and Fiona said the rosary together. When Fiona's arm shot out to grab me with its characteristic tinkle of silver bangles, I noticed the three pencils stuck in her hair. A three-pencil day is a "ten" on the stress-meter. "Here, link up with us, Cass," she muttered. "All sincere prayers have healing power."

But I slid away, whispering, "Let me see what I can find out about Raoul. Don't you want to know if there are aliens with sunray guns roaming around Brant Rock?"

She let go. Good thing, because Fiona really does have an irresistible grip. I wondered if she'd ever taken up arm wrestling.

Omerta was in full force in Emergency; the gals there were as tight-lipped as the *Cosa Nostra*. No one would even verify that Lazaro had been treated there recently. That's because I made the mistake of answering truthfully, "No, I'm not a relative, just an acquaintance." I thought perhaps Lazaro was still languishing in one of the curtained cubicles, waiting for a ride home from Sister Mary Vincent.

The girl at the computer looked at me suspiciously. "Where's Sister Mary Vincent who brought this guy in, if he's here?"

"Visiting another patient, her cousin. Can I help?"

"What's your name?"

"Cassandra Shipton."

"Wait here a minute!" She moved away from the desk, walked briskly back to the rear of the corridor, and disappeared from view. When she emerged a few moments later, she nodded to me.

"Yes?" I said.

"Mr. Lazaro says you're a friend. The doctor gave Mr. Lazaro an injection that might make him drowsy. He'll need a ride home. Can you find Sister Mary Vincent and ask her to drive the patient home, or maybe you...?"

"She's saying the rosary. I'll do it." What better way to hear about that mysterious Will-o'-the-Wisp than from the poet's mouth? I followed the girl back to where Lazaro was sitting on a gurney, his legs dangling over the edge.

"Change of drivers," I said. "Okay?"

"I'm delighted," Lazaro said with a hint of his old suaveness, but in truth, he was looking blotchy and uncomfortable.

I couldn't very well give Joe a call on his cell to tell him I'd be back later—not in the middle of a rosary—he'd have to take my disappearance on faith, I thought as I brought the Jeep around to the Emergency exit door where Lazaro was waiting. He got in—gingerly, I noticed. He was not too far gone, however, to smile at me. Even in his disfigured state, he had a devastating, seductive smile, reminding me of a sexy vampire of the Hollywood persuasion. "Ever see a Will-o'-the-Wisp, Cass?" he asked.

"One rarely sees that phenomenon in winter," I said. "It's very strange. Did I hear right, that you tried to grab the thing and got sunburned?"

"It might have been an allergic attack, something I ate," he said. "It wasn't a burn, after all. Just a case of galloping hives. They gave me a massive shot of antihistamine."

"Are you feeling better now?"

"Not really. The hives seem to keep roving to new places. Some of them quite uncomfortable."

"Bummer," I said. "So...did you hear the fire alarms?"

"What fire alarms?" Lazaro said. He was rubbing his left shoe against his right shin.

"Try a cool oatmeal-flour bath," I suggested. "The starch sooths itches."

Lazaro was renting the upstairs apartment in a charming Cape Cod within sight of the shore and some very picturesque fishing boats. The cottage, which was quite near to Fiona's place in Plymouth center, had once been called *Deluca's Sea Garden Gallery and Gift Shoppe* but now housed the *Footloose and Fancy Free Travel Agency*. As soon as I dropped Lazaro off, I drove straight back to the hospital and reported to Fiona.

"Hives," she said dreamily. "And you said that Pieter Brand was burned? Curious that the two of them..."

"Yes."

"Well, this isn't the Middle Ages," she said cryptically.

"Middle Ages?"

"A sudden physical reaction is not evidence of guilt. Cass, you really need to start focusing on these fires, my dear. We need to know who, why, what, and where, before there are any more tragedies. And poor Will, a victim just as surely as if he'd been injured in the fire itself."

I don't know how many times I'd explained to Fiona that these revelations are never voluntary and rarely complete. My man-in-the-balaclava vision was a case in point. We still didn't know who he was. Something would come to me, but I didn't know what, and I didn't know when. It would depend, too, on my interpreting whatever I "saw" correctly.

And besides, the future wasn't looking good to me right then. All through that day, after only a few hours sleep, while we took turns hanging around the family waiting room at the hospital with Deidre, I felt myself going directly against Fiona's suggestion and trying *not* to envision the future.

CHAPTER TEN

My object all sublime
I shall achieve in time—
To let the punishment fit the crime.

–Sir William Schwenck Gilbert

Bedlam at Animal Lovers did not faze Heather one bit, and her live-in manager Grace Hulke, a large untidy woman with long gray braids and a knitted cap, shambled around imperturbably as usual, looking like a street person sans supermarket cart. Although she avoided all eye contact with humans, Grace was a tender caretaker to the sanctuary residents, which was what counted after all. Fred Crippen, a cadaverous taciturn person who might have been drawn by Toulouse-Lautrec, assisted her by day. Both these regular employees had the air of being abandoned souls themselves. When the physical responsibilities of operating the shelter were becoming more than even this redoubtable couple could handle, there were always volunteers to be marshaled into action.

Heather was in her glory, pressing these good temps into extra hours and ordering the finest modular dog kennels and shelters to house the thirty-seven new residents as Animal

Lovers underwent an immediate expansion. I marveled at Heather's largesse with her blue and gold Mont Blanc pen and leather-covered check book three times the size of mine, but she merely waved airily at the portrait hanging on the wall, her great-great-grandfather, Captain Nathaniel Morgan.

"Who knows what my revered ancestor was *really* trading in China? The opium trade was, after all, one of the most lucrative. Perhaps his funding of this sanctuary will ratchet up his and the family's Karma for many lives to come. Kindness to innocent dumb animals, after all, is the most basic and laudable of human virtues. We ought to be stewards of the planet and its myriad creatures, not exploiters. And by the Goddess, this is the year I *am* finally going to become a vegetarian!"

She waved her Forker's Farm chicken salad sandwich in the air to emphasize her point. We were having a quick lunch in her office before returning to the fray. I had been pressed into service as a volunteer to help feed, water, and walk the barking horde, at least until Heather could hire another full-time caretaker or two and give us volunteers a break.

Every time I arrived home after a stint at Animal Lovers, Scruffy sniffed my shoes and jeans in deep disgust. *Hey, Toots, where have* you *been slumming? I've met a better class of mutts at the town dump.*

Raffles, however, simply greeted me with the joyous abandon and leaping kisses that humans have a right to expect from their canine companions—rather than a lot of smart remarks.

While I was filling in at Animal Lovers, M & Ms had rushed home to take over Deidre's menagerie, and Betti Kinsey returned from her weekend in Wareham. Although she had the status of an au pair, Bettikins, as she was affectionately called, didn't live with the Ryans but had rented a cottage on Crooke's Lane, so tiny that it looked like a playhouse, and she got around town on a Moped. Will was still in the hospital while various treatment options were being considered. One thing was for certain, his days as a firefighter were over. With their financial future so uncertain, Deidre continued to work—albeit, a bit feverishly—and actually held a grand opening of *Deidre's Faeryland* at the mall.

Heather and I talked about all this at lunch. She said: "Personally, I think focusing on that shop may be saving Deidre's sanity. We ought to drink to Will's recovery and her success!" She took a split of Veuve Clicquot out of her mini refrigerator, opened it expertly, and divided it between two plastic glasses. "I only wish Deidre were here to join us. I agree with Bette Davis that there comes a time in every woman's life when the only thing that helps is a glass of champagne," she said, handing me one. "Here's to all good things for Deidre and her family! May all that's best come to them in magical, marvelous ways."

I toasted with all my heart, and we clinked glasses, although it wasn't a real crystal *clink*. I sipped my champagne. The plastic took something away from the experience, but it was still an enervating beverage. Yet, I was aware of a nagging presentment.

"Did I tell you that the Kellihers are taking a sabbatical?" Heather said. "Gone back to Ireland to draw inspiration from the great Druid sacred sites, whatever they are. Won't be back until the Spring Equinox. I offered to take the cats, but of course Maeve said no, they are wild-spirited creatures who would pine away in confinement. That's so wrong! Cats are in danger every moment they are out in the so-called natural environment."

"So what did they do? Hire a cat-sitter?"

"You got it in one, Cass. And you'll never guess who it is?"

Not a question to ask a clairvoyant, even a "sometime" one like me. "Oh, Sweet Ceres! They've hired Sylvie away from Floribunda? But what will that poor wan thing do when her stint with the kitties is over?"

"The way we've got it figured, the job Dick was angling to get her, at the Nature Conservancy, will be open by then. Very neatly arranged, if I do say so myself. Working for the Finches, that girl is paying almost as much for her apartment as she makes in the store. What a rip-off. At the Kellihers, Sylvie has a pleasant place to live, light duties, and a decent wage she won't have to spend on anything. Can you guess why the sudden urge to revisit their Druid roots?"

I sighed. "It's Pieter Brand. Brian senses that Pieter is carrying the torch for Maeve."

Heather groaned. "I don't know how you do that."

"Sexual attraction and a cough cannot be hid," I said. "Say, I want you to do me a favor."

Heather looked at me doubtfully. "Sure, Cass. Anything I can fit into my present killer schedule."

"Invite Pieter Brand to dinner. Then let me know what night so I can set up a little caper with Fiona."

"Fiona? Set up what? I thought that *I* was your regular partner in crime."

"I need you for a diversionary tactic this time. Here's the thing, Heather. Remember that we did that mirror spell on the same night as the Shawmutt Pound disaster.

And it's a spell designed to reflect fire back to the one who sets it. There were two curious maladies that night—ones we know about, that is. Pieter's arm and Raoul's hives. Now I realize the arsonist may very well be some nerdy guy we never met who lives in the wilds of Carver or Kingston and gets his jollies from setting fires that destroy living beings. Nevertheless, Pieter gets to be a person of interest because *he was there* "just driving by" and helped to rescue the animals, like the hooded guy who was seen at Fresh Meadow. And Raoul was out that night, too—'communing with nature,' as he calls it, and claims to have run into a Will-o'-the-Wisp in February, which gave him a sunburn that turned out to be hives. Two suspicious occurrences that I feel bound to investigate. After I rule out Pieter and Raoul, I'll branch out to the usual suspects, your local vicious villains. But I believe in an intentional universe, so I'm inclined to think I'm on the right track already."

Heather sighed and emptied the rest of the champagne into both our cups. "You expect me to be a gracious hostess to someone who may have been burning up animals for sport?"

"It's in a good cause. While you're wining and dining the suspect, I'll be having a look at his things in the Craig place. Maybe find a clue. I can't ask Deidre, for obvious reasons—she's running herself ragged between the new store and the sick husband. Good thing she has such excellent help. I can't ask Phillipa because she gets all-over law abiding whenever I mention an expedition of this nature."

"Well, no wonder. She's married to the Law. Breaking and Entering, I believe Stone would call it. What exactly do you expect to find—a can of gasoline on the kitchen table?"

"Not unless I'm incredibly lucky and Pieter is extremely stupid. All I expect to do is breathe in something from the atmosphere of his living quarters. You know how it is when you enter someone else's house? There's a real aura? Well, for me that aura may be a bit stronger than for most. Sometimes nearly overwhelming. As for the legalities, I'm hoping to locate an unlocked access. Remember when we were there before? I've got my eye on that little high pantry window. No one ever locks a little high pantry window. So then, I figure, it's only *Entering*. I'll bring a Welcome-to-the-Neighborhood bread in case I get caught red-handed and need an excuse for being there. Do you think Pieter would like my Banana Surprise?"

"And you're taking Fiona?" Heather's tone was incredulous.

"Fiona is game for anything. I don't want to go alone, and there's no one else, since you're going to be getting the suspect out of our way. I'll have a look at Pieter's books, too. That's always so revealing."

"Don't forget the medicine cabinet and the refrigerator. But I'm asking you again, Cass—*Fiona?*"

"I'll need a lookout. And I won't let her bring the pistol. Be a shame if Pieter got shot trying to get into his own house."

"What about Raoul?"

"I'll burn that bridge when I get to it. You know where he lives? DeLuca's."

"Hey, small world. It's the *Footloose* travel agency now. And I know the gal who runs it, Wendy Windsong, so maybe we can work something out there later. Whoever did the deed, I'd like to see him buried in the same pit with the animals he torched."

"Banish that thought. What we'd like to see is an evil arsonist handed over to the law."

"Yeah. After he's buried," Heather said.

That night Heather called me to say that Pieter Brand was coming for dinner at seven on Thursday night. "I'm serving him truth serum," she said. "Honestly, though, he has rather a charming way about him. I find it hard to believe..."

"Take a look at that burn, how it's healing and all," I suggested. "Remember the poisonings at the church? I think that was a lesson in not being a sucker for innocent charm."

Fiona would be glad to come with me, she said, providing she could get a sitter for Laura Belle. No, she would not be bringing the pistol, which she now kept locked up in the glove compartment of her old baby blue Lincoln Town Car.

That left only the problem of Joe, who took a dim view of any overtly illegal activity on my part and tended to lecture me on sensible behavior and staying out of harm's way because he couldn't live without me, et cetera, et cetera. Those loving arguments that were difficult to refute when he was holding me in his arms and addling my reason so that I wouldn't think about those many times he got himself thrown in jail in some foreign country. *Talk about double standard!* But in this particular questionable endeavor, the Goddess smiled on me with one of her left-sided smiles. As it turned out, Joe would not be a problem because of the Korean whales.

The *Rainbow Warrior* was on a month-long campaign in Inchon Harbor to protect some of the world's most endangered big mammals and the ocean they inhabited. The ship had been greeted by the Korean Federation for the Environment, a phalange of Buddhist monks, and children who danced and handed out *I Love Whales* t-shirts. Two marine biologists on the ship were conducting a whale survey, and a Greenpeace volunteer cyber-activist was keeping a daily computer log for the rest of the world to read. It was, all in all, a very successful publicity campaign. But then the guy responsible for running the ship (Joe called him the equivalent to Scotty on the *Enterprise*), the engineer out of Amsterdam, got a ruptured appendix and had to be taken on shore for an emergency operation. Greenpeace headquarters called Joe to fill in, and he agreed to take over the job.

He broke the news of this unexpected assignment gently to me on Tuesday, and I tried not to appear too agreeable about the cutting short of his leave, even when he said, "I'm really sorry I couldn't get to those countertops this time." By Wednesday, his battered old duffle bag was packed and he was on his way to the airport for the long flight to Korea.

I said as I often did, "Stay on the ship, love. Don't be a hero with those college volunteers who'll be bouncing around in dinghies and holding up banners."

"Don't worry about me. I'm wise, mature, and getting a touch arthritic. Just concentrate on keeping yourself out of mischief while I'm gone. There are only two weeks of this tour left, so I'll be back before you know it." His usual parting cautions and promises.

"I'll be the model of a prudent *herb wyfe*, just keeping the potions perking and the home fires burning." *So to speak.*

Pro forma. Neither of us really believed that. Might not be the best basis for a mature marriage, but it didn't matter because we were still irresistible to each other. And the good-bye kisses were very sweet. The only thing sweeter would be our hellos.

CHAPTER ELEVEN

Like a wild stranger out of wizard-land
He dwelt a little with us, and withdrew;
Black and unblossomed were the ways he knew,
Dark was the glass through which his fire eye shined.

–Edwin Arlington Robinson

Nick Deere was no fool. Parking his Harley in a municipal parking lot around the corner, he'd walked stealthily back on the shadowed side of the street toward Pryde's Video Place, where he'd lounged in the shadows of a narrow alley across from the store. An hour later, at five, a skinhead wearing a skull and crossbones shirt had entered the shop and replaced Pryde at the cash register.

Nick watched as Pryde hustled down the street. Grinding the unfiltered Camel he'd been smoking under the heel of his boot, Nick followed the porcine little body. Pryde hurried into the Floribunda Flower Shop. No way was Luke there to buy someone a floral tribute. Nick was a cool hand at reading faces, and he'd detected the evasive look in the man's eyes when he pumped him about Syl.

Nick had some unfinished business with that fucking broad. Claiming he'd owed her some pitiful savings she'd got from working at the 7Eleven, she'd taken a couple of hundred from his stash in the trailer—what a wimp. If she had any guts, she'd have snatched the lot. But no one ran out on Nick until he was damned good and ready to dump her. Like that Pauline. She'd tried it, and Nick had taken care of her good. Not a trace, either.

Nick figured he was hot on Syl's trail now. Grabbing a cup of coffee and a slice at the pizzeria opposite, he studied the flower shop while waiting for Pryde to leave.

Careful and casual though he'd been, when he asked about Syl, that red-haired bitch at the counter had squinted at him suspiciously. Eyes narrowed, lips pressed together. She knew Syl, all right—no fucking doubt about that. Once he'd caught her glancing up the back stairs. Just a flicker, but it hadn't escaped him. Those windows above the shop—looked like an apartment up there.

Later that night, Nick had returned. Easy enough to break in the back door. The rooms upstairs were clean, neat, and empty, no sign of occupation, but Nick knew Syl had lived there recently. He could smell her.

On his way back through the store, Nick had scooped up all the cash he could find—which wasn't much. He'd smashed the thermostat regulating the cooler where perishable flowers were kept fresh. Breaking the glass case in the show room, he'd dumped water out of those containers, and as a parting shot, left his burning cigarette on the wooden counter.

Best to stay away from his trailer for a few days, in case Syl put the finger on him for the damage. Nick was on the outs with his old man again, but he knew a guy at Johnny D's Garage in North Plymouth. Bruce the Greaseball. Maybe he could crash at his place for a few days. Only a matter of time before he got a chance to settle with Syl.

༄

As soon as Joe left on Wednesday morning to save the Korean whales, I made my Banana Surprise breads. After they cooled, I wrapped one of them in cherry-colored plastic wrap with matching ribbons, adding a *Welcome to Plymouth* tag. I figured this was as good an excuse as any to walk into someone's house. If I got caught, that is.

Heather called and we synchronized our timing. "Carry your cell, Cass, just in case something unexpected happens and I need to get in touch."

"What can happen? Keep the guy there until nine-thirty or so, and the deed will be done."

"Are you still taking Fiona?"

"Yes, I'm taking Fiona. She'll be fine. We've done this before with Fiona, if you recall."

"But the thing is, I was there with you to keep Fiona from screwing up the search."

Obviously Heather didn't remember that it was she and I who had spooked the target, not Fiona.

The next night Fiona arrived at my house twenty minutes after seven, breathless, with only one pencil in her hair—a good sign. I was already pacing the floor because I wanted to get to the Craig place around seven-thirty. Even if Pieter was running late, he would have left for the Devlin's place by then, probably on foot because their houses were less than a quarter of a mile apart. I figured I'd need an hour or more to soak in the atmosphere and poke around—just a quick psychic hit—and I didn't want to cut things too close.

It was seven-forty by the time I parked the Jeep on a broad shoulder of the main road a good distance from the house. Fiona and I crept down the long driveway, keeping to the shadows of tall pines. The front light was on, and I could see the formerly rotting porch floor, which went around three sides of the house, had been replaced and painted. And there were other signs of recent renovation in the tumbledown Victorian mansion, including a new roof and the removal of the catalpa tree that had crushed it last year. A light was burning in the kitchen and in another downstairs room, perhaps the library.

"Let's go around back and see if he's left a window unlocked in that pantry," I whispered.

"If that's how you want to do it," Fiona said. It was then that I noticed she was carrying her reticule.

"I'm going to need you to keep watch and tell me if anyone comes," I reminded her. "Now, you don't have anything in your bag that I have to worry about, do you?"

"I think it would be better if we went around through those bushes on the dark side," Fiona said. "This side is too well lit."

She had a point. The ample circular driveway was plainly visible in the glow of the front light. *What was that—a thousand watts?* I wedged through the bushes on the wooded side with Fiona closely following me until we got to the back of the house. Through the kitchen windows we could see that the remodeling bug hadn't yet bitten that room, where ancient pine cabinets and counters had turned as dark as molasses and were probably just as sticky. Sidling a bit farther, I found the pantry was dimly illuminated by a light in the kitchen shining through the open door.

"Can you give me a hand here, Fiona? This is the window I thought might be unlocked." I indicated a rubbish bin—square, like a smallish dumpster—which we struggled to push under the window. When we'd shoved it into position, I got a leg up from Fiona and teetered on the rim of the bin, trying to push up the window. I thought it gave a half inch but was perhaps too grimed up with dirt and old paint to budge easily.

"Here, use this," Fiona said, reaching into her reticule. She handed me a putty knife—perfect! I used its flat blade to loosen the window, jimmying it up an inch at a time. It took a great deal of effort, the parka I was wearing made me feel much too warm (or was I having a hot flash? *Of all the times....*!) I edged out of the coat and let it drop to the ground. Then one more mighty shove, and...

...*Oops!* The cover tilted and I fell ass-backwards into the rubbish bin! Fortunately, some unsavory bundles cushioned my fall, and I struggled out of there with only a bruised elbow and mashed foot. Maybe I would look through that trash for evidence when I was through in the house.

"Okay, give me another hoist here," I muttered to Fiona.

"Better to use this, I think, dear." Out of her reticule, she pulled a slim nylon rope ladder, just room for one foot after another—the kind of thing that Boy Scouts probably got a badge for making. Next she fished out an S-hook to fix it to the windowsill.

"Geeze, you could have clued me about the ladder. What else have you got in there, lady?"

"What else do you need?" she asked, while I threw the hook over the rim of the window, attached the little rope ladder, and tested it with my weight. It seemed to hold just fine, and I eased my way up and over the sill. Except that my butt got stuck halfway through the small window.

"Need a push, dear?" Fiona asked.

But just then I tumbled through, cruelly scraping my hips, onto a cabinet built in under the window. A basket of apples cascaded onto the floor as I leaped to my feet. I leaned my head back through the window. "Better keep an eye on the driveway and hoot or something if you see Pieter coming home."

"You mean like this?" Fiona did a good imitation of the Great Northern Owl celebrating a successful mouse hunt.

"Great! Very authentic," I said. "Hand me up that banana bread, will you? Just in case. And the pen light. I think I left that in my Parka pocket."

Fiona stood on tiptoes and I reached down to take the two items. I left the bread on the pantry shelf and moved forward through the kitchen. A cold cheerless room, no "heart of the home" at all. I shivered, opening the ancient refrigerator to have a quick look. A bachelor's refrigerator. Carton of orange juice, piece of beef sausage, wedge of Gouda that looked gnawed, half-empty tin of beans, and four bottles of imported Amstel Bier. Good thing he was getting a decent meal at Heather's.

Closing that pitiful appliance, I moved down the dark hall to the other lit room, the library. No more a shadowy mausoleum of mildewing books and shrouded mahogany furniture, the library had undergone an amazing metamorphosis. Now the lighting was bright and the furniture functional and highly polished, although rather too modern for the room. There were library tables, a drafting table, an easel, artist's supplies—oil paints, watercolors, palettes, jars, old flannel rags—in colorful profusion. The book shelves were filled with art books and children's books, although the higher shelves still held some of the old leather volumes. Sketches for what I assumed was Pieter's new book were laid out on one of the library tables.

That's when I really felt like a rank intruder!

Nevertheless, I had a look. A maiden running through a tangled wood, Munch-like screaming faces emerging in branches. A medieval soldier on horseback with armored cap, short cape, sword, and shield emblazoned with a red cross, accompanied by a fire-breathing wolfish dog chasing the girl. A woodsman in a green tunic that looked made of leaves, a bow over his shoulder, a dagger at his twisted vine belt. Gazing at the watercolors, I felt light from one of the brilliant desk lamps penetrating my eyes, bouncing me out of the room into the world of the illustrations. Was Pieter Brand the menacing soldier or the green woodsman?

Could he be both? Predator and savior. His mild, fair exterior and the deceptive studious glasses masked a hot depth of passion, flaming in the breath of the slavering dog, more violent even than I'd felt when I touched his hand at Heather's. I quickly withdrew from that image and stepped into the drawing of the huntsman, where I felt a whole different thrust of emotion. This was a knight without armor, a crusader, a righter of wrongs. *Pieter must be a Gemini*, I thought. *Of all the sun signs, the most difficult to read. Always charming, always unpredictable. If he's the arsonist, no one would ever guess. It's a Dr. Jeckle and Mr. Hyde thing.*

Since I'd promised Heather that I would inspect the medicine cabinet, I used a pen light to find my way down the cavernous dark hallway, and then to maneuver my way around the unlit room. I took in gauze bandages and disinfectant standing out on the marble counter as if recently used. An aloe plant. *Excellent treatment for a burn.* Inside the mirrored cabinet, shaving supplies and prescriptions. Valium. Percocet. Tylenol with codeine. He must be hurting a lot. I closed the door. The john had a great old mahogany seat with a pull chain. I realized I needed to pee.

I was sitting on that wooden throne when I heard Fiona hooting outdoors. Never have I moved so fast off a john! Pulling up my jeans, I raced down the hall to the kitchen, geared up to throw myself through the pantry window. But I paused long enough to toss the banana bread into the trash bin outdoors, then release the hook and let the rope ladder fall to the ground. I executed a Wonder Woman leap, and a moment later was on the ground with two aching ankles but all in one piece. Fiona was hurrying to meet me through the bushes, holding my parka. I slipped it on while she picked up the ladder and hook and stashed it in her reticule.

"Your cell phone was in your coat pocket, dear. Heather just called. Her guest claims to be feeling a bit under the weather and is ready to leave. She's insisted on giving him a cup of peppermint tea, but that won't delay him more than a few minutes. Where's the banana bread?"

"Won't need it, might weigh us down—got rid of it. *Let's go, Fiona!* You did great with that hooting, by the way. Even in the bathroom, I could hear it." We dashed around the dark side of the house the way we had come, took a short cut

across the porch, and made it to the car in record time for two
middle-aged witches caught without their brooms.

"Whew! That was great." Fiona heaved a sigh of
satisfaction while I revved up the Jeep and high-tailed it out
of there. "Brought me back to the joys of my misspent youth,
all those government offices we broke into, burning draft
records and whatnot. By the way, I didn't hoot."

"You didn't hoot! That wasn't you??"

"No, that was a real owl, dear. A magical bird, symbol of
the transforming power of spirit, cherished by wizards and
wise women the world over. I have a pamphlet on owl magic
at home that you might like to read."

"No room for it in your reticule with that assortment of
illegal entry goodies?"

"I like to be prepared," Fiona said. "I'd decided there was
no need to hoot when all I had to do was to rush back to
the window and call you. Just on my way when I heard our
feathered friend give warning. I'd like to call that wonderful
creature to my place, but I fear that Omar....he's such a jealous
little darling."

I had a sudden image of Fiona in my mind's eye. She
was wearing a fur-trimmed, hooded cloak, a basket over her
arm, an owl on her shoulder. Sparkling lights shone around
her, the very image of a fairy godmother. "Maybe Omar could
learn detente," I said. "Because I see you in some other life
with a companion owl. Do it, Fiona. Call an owl to your own
trees."

"Maybe I will. Let me think about that. But Cass...what
did you learn about Pieter? Is he the evil soul who set the
fires?"

"I learned only that he *could* be. The dark force burns within him with the heat of Hades. But somehow, I'm not convinced. He may be channeling all that personal electricity into his work. Art grounds the artist, you might say."

We were silent and companionable for the rest of the ride. I parked in front of Fiona's fishnet-draped cottage. Watching her carry the green reticule as if it were no weight at all, I couldn't help but wonder what other useful items she'd tucked in there. I decided not to ask, preferring to think that whatever was needed simply materialized within its mysterious depths.

After the kind neighbor who was watching Laura Belle scooted home, Fiona and I shared hot cups of cocoa and a few chuckles over my merry mishaps at Brand's place. "Uh-oh, I'm afraid I forgot to pick up those apples, too. They're all over the pantry floor," I giggled. "What ever will he think happened?"

Fiona said, "That's what I wondered, dear. Why go in the pantry window when we could have simply unlocked the front door?"

"What...what do you mean '*simply unlocked*,' Fiona?"

"Well, I did bring my master key and my lock picks, the set I've had since the Sixties. We used them when we broke into the Craig place the first time, don't you remember? You are taking your ginko biloba, aren't you?" She reached into her reticule and drew them forth.

Real burglar's tools, I thought. *A felony simply to possess them with intent to use.*

Fiona continued unperturbed by my expression, which was certainly registering vexation and chagrin. "But you seemed set on going in through that pantry window, so I thought there must be some magical application to your plan. I didn't want to interfere.

Chacun á son gout."

I was truly speechless for some time. Then I said, "Fiona, you won't let anyone outside the circle know that you have that stuff, will you?"

"Not to worry, dear. I've said a few words over this set and consecrated them with the four elements. So I very much doubt that anyone would recognize them."

"You mean you put an invisibility glamour on your burglar's tools?"

"These things are so difficult to put into words," she sighed. "Let's call it a Magical Misplacement. You know how it is when you're looking for something and it's right there in front of your eyes but you keep missing it?"

"Yes, sort of," I said.

"Like that, dear. See, first you bless the item with salt water and incense—the incense represents air, you see, and the water, of course, is water."

"And *they call the wind Mariah*," I muttered.

"Then you pass it through a fire. Best to use a potholder there. Finally you bury it for about...." Fiona continued with her recipe, lulling me with her calm tones. I actually forgot to be annoyed that she had let me fall into the rubbish bin without ever mentioning her keys.

❧

As to what Pieter Brand thought about the scattered fruit and whatnot, I got an earful about that from Heather the next day. "Pieter just called me, wondering if he should call the police or the animal control officer!" she began in an accusatory tone.

"Oh, don't be a worry-wart. I may have left a few apples on the pantry floor."

"And the window open?"

"Oh, Sweet Isis!" I felt that sudden chill that signals one has just committed a major stupidity, like dropping heirloom silver down a running garbage disposal. "Maybe I did forget to close it all the way. I never gave it another thought. *Stupid, stupid...*" The last was addressed to myself.

"Late last night Pieter went into his pantry to get an apple and guess what he found?"

"Apples?"

"He found two raccoons having a party, can you imagine that? Not only had they munched up most of the apples, but one of the raccoons appeared to have unwrapped a pink-plastic package with some sort of bread inside it. This fellow was stuffing himself and having a bit of scuffle with the other raccoon who wanted a handful for himself."

"Everybody loves my Banana Surprise—chocolate chips and cherries," I said. "Well, thanks be to the Goddess he's attributing that mess to the raccoons."

"*But wait, there's more.* After Pieter got the raccoons out of his pantry—he jousted them through the window with a push broom and a spray bottle of vinegar, he said—he found a *Welcome to Plymouth* sign on the floor. He wondered if the local Welcome Wagon had made a late call. So then next morning he went outside looking around for any other raccoon damage or signs of two-legged visitors."

"Shrewd move, but probably he didn't find anything, right?"

"He found footprints—human footprints—on one side of the porch where the paint had not quite dried. Two persons appeared to have run across it at top speed. He could tell that from the length of the strides. One woman, he said, might have been wearing orthopedic walking shoes; the other wore boots with one chipped heel. Pieter figures if he could find someone with gray paint on orthopedics, or the chipped boot, he may have caught himself a burglar."

"A regular Sherlock Holmes. And what did you say?"

"I said it was more likely that the Welcome Wagon ladies had been surprised and attacked by the masked critters, and the gals had made a run for it. I told him to put mothballs in his rubbish bin, and to keep it tightly covered, to discourage future visits from wild animals. Next time it might be coyotes. They have been sighted in this area, you know. And above all, to shut that pantry window and lock it."

"Good advice. I think you saved my bacon there."

"I'm not sure he believed a word I said. Just a feeling I had. Made me rather nervous."

"You were very plausible. And quick. Thanks."

"So...when's your next caper?"

"Why do you ask, as if I don't know?"

"Because I want to get into Raoul's apartment with you, of course. I can't let Fiona have all the fun."

"Would you believe that Fiona has a perfect set of burglar's tools?"

"Yes, I would believe that. Surely you remember that she used her lock picks when we got into the Craig place last year. But let's not tell Phillipa. It would be just one more item in the long list of our little secrets that she has to keep from her beloved detective."

"Right. So, when do you want to go?"

"Let me have a little chat with Wendy Windsong and see if I can figure when the coast might be clear."

"You go, girl." I was feeling better already. Perhaps Heather *would* be a more reliable partner in private investigations than Fiona.

ESBAT OF THE CHASTE MOON
CHAPTER TWELVE

Where are your books?—that light bequeathed
To Beings else forlorn and blind!
Up! Up! and drink the spirit breathed
From dead men to their kind.

—William Wordsworth

Before Heather could work out a way to investigate Raoul's place, a few other matters took center stage.

The first was my daughter-in-law Freddie—Winifred, married to my second child, the handsome computer whiz with green eyes just like mine, Adam Hauser. It's a long story, but in short, Freddie had come into our lives because she's gifted with an amazing talent for psychokinesis, which is the art of "mind over matter." Just by concentrating in her own intense way, she can addle a delicate machine, and in fact, had once saved our lives with that useful ability by altering the timer on a bomb. She can also move small objects (but only with extreme effort) and warm a metal spoon in her hands so that it bends like putty. Although I've done my best to instill ethical and protective controls in that girl—like

never, not ever trying to break the bank in a gambling casino—
she has slipped up a few times.

Not long after Fiona and I escaped from the Craig
place, Freddie called me, which in itself is unusual. Email
is her preferred mode of communication, and I do love her
brash, breezy style. Although I have two daughters of my
own—smart, warm, reliable Becky and theatrical, ephemeral
Cathy—I must have needed another, for Freddie has claimed
her own special place in my heart.

After the customary chit-chat about Adam, his job, her
job, their apartment, and a general inquiry into what mischief
I'd been up to in her absence, we got down to the reason for
her call. "I'd like to consult you on, like, an *awfully* delicate
matter," she said. "It's a surprise for Adam's birthday next
month."

*Next month? March? Freddie knows very well that Adam was
a July baby. Why the ruse? Does she think my phone is bugged? Or
hers?*

"Wouldn't it be nice if we could get together for a mother-
daughter consultation," I suggested.

"Cool! I knew you'd understand." I could feel Freddie's
grin through the phone. "You're the best, Cass. Listen, I have
to be in Boston for a conference next week. What if you, like,
threw caution to the winds and met me for dinner after I've
survived the day's boring meetings and speeches? I know that
would be a lot of night driving for a lady of your age, but..."

"I'm not doddering yet," I interrupted tartly. "And I'd love
to see you. To discuss Adam's birthday gift. And whatever.
But isn't this an Iconomics, Inc. conference? Won't Adam be
coming, too?" I asked. Freddie worked for the same Atlanta
computer firm as did Adam, who had recommended her for

an entry-level job. With her particular talents, however, she had soon risen through the ranks to become a *Troubleshooter Extraordinaire*

"Just me, not Adam. He's so senior now they're sending him to Britain on some awesome government project I hardly understand. As far as this being an Iconomics show, yes and no. *So*...how are all the other good witches of Plymouth?" Freddie changed the subject deftly. Okay, I would wait, but impatiently.

"Pretty much as you left them. I'll catch you up on everything later." I could be as mysterious as my daughter-in-law, after all.

"Yeah? What about all those fires I've been reading about. The stable, the mill, the dog pound—ugh! so awful to think of those little doggies. I keep tabs on crime in Plymouth, you know, just to see who my favorite crime-fighters might be hexing. I bet Heather's gone berserk over someone frying those poor animals. Up to your necks, are you?"

"That's a matter for the police now, my dear."

"Ha ha. You know I'm a whiz at reading people, just like you, Ma Soothsayer."

"Well, I guess we'll have a lot to talk about. But not on the phone." The rest of our guarded conversation was spent in setting up a time and place to meet. The lobby of the Taj, which was the old Ritz-Carlton (Freddie must be doing very well indeed!) at seven on Friday. She'd make a dinner reservation somewhere and surprise me, she insisted. It all sounded intriguingly clandestine. I should probably wear something black and elegant, meaning I'd better borrow an outfit from Phillipa whose wardrobe of slinky black stuff rivaled that of Morticia in the *Addams Family*.

ᑎᕉ

Another distraction was the demise of *Ye Olde Curiosity Shoppe Fine Antiques and Collectibles* on Court Street. It went up in a fast, fierce blaze, clearly arson, badly damaging both of its neighbors, *The Plimouth Art Club and Gallery* and *Winkenwerder's Used and Rare Books.* The book store happened to be a favorite hangout of Fiona's who never saw an ancient leather-bound volume or mildewing pamphlet she didn't love.

This being the fourth suspicious fire in a couple of months, state fire marshals and their insurance counterparts now descended upon Plymouth like vultures circling carrion. The term *serial arsonist* was being bruited about Plymouth, from the firehouse and police headquarters to the town hall and the *Plimouth Times.* Speculation moved along up to the *Quincy Ledger* and the *Boston Globe.* Fire Chief Mick Finn became ever more taciturn and surly at being bugged by both the arson specialists and the media.

Naturally, investigators weren't the only ones hanging around the smoking ruins, hoping to pick up clues. Heather, who had purchased a set of dining room chairs from *Ye Olde Curiosity's* proprietors Clive and Bev Cleverly, was able to ferret out the interesting tidbit that several rare and valuable first editions had disappeared from Winkenwerder's place in the massive confusion of the fire. Apparently Wink had been rushing back and forth with boxes of books he wanted to save in case the fire leaped over to his building, which it did in short order. Passersby offered to help load the books into his van while he dashed back for more.

"Does he remember what those good Samaritans looked like?" I asked Heather.

"Are you kidding? In the midst of imminent disaster, all he saw was another pair of helping hands. Now he's crying, where's my *Alice's Adventures*, my *Pinocchio*, my *Peter Rabbit*? When I told Fiona, she practically went into mourning over the lost treasures. She vows to dowse out their whereabouts, and you know, there may be something to that."

"You mean all the missing items were children's books?"

"Well, no, he mentioned Walt Whitman, too. *Autumn Boughs*, I think it was. And a first edition Keats' *Eve of St. Agnes* et al ."

"Any chance those books were cremated in the shop?"

"They were all in one special locked case, rare firsts in prime condition. Those were the books he was trying to save."

"Interesting," I said. "Didn't *anyone* see who was helping Wink?"

"Believe me, I'm asking. Maeve doesn't know if Pieter was there. Phil doesn't know if Raoul was there, and she really pinned me down about why I wanted to know. Finn has no idea, either, but these disaster scenes have been so jam-packed with TV crews and onlookers waving every time they see a camera, it's a wonder to me that the firefighters functioned as efficiently as they did. The worst are the busybodies who have no business getting in the way but simply swarm around all bug-eyed, adding to the chaos."

"Yeah, I'm glad we're not like that."

"Right."

∽

Even after his discharge from the hospital, the news about Will continued to be worrisome. A cardiac catheterization was scheduled to learn more about his specific arrhythmia. Running herself ragged between shop and home, Deidre was losing weight from her already petite frame. A tense double line appeared between her eyebrows, as if she couldn't quite see where she was going anymore.

"We've got to do a serious healing ceremony," Phillipa said. We were having a kitchen table conference about Deidre's troubled situation. The aroma of my Wise Woman tea blend wafted around our heads, while the two dogs settled down at our feet, smelling of wet fur from the cold, wild rain outdoors. "Put all this fire business aside and throw our energy into averting a tragedy right here in our own circle."

Put all this fire business aside? Heather and I glanced at each other in silent agreement not to bring up the touchy subject of our planned investigation of Raoul.

And so we agreed that the March Esbat would be entirely devoted to the Ryans. Esbat of the Chaste Moon, a time of rituals for banishing ill health and for promoting the life force, as well as honoring families. It would be perfect.

Only Fiona said, "You never know which way these things are going to work, my dears. All we can do is to channel our energy into Will's ailing body. We can't predict how that energy will be used."

"But he's always been so strong and robust," Heather mourned. "We have to do everything we can. This will be a real test."

"They've all been real tests," I demurred, breaking one of my oatmeal crunchies and handing the halves under the table where they were devoured appreciatively but noisily.

"Chocolate is a poison to dogs, you know." Heather scowled at the dish of cookies.

"Mostly raisins and peanuts," I defended myself.

"Or any sweets, for that matter," Heather declared, and not for the first time. "Dogs thrive best and are more disease-free on an unvaried, nutritionally balanced dry food. Table scraps are taboo."

Barks and twigs, that's all she feeds her mutts. Poor bastards. How about another cookie, Toots? I promise to spit out the chocolate chips.

"Yeah, yeah. You don't think I'm dumb enough to believe that, do you?" I replied.

"Well if you don't believe me," Heather said huffily, "ask Dick. He gets all the latest veterinary journals."

"For heaven's sake, Heather," Phillipa said. "Cass is talking to the dog not you."

I ignored them both and continued with the subject at hand. "Think about the changes we've brought about among ourselves, the seeds of wishes that have grown and blossomed. Surely we believe that our intentions have a real influence on events."

"When you open that door to the universe, you never really know what will walk through," Fiona said.

"Hey, Fiona," Heather said. "Enough with the doom and gloom. If prayers, wishes, and a few well-woven spells can do it, consider it done."

౪◡౨

Later I told Deidre what we had planned for the March Esbat. After she'd cried and then mopped up the tears, she said, "I suppose this was something I had to learn."

"What?" I asked.

In the living room of the Ryans' brick-fronted garrison Colonial, we were surrounded by Deidre's handiworks— framed embroidered mottos (*Love Me, Love My Poodles* and *Flowers of Friendship Never Fade,* and more in that vein), needlepoint pillows depicting angels and fairies, charmingly restored pine furniture Her restless energy never seemed to burn low, except perhaps when it came to cooking. We sipped from mugs of tea made with supermarket brand tea bags, now limply languishing in a ceramic poodle dish beside a plate of arrowroot cookies.

She glanced at the stairs and lowered her voice. "Will's resting. Oh, Cass, I feel so rotten. I've been, you know, *careless* about him. He's always been there for me since we were kids in high school. I never even went out with another guy, and that can make a gal really restive as the years go by." Her voice faded to a whisper. "What might I have been missing? I know Will's been a caring husband and father to our children, but somehow, I can't say I've cherished him. I have to admit that I've always found him to be a little slower than I would wish."

"You've made Will very happy, Dee," I said. That was true until recently, when I had actually detected the dark emptiness of depression in Dee's husband. "And he's so devoted to your family." Such comfort was thin, I knew. Deidre's dissatisfaction and unspoken longings had always been clear to me, too, whether through friendship or clairvoyance I couldn't say, they so often overlap.

"Oh, he's worked hard for us and made a good living, especially since he was promoted. Still, I found his eternal good-nature to be so tedious there were times I just wanted to punch him. And I know I took that strong silent strength stuff for granted. But now that he's become so frail, it's made me realize how much I really do love him. Always have. That must sound like a cliché reaction, but it's real, it's true. I love Will with all my heart and soul, and it's taken this catastrophe to make me realize it."

By now we were both crying, of course. Deidre got out the Irish whiskey and poured jiggers of it into our mugs of cooled tea   her favorite attitude adjuster.

Before our crying jag got too far along, however, the children descended on us from their Easter clothes-buying spree with Will's mother, M & Ms. Baby Anne woke up from her nap, at first sulky, but then clapping her hands with glee over the new hats. The resulting clamor had its own healing affect.

Finally, after M & Ms left, Deidre said, "Hush, you lot.Your father's having a bit of rest before dinner. Jenny, why don't you take everyone into the den. There's the new Pinocchio video you can watch."

That reminded me of Winkenwerder's missing books, so I related the news of that theft to Deidre.

"Are they very valuable, do you think?" she asked. "And could they be sold without the thief getting caught?"

"Sure, if you get the right buyer, an overseas collector maybe. Unless the arsonist took them as trophies of his night's work."

"Well, then, we should be able to find them and him," Deidre said, a little of her old sparkle coming to life in her blue eyes. "Fiona's our finder. Put her on it."

"That's what Heather suggested, too. Great minds run on the same ley lines. But Fiona was far ahead of us, as usual. You know how she values first editions. She began dowsing for the stolen items right after the fire at Winkenworder's."

"And?" Deidre asked eagerly. It was good to see her cheering up, even if it took a crime to do it.

"Fiona says the books have been sent out of Plymouth and are now located somewhere in the Boston area. More than that she doesn't know. She said she's a finder not a clairvoyant like me, and that I ought to get cracking and 'see' in what kind of place the books are stored."

"Have you?"

"I've tried. And I'll tell you what I've seen. Shelf after shelf of books in a kind of moldy old room. A real hodgepodge. So I'm assuming the books have been hidden among many others. Needles in the book stacks."

"You know what I think?" Deidre's old enthusiasm had definitely returned. "The thief has already sold the Winkenwerder books to a dealer in the Boston area. What you're seeing is a typical used book store."

"Maybe even on consignment. But Wink has circulated a description of the stolen items to every book dealer in New England."

"You're assuming they're all honest," Deidre said. "But maybe if you bring in a priceless rare book claiming it just fell off a truck, no questions are asked."

"Maybe we *should* assume the best about others. Isn't it the Wiccan way to honor the light of truth that shines in every soul?"

"Yeah, yeah. But not necessarily to cash their personal checks," Deidre said. "It's the Wiccan way to honor justice, too. And no one cares more about justice than you do."

"So the dealer must know, then, that he's selling hot books. But he's doing business very quietly with unscrupulous collectors," I said. "Maybe something more will come to me."

"The name of the shop would help," Deidre said.

CHAPTER THIRTEEN

Sweet is the swamp with its secrets,
Until we meet a snake;
T' is then we sigh for houses
And our departure take.

–Emily Dickinson

Hunched over the library table, Pieter Brand paged through of the 1917 Creswick *Robin Hood*. The Wyeth illustrations were a formidable challenge to the new version on his drawing board. Huge ancient trees with their powerful gnarled roots, a heavy dark forest that managed to be mysterious without menace—truly a hard act to follow. Clever Robin Hood with his Merry Men weaving their way out of Nottingham. Delightful work that time had invested with increasing value.

But Pieter knew that his own Maid Marian would be unique. Not just a lady wedded to a forest outlaw, but part of the greenery herself—so perfectly modeled by Sylvie; every pose of her body as graceful as a sapling birch. He glanced with satisfaction at the latest illustration clipped on the easel. The tendrils of pale brown hair curling away from her face as she melted into the trees. His Robin Hood, too, would be less a rascally brigand redistributing wealth and more a mythical Green Man, king of the woods. Pieter knew this would be his most original work yet, finer even that the Dragon that had fired his imagination two years ago.

Brand's Robin Hood, Pieter said to himself, *like no other in all the world*—and it had better be a commercial success, too. He couldn't remember what had possessed him to buy this grand old money pit that now was sucking up all his royalties. And the royalties were drying up, too.

Thinking of his dwindling bank account somehow made his arm start smarting again. Such a stupid thing to have happen. None of the salves and medications seemed to dry up the oozing mess. Pieter tried to remember what remedy his mother used on burns. He could call and ask, but it would only worry her. And she'd be after him again...*when are you coming home? When are you coming home?* The endless refrain. Utrecht was no longer home to him. Once it had seemed such a welcome refuge when he and his mother had fled there after that wicked old man burned up in his chair. Now it was far too narrow a place, too conventional and restrictive for the dreams and desires he needed to fulfill.

∽

I parked in the garage under Boston Common, a vast catacomb of chilly gloom, not a little scary to a woman on her own at night. Of course, I had my usual amulets: silver pentagram, a drop of sage oil on each wrist, a dusting of ground cloves on the soles of my new patent leather pumps, and a cayenne pepper spray in the stylish Gucci bag that Joe had brought me from Rome.

I walked up the stairs with brisk purpose (to discourage muggers) and strode through the Common, across Charles Street, and into the Public Gardens, rejoicing in the lights and festive crowds, heading toward the Taj, which would always be the Ritz to me, on Arlington Street. As I gazed at the Boston skyline, I had the strangest feeling that the city itself was about to give me a gift. Now what would that be about? I stopped for a moment, leaned against a verdigris bridge railing, and closed my eyes. *Yes!* It was Adam. This wonderful place was going to present me with my son. How and when I didn't know, but I continued my walk smiling hugely to myself.

My daughter-in-law, seated in the hotel lobby where she could watch the door, jumped up to greet me, smile meeting smile. Freddie, who at one time had affected a punk style, complete with gelled spiked hair and multiple piercings, even a nose ring, was now as chic and sophisticated as a model in *Elle* or *Vogue*. Her skirts were still mini, but she wore a sleek, ankle-length leather coat over the short wool sheath of a color probably called "mango" that brought out the amber of her eyes. *Tiger eyes*, and she wore earrings to match. A single pair, not like the old days of five gold rings on one ear and a pentagram dangling from the other.

I was glad I had borrowed Phil's jet-beaded black cocktail dress. The classic empire style didn't require too much of my waistline. Swanning into the posh hotel wrapped in Heather's Versace cashmere coat, I'd thought I looked quite as if this were my natural habitat.

As we embraced enthusiastically, I felt the uplift of spirit, like a fresh April breeze, that Freddie always brings with her. I wondered why I'd worried so about this amazing young woman setting her sights on my son. I'd been there, so I knew that for Freddie it had truly been love at first sight, struck to stone by the vision of my son descending the stairs wrapped in a towel, whereas it had taken Adam much longer (after how many love spells and potions?) to embrace his fate. She'd been a mere teenager, after all—but how elegantly she had turned herself out for Adam! *The transforming power of love,* I thought, remembering when I'd first met Joe, how empowered I'd felt, blazing through everyday chores like Zena the Warrior Goddess. A combination of sexual and magical energy burned like a fever in women in love. They can be anything, do anything for the object of their desire.

"Let's get a taxi," Freddie suggested after a suitable number of air kisses. "The Taj's dining room's open, but you never know who may be listening."

Curiouser and curiouser. I noticed that Freddie didn't give our destination to the driver until we were well on our way. And I actually saw her looking back out of the cab's rear window—checking that we hadn't been followed?

There was a light rain—thanks be to the Goddess it was too warm to turn to ice or snow—and the beams of the headlights coming our way flashed into my eyes, lulling my senses. Just the kind of stimuli that often bounced me into La La Land. Our hands resting on the seat of the car were touching as well, so I felt the surge of Freddie's electric aura. And sure enough, for just a nano-second, the wet street faded and I saw her in a room with a white-coated professorial type. There were beads of sweat on her forehead. She seemed to be concentrating on a number sequence being generated every second or so by a machine that looked like a black box. Then the vision faded as instantly as it had appeared, and we were stopping at a restaurant in the North End.

Luciano's Villa. I felt a flash of deja vu. Had I been here before, or seen this place in a vision? It was large, well-lit, with a pleasant ambiance of marble statuary and Pompeian murals. Freddie passed a rather substantial tip to the maitre 'd and requested one of the secluded tables in the balcony niches. Soon we were whisked away upstairs, looking down on the noisy diners below, our table as private as a box at the opera.

The waiter served our drinks and departed. "Okay, daughter in law..." I sipped a dry vermouth aperitif. Freddie had a single malt scotch with soda on the side; Adam's influence, I thought. "Spill it."

Freddie leaned over and smiled conspiratorially. "You'll never believe this, Cass."

"You've been tapped by a psychic think tank?"

She sat back abruptly. "Jesus, Cass. That's almost exactly on target. Awesome, but I wish you wouldn't steal my thunder like that."

"Oh. Sorry. So what think tank is it? Rand?"

We paused while the waiter made and served our Caesar salads and departed. Essence of garlic and anchovy wafted up from our plates. Tearing apart our loaf of warm Italian bread, we dug in.

Spearing a crouton and a leaf of romaine, she leaned over again. "Have you ever heard of the CIA's Stargate project? It's a top secret remote viewing program the agency ran some decades ago, very hush-hush until the investigative reporter

Jack Anderson exposed it to the world's ridicule. No longer operative, supposedly. Really a *me-too* deal anyway. We knew the Russians were using psychics, so our guys wanted to go them one better."

"The CIA!" I took a large gulp of the drink I had planned to nurse cautiously, mindful that I would be driving myself home. "Ceres save us—the agency still has a psychic think tank? Didn't all that go out with the Cold War?"

"Awesome, isn't it? I haven't given them an answer yet. Somehow I wanted to hear what you had to say before I, like, signed my name in blood and handed over my soul."

"Does the Christian Right know about this? Our own government dabbling in the paranormal! Oh, sorry...I guess I'm digressing. What would you have to do? Quit your job at Iconomics and head for Afghanistan? I imagine you've consulted Adam about all this?"

Freddie laughed merrily and kicked me under the table in case I hadn't seen the waiter approaching with our entrees. She waited until he'd served the saltimbocca, asparagus, and roasted potatoes. The aroma of the rich brown wine sauce was divine.

"Never, never tell Heather that I ate veal," I pleaded. I'd quit buying veal myself, but occasionally succumbed to a restaurant's lack of animal rights' sensitivity.

"Yes, of course, Adam and I have talked about this. Here's the thing, Cass. He's been tapped, too. Not to leave Iconomics but to use his position and his overseas assignments to do a few minor jobs, gather a little information, that sort of thing?"

My son, the CIA operative? "I'm astounded. And I don't astound that easily. How did they get onto you, anyway? Oh, Great Goddess, have you been gambling again?"

If Freddie could blush, she was doing it now. Just an attractive flush across those gamin cheekbones. "Oh, Cass. Just for fun once in a while. I don't stay long, and I don't go back to the same place twice. But it's mighty tempting to see if I can turn on those bells and whistles in the Big Bucks machine."

"Just the slots then, and only once?" I didn't believe that for a moment.

"Well....how's your veal?"

"Heavenly. Don't change the subject."

"Now and then I try my hand, so to speak, at the roulette wheel. But I really don't know if it was that, or some of the things I've done at Iconomics, or even the media hubbub about me and that bomb—you remember the one I addled?"

"As if I could ever forget. We owe our lives to that useful little talent of yours. For all we know, the CIA. has a fat dossier of your accomplishments. How did you do in the test?"

"What test?" Freddie topped up my wine glass with the pleasant Chardonnay she'd ordered.

"White-coated bearded guy. You were trying to influence a number sequence, I think."

"*You saw that, too?* It's called a random number generator. RNG. Often used in modern cryptography, but apparently none of them is perfect, and it's useful if someone can spot the weak link. I did the compass needle thing, too. Magnetic North 'r Us. And just for good measure, I hexed the laptop the guy was using to record his notes of our interview. His jaw dropped—literally. But, hey—just imagine if he knew about your visions. Maybe it's you and your merry band of witches who should be recruited by the Company."

"Perish the thought. I wouldn't exactly say that Joe is an anarchist, but he does make his living by continually protesting some government or other, often our own, on environmental issues. Which means, I hope you're going to cool it in all future emails. I'd hate to think of the notes in your dossier already, culled from our emails, referring to the circle and its activities. Good Goddess, what a nest of scorpions!"

"Sounds as if you're not much in favor."

"I didn't say that. Let me meditate on it. I know it seems like the Grand Game to you right now. Maybe a chance to do something useful as well. And I'm especially grateful that you decided to fill me in. Otherwise I might have been getting those flashes of insight that drive me crazy when I don't know what they mean. The bottom line, though, is that you have to do what you think best, both of you. Regardless of how I might feel about it."

"After this, I won't be telling you every little detail, you realize that, don't you?" I laughed.

"Don't worry, honey. It's my Karma always to know more than I want to, not less. Well, except in something like identifying this arsonist. In pursuit of a criminal, I never 'see' all I'd wish to know."

"Yes, but in time you get your man—or woman—you always do. Although I guess most arsonists are men, aren't they?"

"I'm pretty sure this one is. In fact, I may be hot on his trail right now."

"I have the utmost faith in your psychic deductions, Cass. So if the agency was going to, like, get Adam and me wasted in some foreign desert, you'd probably sense that and clue me in, right?" Freddie picked up the wine bottle to refill my glass.

I put my hand over my glass. "Of course. That's what moms like me are for. But let me ask you this, are you talking occasional mission or full-time career as a spook? Would you still be at Iconomics with Adam? And where would you be based?"

Freddie grinned. "Adam and I will be working together—do you think I'd agree to anything else?—and that brings me to the good news. Iconomics is going to open up another facility, guess where! Right here in Boston! And we're being transferred with a few other key people. Won't that be divine?"

I've learned to do a great "surprise face," and I put it on now—easy enough, since I was truly delighted. "Wow! That's the best news you could have given me. It will be so wonderful to be able to see more of you two! And about the other thing, I don't feel any danger around you *right now*. Just your usual electricity. I wonder if that's not the source of your psychokinesis, although you probably don't realize you're throwing off sparks. But I do suggest, in your new avocation as a spook," I leaned over and fixed her with my "mother-in-law" meaningful gaze to emphasize the point, "that you *never, never* try to slip in anywhere undetected. You just can't help lighting up the place, wherever you are."

"Don't worry, Cass—I hear you. But remember, Adam and I will continue to be employed at Iconomics. It's some kind of deal with management. They'll parcel me out as needed. Like next week, supposedly I'll be on unpaid personal leave but actually at Langley. Working for the Directorate of Science and Technology."

"Could be worse. Maybe you'll just be holed up in a lab occasionally, safe and sound. Anyway, I think you ought to rely on your own sensors more than mine to sort out assignments. Also, I think I need a double espresso, not more wine."

Freddie put down her fork and signaled the waiter. I watched the fork make a little hop as if wanting to get back into her hand. She never even noticed. "Tell me about who you've got in your mind's eye for those hometown arsons—surely someone is on the griddle!" Freddie said.

As we finished our dinner with espressos and almond pastries, I regaled Freddie with my investigations and suspicions.

Her eyes sparkled with excitement. "I know *The Dragon of Utrecht*, as a matter of fact. Lovely book. Pieter Brand's the author? And the other guy, Raoul Lazaro? Oiling his way around the Plymouth lady-poets, is he? How's his poetry, any good? Another Bob Dylan maybe? "

"Not Bob Dylan, *please*. At least never mention Dylan to Phil in the same breath with Raoul. Lazaro's stuff is heavily political and very angry. He's an émigré from Cuba."

"Political? So you've targeted two guys, one an artist who's specialized in drawing fire-breathing dragons, and the other a poet who's deep into fiery politics. *Cool.* You just have got to keep me posted on what you find out. At least no one's been murdered—yet—but those poor animals! I bet Heather is getting out all her black candles for this one."

"I will keep you posted, but very cautiously. Our future communications are going to have to be models of reticence. And I'm going to send you a protective amulet. It looks like a Lucite bracelet with a tiny sprays of dried herbs inside. Something to wear when the going gets tough."

"Awesome! What's in it?"

"A few protectors. Mistletoe. St.John's Wort. Sage. Other stuff. And Freddie..."

"Yes?"

"Don't let Adam get in over his head, okay? He's so idealistic."

"Not to worry, Mom. I shall watch over him like a tigress." Her amber eyes gleamed with feline intensity.

CHAPTER FOURTEEN

Lo, the herb of healing, when once the herb is known,
Shines in shady woods bright as a new-sprung flame.

–George Meredith

March came in with its usual icy gales off the Atlantic that made me feel winter was never going to give up its leonine grip. Holding our Esbat of the Chaste Moon at Phillipa's house, however, helped dispel the shivers. A blazing fire in the copper-hooded fireplace that occupied most of one wall thawed the chill in our bones. Apricot and cream silk cushions, golden Afghan rugs on the slate floor, and Moroccan brass tables warmed our souls. From the kitchen wafted the spicy scent of freshly baked Double-Gingerbread—balm for our noses.

"There's healing in this room already," Fiona pronounced.

Deidre said: "So many of our spells and prayers have been hit-or-miss..."

"Oh, I don't know about that," Heather interrupted. "Remember the serendipitous arrival of our eagles. And Captain Jack, who's been such a Goddess-send to Dick and me. Although I have to admit, I hadn't counted on that pesky parrot. Then just recently, the rather continual rain we got after that quenching spell on Cass's porch."

"What quenching spell?" Fiona asked.

"Well, now," I said briskly, "let's get on with this one, which is so important."

"As I was saying, so many have been hit-or-miss," Deidre continued her train of thought, "but the way I feel is, it's better to have faith that our intentions can influence the world of form than just to accept whatever miseries are thrown our way as the will of the universe." She kept her hand on the cell phone that linked her to home where her au pair Betti was watching over Will.

"Witches believe in magic, that's the thing that sets us apart. Sounds simplistic, but in fact it's a profoundly different philosophy from the mundane acceptance of fate, a.k.a. *God's will*," Phillipa said. "Okay, sometimes spells don't work exactly as we imagined they would, but they sure make things happen." She began casting the nine-foot circle, our sacred space between the worlds, with the no-nonsense 19th century dagger that was her athame. We used no chalk or other markers; the circle is imagined into reality—like the equator—except that we indicate the four directions. On this Esbat, smoldering myrrh symbolized the east, a chalice of water the west, a crystal bowl of salt the north, and one of Heather's special candles (red for health and energy) the south. I added branches of dried sage to the logs in the fireplace, a healing scent, and we proceeded with our ritual and special prayers for Will Ryan's recovery.

We invoked the Goddess whose abundant energy creates, sustains, and evolves all life, and the God whose force is the changer, catalyst and defender of life, and we asked that these two aspects of the universe would guide and guard the Ryans, specifically to resolve Will Ryan's health problems according to his free will and for the good of all. Free will is essential, for every soul must be free to work out his or her own destiny. As Fiona often reminded us, each of us has a unique path to follow, which may or may not include what someone else believes is for the best.

Each of us held Deidre's hands and spoke a few words of hope and healing, after which, of course, there were tears all around and the catharsis of a good cry made us all feel better.

"How I wish I could bring on visions when I need them," I complained when we were into the "cakes and ale" part of our Esbat, tucking into gingerbread and hot cider with a dollop of rum. I was thinking particularly of being able to see what would happen with Will and to discover the identity of our arsonist.

"I've always thought you'd come to that one day, Cass," Fiona said. "When you want to, deep down. But right now, you're of two minds."

"Better than two heads," Phillipa said. "But I understand very well why a person may be reluctant to take on the *responsibility* of second sight. Many times, while reading the tarot for someone, I've been entirely appalled at what the cards revealed to me. Usually I fudge the results, put a good face on it, even if it's the Ten of Swords. After all, I can't very well say, *uh-oh, looks like you're going to be pierced with many swords of disaster and depression.* But the problem is, *I* know. Sometimes it makes me quite hesitant to give readings at all."

"I've noticed that," Deidre said. "So I don't suppose there's any point in asking you to do a tarot lay-out for Will?"

"Oh, sure...but not right now because I don't think my energy is at the right level for a proper reading."

To me that meant Phillipa was still rather worried about Will's future. As I was.

෨

Joe got home from saving the Korean whales before Heather and I had a chance to look around Raoul's apartment. This posed the small problem, *where would I say I was going? Hey, honey. I'll be doing a spot of Breaking & Entering with my circle sister this evening. Don't bother to wait up, but have the bail money ready in case I call. No need for concern, though--we're counting on our sixth and seventh senses to see us through.*

Other than that nagging worry, it was a reunion of blissful abandon. You'd have thought we'd been separated for three years not three weeks. Joe's return made me realize that I'd never really felt true grown-up happiness until he came into my life. All the more reason for not causing him any unnecessary concerns about me. I would follow one of Fiona's guiding principles of marriage: *it's wiser not to burden a husband with too many details that are best handled by a woman.*

Leaving Joe happily occupied in measuring my cabinets— after he'd promised to negotiate with me what countertops we would choose—I dropped into the Devlin manse to see how plans for the Raoul gambit were progressing. Heather thought I looked peaked and needed a bit of a pick-me-up. Opening the walk-in wine "cellar" off her kitchen, she selected a Prosecco and removed the cork with the ease of

long practice. Soon we were sprawled on cushioned wicker
chairs in the conservatory, our feet up on the same hassock.

"If I hang around Wendy Windsong's travel agency much
more, I'm going to have to book a world cruise." Heather
filled two flutes with the Italian sparkling wine and handed
me one. "Which by the way, got me to thinking we ought to
take the circle on a cruise one of these days. There's something
about being out there on the ocean with no land in sight
that's utterly magical. Picture it, Cass. Nighttime, full moon,
an orchestra playing."

"Yes, yes—*An Affair to Remember*. Joe certainly seems
to be enthralled with life at sea, sans orchestra I've noticed.
Super idea, though. Maybe in the fall?"

"Ah yes, the Bermuda Triangle might be a trip, especially
during the hurricane season."

Several of the Devlins' canine charges were milling
around us, along with Scruffy and Raffles, whom I had
brought with me, thinking maybe Honeycomb would relent
and give them a nuzzle. But no. When Raffles, with youthful
naivety, chased after his mama and butted her playfully with
his head, she merely caught him by the leg and tossed him
off his paws, even though he was now taller than she. Then,
with a withering glance at Scruffy, she'd stalked off into the
potted palms.

Is it something I've done? Scruffy gazed after her retreating
golden backside, his expression wistful, while Raffles righted
himself with a bewildered look.

"*Is it ever!* Why don't you guys go out for a while and
run with the big dogs," I suggested. Opening the French
doors to the "dog yard," a lavish fenced paddock with several
hospitable trees, I booted out my two fellows, who were

instantly followed by all the others except Trilby the aged bloodhound and Honeycomb in her Garbo mood.

"I think I may be getting a case of cold feet," I said. "But now that you've cased the joint, what do you suggest?"

"Wendy's no problem. She doesn't reside on the premises, goes home right after she closes *Footloose*. And she did mention to me that her renter, Lazaro, is going to New York next weekend to join in a solidarity-with-Cubans-in-exile reading sponsored by the American Poetry Society. If you're nervous, we don't have to get *inside* Lazaro's apartment. Because I know just how you're feeling right now. I often experienced a case of nerves when I was planning to break into some horrid lab to rescue the dogs who'd been shipped in for experiments. But those good old days are over now. Dick has made me swear on the heads of my favorite doggies, which are all of them, that I will never, never break into a lab again. *Into a lab.* You note the loophole there?" She leaned over and topped up our glasses. "Anyway, we can just wander around outside, maybe look through a few windows, shake the door knobs, et cetera, to see if you catch any vibes, how would that be? Or I might borrow Fiona's little set of lock-picks in case you have a change of heart."

"Okay, as long as you remember that carrying that gizmo with the intention of using it illegally is considered a felony," I said glumly. I had this uneasy feeling I couldn't quite pin down; a vision would have helped at that point, but they hardly ever appear when they're really wanted. "Next weekend then. Let's say Saturday after *Footloose* closes. But what in Hades will I tell Joe?"

"The same thing I'm going to tell Dick. *Shopping.* Shopping for new spring outfits. Nordstrom's at Massasoit Mall should be perfect."

"Joe knows I never shop for new clothes. Oh, sometimes I buy online, of course. But I can only tolerate new clothes that feel like old clothes the minute I put them on." I looked down at my L. L. Bean twill pants and Lands' End "Purple Sage" drifter sweater with satisfaction—perfectly Plymouth matron.

"And it shows, girlfriend. It shows. That's why you have to borrow stuff from me or Phil when the crunch comes. What about when you go shopping with Becky?"

"Yeah, Bloomingdale's. That's where I got that pale green Grecian dress I sometimes wear on Sabbats."

"Okay. Makeover time. Not extreme makeover, you understand, but definitely a new Cassandra."

"I thought we were going to be lurking around Raoul's place?"

"We are, we are. But first we're going to shop till we flop. Department store bags, my dear—we need bulging bags for camouflage. Earlier in the week, you know. I'll hide them in the Mercedes trunk until Saturday."

"A research caper and a new look, too. Sounds like a plan."

"Naturally. Magic is all well and good, but the Goddess helps those who help themselves.

∾

When it comes to a subject I know little about, such as fashion style, I'm a pushover for whatever I'm told to buy. Heather had no trouble laying garments across my outstretched arms and steering me toward a fitting room. She was flashing her

Way-Beyond-Platinum credit cards, too, but I couldn't allow her to pay for my new spring wardrobe. So we compromised on a sophisticated Maggie London green skirt suit, a makes-you-look-tall-and-slim Donna Ricco 3-piece pants suit, a rainbow of Anne Klein silk shells, two tailored shirts, and a lilac sheath with matching fringed poncho from Liz Claiborne.

"Sweet Ceres, I'm going to have to go on that *Footloose* world cruise with you, now that I have all this finery," I said. "I mean, wherever will I wear this stuff in Plymouth?"

But she wouldn't let me buy the boots I wanted to go with the slacks outfit because they were genuine leather. "I'll get you a nice faux alligator pair from my own bootery, Friendly-to-Reptiles Footwear. And a handbag to match. Goes with anything, and roomy enough for all your housebreaking gear."

"Oh, thanks. I think you have me mixed up with Fiona. A faux alligator reticule is it? I think I'll stick with that lovely soft Gucci bag that Joe brought me from Italy."

"Okay, but remember I have only your own good looks at heart."

The important thing was that we had armfuls of impressive Nordstrom shopping bags to serve as cover for our Saturday caper.

CHAPTER FIFTEEN

One little prayer, and then—what bitter fight
Flames at the end beyond the darkling goal?

—Aleister Crowley

Saturday afternoon, leaving Joe a plate of left-overs to nuke when he got hungry, I got ready to join Heather around four. A strange hour for a shopping trip, I would have said, but Joe never blinked an eye, immersed as he was in the problems of kitchen remodeling.

That's the different thing about men and women. Men concentrate on their goal of the moment to the exclusion of all outside incidents, whereas women don't want to miss anything—not a single thing. It's not that they're from different planets, the Mars vs. Venus theory—it's just that men have a singular, silent, straight-to-the-mark arrow mentality whereas women enjoy a chatty, circular net-all-the-fish approach. And if something smells a little "off," they notice it.

"Sure, sweetheart. Have fun," Joe murmured. Chances are he didn't even know what time it was. Having pinned me down to antique longleaf pine countertops, he was drawing a plan to scale with ardent attention. The order would have to be custom milled and finished, buying me another month or more before chaos reigned in my kitchen. Anyway, the pine was gorgeous and matched my wide-plank floors.

Before I left, I sat Scruffy and Raffles down in front of me. "Listen, you guys. You're going to have to nudge the boss when it's your dinnertime. He's really busy and may not remember that everyone has to eat."

Not to worry, Toots. I'll see that old furry-face feeds us on time or sooner. What's for dinner?"

"Dog food—what do you think? Oh, and there's a little dish with two leftover chicken livers."

"Dog food?" Joe said wonderingly, chewing the end of a pencil.

"Not you, honey. You get the chicken and vegetables covered plate, takes three minutes to heat in the microwave, the dogs here get the dog food and the two chicken livers, cold."

Okay by me if furry-face would like to switch bowls. Makes a change,

"In your dreams." I patted both doggie heads, kissed Joe, and slipped away guiltily.

When I arrived at Heather's, I found her already wearing the camouflage suit with matching cell phone that she favors for break-ins, but which I thought made her stand out like a Green Beret at the opera. Personally, I'd opted for a head-to-toe black "cat burglar" outfit, a much better choice for blending with the shadows of the evening. I might have blacked my face a bit, too, but how would I have explained that to Joe?

Not having "sprung ahead" to daylight savings yet, we only had to wait until six for it to be dark enough for our covert activities. We took Heather's Mercedes and parked it at Fiona's, close enough for walking to our destination.

With a little twilight still gleaming, we took a tea-and-scandal break with Fiona, who'd been researching Pieter Brand and Raoul Lazaro during slow hours at the library, which were most of them. Two things she'd learned so far. As a Cuban refugee and a writer, Lazaro had been sponsored by a rich old gal living in Brewster on the Cape. When she died, his patroness had left Raoul a legacy that enabled him to live comfortably and pursue his poetic career without worrying about a "daytime job." And as we knew already, Pieter Brand had been ostracized from several major architectural firms in a dispute over supposedly plagiarized plans for a model "city village"—really an apartment complex with shops and a park. What we hadn't known was that, when construction began on that complex a year later, there was a disastrous fire at the site. Fiona said that the project was still in limbo, and now might never get built unless new funding came into the picture.

"This is only the start, girls," Fiona said. "There's no end to the personal information that can be unearthed on the Internet, as anyone who's had her identity stolen would verify. I'll keep working on Brand and Lazaro. And Omar will, too. When I get truly stuck, I depend on Omar to walk across the keyboard, just to get me off on a new track. It's so utterly random, it works."

Heather and I looked at each other over our teacup rims. "It's the kind of thing that would only work for you, I think, Fiona."

"We're assuming, of course, that the arsonist is one of these two guys and not some weirdo who wouldn't be caught dead traveling in our particular social circles," I mused.

Fiona put a be-ringed hand on mine; her touch always had quieting effect. Contemplating another urban commando raid had rather jangled my nerves. "Have faith in your powers, dear," she said in her reassuring glamour voice. "At the deepest level, we usually know what we're doing."

"Right. Well, tell Omar, if he makes a real important hit, I'll send him a catnip bouquet," I said.

The Persian at that very moment was sitting on the top of a freestanding bookcase, hissing with derision. I'd never tried to talk to Omar, whom I suspected thought himself too highly bred to converse with the ordinary animal talkers, but I had spoken a few words with Patty Peacedale's coon cat, who had been dubbed Buster by his former owners. But in our conversations, the cat had insisted that his real name was Loki of Valhalla, and after I'd explained the situation, Patty obliged. It's interesting to note that animals have their own ideas about names, a lesson I'd learned from Scruffy, who'd adamantly refused to answer to *Lancelot du Lac*.

Heather persisted in her plan to borrow Fiona's lock-picks, which I swore we were not going to use. Fiona sprinkled us with some of the precious corn pollen she'd brought home from the Navaho reservation and pronounced that we would be just fine as we took off into the twilight. We soon discovered, however, that the *Footloose and Fancy Free Travel Agency* (formerly *Deluca's Sea Garden Gallery*) was a rather well-lit establishment with an excess of floodlights in Colonial guise all around the outside of the shop (a converted Cape Cod cottage with a two-story extension).

Slinking around to the back, which was more like the front to me since it overlooked the ocean and a picturesque marina, we peered in the windows and tried the back door.

Subdued night lighting inside the travel agency showed that it occupied less space than had the shop and gallery preceding it. Thus the Lazaro apartment was now on two floors—a stove-light dimly revealed a first-floor kitchen behind the travel agency offices with a stairway that we deduced must lead to the rest of the rooms on the second floor. Heather jingled Fiona's housebreaking tools.

"No, wait," I said. "First let me try to take in some simple vibes, as we agreed."

"Okay. You go, girl."

We sat side by side on the back stoop. The moon, a tipped golden bowl, had just appeared, still veiled in amber mists at the Atlantic's horizon, such an inspiring sight making it easy to be silent and meditative.

But nothing came to me. *Nada.* A perfect blank where my mind's eye should be watching a kaleidoscope of pictures.

"I wonder how she died," Heather said.

"Who?"

"Raoul's patron saint, the rich widow."

"Good point," I said. Then, as I allowed my gaze to fix on the rising moon, I began to get the faintest glimmer. Something to do with a Rolls Royce. But before the image came sufficiently into focus, Heather nudged me The inner image I was concentrating on shattered into a shower of light fragments, becoming once more, the star-lit sky.

"Well, shall we break in, then?" Heather grinned and started poking around in the lock with her tools. I've found that time really slows to a crawl when you are in the act of committing a crime. So it was definitely an eternity later that the lock gave a submissive click, and Heather cautiously opened the kitchen door. No one appeared outside or inside.

"Looks as though the coast is clear," I said. "But you know what? I wouldn't go in there if I were you. Or me."

Heather looked back at me sharply. She already had one foot over the threshold while I was getting two cold feet. "Listen, Cass, don't you want to have a look around in case Raoul lifted Wink's rare books at the Court Street fire? You said maybe the arsonist took them as a kind of souvenir. If we found those, well...what a coup! But that's okay... you just look around here in the kitchen, and I'll go upstairs. Whistle or something if there's a problem."

"No, there's no evidence on the premises," I said firmly. "Let's just say I know this in my bones. Breaking in here tonight is a dumb idea. So come out of there, and lock the damned door. We're Wiccans, after all, not burglars. Why should we put ourselves on the wrong side of the law? Let's investigate these men by spiritual means."

Heather groaned but she stepped back out of Lazaro's kitchen. She stood there rattling the keys and musing. "I *suppose* we could keep Googling them. Some dirt is bound to turn up. But we've already done the clothes shopping," she complained.

"Yes, and I just adore those pricey outfits you picked out, makes a change from the L. L. Bean catalog. And now I'll be able to model them for Joe, although I'm really sorry that I'll have to pretend our 'shopping spree' was tonight. I loathe lying to the love of my life except as a matter of absolute necessity. But wait," I whispered. "Quiet! Listen. Do you hear something?"

We were both silent for a moment. A splat of gravel, a motor purring. We peeked around the corner of the building. A gleaming Jaguar of a color called "salsa" red, stood under a Colonial lantern, and getting out of it was our handsome local poet. He was wearing the romantic outfit he'd worn to the poetry reading at the library, complete with paisley neck scarf tucked into his open-necked shirt.

"Shit!" Heather whispered fervently. "Let's beat it out of here the other way, then."

The "other way" cut through a thicket of bushes that grew between the travel agency and what was formerly a small separate art studio, now a storeroom. Below was a steep slope to the shore and the marina. We got through the tangle, somewhat mauled by unforgiving lilac branches, and ducked around the corner just before Lazaro reached his kitchen door. He was whistling some old song with a Latin rhythm that I almost remembered. *We're having a heat wave, a tropical heat wave.*

It seemed as if the coast was clear for a clean getaway, and it might have been if Wendy Windsong had not chosen that moment to tool into the driveway, catching us squarely in the headlights of her silver Passat. She rolled down the window.

"You two looking for a cruise?" she inquired with an undertone of suspicion in her normally perky voice. For one wild moment, I thought she had said "bruise."

Heather looked as guilty as I felt. "Just out for a walk," she said brightly. "Cass wanted to have a look at the marina by moonlight."

Very inventive, I thought. It was clear enough, though, that Wendy wasn't buying it.

"I see that my tenant has returned unexpectedly," Wendy said. "I remember your asking me about his schedule." She looked accusingly at Heather.

"Oh, yes, so he has," Heather said, as if just discovering the flaming red Jaguar in front of our eyes. "Well, lovely to see you, Wendy. We must go on with our walk before we cool down. Got to get that heart rate perking." She grabbed by arm and pulled me out onto the dark road. My heart rate was perking just fine. *Aerobic burglary—a new pulse-pounding exercise.*

"I suppose you're going to say I told you so," Heather muttered at we hotfooted it back to Fiona's and the Mercedes.

"It wasn't just because of Lazaro," I said. "Although I did have a twinge of apprehension when you unlocked that door. But..." It was proving difficult to wax philosophical while huffing and puffing my way through the dark. *Another time.*

The instant we reached her front walk, Fiona threw open her front door, as if she'd been standing there waiting for us. "Come in, come in. Are you all right? You're looking a little bushed, my dears. *Now, tell me everything.*"

"I'll tell you this," I wheezed. "I'm no longer in the break-in business as of this evening. We almost got caught...*again.* Not only by Lazaro, but by Wendy Windsong as well."

"Yes, yes...but what did you find out?" Fiona urged.

"Nothing," Heather said morosely, throwing herself onto the sofa. "Cass got into one of her doom and gloom moods right after I got the door open. Here." She fished out the lock-picks and handed them to Fiona.

"I wonder if his hives got better," I mused. "I couldn't detect any blotches under those yellow lights."

"You saw Lazaro?" Fiona's mouth formed a perfect round O.

"Yup. Got out of there just in time. The bastard came home early. Poets can be so unreliable. Except Phil, of course."

"Well, you did right then, aborting the mission." Fiona looked over her half-tracks from me to Heather, who was still scowling. "But there's more to it."

"I'm a reformed woman," I said. "Let's pursue these guys with Wiccan ways from now on. Not hexes and stuff like that. All good white magic. And no embarrassment for our nearest and dearest. What do you say, Fiona?"

Fiona sighed and dropped the lock-picks into her reticule. I looked at her sternly. "So? I might lock myself out by mistake sometime. Okay, okay. I'll get back to my Internet searches. No more walking on the wild side, then. Damn—it's like the end of the Sixties all over again."

"Yeah, I know what you mean, Fiona," Heather moaned. "Dick's made me swear I'd give up rescuing animals from research labs. I mean, I can picket, petition, harass, and write letters to political figures all I want, but I miss the good old hands-on days of actually breaking in that door with a sledge hammer."

"Let's cut short the nostalgia trip, gals," I said. "What I'm wondering is, how did Lazaro come to America? And I'd like to know more about that rich angel who sponsored him."

Fiona, who was fussing around her liquor cabinet, came out with a bottle of Glenfiddich single malt Scotch whiskey. After dusting it off with the hem of her coat sweater of many colors, she insisted we all have a "wee nip" to buoy us up. "I gather you've not read his book *We Drowned at Dawn?*" she said, pouring generous dollops of the golden liquid into heavy glass tumblers. Then she wandered in a bemused fashion over to one of her wall-to-wall bookcases, pulled out two identical volumes, and handed us each one. "If you want to know a poet, read his poems, my dears. Believe me, it's even more revealing than breaking into his house."

"Now she tells us," Heather muttered.

"Apparently Lazaro escaped with a number of other refugees on a ramshackle fishing boat," Fiona paraphrased the cantos. "The boat capsized, and he alone was saved. In a rather wobbly iambic pentameter. Mostly unrhymed blank verse but with the occasional rhymed couplet. Rather a Shakespearean technique, although if Shakespeare were writing now, he might have been a rapper."

I was getting that dazed feeling that sometimes comes over me when I'm listening to Fiona. Perhaps I would rather break into a poet's apartment, with all the risk of legal hassles and bad karma that entailed, than be condemned to read his slim volume of precious verse. Nevertheless, I paged through my copy in an idle fashion. No pictures, alas. My gaze fixed on the last lines at the end of a longish poem.

My salamander love,
With your hot hands, set fire to my soul,
Release desire, let my flesh feel purged
And purified. White ashes be my dirge.

I read those four lines aloud, and said: "We ought to get in touch with Sylvie, and see how she's faring. I wonder if she's still channeling that fire spirit, don't you?"

"Well, what you recited is metaphoric, of course," Fiona said. "Not hanging evidence. Phillipa says that these poems are moving testaments to the Phoenix-like qualities of the human spirit, and that Raoul's sensual and visceral language gives his poems their power. And I have noticed that Raoul rates very high on the swoon-meter with the ladies who come to hear him read."

"Two things, then," Heather said. "Get in touch with Sylvie, and reel in Phil. How can any plain old husband be expected to compete with a sensual poet in a silk shirt and a damned paisley cravat? I'll wager there's not another guy in Plymouth who'd measure anywhere near Raoul on Fiona's swoon-meter."

"Oh, I don't know," I said. "Joe is much, much sexier, which is why he's in such great demand for Greenpeace fundraisers."

"And that's your perfectly objective opinion?" Heather asked with a wink at Fiona.

"Never mind your snide remarks, dearie. Let's concentrate on what we can do magically to get rid of this firebrand, whoever he turns out to be. Fiona?"

"Let me have another look in *Hazel's Book of Household Recipes.*" She wandered over to another of her wall-to-wall bookcases, an eclectic assortment, none of them built-in, all of them having an antique mystique, with different woods and finishes. This one was constructed of fine golden bird's eye maple with protective glass doors over every shelf. Here Fiona kept her more esoteric volumes. *Hazel's*, although covered in moldy leather, no longer reeking of mildew since it came into Fiona's possession from a yard sale, but still was much thumbed and bookmarked.

"You know, we could simply try to get those two to move far, far away—preferably to another country," Heather said. "Isn't it bittersweet branches, Cass, that are used to rid oneself of a troublesome neighbor? Just toss it into their yards, right?"

"Maybe," I said cautiously. "But you never really know how herbal magic will work itself out. For instance, you might find that *Footloose Travel* was inspired to move elsewhere while Raoul stayed put. But I do have some dried bittersweet sprigs with their berries. Very potent stuff, but the scourge of a garden. Tries to take over the world."

"Or I could do a candle spell, something specially made with bits of foreign soil and tickets to Timbuktu," Heather suggested.

"No, I wouldn't feel right about just foisting a pyromaniac onto another community somewhere, it would be like transferring a pedophile priest to another parish or a deadly nurse to another hospital," I said.

"Divination!" Fiona said. "For Goddess' sake, this time let's do a bit of scrying before we do the spellwork. You gals tried a quenching spell after the Esbat of the Wolf, while I was driving Sylvie home—yes, yes—you thought I wouldn't know?—and what you got was *le deluge.* We must learn to look ahead and assess the consequences." She paged thoughtfully through the pages of handwritten recipes, many of them with dramatic little flourishes such as exclamation points that appeared to be daggers dripping drops of blood. The daggers were in the section titled *Just Desserts.* That Hazel must have been a devious soul—just our kind of gal.

"I guess we ought to have the full circle for this one," I said. "If I can't scry properly, we'll get Phil to read the tarot. But we need to take some action as well. I can't bear to think of those poor animals. So...have you found the right spell yet?"

Fiona laughed deeply and with her many-ringed hand, patted the open page she'd been perusing. "*Hoist by His Own Petard,* this one is called. Don't you love it?"

"What's a petard actually?" Heather asked.

"French originally, my dear—it means a loud explosion of intestinal gas," Fiona said merrily. "But once it got into English, via Shakespeare, a petard was a small bomb that might be used to take down a city's gate, so the phrase meant to blow one's self up with one's own bomb."

"Sounds like a plan to me," I said. "What herbs do we need?"

"Same as the Dispelling Demons recipe but without the blue candles." Fiona read the esoteric list aloud.

I would find them all at home in my cellar workroom, but some botanicals with a deadly duality—curative uses combined with poisonous properties—were in coded jars so that the casual observer wouldn't be alarmed. "You make pressed incense out of the stuff that you burn on nine nights."

"I have some splendid blue candles. Let's use them anyway," Heather said. "Any words?"

"You know how careful Hazel was. It's quite cryptic," Fiona looked pleased with this chance to decode Hazel's old English charm.

"I wonder what happened to her. I hope she lived to a ripe old age surrounded by loving and respectful descendants," Heather mused.

"And I hope she's been reincarnated into our world. I'd love to meet her," I said, but then I sighed, thinking of how in some delicate way I would have to get Phillipa's cooperation in this newest endeavor. I didn't believe she would be able to think any evil of handsome Raoul. For her sake, I hoped someone, anyone else would prove to be the guilty party and true target of our "hoist" spell.

OSTARA, THE SPRING EQUINOX
CHAPTER SIXTEEN

Come fill the Cup, and in the fire of Spring
Your Winter-garment of repentance fling;
The Bird of Time has but a little way
To flutter—and the Bird is on the Wing.

–Omar Khayyám

Whatever Sabbat is approaching, I feel it's my favorite, immersing myself wholeheartedly into the mood of the season. My Libran personality, I guess, always in love with the beauty of the present moment. Ostara this year was no exception, fulfilling my bone-deep aching desire for a hint of spring. Yellow branches of willow were thickening and brave crocuses pierced through the cold earth. Joe obligingly cut armfuls of forsythia and brought them into the house to force into early blooms, and that wasn't all that got an early start on the season's awakening pleasures. *Yes!*

On March 21st, the Vernal Equinox, the circle celebrated Ostara in Heather's conservatory, its greenery a perfect expression of our spring longings. Our hostess's canine companions were all ensconced in their kennels, and Captain Jack was tucked up with his parrot Ishmael in the apartment above the former garages once home to automobiles of the thirties with their gleaming Art Deco styling. The Morgan family had been partial to Mercedes Benz even then, and it was still Heather's car of choice, albeit with windows nowadays spotted with dog drool.

The plastic bones and chew toys had been swept away for this occasion, however, allowing potted ferns, ficus, palms, and avocado to work their green magic. The tall Japanese vases were filled with creamy lilies. An altar had been arranged at one end of the long, glass-windowed room, decorated with pots of white and yellow tulips and Heather's spring candle creations, pink embedded with sea shells, pale blue with dried lavender flowers, and a white work candle with silver runes. The Goddess was represented by Heather's triptych of Hecate, Queen of Witches and the Underworld. Hardly springlike, but this particular triptych had a history with us and our sorties into crime-solving. Hecate was said to know the names and properties of all the plants (knowledge which she imparted to her spiritual "daughters") and her sacred animal was the dog, which especially appealed to Heather. Also lending her fertile presence to Ostara was the bronze statue of Cerridwen, looking remarkably like Heather herself, who was also bronzed and beatific, especially on this occasion.

Fiona added a verdigris garden statue of a bunny and a wooden sculpture of the Green Man, a copy, she said, of the leafy face so often carved into medieval church roofs. All else that was needed, she declared, was to open our hearts and minds to the freshening breezes of spring. Wearing a garland of wild violets only slightly askew on her coronet of braids, she was looking the very picture of a mature Titania. I noted a small silver owl pinned on her coat sweater of many colors. Perhaps, as I had suggested, Fiona was "calling" an owl into her life. Associated as it was with Athena and wisdom, the owl would be her perfect familiar. I hoped Omar would adjust.

Heather presided over our invocation and ritual. We wrote our various hopes for the season on painted eggs and buried them outdoors in the soft earth of the flower garden so that the Earth Mother would know our dreams; then we scooted back inside to warm up. Hand holding hand, we raised the energy within us until it could no longer be contained, then let it go all at once. *May the Spirit be with us. May our wishes be fulfilled in the Universe of Infinite Solutions.*

At that moment of release, I noticed Diedre's expression was particularly wistful, and I thought how difficult her home life had become, even with help from her au pair and her mother-in-law. Even more worrisome, I could feel an aura of despair around Deidre that was foreign to her usual merry, energetic self.

After our solemn ceremonies, came the traditional merry feasting, which at Heather's was translated into a fine old sherry and Phillipa's Easter almond bread with whole eggs baked into its golden braid. That was my opportunity to probe a little deeper into Deidre's problems, and it didn't take too much urging to have it all out on the table.

"Will is getting so restless. I have to admit I think he's drinking too much lately," Deidre confessed. "He's a sweet-natured drunk, but it's not good for his health. The cardiologist has warned him that he ought to give up hard liquor and be satisfied with a glass of red wine at dinner. But Will won't listen—you know the Irish and their whiskey! He says after working his way up to Deputy Fire Chief, he can't abide not being part the action with all these suspicious fires, and he needs a few drinks for solace. What's life worth, he says, if he can't do a man's job? Well, you know how men go on when they're laid up with some ailment, no patience at all. So I guess I've been worrying myself into a state over what I can do to make him realize that drinking himself into a stupor every night could be the death of him. And then there's the problem of getting him into bed without distressing the children. I should be able to reach Will, make him see reason. He's always listened to me in the past, even let me make all the decisions. Oh, sorry... I don't mean to go on and on with a long face at this lovely Sabbat."

"Oh, fiddle! What do you think friends are for if not to listen and help?" Fiona shook her silver bangles in exasperation. "Now here's what you have to remember, honey. It's the saddest, most important lesson in life. *You can't change other people.* You can offer sympathy, advice, remedies, and alternatives—the lot! But all real change comes from within the person himself. So you cannot take the blame or responsibility for Will's drinking. That he has to do for himself."

I was silent, my thoughts clouded with memories of my own struggles with an alcoholic husband. Well do I remember trying to get him up the stairs—and he wasn't the "sweet-natured drunk" that Diedre described.

"If you need any help with the children—I mean, if you need a break at any time—I'd be glad to take them," Phillipa said. Since she'd never been particularly nurturing, her offer surprised me—until she added: "And Cass will lend a hand, too, with the kids or the dogs, whatever."

"Or any of us could spell you at the store," Heather said. "The most important thing is to get Will through this bad patch. And yourself."

There's nothing like an outpouring of real concern to get everyone crying, but it was a short-lived squall, soon ended in smiles, hugs, and farewells, *Merry meet and merry part, and merry meet again.*

ᘒ

The next suspicious fire in Plymouth would forever be called The Good Friday Fire. Easter, the first Sunday after the first full moon after the Vernal Equinox, came early this year. Easter week vacations began and schools were closed.

Blustery March was warmed for me when my young Native American friend Tip (Thunder Pony), a boy I had once fantasized about adopting, visited me during his week off from high school in Wicasset. He'd metamorphosed, it seemed overnight, into a muscular young man with a square jaw and broad cheekbones. He'd never be a six-footer but he'd certainly outgrown by leaps and bounds the slight boy I'd befriended. His grin hadn't changed, though, and the way it gave his gray eyes an Asian look.

"Are you the lady that advertised for a handy man?" Tip always greeted me as he had when he'd first appeared at my kitchen door a few years ago while he was still living in Plymouth with his drunken father and needed to make some money.

"Oh, Tip, it's *so* wonderful to see you again," I said, noticing with his bear hug that he was nearly as tall as Joe now.

It's the boy! The boy who plays ball is back. He should stay here with us. Scruffy danced around the two of us in a canine ecstasy of hope. Raffles cavorted around the perimeter of the huddle, prepared to love whomever his sire loved.

Tip crouched down to greet the two dogs, nose to noses. "Still got that orange spongy ball, big fella? I promise we'll have a good ball game outside before I leave today." Tip was the one person in the world who seemed to communicate with Scruffy in the same way that I did. "And who's this chip-off-the-old-blockhead?"

"This is Raffles, son of Scruffy. Surely you remember the day that Honeycomb whelped, you rushed over to see 'the miracle of birth' and nearly fainted? Heather wouldn't let me get away without adopting one of that litter, and besides, once I looked in Raffles' eyes, it was love at first sight."

You should have left well enough alone, Toots. We were doing just fine on our own, you and me. This dumb pup keeps trying to push his nose into my business. Having found his decrepit old orange ball, Scruffy pushed it eagerly into Tip's hand, positioning his rump so that Raffles was relegated to the outskirts of the action.

Raffles was only the beginning of all we had to catch up on. After his father's death, living with his uncle John Thomas in Maine had opened a world of opportunities for Tip to follow his heart into his favorite pursuits—Native American music, forestry and tracking (an art at which he was especially gifted), and competing as a long-distance runner in state competitions. Tip shared his exploits and successes with me, and I told him about our latest crusade to catch the Plymouth arsonist. After all, he already knew about the crime-fighting activities of me and my "medicine women" friends, as he called them, and had in the past shared some of our misadventures.

"What a creep this guy must be, getting off on burning up animals like that. I bet Ms. Devlin has been pretty wild," Tip said.

"You're right about that. He's Number One on her Most Wanted list."

"Here's my cell number." Tip jotted it down on my kitchen memo board. "It's always on, so you can reach me anytime. If something comes up that you need help tracking that felon, I can be here in a few hours. I've got wheels now— Uncle John's old motorcycle, but I fixed it so it works pretty good."

A tiny *zinger* of prescience told me I'd been taking Tip up on that offer not too far into the future—but in a different sort of crisis entirely. Great Goddess, wasn't the arsonist trouble enough? I shook my hands to cast off the negative vibes.

Meanwhile, Tip got a taste of our firebug before he left for Maine. Some teenagers having a spring break and Lenten beer party in the parking lot behind Bishop Angell High School at 3:00 AM on Good Friday, were startled out of their boozy bonhomie when the back entrance of the school went up in a quick burst of flame. Although most of the youngsters made a fast getaway, one teenager, Judy D'Marco, plumped down on a broad stone wall that circled the lawn, called 911 on her cell, and reported the blaze. She wasn't feeling up to running anyway.

The building should have been empty. School was closed for Easter week, and the janitor made it a point to finish his allotted spring cleaning chores by four each afternoon of the break. But Judy, remaining at the scene, told Mick Finn that she thought she'd seen two classmates at the window. Perhaps they had broken into the empty school on a lark and set the fire, and now they were trapped inside. Judy had been drinking beer steadily all afternoon, but she had an amazing capacity for looking and acting nearly normal (unless you peered really closely at her eyes) until at some point in these binges she suddenly dropped to the ground like a sack of potatoes. But Judy had not yet reached the point of oblivion so often observed by her peers, who fondly nicknamed her Dead Drunk D'Marco, or D.D. for short.

Hearing her slightly hysterical report, two volunteer firefighters standing nearby, themselves fathers of teenagers, took off running into the school. After searching through the blazing rooms to which Judy had pointed with a finger only slightly wobbly, one of the men staggered out with his face blackened with soot and his lungs filled with punishing smoke. "Ceiling's falling in that side. Rooms are empty," he gasped, pushing away the oxygen mask offered by paramedics. "Where's George? We got separated. Did he get out okay?"

But George Dufy, father of three, did not get out of the burning school on his own. Other firefighters rushed in to find him pinned under a collapsed beam. No evidence was found that any youngsters had been in the school at all, and finally Judy admitted, in floods of tears, that she herself was no longer sure of what she'd seen.

It turned out that Tip had known Judy in Middle School, giving us an excuse to drive over to the D'Marco's place so that he could say "hey" and invite the girl to tell us her version of events. It appeared, however, that Judy could no longer think about that night without crying. With much prompting, through her sobs, she said *maybe* she'd seen some guy running away from the back of the building and *maybe* he had some kind of hood over his face. It was hard to tell at night. She didn't add that she was too drunk to know what she saw, in or out of the burning school.

Dufy's leg was badly crushed and broken, but somehow the doctors managed to patch him up without amputation. It would be months, however, before he could go back to work. Mick Finn attempted to keep Judy's involvement under wraps, but the Plymouth grapevine being what it was, one of the Dufy girls, after visiting her father at the hospital, waylaid Judy behind a local hangout and blackened both her eyes.

Mick Finn reasonably pointed out to the Dufy family that Judy had not set the fire. But someone had, because traces of a common accelerant were found inside the building near the back doors where the janitor had left two barrels of trash for later dumping. It was mineral turp, an artist's staple, the same accelerant that had been found in the Shawmutt Animal Pound.

"Mineral turp!" Phillipa exclaimed to me when Stone finally told her. He and his partner Billy Mann had been assigned to work with the Massachusetts Fire Marshall's office in determining the causes of this series of Plymouth fires. So Phillipa's husband was getting a crash course in arson, and we were getting another direct pipeline to whatever evidence was discovered.

We were sitting in Phillipa's kitchen while she tenderly gave her puff pastry another turn. "Now that pretty much

underlines the name Pieter Brand, doesn't it?   Because
I know you've been sniffing around Raoul, Cass, which is
plainly ridiculous, a sensitive artistic person like he is. No
one could write such insightful poems and..." She left the
sentence unfinished as she slapped a marker on the pastry
and rewrapped it with a patience she reserved only for the
culinary arts.

"Okay, suppose, just suppose, it turned out that our
arsonist is Lazaro." I stirred honey into my Earl Grey tea.
It was local honey, nature's homeopathic remedy for pollen
allergies.

"Believe me, it isn't Raoul. Even Stone doesn't believe
that. Oh, he did ask me what you'd come up with—he's
become a believer in your psychic acumen—so I told him
about your current fixations."

"What about that strange case of hives Lazaro got after
the Shawmutt fire? The way hives move over the body is like
a flaming itch," I said.

"Hey, listen up! It was Brand who actually got burned, a
perfect working out of our mirror spell. *Let the evil be reflected
back upon the evil-doer.* Not only that, he was *there,* pretending
to be a rescuer, that pervert."

"Heather isn't convinced. He's her neighbor and new
friend, so she feels about Brand as you do about Raoul."

"Well, Goddess help him when she gets it. Heather's
never been as hesitant as the rest of us to brew up a good
old-fashioned hex." She sat down across from me and poured
herself a cup from the Chatsford teapot. Hers was the graceful
lily design. I had the verdant herbal pattern, a gift from
Phillipa last Christmas. Perfect pourers, those Chatfords. Tea
was such a satisfying ritual, rich in magical implications: a

communion of friends, a healing breath of leisure, a quiet time for ladies to concoct plans or to defuse anger.

We sipped in armed silence for a few moments. Then I steeled myself and took a copy of Lazaro's book out of my handbag. "Then, how do you explain this?" I read, "*My salamander love, With your hot hands, set fire to my soul...*"

"I wonder if you have any poetic sensibility at all," Phillipa interrupted me. "That's called *metaphor*, my dear." A flush of color spread across her cheekbones as she looked down into her cup, swirling around the last drops in the bottom of her cup.

"Want me to read your tea leaves?" I offered.

"What! You read tea leaves now? That's new."

"Another gift from my grandma. And the mood is on me. Don't finish that last sip. Hold the cup in your left hand and swirl it around three times clockwise."

Of course she couldn't resist. She followed my directions exactly, mumbling under her breath.

I continued. "Now invert the cup over the saucer with the handle toward me." I counted seven breaths dramatically, then turned the cup upward and gazed into it.

"Ah..." I said in my most mysterious tone. "I see a book in your future, perhaps a volume of your poems since you're not doing cookbooks anymore?"

"That would be lovely. Raoul says....oh well, enough of that. What else?"

"Well...I....there's something coming between you and Stone. See right here?" I pointed to a hopeless muddle of wet leaves. "Shaped like a cabbage, sort of—that means jealousy. And this wasp thing over here could be another man pursuing you. Can you imagine that! How very romantic. But if you don't turn away, there's a possible break-up, see right here near the top of the cup, which means sooner rather than later. A dish sliced right in two, trouble at home." I indicated two globs of tea leaves branching away from each other. "But the trouble can be prevented if you draw away now."

"Where? Where? You don't really see that, do you? Well, Raoul, you know, is so flattering. I have to admit he has tried... He's been sending me poems, very lovely ones, too, about his 'dark winged lady of desire.'" Phillipa blushed and looked down at her fingers, which at that moment were twisting her wedding ring around and around.

I glanced toward the long herb planters under her two kitchen windows, filled with a cascade of lush herbs ready for snipping. A copper mister was perched at one end. Gazing at its bright reflection, there was a sudden flash in which I saw Phillipa and Raoul bending together in a passionate embrace, the image fading as instantly as it had appeared in my mind's eye. Good. I didn't want to know any more.

"Just a warning, but if I were you I would take it to heart," I said. "Fortunately, the future is always malleable, as you know. There is still time." I was remembering how my grandma's readings had so often deftly brought up matters of her concern about me. Work harder at school. Eat properly. Stay away from low-class companions. *Good show, Grandma!* "Does Stone carry a weapon, by the way?"

"Yeah. Sometimes. Depending. Often it stays locked in his gun safe. He doesn't realize that I know the combination. You never can tell when a girl might need a gun."

"So Fiona has always said. How did you find out?"

"He kept practicing, in case he would need to open the safe quickly in an emergency, like a home invasion thing. Timing himself. Sitting in the living room, racing up the stairs, opening the closet, and taking the gun out of the safe. He even practiced using the keypad in the dark. So I thought, what if there really is an emergency and Stone isn't here?"

"Yes? But how did you get the number sequence? You've never claimed to be a mind reader."

"True, but Stone was so absorbed in his stop watch, he hardly noticed me putting away laundry in the bureau drawers or changing my earrings while he fiddled with the lock. Once I even sat on the bed beside him and he didn't even seem to notice I was there. In short, I memorized the combination. Anyway, why do you ask?

"What if the trespasser were more of a Don Juan than a mugger?"

"Oh, you worrywart. Stone would never shoot anyone in anger. And besides, I'm not about to invite a Don Juan in for tea." Phillipa looked out the window, musing, then abruptly charged me. "You've got Raoul and Brand buzzing around in your peaked hat, I know. And I know it's not Raoul. He's really a lovely man—a tormented genius. So what can we do to pin down Brand?"

"Well, Fiona has got some spell out of Hazel's book. It's called *Hoist by His Own Petard.*" I couldn't help chuckling, but continued more soberly. "I'm pressing some incense for this event—has to burn for nine days—and Heather is bringing blue candles. We'll need all five of us, and we're going to do a divination first to make sure the outcome will be desirable. So bring your tarot."

The best laid plans of witches and women "gang aft a-gley," in the words of Bobbie Burns. It was weeks before we got a chance to Hoist the enemy, and after the ensuing tragedies, it seemed almost too late.

⁐

After another rollicking lunch with Heather during which she had discussed her plans to lobby for the rebuilding of the Shawmutt Animal Pound into a No-Kill (or at least, Low-Kill) Animal Care facility, I decided to stop by the Kellihers and see how Sylvie was faring.

My dryad girl was a nice surprise. Getting out of the Floribunda apartment and into her interim job as a house-sitter for the Kellihers, she'd blossomed like a flowering tree in the spring sunshine. Her long light brown hair had taken on a waving sheen when she tossed her head, like one of those improbable shampoo ads. Her moss-green eyes with their barely brown lashes looked as serious as ever but somehow less shy, and there was an attractive pink blush over her cheekbones. And she seemed very pleased to see me.

I'd had to leave Scruffy and Raffles in the Jeep because of the thirteen-something felines in residence, plus Sylvie's Misty. Raffles settled right down, nose on paws, worn out from larking about with the Devlin menagerie, but Scruffy made his usual protest. *Well, don't blame me, Toots, if you get over-run by those hairballs up on the roof. Someone ought to call pest control to get rid of those crazies.*

"Now, now. Cats are our friends, too," I'd said, firmly shutting the Jeep door on Scruffy's indignant snout.

"No, thanks," I declined Sylvie's offer of refreshment. "I've just been stuffed with lunch at Heather's. Thank Goddess for Captain Jack's wake-up mug of boiled coffee, or I don't know how I would have driven without falling asleep over the wheel. So, tell me how it's been going with you. I must say you look wonderfully rested! And so pretty, too."

We sat in the Kelliher's rambling ranch-house living room, which was decorated with Celtic weavings and artwork. The chair I chose was an embrace of soft cushions. Several cats were lounging at ease on wide, padded windowsills. There was a soothing sound of running water coming from a corner of the room that housed a floor-to-ceiling greenhouse, protected from the felines by glass walls. The stone floors were smooth and rugless so that Maeve could get around in a walker or wheelchair with ease.

"I'm really enjoying myself here, like an imposter queen in these palace surroundings. So peaceful without.... Well, no one knows where I am." Sylvie sat primly upright on the sofa.

"It's your old boyfriend that worries you, isn't it? What's his name?" I didn't need a teacup to read Sylvie.

"No, no, I'm not worried. I'll be all right. Nick won't even know where I'm living."

"Nick who?" I insisted.

"Nick Deere, but you mustn't worry about him. I'm definitely through with his jealous tantrums." The usually pliant Sylvie was showing a new strength of purpose. "Of course I'll have to find my own rooms as soon at the Kellihers return in late summer. But that's weeks away yet. I'm just waiting for that Nature Conservancy position to open up. Meanwhile, I have accepted another job that doesn't interfere at all with my house-sitting and gives me a chance to put away a nest egg. And that's thanks to Mrs. Devlin, too."

I knew about this but I asked anyway.

"Yes, it's called Pet-Meals-on-Wheels. I drive the Animal Lovers van to deliver meals for pets to elderly or handicapped people or any person who can't properly care for their furry friends. And if it's a housebound dog, a nice walk is included as well. Or sometimes I clean out a cat's litter box, ugh, not my favorite thing. Thank heavens the Kelliher kitties have the run of the outdoors. We have a dozen clients, mostly seniors, signed up already. It's funded by Animal Lovers for anyone who's in need. She's thinking of funding a veterinary van, too—called Heals-on-Wheels. Mrs. Devlin says we'll encourage people not to give up their loyal companions in hard times. Most of it is fun, really, and everyone is so grateful. The animals, too, get to know I'm bringing their dinners, so you can imagine..."

"Heather has the most amazing ideas," I murmured, watching three of the Kelliher cats avail themselves of the pet door, sailing from house to yard in a royal procession. "Do the kitties come and go all night, too?"

"Yep, but very quietly," Sylvie said. *"On little cat feet,* like the fog, you might say."

"So...have you been too busy for automatic writing then?"

Sylvie looked down at her lap. A sleek gray fellow leaped up on the sofa and availed himself of her warmth, turning around twice before settling down with loud purrs.

"This is Fomoire, the Phantom. They're all named for Celtic gods and goddesses. Mrs. Kelliher wrote down their names and descriptions before she left so that I'd know what to call the little critters. She added a note on how to pronounce each name, too—Celtic spelling is unbelievable. Yes, there's nothing like holding a pen and pad of paper while sitting with a cat in your lap to bring on the vague writing state."

"You've decided to seek it out, then. Otherwise..."

"Yes, Cass, it's me who takes the pen in hand, so I must want to see what happens after all. I kept getting the scary fire stuff for a few days after I arrived here, and then something changed. I don't know what. Maybe it was being here in this quiet place with all the cats milling around me, almost as if they were protecting me from that scary entity who wants to purify everything with fire. Because I began to get messages from someone who calls himself the Green Man. He's mythic and fascinating and much less frightening. All the channeled messages are hard to read, of course, but I've managed some translations. Mr. Kelliher said to go ahead and use his computer if I wanted to type anything."

"The Green Man's a classic symbol of this time of year when everything is bursting into new growth. I'd love to see what you've received, if you feel like sharing."

Sylvie smiled, a warm shy smile. "Of course. I came to you for help, didn't I?—Mrs. Peacedale suggested it—and my life just seems to have got better ever since. Maybe it's the Wiccan thing?"

"It's possible that, by reaching out to us, you've put yourself into a new path toward good things, which would be a Wiccan thing to do. But Wicca can't always prevent the bad things from happening." Even as I said that, I felt with a cold shudder some shadow standing in back of me waiting to fall. *Now what was that?*

Sylvie got up in her graceful way and went over to a curved desk facing the backyard window, a pine-encircled clearing where cats roamed free, stalking small prey or reclining on wooden benches at their ease. Bringing back a sheaf of neatly typed pages, she handed them to me without comment. Then she went back to gaze outdoors while I read.

"Misty loves it here," she said dreamily. "She's never had a chance to be her wild self before. I know how much Mrs. Devlin is against it, but I wonder—a shorter life but a sweeter one?"

"I'm glad I have dogs so there's no question, although I suppose if they were Heather's, she'd insist on having them fenced in at all times, whereas I do sometimes let my two pups frolic in the pines unleashed. And she's much in favor of having the males neutered as well, but Scruffy isn't having any of that. Threatened to leave home and run away." I settled back into my chair to read.

"You mean he knows what Mrs. Devlin is suggesting?"

"Of course. Dogs don't have a wide range of interests, but they certainly have a keen grasp of matters that concern them. It's almost telepathic."

We were silent then as I perused the pages, which had seemed so different when they were scrawled with big, crude words running all over each other. The fire messages, now that they were typed, read more like prose-poems, a curious point.

I am the winged phoenix, I am the blaze of death. Come to me, all ye who are impure and infirm, all ye who are afflicted with sins of the flesh, and I will renew you through the transforming flame of my desire.

Well, sure, mostly the same weird stuff I'd read before. Three pages of it, and no hints about who was the author. It was a cool relief when I got to Sylvie's Green Man, who signed himself *Robin the Green. I am the face in the oak tree, clothed in hush of shadow, in the lush leaves of deep summer. It is I who drive the cycle of seasons, and with my endless energy bring to life all growing things. Merry men and merry maids, follow me into the forests. I will teach you to draw the bow of desire, to let fly the arrow of truth, to pierce the heart of evil, to live in harmony with the natural world.*

This mythic figure, King of the Wood, was quite familiar to me as a representation of the pagan God of fertility, so dear to the hearts of the people that he'd often been incorporated into European cathedrals. The Green Man always made me think of Greenpeace, and dear Joe, my own green man. But somehow Sylvie's new communicant had overtones of Robin Hood—the merry men, the bow and arrow, the guardian protector of the land and the lady May. The illustrations for Brand's new book that I'd seen in his library came back to me now. Was it Brand's Gemini personality to whom Sylvie was connecting. Could he be the source of both messages?

"What an interesting person you're channeling," I said when I had reached the last page.

"It's so strange, though," Sylvie said. "Coincidental, I mean. Pieter Brand stopped in to visit me—it seems he'd promised the Kellihers that he'd see if I needed anything taken care of—and he asked me if I'd pose for a few sketches. He said he's working on a new version of Robin Hood. More magical than historic, he said—and he likes me for a different sort of Maid Marian."

"And did you agree? So-called coincidence is often nature's 'on purpose'."

"Oh, sure. I didn't have to go over to his place, which might have made me nervous. He had a sketch pad with him and did a few quick drawings of me standing between those pines out there in the backyard. Pieter said I kept disappearing, how did I do that? and I really didn't know what to tell him. I never moved actually."

"That's one of your dryad charms, Sylvie. Fiona warned us that you'd be nearly invisible whenever you were among trees."

"She did? Gosh, I don't know if I believe that. Anyway, Pieter was so pleased with the sketches, I let him come over again and draw me with pastels instead of charcoal. Do you think that was all right? Would the Kellihers mind?"

"It was they who suggested he call, remember, so I wouldn't worry. But keep in mind if anything, anything at all, happens with Pieter or with anyone, that worries or frightens you, it's okay to call me. I don't live far and I can come to you quickly. Or if I don't answer, call Phil. She's just on the other side of Jenkins Park, and I'll alert her that you're alone here. Or in a pinch, if you ever have to hide from anyone, run out among the trees—even though you don't believe it, that's where you'll be the least visible."

"I suppose trees are a natural haven. At least, they've always been so for me. Anyway, thanks, Cass. But now I feel I'm making a fuss over nothing. I really like Pieter, he's like a real gentleman."

Even if this weren't already Deidre's handiwork, our redoubtable matchmaker would love to hear that Sylvie was posing for Pieter's new book. I couldn't see Sylvie and Pieter

Brand as a couple, though; he must be at least fifteen years older than she and from an entirely different culture. Also, no matter how harmless he appeared in company, Brand had been on the site of the Shawmutt Animal Pound fire, and was himself burned, which could have been the affect of our mirror spell.

Brand's retelling of the Robin Hood legend with magical elements intrigued me, but I mustn't lose sight of his earlier work, the fire-breathing *Dragon of Utrecht*.

Why didn't the unconscious forces that had drawn me to investigate Brand and Lazaro go that one psychic step farther to point the finger of accusation at one or the other? Was there some reason I had to keep them both simmering in my thoughts?

CHAPTER SEVENTEEN

Yes, it is the witch's life,
climbing the primordial climb,
a dream within a dream,
then sitting here
holding a basket of fire.

–Anne Sexton

My oldest child Rebecca – Becky – is a reliable, sensible Taurus, so inflexibly methodical that she just naturally alphabetizes everything in sight, from the books on her shelves to the spices in her kitchen. Even the clothes in her closet are color coordinated, with a heavy emphasis on the navy blue so often favored by conservative female lawyers. My daughter had grown plumper since her divorce from the philandering Ron Lowell, but her shiny chestnut hair had been treated to a trendy asymmetrical cut, and she was looking quite stylish when she jumped out of her Volvo and gave me a great warm hug.

Becky had come for lunch, as she did once a month now. I imagined that I was neatly jotted in her planner. *Check on Mom. What's she up to now?* In the past, when Ron had been involved in politics, she'd worried greatly and lectured me about my getting locally infamous as a Wiccan and a crime-solver. These days, perhaps because of her work in family law, she'd seen enough of dysfunctional families to make her own mother look pretty near traditional. After all, I even baked cookies.

But not today. Joe had the kitchen in handyman's chaos and was installing the new countertops, so we went out for lunch to The Walrus and the Carpenter, a cozy restaurant specializing in a raw bar and lobster so fresh it was fished out of a tank to be boiled alive for your pleasure, something we couldn't bring ourselves to do. But the crabmeat rolls were fabulous; I wouldn't dwell on the crustaceans' origin as free denizens of Alaskan waters. Becky ordered a Cosmopolitan and I asked for a glass of the house Chardonnay.

"What shall we toast?" I asked.

"Oh, anything but work," Becky sighed. "You never know how much preventable misery there is in ordinary life until you specialize in family law."

"Well, let's drink to harmony in our own lives, then," I suggested. "I suppose you get lots of heartbreaking custody battles."

"You bet, and not just the kids, either. With many childless couples now, it's a knock-down-drag-out fight over the family dog. Visitation rights and all. Okay, here's to hope, harmony, and happiness, then." We clinked and sipped. Becky was looking over my shoulder in a speculative way. "Now I wonder who's that over there giving us the eye? No, don't turn around. He'll know we've been talking about him."

Taking out the small mirror I keep in my bag for averting the evil eye or putting on a dab of lipstick, I studied my face and the room in back of me. Pieter Brand, leaning on the raw bar with a plate of oysters and a glass of beer, was gazing directly our way.

"That's Pieter Brand, the children's author," I said. "He bought the old Craig mansion, and he's restoring it on the profits from his Newbury Award." No sooner had I got the words out of my mouth and stashed the mirror, than Brand strolled over, apparently finished with the poor raw fellows, the beer still in his hand. He tapped me on the shoulder. I turned and feigned surprise, but a flush of guilt ran through me. I hoped he hadn't ever figured out whose boots had left footprints on his newly painted porch.

"Hi, Cass. Nice to see you again. May I sit with you for a moment?" he asked.

"Of course. I'd like you to meet my daughter, Rebecca Lowell. Joe has our kitchen torn apart, so we've escaped for a quiet lunch. Becky, this is Pieter Brand, a new neighbor of the Devlins and the Kellihers." It did not escape my attention that Brand and Becky were smiling at each other with quite a lively interest for two strangers barely introduced. It's the kind of thing mothers and clairvoyants never fail to notice, and I was both. *Oh, dear.* "We're having sort of mother-daughter tête-à-tête," I added.

"Which I wouldn't dream of interrupting." He started to stand up but I waved him back, wanting to pry a little first.

"I dropped in to see Sylvie last week," I said. "She told me she's been modeling for your new book."

"Ah, yes. The tree sprite. She seems lonely there all by herself."

"I think she's relishing the freedom," I said. "I believe there's a disgruntled boyfriend somewhere in her recent past. But she never talks about him."

"Except to you?" Brand's smile was quizzical.

"My mother has a talent for knowing things she's not supposed to know," Becky said with just a hint of pride.

"I remember our discussion at the Devlins' dinner party. So many psychic whammies in one room, I nearly fled in panic. So then, Rebecca, have you inherited your mother's clairvoyance?" Brand just wanted an excuse to look deeply into Becky's eyes.

"Not a speck of it, I'm afraid. I'm all logic, she's all intuition. Or you could say, sense and sensibility," Becky affirmed. I wasn't as sure as she that nothing otherworldly would turn up in her psyche, but I didn't demur as I might have if we were alone.

"Then I need have nothing to fear from you?" Brand said.

"Do you have something to hide?" Becky was shrewd enough to ask.

"Oh, everyone has a secret. Like Sylvie and the abusive boyfriend." I said, wanting to get this intimate little chat on broader ground.

"Cass, you're her friend. You must insist that Sylvie call me if there's any sort of problem," Brand said. "The Kellihers asked me to keep an eye on her in case of burnt fuses or other domestic crises."

That might be a leap from the frying pan into the fire, I thought. "Sylvie said you're drawing her as Maid Marian?"

"Yes. Well, as you know I don't like to talk much about a work in progress. But it's not your usual Marian, or a typical Robin Hood tale for that matter. But I mustn't intrude on your luncheon any longer, which I see is headed this way."

The waiter appeared at our table with the heaping crabmeat rolls and bowls of coleslaw.

Before leaving Brand turned his full charm Becky's way. "Is it Miss or Mrs. Lowell?"

"*Was* Mrs. Lowell," Becky said. "Mom forgets that I've gone back to my maiden name, Hauser, ever since I went to work at Katz and Kinder."

"Katz and Kinder—is that a law firm?" Brand asked.

"Yes, I'm a family attorney." Becky was still smiling and might even have been fluttered her long brown eyelashes. Brand looked at if he was going to fall forward any moment. Maybe his dark-framed glasses were steaming up a bit. By the time he actually took himself back to the bar to pay his check, the two young people had managed to exchange quite a lot of information.

"You found him very attractive? You go for that blonder-than-blond look?"

"Oh, Mom, cut that out—I don't even know him. I mean, we just this minute met, and you're already doing the psychic thing, aren't you? Pieter Brand—is that a German name?"

"Dutch, I think. I wager he'll find some reason to call you at Katz and Kinder, which you just happened to let slip was your place of employment. And if he does, I want you to be very careful, very reserved."

"Good Lord, what do you mean? You *don't* think he's the South Shore arsonist you've been telling me about, do you?"

"Let's just say I haven't ruled him out yet."

Later, after Becky left with promises to call often that she would forget as soon as her busy life consumed her again, it was nearly three, a difficult time of day to begin any new activity. So I took Scruffy and Raffles for a walk on the beach, then whiled away some minutes admiring the way my new countertops were shaping up. I also admired the brawny shape of my husband who was looking pleased with himself, as well as jaunty and sexy. Then I tore myself away from the notion of an afternoon siesta and went to work on my new Psychic Visions dream pillows. Not being much of a seamstress, I had bought the pretty pillow covers patterned with herb designs and would now proceed to fill them with soft natural cotton and fragrant dried herbs for pleasant sleeping and a hint of prophetic dreaming. Sales for the Psychic Vision were always brisk, but I couldn't resist experimenting with the formula. Now the catalog entry would be emblazoned with a banner, "New and Improved." Maybe stir up even more orders.

Fortunately, considering the state of my kitchen at present, I still had a cellar workroom with its well-stocked shelves. Joe had built me a grand new worktable to replace the old gate leg missing its leaf, and installed new track lighting. I'd kept my former lamp still hanging above the work area, however; there were meditative moments that somehow called for a single shadowy light. I had a huge old wooden bowl in which I was combining dried herbs for visionary dreams—lavender, rosemary, aniseed, bay leaves, mimosa, and other soporific scents. In a general way, I drew on old recipes, some from my grandma's notebooks and some from Hazel's Household Recipes, but relied on my own intuition to personalize the product.

Just breathing in the hypnotic fragrance after a big lunch and midday wine was enough to put me into a pleasant doze, and yet the lavender added a refreshing note that kept me from descending into an actual stupor. *Good mix*, I thought.

The better to consider its merits, I turned off the raucous track light, and rocked quietly for a while in the oak rocker I keep in my workroom, inhaling the drifting scent and gazing at my swinging, shining green-shaded lamp.

In the next blink of an eye, the cellar faded away and I was in some foreign kitchen, a pleasant spotlessly clean room with the sun streaming in small high windows and Delft tiles decorating the walls. A woman was sitting at the kitchen table shelling peas and humming to herself. Round face, shining brown hair, looking very familiar to me. And then I had it. She was the very image of my daughter Becky! As I watched, a fair-haired boy ran into the room with a paper in his hand and leaned against the woman's knees. "Oh, het mooie schilderen," she said in quiet praise for the watercolor the boy held in his hand.

The image paled and disappeared, but I could guess what—who—I'd seen in my mind's eye. Brand's mother or grandmother, or even an aunt, the source of his instant attraction to Becky, maybe something he didn't even recognize himself. I must remember to ask him about his family. Was his mother still alive, I wondered. What did she look like now? Or could the little boy have been Pieter's father, was he also blond and a painter? The image of the woman in the scene I'd just witnessed must be part of Pieter's conscious or unconscious memories. Or even a past life memory. Yes, it could be that, too. How often are we instantly attracted to someone with a sense of having known and loved the person in previous existence. I remembered how it had been with Joe and me. Irresistible. Love at first sight. Not to mention, lust at first date. And the sweet familiarity of his body, surely we had been together intimately in many other lives. Or was it as Fiona believed, that we connect with past lives without having lived them?

"I've just laid the last countertop in place," Joe's voice called down the cellar stairs, jolting me out of my metaphysical speculation. "Don't you want to see how it looks?"

"It's just gorgeous," I said when I'd got myself upstairs. Scruffy and Raffles were sitting on the threshold between the kitchen and living room, viewing the wreck of the kitchen, their favorite room, with some alarm, their ears pricked up and expressions wary. *Furry Face has really messed up the good food place this time. Where's our chow crock, our dishes with our names on them? Are we going to be starved and forgotten just as I've always feared?* Scruffy didn't even scold Raffles for leaning against him as he normally would. There was creature comfort in closeness.

"Don't worry, you guys. You'll be fed royally just as always." I patted the anxious heads, then coaxed the two dogs out onto the porch where they could avail themselves of the pet door.

"Love the way the wood tones match my pine floors," I praised the master woodworker. Putting my arm around Joe's waist, I nuzzled his neat beard. The next thing we were kissing for a pleasant interlude which might have gone on longer if he hadn't reminded me that it was possible to have most of the debris cleaned up before dinner.

"Oh, joy. Not that I mind cooking in bedlam, but it would be a treat not to have to step over planks and stuff. I'll stay out of your way, then. I've got some dream pillows to finish in the workroom."

"Save one for us," Joe suggested. Oh sure, but I had a whole other bouquet of herbs and scents in mind for our bed.

Rose petals, trumpet honeysuckle, hibiscus... I recited the list to myself as I descended to the cellar again.

Fiona has often urged me to get control over my visions so that I could summon them at will, and it occurred to me now that this new blend had sent me winging into the Netherlands and was perhaps the way to do it. Nothing goes to the brain quicker and more evocatively than odors. Perhaps my visionary dream potpourri was really a clairvoyant boost as well. Maybe I'd keep this mixture for my own use but defuse it for general consumption, less mimosa and bay perhaps. Carefully, I chose a predominantly blue (for clairvoyance) pillow cover for myself, filled it with soft stuffing and the new herb blend. I set that one aside to sew closed later, then added lots of dried chamomile, valerian, and hops to the bowl for the rest of the pillows—sleepy stuff to neutralize its potency. Soon, very soon, I would lay my head on the pillow I'd made for myself and see what would happen.

CHAPTER EIGHTEEN

I called on dreams and visions, to disclose
That which is veiled from waking thought; conjured
Eternity, as men constrain a ghost
To appear and answer...

—William Wordsworth

At the table in the little Ritchie kitchen, Laura Belle was mixing raisins and brown sugar into her bowl of oatmeal with quite a self-possessed air for so small a body. Whereas most children are clearly works in progress, there'd always been something oddly mature about this little girl; an "old soul" my grandma would have called her. She looked at me with her amazing morning glory eyes and gravely said "Aunt Cass" by way of greeting, then turned back to her breakfast. Laura Belle was not a gabber.

Fiona gazed at her fondly and filled thistle mugs with coffee which we took into the living room. My hostess settled into her accustomed reading chair, and I sat on the sofa. Omar lay prone across the scarred coffee table, basking in the rays of morning sun that burnished it. I noticed how the panes of glass in the casement windows sparkled in the light. Since

Laura Belle had been sent back to Fiona, the Ritchie place had assumed the ambiance of a cheerful Disney cottage.

"My little Tinker Belle speaks very little, but she seems to choose every word for its truth. I believe she has the gift the Egyptians called Ma'Kheru, a state of grace. Possibly related to Logos, the word of creation. And if she's Ma'Kheru, according to the old beliefs, whatever she says will come to pass in the world."

That sounded to me like a rather oppressive gift. "It's too great a responsibility for such a little girl. One needs the occasional prevarication just to be a civilized person. Perhaps Laura will tell her share of fibs later, especially when she's a teenager." I said. "Now you said you've some research results for me on Brand and Lazaro?"

"Wait and see. She will never tell a lie; she will be a Sybil." Fiona drew herself up into that queenly glamour that will not be gainsaid. Then she reached into the greenish reticule leaning against her chair and took out a stack of three-by-five cards. Wearing her half-tracks low on her nose, she absent-mindedly stuck a pencil in her coronet of braids beside the crochet hook that was already there and peered at the results of her research.

"Lazaro, as we know, claimed political asylum when he arrived here, the only survivor of a flimsy fishing boat that sank off the shores of Miami. He was reported to be an anti-Castro activist who would have been arrested and executed the moment he put a foot back in Cuba. Nothing extraordinary in that story. Many others have made similar claims. But there is something irregular in the level of support he received. Top people in the government took an interest. Then, of course, there was his patron."

"Did you find out her name?"

"Yes, I did, dear. And I also found a brief account of her accident in the *Miami Herald*, and her obit as well. From there I accessed probate records of the estate to follow the money, as they say." Fiona beamed proudly.

"So, spill it please..."

"Frances Dickinson Lowell! And before you ask, yes I did check, she *was* a distant relation to your daughter Becky's ex-husband. Rich, eccentric, and childless. But any hopes that she would favor a cousin or nephew with a bequest were dashed when she died. The bulk of her estate was bequeathed to her favorite charity, the Jamaica Plain Home for Wandering Artists, where painters, writers, and musicians who have fallen on hard times can rest and work with dignity. It is not, by the way, a substance abuse rehab facility; you have to be clean to get in. If you think this leaves Lazaro out in the cold, wait, *there's more.*" Fiona paused and consulted her notes with an enigmatic smile. She knew I was hanging on her every revelation. "Lowell's protégé did get a separate bequest right off the top of the estate. Lazaro was set up quite comfortably with a trust that will keep him out of the J. P. Home for the rest of his life, gilt-edged securities held by the Boston Savings and Fiduciary Trust where Mrs. L was on the Board of Directors. He was also invited to select among the household inventory any items that might have had sentimental value for him."

"Yeah? What did he choose? Her diamonds, perhaps?"

"No, nothing as obvious as that. Just a few books. Apparently, he cherry-picked his way through her collection of modern first editions. That Jaguar he's driving now could have been paid for by just one of them—a 1937 first edition of Tolkien's *The Hobbit*.

"And the accident, if that's what it was, freed him from his patron? I'll bet that Lazaro got tired of playing the artiste in her entourage. That trust would have given him an excellent reason to arrange something for Mrs. L."

"Let me freshen your coffee first." Fiona struggled out of her reading chair and limped into the kitchen. Her arthritis was bothering again. When she returned with the refill pot, Laura Belle, all three and a half feet of her, trotted confidently alongside carrying a plate of shortbread. Omar lifted his head and delicately sniffed the air. After offering the plate to me and her aunt, the little girl shared her own shortbread with Omar, then carefully put the plate on the pedestal table beside her great-aunt. Omar leapt gracefully off the coffee table and smoothed himself around Fiona's legs.

"Ah..." I said in a warning tone, not wanting anything too scary to be discussed in front of Laura, who had hopped up beside me and was listening intently.

"Mrs. Lowell and Lazaro were staying in Newport, Rhode Island, for some social and charity events," Fiona glanced again at her cards and took up the story."Late at night after one of these parties, Mrs. L. ordered her car for a drive into Boston where she had reserved a suite at the Ritz. Suffice to say, the Rolls careened into a row of Jersey barriers on Route 95 and flipped over several times. News accounts suggested that the chauffeur was under the influence of drugs or alcohol or a combination of both, but the autopsy report confirmed only an illegal blood alcohol level. Both the chauffeur and Mrs. Lowell were...." Fiona's voice trailed off as she encountered her grand-niece's big eyes and solemn expression.

"Killed," Laura Belle said.

"Yes, dear one. When people pass away, they journey to a beautiful place called Summerland. Even beloved animals."

Laura Belle hopped off the sofa. "They put them in a box. In the ground with dirt on top. Outside now, Fifi," she said, heading for the back door in the kitchen. Omar slunk after her devotedly.

"Mind you wear your jacket and hat, and don't go out of the backyard," Fiona called to the little girl. Laura Belle glanced back, nodded, and smiled her sweet rosebud smile.

After Laura Belle had departed, I said, "I see what you mean about Word of Truth. A very clear-sighted child. You may have to talk to her more about the concept of Summerland. Too much mundane truth can be hazardous to the psyche. Now where was Lazaro when the accident happened?"

"Lucky guy. He had stayed to commune with the ocean while Mrs. Lowell attended to business in Boston. An appointment had been scheduled with her financial planner, and there was a meeting of the Board of Directors in the afternoon. She was to have returned the next day to continue their round of parties before spending a few weeks in her New York apartment at the Dakota, then back to the West Palm Beach house for the winter season."

"Lucky guy or guilty guy. That remains to be discovered. Okay, what about Brand."

Fiona took up another set of cards and readjusted her half-tracks. "On his father's side of the family, Brand's lineage dates back practically to the Peter Stuyvesant era. But his mother, Johanna, who was much younger, not a beauty but fresh-faced and pretty, came from Holland." Fiona handed me a copy of a newspaper wedding photo circa 1960s, "Mr. and Mrs. Willem Brand."

"She's very charming though. Reminds me a little of Becky. Lovely hair. Chestnut brown, I'm guessing, with those highlights," I commented. "Apparently Pieter got his fair coloring and poor vision from father Willem. You know, Fiona, I will forever marvel at the way you gather information. You could have had quite a career as a P.I."

Fiona smiled enigmatically."That's what I'm doing now, Cass. In an informal *pro bono* way, of course."

"Informal and unpaid."

"Ah, but you can't buy the satisfaction I feel when we track down malfeasants. Well, to continue. Johanna's family included some minor artist and artisans, but Willem's were all businessmen. Not surprisingly, the union proved to be an incompatible one. We know that because I have court records of Johanna attempting to obtain a separation from Willem which was foiled because Willem was somehow able to retain sole custody of little Pieter. So Johanna stayed and took who-knows-what abuse to remain with her only child. Then, when Brand was eight, the father died in a little home accident. Fell asleep smoking his pipe—dead drunk, I would guess—and set fire to his chair, so the story goes. Johanna, now a well-to-do widow, took Pieter back to Holland where he remained until the age of 18. Since he's an American citizen by birth, he chose to attend college and architectural school here. And there you have it."

"I wonder...another lucky accident or did Johanna...the little boy...? Becky and I ran into Brand at The Walrus and The Carpenter a few days ago. The two of them seemed to take quite an instant interest in each other. Something else to worry about."

"We will say good words for Becky," Fiona assured me. "She will find the right person to heal her heart. I wonder how he could bring himself to sell."

"Who? Sell what?"

"Lazaro. *The Hobbit*. I'm afraid I'd have a difficult time parting with that marvelous book—and *The Wind in the Willows*, of course."

"*The Wind in the Willows?* Kenneth Graham?"

"1st edition. Paid for his computer and all those silk shirts, I'll wager. Still, Raoul is the biggest draw I have at our local poetry readings. I will choose not to suspect him unless I must. After all, it was Brand whose history was tainted by a flaming father. And that mysterious construction fire—his failed "city village." And *The Dragon of Utrecht*, of course. Breathing the stuff all over the villagers. And he has shown up pretty handily at our local conflagrations. Got burned even. Also, those pale eyes."

As is often the case with Fiona, I was feeling dazed with an overload of data before I left. Driving home in that bemused state, I thought this might be a good time to try out my new personal psychic visions pillow, maybe sort out the truth between our two likely candidates for local arsonist.

After lunch, Joe went outdoors to rake out my herb beds. Among the many mundane joys of marriage, having a guy willing to take over the heavy gardening chores is high on my list. I looked out the window and sighed—should I go out and help him? Or should I take a little nap?

Hey, Toots. Let's go snuggle on the big bed. Scruffy cocked his head at me invitingly.

"Good idea," I agreed. Raffles trotted after us with a hopeful air, but a low growl from his sire—*Get lost, Omega Pup*—relegated him to the braided rug on the floor at the foot of the bed. Scruffy hopped up on the bed and settled himself comfortably with his head on Joe's pillow. From the high shelf in my closet, I took down my blue-bordered dream pillow sprigged with a lavender pattern, lay down with my cheek against it, and thought about my conundrum: Lazaro or Brand? Soon I drifted into a pleasant doze.

I don't know how much time passed and whether I was actually asleep or merely skimming along the edges when I found myself at the scene of a fire. An old brick building was ablaze, flames and smoke shooting out of the rear windows. Beside the building, there was a handsome stone church. It was a church I'd seen but not one I knew well, as I did the Garden of Gethsemane. Fire trucks careened into the driveway, followed by the Fire Chief's bright red Pontiac and several civilian vehicles, perhaps some of the volunteer firefighters. Men shouting to one another were soon scurrying in all directions.

A priest rushed out of the church. A black SUV careened into the driveway. The big redhaired man who got out of the Bronco seemed at first to be stumbling. Then, with some lingering aura of an athlete, he sprinted forward toward the burning building just as three women ran out from the back, one of them sobbing. But before the big man could reach the front door, he collapsed on the ground. Mick Finn yelled for the medics who came running with a stretcher. The priest hurried over to join them.

The fallen man was taken into the rescue vehicle, which did not leave the premises. With my dream powers, I was able to look inside the van. One medic was manning a fibrillator, while the other checked for vital signs. The priest was administering the last rites. The second medic shook his head, but they kept trying to revive their patient. I saw the red hair, the slightly florid face—the man was Will Ryan. I sat up on my own bed and screamed.

Two mighty frightened dogs hightailed it for the kitchen as I threw the vision pillow as far from me as I could. It bounced off the window, struck a bowl of potpourri which fell off the piecrust table and hit a leg of Grandma's rocking chair just right to splinter into a thousand pieces. Shards of Meissen china and fragrant petals flew everywhere. I would mourn for that bowl, but I never wanted to lay my cheek on that damned pillow again. Good riddance to bad vibes.

Evidently it was a quite a piercing scream, because a minute later, Joe came running into the bedroom, a panicked look on his face. "Cass...Cass...what happened?" He looked at the shambles on the bedroom floor with dismay, then stepped over it gingerly to gather me into his arms. "Are you all right, sweetheart? What happened to that pretty bowl?"

Feeling the warmth of Joe's comforting embrace somehow brought on the hysterics. Between sobs and hiccups, I managed to say, "I had....a dream....a bad dream...Will Ryan...oh, Joe, he was dead! He tried...he never should have...what was he doing there at a fire, for Goddess's sake?"

"But, sweetheart...you're saying this was a dream...not one of your visions?"

"No...yes...it *was* a vision, Joe, but it was a dream, too. Oh, let's find out if there's been a fire today...we have to call...the station...did you hear...was there an alarm while I was sleeping?"

Joe stroked my hair softly. "Hush now, sweetheart. It's probably not true, you know. There are dreams that are simply an expression of our fears. Not a glimpse into the future. I want you to calm yourself now. Whatever's going to happen, you'll be no good to anyone if you're hyperventilating—right? Now get down off the bed very carefully, and *wear shoes*. I don't want those pretty feet all cut up. Then you go splash your face with cold water while I call the fire station. Will that do?"

"Yes, okay. But you'll come and tell me no matter what, promise?"

A few minutes later I was in the downstairs lav, pressing a cold cloth on my blotchy face, when Joe leaned in the door. "There have been no fire alarms in Plymouth County today. The last incident was a report of dark smoke pouring out of the firehouse itself. Apparently, the guys all rushed off yesterday to put out a small brush fire in one of Finch's cornfields, forgetting that they had a chicken frying on the stove. A neighbor saw the smoke and called in the alarm."

It was a relief to laugh. Situation normal, another small town crisis averted. "There must be some mighty red faces at that firehouse!"

I insisted on cleaning up the mess in the bedroom on my own—after all, it was my vivid imagination that had caused the breakage. As always for persons who live with pets, there's the broken china paranoia. I swept three times, then vacuumed everywhere thoroughly, and finished up with a thorough wash of the floor before I would let the two concerned dogs back into the house.

CHAPTER NINETEEN

Who gave thee such a ruby flaming heart
And such a pure cold spirit?

–George William Russell

I needed to talk to someone with an understanding of the helplessness and frustration of precognition and a clear view of the realities. So it was Phillipa to whom I confided my vision of Will Ryan's collapse at the scene of a fire that apparently had not yet happened. Cardiac arrhythmia is a leading cause of sudden, unexplained death, and I feared that's exactly what I had witnessed. Phillipa's thinking processes are straight as an arrow (providing no sexy guy is involved)—with none of Fiona's unsettling digressions or Heather's unruly passionate, unreasoned reactions.

"Well, first of all, we ought to find out if you saw a real or imagined church."

"The fire wasn't in the church—it was in the brick building beside it."

"Priest, you said a priest ran out of the church." Phillipa was already punching keys on her kitchen computer, Googling for Catholic churches in Plymouth. "Ah ha! Eureka!" she caroled. "How about St. Catherine of Siena's Convent in Pinehills?

There's a chapel next door, also called St. Catherine's. Oh, Blessed Brigit! You know who lives at that convent? Sister Mary Vincent, my partner in rhyme."

"And Sister Mary Vincent, I discovered at the hospital, is a distant cousin of Will's. Shouldn't I warn her? Or tell Mick Finn? Or ask you to caution Stone, now that he and Billy have been tapped as arson investigators. Do you think I should alarm Dee? Oh, I really hate the idea of burdening her with such a horrifying vision. She already has so much to deal with since Will got sick."

"*Dream.* You said it was a dream that *might* be a vision because you were napping on that new vision pillow. Which is where, by the way?" Phillipa asked.

"I stuffed it into the back of my clothes closet. I'm thinking of burning the damned thing. Because I'm never going near it again."

"Now, now, *never say never.* You might need to summon a vision again before all this is over. But if it truly was a dream and not a vision, it might be better *not* to say anything to Dee. It would be like panicking her with some personal nightmare. It isn't as if a warning from you might make her any more careful of Will. She's already worrying about his every breath. More tea?" Phillipa held up her Chatsford teapot.

"Thanks, is this Assam? I guess you're right."

"The coffee-lover's tea, yes. I thought you needed to be perked up. On the other hand, if it was a *genuine* vision, then a warning from you might prevent a tragedy."

"You're a great help. I'm damned if I do and damned if I don't."

"I tell you what—why don't I read the tarot for Dee and see what turns up? I'll just ask the question and lay out three cards." Phillipa went to fetch the red silk bag in which she protected her tarot deck from negative vibes. Blue soladite, a stone of the sixth chakra, was kept with the cards to enhance psychic awareness. I thought that I would rather have carried a stone that *diminished* such knowledge. Well, maybe...maybe not.

We both took a deep breath. Phillipa shuffled with that faraway look in her eyes that comes over her before a reading. "What will happen in the life of our dear friend Dee?" she asked, and swiftly drew three cards from the deck, laying them down between us.

The Moon, the Three of Swords, the Nine of Swords.

"Oh, shit," Phillipa said.

"I believe the future can be altered," I said stoically. "That is, I believe that by concentrating, we can step from a disaster in one universe into a parallel universe in which that misfortune does not occur."

"Weird theory. You've never said that before. I didn't know you were conversant with the new physics." Phillipa looked at me keenly.

"I just adopted it. I mean, the existence of parallel universes explains how I feel about changing one's fate. That it's just a sidestep into a different dimension."

"You know what they say, *a little physics is a dangerous thing.*" Phillipa studied the three cards of unforeseen peril, heartbreak, and sorrow over the fate of another. She shook her head sadly. "But I'll take any theory that can avert the danger in this layout."

"Anyway, your reading has convinced me that I must have that talk with Dee about keeping Will completely away from fire scenes. I know he's on medical leave, but I mean not even as a spectator. I may even speak to Will himself," I said more confidently than I felt.

"We have to make some effort to prevent that fire, too, if that was a vision and not a nightmare. Now that we have an idea where it might be."

"If only we knew when..."

"Don't you have any idea at all?" Phil asked.

I searched my memory to restore the vision. Or dream. As always, the particulars of the scene were already fading. I should write down exactly what I see when I see it. But in this case, not only had I been in shock, I was faced with the wreckage of the Meissen bowl. "Not a clue," I said regretfully.

Phillipa said she would definitely tell Stone to keep an extra close watch on St. Catherine's—that I'd envisioned a fire there, although we didn't know when. "*Who, what,* and *where* are the easy ones, but *when* is nearly impossible," she said. "It's the thing we so often get wrong, because our precognition is a glimpse into a timeless dimension where past, present, and future no longer exist."

"I'm not having too much luck with *who*, either," I said.

᠗

Before I could have a talk with Deidre, or even thought how I would word the warning, Heather called to say that Sylvie was in the hospital. And so was Oisin, one of the Kelliher cats. "Not in the same hospital, of course," she said. "Sylvie's in Jordan, and Oisin's at Wee Angels. Punctured lung but expected to recover if all goes well.

"Sylvie?"

"No, Oisin. Sylvie's only got contusions, abrasion, scratches, and bites. Had to have an antibiotic IV, tetanus shot—the works. She'll be out later today probably, and she insists on going back to the Kellihers' to keep an eye on their feline family. Well, you can't say I haven't warned them again and again."

"What? What? What?" I yelled over my cell phone with increasing confusion.

"If you're going to let cats run wild outdoors, you're going to have to expect some nasty encounters. This was a coyote— a pair of them actually. All these blasted developments going up, woodlands disappearing—the poor animals are forced to forage in suburbia. It's not fair to the wild things or to the small neighborhood pets they prey on. Did you hear about the Yorkie named Baby?"

"For Goddess's sake, will you tell me what exactly happened?"

"Can you believe it one of the creatures actually had Oisin in its mouth when Sylvie attacked it."

"Sylvie attacked a coyote?"

"Yes, with a broom, I believe. Always has been a good weapon for women—sweep away many kinds of negativity. Dick said it looked like a CSI crime scene with all that blood and slime on the patio. Patty Peacedale's with Sylvie now at the hospital, and so is some reporter from the *Pilgrim Times*. I was there, too, for just a few minutes earlier, and naturally I asked Sylvie what happened. She says she doesn't really remember much about it. Went out to sweep catkins off the patio and saw this animal at the edge of the pines with poor Oisin hanging out of its mouth crying pitifully. I don't think

Sylvie could have given much thought to what she did next. Just charged the coyote, probably beat it over the head with the broom, and grabbed the cat out of its mouth. Got a few bites and scratches in the melee. What a crazy thing to do!"

"Crazy brave. Just like something you'd do." Where animals are concerned, Heather, too, rushs in where angels fear to tread. "I wonder, if I go over to Jordan right now, will Sylvie still be there or on her way home?"

"I'm not sure. I know that Dr. Blitz is set on keeping her under his observation overnight. I've called Pieter Brand and asked him to feed and water the kitties. He was quite nice about it, which may set Sylvie's mind at rest."

I decided to zip over to Jordan anyway. When I got there, I discovered that not even Dr. Blitz could keep Sylvie from her cat-sitting responsibilities. She was up and dressed, waiting for Patty Peacedale to give her a ride.

"Sylvie!" I exclaimed, gingerly hugging the pale girl. "Hardly anyone would have done what you did. I don't know whether to praise you or scold you."

"Dr. Blitz said he never saw an animal bite heal so fast." Patty looked up over her ever-present knitting and reported. "If he weren't a man of science, he said, he would have called it miraculous. So I said I didn't mean to jar his agnosticism, but coincidentally I'd got our prayer group working on Sylvie the minute I'd heard about her confrontation with those wild beasts." Her fingers kept working independently on what looked like a long khaki scarf or gorilla sleeve.

"Possibly it was the prayer cycle. Or even a self-healing," I said, remembering Fiona's description of the typical dryad. Sylvie looked down at her green sneakers and offered no comment.

"That reporter was quite taken with our dear heroine," Patty said with a proud smile. "Brought his photographer to take a picture of her right in bed, but wearing a suitable robe which I'd brought for her. I bet you're going to see Sylvie on tomorrow's front page. If tomorrow is Thursday." The *Pilgrim Times* was published only two days a week, Tuesday and Thursday. "I hope it is," Patty fluttered on, "because that will mean I didn't miss the Wednesday Afternoon Parcels for Peace meeting again." Patty ran her hand over her forehead where the usual resistant lock of hair had fallen and glanced at her watch distractedly.

"I'll take Sylvie home, Patty. You go ahead and catch that meeting."

"Oh thank you, dear Cass. Sylvie, if you must go home now, promise you'll put your feet up, have a nice cup of sweet tea, and rest. I wonder if Wyn would mind my having a little prayer vigil for Oisin? I'll ask him." And Patty sailed out of the room on her various good missions.

ᘒᘯ

"'Plymouth Girl Rescues Cat from Coyotes'" Fiona read aloud from the *Pilgrim Times* the next day. She'd stopped in for a cup of coffee while Laura Belle was in nursery school. "If Sylvie were a Native American, she would be named for this event ever after. Woman Who Attacks Coyote with Broom."

"Catchy," I said. "I'm just glad she's not scarred or worse. If she got herself between the trees, I wonder if the coyotes could really see where Sylvie was batting from."

"Good point, but I think animals are one up on humans when it comes to detecting presence. They'd have smelled her whereabouts—and probably her rage as well. Speaking of animals, how's Oisin doing?"

"Heather says the surgery was successful but he'll need a week or two at Wee Angels for his convalescence. She wants Sylvie to bring all the other cats indoors and keep them there, but of course the girl can't do that. The Kellihers left strict instructions for their pets to be given free reign of the backyard."

"Let's say a few banishing words to the coyotes. This is a good day for it—waning moon."

And so we did. Later we wished we'd broadened the scope of our banishing spell for Sylvie's sake.

∾

Before Fiona rushed away to be home for Laura Belle, she urged me not to postpone my conference with Deidre. "The right words will come to you. Trust in yourself," she said, leaving me with a big, warm hug that did indeed inspire me to confidence. Fiona's hugs have a special magic, better than corn pollen or sage oil.

When I called, Bettikins answered; Deidre was at the shop. Joe had taken the Jeep over to Home Warehouse to buy new hardware for my cabinets, antique brass. So I decided to borrow his rental car parked conveniently in the driveway with the keys in it. I walked the dogs, explaining that the mall was not a fun place for them to visit, that Joe would be home soon.

Scruffy sniffed the air, taking in the news with all his senses. *Watch out, Toots. I smell trouble. You better take me with you, never know when you might need guarding. The kid can stay here by himself. He's useless anyway.*

"I'm only going over to the mall, for heaven's sake. I'll be back before you know it." Pushing them both in the kitchen door, I handed out compensatory biscuits, and took off in the rattling red Toyota.

Bringing two coffees from Sweet Buns, I found Diedre just finishing up with a customer who was buying a faery godmother doll, the one that looked so remarkably like Fiona with its little coat sweater of many colors, granny glasses, and miniature green reticule. "Got a tiny gun in there?" I asked when the buyer was out of earshot.

Deidre grinned mischievously. "The doll's not quite *that* authentic, Cass. But her tote bag does have some teeny pamphlets and a bag of faery dust. What brings you here today? Not that I'm not delighted to have company and a coffee break."

It wasn't easy, but I started out with the vision pillow I'd accidentally created and my dream of a fire, probably at St. Catherine's convent. "Stone knows, and he's promised to find some way—short of confessing that he's listening to a psychic—of warning the Chief of Police to keep a watchful eye on Pinehills. The thing is, Dee—I'm worried about Will. He's not been going out on fire alarms, has he?"

"My Will's on medical leave, soon to become a permanent retirement with a fairly decent pension. Mick Finn has cautioned Will that he'll prejudice his claim if he hangs around fire scenes and is seen to so much as lift a hose. But to tell the truth, Will's just like some old fire dog whose ears perk up every time there's an alarm. So far he's only slipped out once to follow the fire trucks, but after listening to Finn and me giving him an earful, I think he'll give it a rest now."

"The thing is, Dee, I'm so sorry to worry you, but I'm afraid something will happen to him if he doesn't stay away from fire scenes."

She looked up at me sharply from her coffee cup. Her face had paled, and for one moment, I could see exactly how it would look when she was thirty years older; the lines that hadn't happened yet were all there. "Exactly what is this, Cass? Are we talking *worry* or *vision?*"

"I don't know, honey. But I couldn't *not* tell you."

"Jesus, Mary, and Joseph," she cried, just as she must have heard her mother exclaim time and again in her Catholic youth. "What am I supposed to do? I can't be in two places at once."

"No, of course not," I said in a soothing tone. "Just reinforce what you've already told him. Make Will promise— swear on the Bible even—not to hang around the firehouse or follow the fire trucks. Do whatever you have to do. And forgive me, Dee. If you only knew how much I *don't* want to be the bearer of ill tidings."

"Cassandra," Deidre said with a bit of her old impishness. "What can you expect but doom and gloom from someone named Cassandra?"

"Maybe I should have stuck with Sandra," I agreed.

The coffee I'd just consumed was sitting in my chest like a cup of acid, and Deidre didn't look much healthier than I felt. We were too far away to hear the Plymouth fire alarm— what if it was wailing right this minute?

My offer to mind the shop open until her assistant would come in at six was gratefully and hastily accepted. Deidre couldn't wait to have a serious talk with Will. There was never any doubt in her mind that I was a seer, and that I'd seen a tragedy. She rushed home, and I rooted around in my woven Libran handbag for antacids and aspirin. A clairvoyant should never be without her over-the-counter meds.

While I was there, Phillipa called me on my cell phone. "Stone says there's no way in hell he can warn the Chief of Police about your vision of a fire, possibly at St. Catherine's. He'd have to manufacture an anonymous tip, and then if the fire actually materializes, he'd be called to account for not submitting an official report."

"Yeah, I understand. And I'm not surprised. Well, I've warned Dee as tactfully as I could. Naturally she got pretty excited, though. In fact, I'm shop-sitting right now, so that Dee could leave early and lay down the law to Will."

"It should be all right, then."

"If he listens."

CHAPTER TWENTY

I've a rendezvous with Death
At midnight in some flaming town
When Spring trips North again this year,
And I to my pledged word am true,
I shall not fail that rendezvous.

—Alan Seeger

The convent fire erupted two nights later just after midnight. Although the main building was constructed of brick, the back entry was a wooden addition that functioned as a combination cloak room and receptacle for trash bags on their way to outdoor barrels, and it was there that the blaze flared up. It got a fast start and easily penetrated the kitchen.

Will, who had slept most of the day, was downstairs watching a late night sports recap and drinking. Although on medical leave, he still had his official beeper, and he called in to find out what was going on. When he heard that it was St. Catherine's Convent burning, his promises to Deidre washed away like a child's sand castle. He slipped away to the garage and was saddened again by the absence of his old Bronco, which had been sold in an economy move. But he had the keys to the family Plymouth Voyager in hand, and he rolled the vehicle out as quietly as possible.

After months of moping around the house, ordered to rest and bored out of his skull, he'd found his own medicine. A drop of the Irish made him feel strong and sure again, like his old self. A few drinks, and he was convinced that nothing was really wrong with him. It was all the fault of women keening and wringing their hands and the doctors looking to make a buck. For Jesus' sake, his cousin was one of those Sisters of St. Catherine. He needed to be there, with his buddies, at the center of action. That's what firemen did. When everyone ran away from danger, they ran toward it. Still, his darlin' Dee would be pissed. Well, she couldn't reach him now. For a few hours, he was free to be a man.

In uneasy sleep, Deidre heard the low throb of the motor, the wheels crunching on gravel, and was instantly awake and alert. But by the time she got downstairs and hollered out the door, her husband was gone, tail lights disappearing in the road's curve. Angrily, she tried his cell and pager, punching in the numbers with furious concentration. He'd turned them off deliberately, not wanting to face his broken promises, but Deidre knew, as she knew Will's soul, he would sense that she was crying out to him, *come home, come home before you kill yourself.*

No one answered at the firehouse. There should at least be someone to take calls, she thought angrily—there must be a terribly big, important fire. But where, *where?* Her call to Chief Mick Finn went unanswered, too. Well, him she could forgive. Finally, in desperation, she called the police station. "Oh, hi, Dee," a familiar voice said. It was Bunny, a school friend only recently graduated from the police academy. "Sure, there's a fire. It's over in Pinehills, and a bunch of officers rushed over there in case it's suspicious. St. Catherine's. Those poor nuns! God protect them. I pray they all got out okay."

Feeling cold and frustrated, Deidre wrapped herself in a handmade afghan and sat down to wait in the living room, rocking silently in the rocker she'd stenciled with entwined hearts and flowers. In her lap, she held one of the many stuffed bunnies with which she'd decorated the room for Easter. This one wore a smocked daisy-sprigged dress and a straw hat with yellow ribbons.

Deidre never saw Will alive again.

∾

About two hours after the Bronco's taillights disappeared down the road, Mick Finn's red Pontiac appeared in the neat little garrison colonial's driveway. His eyes reddened with smoke and tears, he pulled himself together to face Deidre. This tragic news he felt compelled to deliver himself.

As soon as all the nuns were accounted for and the fire contained—it hadn't got much past the kitchen and the rooms above—Finn had left Will's replacement, the acting Deputy Fire Chief, in charge at St. Catherine's. He would soon be back to supervise the clean-up, he thought, but that was not how events unfolded. Fortunately, the new man was solid and competent. The fire was reduced to a smoldering, steaming mess soon after Finn had driven away.

When he'd turned off the motor, Finn stood still for a moment, taking deep slow breaths for courage. He would rather have faced a raging inferno. Before he had a chance to knock, Deidre had flung open the door. "Where's Will? *Where's Will?*" she screamed at the harried man on her front step.

"I'm so sorry, Dee. The fire's at St. Catherine's Convent. We never called him, you know that, but he came anyway. Will only wanted to help with the nuns. It was his dear good heart gave out." Tears ran down Mick's craggy, smudged face. "The medics got to him fast, but even with the defibrillator... I'm so sorry, darlin'. At least, there was a priest, though. A priest was with Will at the end."

The blood drained out of Deidre's face, and Mick Finn caught her as she fell. Fortunately, he'd had the presence of mind to call Fiona on his way to the Ryan home, and Stone, who'd been summoned to the scene of a possible arson, called Phillipa.

Fiona, with Laura Belle hastily bundled up in a blanket, was the first one there, finding smelling salts in her reticule, holding Deidre fast in her plump arms when she woke to all the woe in the world. Soon after, the rest of the circle arrived.

CHAPTER TWENTY-ONE

Yet has she'a Heart dares hope to prove
How much lesse strong is Death then Love...

–Richard Crashaw

All of us, including Joe and Dick Devlin, gathered around Deidre with an up-rush of love and support. When she was coherent again, she insisted on being taken to the hospital to see Will one last time. Mick Finn phoned ahead and asked the morgue attendant at Jordan hospital to prepare for a family viewing.

Phillipa stayed at the house with the children. Phillipa had brought her big chef's apron and was putting it on as we were leaving. In times of crisis, Phillipa placed her faith in food. "If people will only eat something and drink a hot cup of sweet tea, they can get through anything," was her philosophy.

The Ryans were still asleep, all except Jenny, who'd been woken by the commotion downstairs. With the pale, grave demeanor of a little nun, she sat at the kitchen table watching Phil work. It was Jenny who'd thought to call Betti. The au pair was on her way via her moped to care for the children.

Finn drove us to the hospital in his flaming red "Chief's" car; Fiona, Heather, and I accompanied our friend, who had dissolved into weeping and keening. Joe followed in the Jeep. By then, it was just before dawn. Cool, gray light extinguished the stars one by one, and the sea gulls began their morning clamor as we drove along the coast to the hospital.

My heart was hammering with absolute grief when we followed Deidre and Mick down the cold corridors of the hospital's lowest level. What good was precognition if you couldn't prevent a tragedy? Had I tried hard enough? Or had I worried too much about frightening others, and so weakened the curse and blessing of my inner knowing?

"Cassandra," Joe murmured in my ear, his warm, comforting arm around my shoulders. "*Cassandra* is fated to glimpse but not to change the destiny of others."

"I don't know if I can bear it," I whispered back.

Will was laid out decently with a heavy sheet over him. The attendant pulled back a corner and revealed the pale face beneath. Although Deidre seemed calmer suddenly, her face was like a crumpled rose from continual weeping. I like to think our embrace of loving thoughts was helping to ease her misery, if anything could.

"Yes, that's my husband, Will Ryan," she said formally, her voice catching a sob. Gazing long and tenderly at the aging warrior, she touched his fading red hair, kissed his forehead, then knelt and said a prayer. Before we urged her away and home, she told the attendant to call Dyer and Dyer, to tell the funeral director that the Ryans would be in touch soon to make final arrangements.

"Now I have to find Will's mother and tell her," Deidre said in a small, tired voice. "I think she's at the Mohegan Sun this weekend. Somewhere in that sea of slots."

"I'll do it," Mick Finn said. "I can take a few of the guys to help locate Mary Margaret. That way, it won't be like getting the news from a stranger—we feel as if we're brothers. And you've got the children to tend. It's a sad, sad thing, and you need your strength."

"Yes, the children." She seemed to square her shoulders a bit and pull up her chin. Almost her old gutsy self. "Thanks, Mick. It's good of you, and I'm grateful. I'll be all right now."

Brave words, but we knew better. Fiona and Phillipa stayed ; Heather and I went home around six.

☙

The wake continued for two days. Deidre remained composed during viewing hours while it seemed as if Will's mother cried enough tears for everyone. At home, of course, it was a different story. Deidre walked the very fine edge of near hysteria, collapsing from time to time into sodden misery. One of the circle was always with her; we'd worked out a kind of rough schedule. Phillipa simply took over the kitchen, making coffee and tea, sandwiches and sweets for everyone, and feeding the children their proper meals. Betti kept the youngsters upstairs for the most part at quiet pursuits. Good thing, since it appeared that Deidre hadn't enough energy left in her small body to give consolation and nurturing.

It wasn't until after the burial that somehow she came back to herself.

Will was well-known and well-liked, and although he'd been on leave, Mick Finn declared he'd died a hero in the line of duty, trying to rescue nuns trapped in St. Catherine's when it was set afire. A fireman's funeral with full honors was arranged. The procession stretched all the way through Plymouth center, firefighters clad in formal navy with white gloves and uniformed police from all of Plymouth County. Will's casket was carried to St. Peter's on top of the new Engine 1, surrounded by masses of white and yellow flowers. Two extended fire ladders were arched over the route near the church with a large American flag suspended between them. Engine 1 passed between the ladders as the firefighters along the road stood at attention.

Bagpipes played while the mourners, including the Town Manager and other dignitaries, entered the church. The overflow was seated in the room below, or stood outdoors. Speakers broadcast the service to those who weren't on the main floor. The church was adorned with simple displays of spring flowers. Firefighters placed a medal and a flag on the casket, and a shiny yellow Engine 1 firefighter's hat, inclined toward the congregation.

The sky was overcast, but thank the good Goddess, the threatened rain never materialized. Deidre was grim, steadfast, and dry-eyed throughout the long service, during which Finn and several of Will's other friends reminisced fondly about their lost brother. Then the long procession of cars wound its way to the burial at St. Patrick's Cemetery. I thought Deidre must be promising herself a nervous breakdown as soon as the public rituals were over; I knew, I would have been.

Even sadder than Deidre's tenuous self-control were the bewildered faces of the children. Baby Anne had remained at home with Betti, but Jenny, Will Jr., and Bobby, dressed in sober little coats, sat between stoical Deidre and Will's weeping mother, watching with awe the pomp and ceremony of their father's funeral. Will Jr. snuffled from time to time, swiping his hand across his eyes and nose. Jenny, who seemed to be determined to emulate Deidre, primly handed him tissues out of her diminutive purse, remaining tearless herself. The youngest son Bobby gazed with awe at the uniforms, the flags, the bagpipes, the casket, the sea of flowers. "Daddy had a parade," he said in a wondering tone.

"You'd better be quiet, Bobby," Jenny muttered, squeezing his hand tightly. "Betti said no talking, remember?"

Fiona leaned over and whispered to me, "We will need to hold our own service, to help Deidre let go."

Later, at the reception in the firehouse, Heather said, "This was murder, you know, ladies."

"Felony with death resulting," Phillipa agreed.

"Perhaps I'll give that damned vision pillow one more try," I said. "Enough of this bouncing back and forth. It's time I got us a name and a face, no matter on whose witch's toes I have to dance."

"Oh, don't be ridiculous. It's can't be him," Phillipa said. "Genius is always so misunderstood."

"And if he's sexy, we gloss over his little foibles," Heather said.

"I don't know, really," I said uncertainly. "It could be Pieter. There were some serious questions about his father's demise. Just touching his hand I felt how hot the passions course through his veins."

"Oh, yeah. But this *fire-Brandt* has a yen for Becky, correct? Right away, you know he can't be all bad, right?" Phillipa glared at me.

"It will be who it will be," Fiona said sternly. "Think of dear Will. And those poor innocent animals. And the nuns, too, of course. Cass is our most reliable clairvoyant, when she's got her courage up."

"Why, thank you for the votes of confidence, ladies." But I could feel my resolve still wavering. I must not be afraid of the depths of foretelling, I told myself. No matter where it led me.

∽

That night, after everyone had gone home except the circle, we gathered around Deidre and held a Wiccan ceremony for Will's passing, as we had once done for Ashbery, Heather's housekeeper. It was a rite of passage we ourselves had created, designed to ease Will's spirit, our way of helping Deidre say good-bye as he journeyed to Summerland.

On Deidre's coffee table, we arranged an altar of white cloth, white flowers, and fine beeswax candles, white with nuances of silver, handcrafted by Heather. The centerpiece was a framed likeness of Will, Deidre's favorite photo. He was younger then; it showed him joyfully leaping to toss a basketball into the hoop, his face radiant. Remembering love's beginnings, Deidre told us, it was often this image of Will that she saw in her mind's eye.

I'd brought traditional frankincense and sprigs of dried rosemary, whose pungent fragrances gave us strength, and a powder made of crushed dried basil, elder, valerian, and marjoram to protect against negative vibrations. We cast the circle, cleansed our hands in consecrated water, and lit the candles. Together we visualized Will rising from his ailing body, young and strong again, melding into the light of pure love and peace. "To die to this existence and to be reborn in the turning of the wheel to a new life."

Quieted by the calming tea I had brewed for us all, Deidre talked about what a devoted husband and father Will had been, and how much she and the children would miss him. We each reminisced, what wonderful a man Will was, always ready to rescue someone else, even an animal, in jeopardy.

We mingled our tears with Deidre's, and blessed her, too, with our healing gifts, a jar of sage-scented balm to rub on her wrists from me. Rosemary for Remembrance candles from Heather. Since the kitchen was now overflowing with food offerings left by well-meaning neighbors, Phillipa had lettered a diminutive volume of spells for faith and cheer taken from *Hazel's Household Recipes*. And from Fiona, another of her mysterious invocations lettered on ancient parchment, its source as puzzling to her as to us. Phillipa, whose voice was trained to poetry, read the verse aloud.

> *Come, winds of the air, and whisper to him*
> *of love's forever keeping,*
> *Come, waters of the deep, and gently bear him*
> *to shores of no more weeping,*
> *Come, seasons of earth, turn and return*
> *his soul's eternal blending,*
> *Come, sun of the spirit, and light his way*
> *to loves and lives unending.*

"Amen," Deidre sobbed, crossing herself. "So must it be."

"So must it be," we echoed in soft voices.

❧

Fiona and Laura Belle stayed in Deidre's guest room. The rest of us went wearily home, Phillipa hitching a ride with me.

"I hope our own thing helped. What an ordeal Dee's been through...but I have to say she was a rock throughout that entire elaborate funeral," Phillipa commented. "She took Communion with Will's family, you know, during the Mass, and I saw her face. Truly, she felt comforted. The Christian rituals have deep roots. As does Judaism. And why not? Let all spiritual paths muddle together into a glorious, nourishing stew, I say."

"Nice metaphor," I said. "I like to think we're following ways even more ancient than the patriarchal religions, just as sacred, and much more sympathetic to our sex," I replied.

"Oh yes, you hedge witch! Well, thank the good Goddess for Unitarians who accept all ideas of the Divine, even godless ones."

"Are you thinking of joining a Unitarian church?"

"Well, if I ever need an indoor place for worship..."

"Patty would be so disappointed. She says she likes to think of us as untrammeled spirits, free of all orthodoxy."

"Sounds like a possible convert to me," Phillipa muttered as I turned into her driveway. "Oh, goodie, Stone's home." Even in the darkness, her smile blazed with happiness. I almost thought I saw her aura flare, but then I really don't see auras.

❧

We took turns keeping watch over Deidre, knowing that the storm of anger, denial, and grief would be followed by a freeze of depression. Inventing reasons to be with her, we listened as she talked out the past, eased feelings of guilt by helping her keep things in perspective. We took her places she didn't want to go, just to keep her distracted. And got her to focus on plots to foil the firebug in our midst. Meanwhile, time passed and the healing began.

"I know what you're doing," Deidre told me fiercely, as I got her to bundle up for a chilly walk along the waterfront.

"Come on," I said as Salty and Peppy launched themselves at the door with gleeful abandon. "These two couch potatoes of yours need a little exercise." Jenny wanted to stay home and help Betti make gingerbread elves, but Willy and Bobby came with us to help manage the toy poodles. Together we tramped toward Plymouth center and the wharf area. My goal was a new "canines welcome" restaurant to which I had not yet dared to bring my own big bruisers.

It was still too early for lunch at the Baskerville Bistro but we ordered coffee, juices, and pastries, along with gourmet dog biscuits for the poodles. A extremely well-behaved German shepherd was lying in perfect composure at his companion's feet, attentively eying Salty and Peppy as if he hoped they were on the menu.

"I'm all right when I'm working," Deidre said, nibbling her chocolate croissant. "I mean, at Faeryland. But once I get home..." Her voice trailed off, but the boys, lost in their own fantasy game, were paying little attention to grown-up talk. "When I think about the future, the children...well, you know. You were a single parent for many years."

"You have such inner strength and vigor, Dee. We've all recognized that in you, and sometimes even envied your boundless energy. Just keep telling yourself that you can handle whatever comes your way. Because it's true. Wiccans believe that our intentions shape our futures."

"If that's true, why did Will want to let go?" Deidre murmured, half to herself.

"Mommy, can we go talk to that big dog?" Willy asked. "He looks lonesome."

"No, dear," said his mom, who was clearly coming back to her role. "We don't talk to strange dogs or people.

"It isn't 'want to let go' exactly." I followed the thread of her central question. "Perhaps he felt that his champion days were gone forever. In this life anyway. And he wished to experience that feeling of youth and power again."

"Do you really believe we come back?" Deidre asked.

"I want to believe it, that's the problem. Because one life is barely enough. And I do know I've *seen* past lives, so that has to count for something. And the future, too. So if I can see the future, it must be that all time somehow does exist in the present. In a multiplicity of versions. Hey, don't you think we five must have been together before, and will be again."

Deidre smiled, her first genuine inner-being smile in a long time. "It feels that way, doesn't it? It's a grand thought. And wherever he's off to, I hope Will finds what he most desires. And never forgets me...us."

"Of course he'll remember. In those 'sweet sessions of silent thought,'" I said.

The smile fled in an instant. "But I am *so* angry with him for deserting me and the kids. Do you think, if we hadn't had...?"

"No, I don't. Not for a minute. Many other women would consider you four-times blessed," I said.

At that moment, the blessing named Bobby was wiggling out of his seat and edging over to the other dog-occupied table with Peppy in tow. As if unaware of his diminutive size, the toy poodle snarled and growled at the surprised shepherd. All metaphysical philosophizing vanished in the resulting melee, but I thought that Deidre was a bit cheerier as we walked home. I even detected a chuckle.

"Peppy must have been remembering his past life as an Irish wolfhound," she said.

CHAPTER TWENTY-TWO

I open and see what no eyes
Save mine have the power to see:
Dead scenes and dead griefs arise,
Dead follies make mouths at me.

–Louis James Block

"Have you seen Sylvie? Has she been staying with you?" Heather's voice on my kitchen phone was sharp with concern.

"No to both. What's happened?" I was making lunch for Joe and me, which I continued to do with the phone held in the crook of my neck. Pumpernickel, corned beef, Swiss cheese, spoonsful of sauerkraut and Russian dressing. I slid the Rubens into the toaster oven. Joe, bless him, was outside laboring on the spring clean-up of my herb gardens. Some of the perennials were already green and fragrant; I was holding a sprig of sage and sniffing it as we talked. Good thing—I would need all the strength and calm that bracing clean scent could impart.

"Pieter's here. He's been stopping over to the Kellihers' place to check on Sylvie from time to time—especially after that incident with the coyotes. He tells me she must not have been around for a couple of days. Pieter's just fed and watered a bunch of very hungry felines, and he's worried. That makes two of us. This isn't at all like Sylvie."

Smells good, Toots. Scruffy and Raffles were lying under the kitchen table, watching me attentively. *But hold that stinky stuff on mine.*

"Sauerkraut," I said. "Awfully good for you."

"I said Sylvie, not sauerkraut," Heather replied crisply.

"Just an aside to the pups. They want their Rubens sans sauerkraut."

"Rubens! Are you out of your mind? Corned beef with all those nasty preservatives? One of these days those two fussy gourmets of yours are going to be brought into Wee Angels with acute indigestion. You know with dogs, that looks a lot like paralysis of the hindquarters."

"Just kidding," I said, dropping shreds of the suspect corned beef into the two salivating mouths. "And you're right—it certainly isn't like Sylvie! She always so careful and responsible, poor little sprite." In that instant, an icy frisson of apprehension prickled my neck and slipped down my spine. "Uh-oh. Something *is* wrong. Just now I can feel it. Look, I'm right in the middle of giving Joe lunch." I looked longingly at the toasting sandwiches. "I'll wrap up my sandwich, and we can meet at Fiona's for a proper finding. If she's available."

"You wrap. I'll call. Get back to you in a jiffy."

☙

When Fiona opened her front door to welcome us, there was only a single pencil stuck in her coronet of braids, a good sign. Her familiar bangle-jangling hug was as reassuring as ever, but I was still shivery about Sylvie, I didn't know exactly why. After all, the girl could have gone off on her own for any number of reasons. Or Pieter may have misconstrued the length of her absence, the kitties simply conning him into an extra meal.

Laura Belle had just had her lunch, Fiona said, and was taking a wee nap in her bedroom with the stenciled magical animals. I remembered that we had talked Fiona out of bats and spiders and got a lecture on what wonderful gifts they conferred on humans. Urging us to get comfortable, Fiona bustled away to make tea.

"How's Dee doing? Is Phil with her today?" Fiona called out from the little cottage kitchen. Surreptitiously, we'd been taking turns keeping tabs on the new widow who alternated between bouts of reckless activity, just like the old Deidre, and fits of melancholy when she could hardly move out of bed. If she did make it to the kitchen, she'd sit at the table with a sodden hanky balled up in her hand, and more often than not, her teacup would be heavily laced with whiskey. Many times it was Jenny who watched over the household when the au pair Betti had gone home to her tiny house on Crooke's Lane.

"Phil's helping Dee at Faeryland today," I said. "And of course Phil's bringing homemade cookies and punch to welcome the customers."

"Great idea...Dee is always so much happier when she's working. It worried me terribly to see her go into one of those near-coma states," Heather declared, curling up gracefully at one end of the sofa. "But no wonder. The awesome responsibility of bringing up four little ones without a father—well, it would certainly overwhelm *me*. Of course, I have been a solo pet parent, but animals are more of a comfort than a care."

Omar stretched, hopped up on the back of the sofa, and walked across its top, his yellow eyes gleaming at us balefully.

"I've done the single parent scene and lived to tell the tale," I said. "You're so busy getting through each day you hardly notice the years zipping by until you find yourself moping around an empty nest. Companion animals are a great solace, but what you really need then is a new man."

"Amen," said Fiona. "I was widowed myself. Terrible jolt to the system when it happens fast like that." She handed around steaming mugs of lapsang souchon tea. "When my Rob got washed off the deck of the *Fiona Fancy* in a September gale, I was in total shock for months. The nights got longer and the veil got thinner. More than once, I thought I saw Rob in his favorite chair or I smelled his pipe smoke circling through the cottage. Never put a foot out of doors until the first of May, when at last I was rescued by a little Beltane magic, although I didn't know then what it was."

I thought there must be a good story there, which I would pry out at a later date. Right now I had a missing dryad on my mind and heart. "Listen, Fiona, I have a very bad feeling about Sylvie."

"When I saw that single magpie in the maple tree this morning, I knew it was an evil omen, and so did Omar. You should have seen him spit!" Fiona declared. "I ought to have taken off my hat to the bird to avert bad luck, but unfortunately I wasn't wearing my tam at the time. In fact, I was just out of bed wearing nothing at all."

Heather and I avoided exchanging glances. We knew it was only a matter of time until Fiona came to the point—and a wonderfully accurate point, too.

"Now here's one thing we know," Fiona said. "Sylvie would never just walk off and leave those kitties, her own dear one among them." She spread a map of Plymouth over the much scarred coffee table, took out her crystal pendulum, and got down to business. In Fiona's hands, the crystal moved without hesitation, starting with a graceful circle then jogging sideways faster and faster toward one corner of the map.

Omar saw this as his opportunity to jump onto the delightfully crackling paper, landing on all four paws with perfect aplomb. At the same time, he jarred Fiona's arm and knocked it to one side. "Didn't I tell you what a prescient pussy he is," Fiona exclaimed with delight. "Look right here, Omar is insisting that I shift onto Kingston." Kingston was a tiny pink triangle at the top of the map. "Mommy's little darling's got to move now so that I can turn the map over."

Apparently, Omar's prescience did not extend to understanding commands. Fiona had to pick him up bodily and set him down on the floor so that she could flip the map. All of Kingston now occupied the coffee table. Omar slunk off to the kitchen, where he had his own personal flat blue pillow on top of the refrigerator, a place of pleasant vibrations and savory smells.

Fiona repeated her pendulum wizardry over pink Kingston. The crystal slowed and began to move in ever smaller circles over the junction of Main Street and Route 3.

"What in Hecate's name is that girl doing in Kingston?" Heather exclaimed. "Can't you zero in any closer, Fiona?"

"I believe it's up to you now, Cass." Fiona hung the pendulum around her neck and began to fold up the map. "I've done all I can do, but have you?"

The thought of deliberately seeking out a vision made me sigh deeply. I'd already been procrastinating on the arson business. But my growing unease about Sylvie was impossible to ignore. "Do you have a Kingston yellow pages?" I asked. "Why don't we try the sorting thing, you know, like Serena Dove and *sortes biblicae* that time we had to find Rose's boy."

Fiona pulled out a phone book from a bottom shelf of the bookcase under the window. Dusting it off with the hem of her coat sweater of many colors, she laid it in front of me on the coffee table.

I hesitated. "I can't remember exactly how this works," I said.

"Invocation!" Fiona declared in a ringing tone. "We must have an invocation for divine help." Taking our hands in her soft plump ones, she said, "Now let's see...which goddess?"

"Hecate always does it for me" Heather said firmly. Throwing her hands and ours upward, her bronze braid swinging, she cried out, "Hecate, goddess of the three paths, you who see in all directions at once, we call on you to help us to find our lost friend Sylvie."

"So must it be," Fiona and I murmured.

It seemed rather an anticlimax, but I flipped open the phone book with what I hoped was suitable reverence. The page that fell under our gaze bore the headings *Cocktail Lounges, Coffee Houses, Coffee Shops, Coins, Cold Storage.* I read them aloud. "Cold storage? Banish the thought. This was not one of my better spells, I guess."

"Wait...wait...wait," Fiona commanded. "Let me dowse that page." Again we watched the crystal pendulum swinging in slow circles, finally coming to rest on a display ad for the Erin Go Bragh Irish Pub and Grille, address Main Street in Kingston, just off Route 3."

"Bingo!" Fiona caroled.

"Bingo?" Heather said. "What would Sylvie be doing holed up in an Irish pub, I'd like to know."

I was leaning over reading the small print. *Proprietor: Pat Deere.* "Uh-oh, here's the connection. Sylvie once told me that guy she was running away from is named Nick Deere. Maybe a relation?"

"Perhaps they patched up their quarrel, and Sylvie just ran off with him and abandoned her charges," Heather suggested, with a frown of disapproval.

"Not a chance," I said. "She was deathly afraid of Nick Deere. More likely, he's forced her to go with him and is keeping her against her will."

"Love slave? Sex slave? It has been known," Fiona said.

"Well, that's a bit over the top, Fiona, but I do think we'd better file a Missing Persons report," Heather said. She already had her cell phone in hand and was calling Phillipa.

"To Hades with that," I said. "Let's go over there and search the place ourselves."

But Heather was already talking earnestly to Phillipa. Ending the call, she said, "Phil says she'll contact Pieter, and with his help, file the report for us. She promises that Stone will take a personal interest and will contact the Kingston police to have a look around the Erin Go Bragh. Also she says, 'Don't let Cass go off half-cocked.'"

"Yeah? What about Nick Deere," I protested.

"I told her. You heard me. She promised that Stone would request that inquiries be made about Nick Deere's whereabouts, too," Heather said.

I was not reassured. I was seeing some dreadful dark, confining place in my mind's eye.

CHAPTER TWENTY-THREE

We saw that fire at work within his eyes
And had no glimpse of what was burning there.

—Edwin Arlington Robinson

I found Joe on the porch with a fresh cup of coffee, his feet up on a wicker table, a dog on each side of his chair. I didn't have to be a clairvoyant to recognize that faintly apologetic smile that belied the anticipatory gleam in his eyes.

Leaning over for a kiss, I said, "I'll get a cup of coffee and join you. Then you can tell me where you're going next. Some luxurious tropical clime, I don't doubt."

Don't worry, Toots. You've always got me to snuggle. Scruffy pushed up my hand with his nose, the better for me to scratch him between the ears. Raffles' tail hit the floor with his own special lopsided rhythm. I knelt down on one knee and greeted both dogs before going into the kitchen for a mug of the strong brew that Joe favored. My mug read: "The Sibyl Is In"—a gift from Phillipa.

When I joined Joe on the porch, a flock of crows had landed on branches of the white birch in the yard. Scruffy dashed through the pet door to defend his turf; Raffles loped awkwardly after his sire.

"Seven crows," I counted, sitting on the chair beside Joe, resting my feet companionably on the same table. *"Seven for a secret that can never be told."*

"Cassandra, you are a walking mythology," he said affectionately. "Believe me, I have no secrets that can't be told. And you needn't envy me this trip. It's the Barents Sea, a part known at the Loophole, international waters. We'll confront the pirating fishing trawlers who are over-fishing the last great fresh cod beds."

"Barents Sea?"

"It's above the Arctic Circle, sweetheart. Think bordering Finland, Sweden, Russia. Think mighty damn cold this time of year."

"What are you going to do?"

"Get the activist volunteers close enough to swarm over the side of the trawler and sit on the nets. I believe we have a banner: *For Cod's Sake Stop Now.*"

"Cute. Better pack those thermal long johns then. And please stay out of small boats yourself. *Promise!* Swear on *this.*" I touched the golden cross that always hung around his neck, nestled on the chest where I loved to nestle myself. Just as I always wore my serviceable silver pentagram as a tangible prayer and charm of protection.

"I promise, sweetheart. I will stay out of all small boats going in harm's way."

"When do you leave?"

"Tomorrow morning. If all goes as planned, I'll be back in two or three weeks."

"Well, good. You wouldn't want to miss Beltane, would you?"

"Not a chance. That's a frolic not to be forgotten." Joe's smile suggested he remember the last Beltane all too well. The weather had been ideal for outdoor romancing. "So what are you gals up to this afternoon?"

"Sylvie's gone missing without a word. We did a finding with Fiona."

"It's not like Sylvie to just take off without telling anyone. Isn't she house-sitting for the Kellihers?"

"Right. That's what worries us."

"So what did you come up with?"

"I can't prove anything—but my clairvoyant self says she's been taken by her old boyfriend Nick Deere and he's got her in some small dark place."

"And you're not confronting this by yourself, right?"

"Who, me? Would I do that? No, Phil has Stone on the case. He'll work through the Kingston police force." I sipped my coffee and thought I'd give those guys a day or so to come up with something, but then I was going to go over there myself.

⁓

April Fools Day. Not a good omen. Joe had driven off to Logan yesterday at dawn in his Rent-a-Wreck, leaving me with a tantalizing memory of the night before and an empty weekend ahead of me waiting for news from Phillipa. If that wasn't nerve-wracking enough, two Saturday morning phone calls stirred even more worries into the stew.

"Mom!" Becky said. "How about lunch on Tuesday?"

Not a surprise invitation. It was that time again; I was jotted into Becky's planner for the first week of every month. "Good timing. Joe just left for a couple of weeks on the Barents Sea, wherever that is—somewhere north, I'm really going to look up in the atlas later. Lunch would be grand, as long as I know Sylvie's okay. We can't seem to find her."

"Oh, yes, Pete told me. He said you've filed a Missing Person report. Sounds serious."

"Pete? Pieter told you?"

"I was getting to that, Mom. Pete called me at K & K one day last week, and well...we've had drinks one time and dinner another. It seems he's had to be in Boston for conferences with his publishers about his new book. Little, Brown, you know. He's been very sweet to me, Mom."

I was silent, thinking how to put a small pin in this balloon. Should I say, *Ask him what happened to his father?* or *How did he get burned at the Shawmutt Pound fire?*

"Mom? You've gone all quiet. You don't still suspect him of those arsons, do you? I mean, that's just crazy. As a family attorney, I have to be a fairly good judge of character, and Pete seems to me to be a really great guy. Talented. Amusing. Mature. And not bad looking, either."

"Becky...he's still on my short list."

"Oh, Mom. Don't you go and spoil this for me. I really like this guy. And I think he likes me, too. Sometimes you just go too far with this psychic mumbo-jumbo."

The only thing to do then was to end the conversation before it got rancorous. If Pieter turned out to be the firebug, I'd banish him from my Becky's life somehow. In a case of danger to my children, I might go for some minor *black ops,*

Wiccan style—just the kind of deviation that I've so often warned Heather against.

"Okay, hon. Whatever you say. See you Tuesday around twelve? Oops, got to go now—the dogs are running up toward the main road."

I put down the phone and poured myself another cup of coffee, as if I weren't jangled enough.

The phone rang almost at once. I seized it eagerly, hoping for Phillipa with a new lead.

But what I got was daughter-in-law Freddie in a manic mood.

"Cass! Guess where I am?"

"Boston," I said definitely. In my mind's eye, I could glimpse the spring sunshine glinting on the dome of the State Capitol building.

"Aw, you're no fun. Couldn't you, like, pretend to be mystified once in a while?"

"I do enough of that. It's a treat not to have to act normal with you."

"Okay, then. Good answer. Listen, if you see something else on my mind, please don't mention it now. Better if we talk in person, you know what I'm saying? How about tea at the former Ritz Carlton?

"I'd love to but I can't. I'm onto something here. A young friend is missing and I fear she may have been snatched by her irate boyfriend."

"At the risk of sounding mundane, how about getting the cops to look into this? Like, that nice guy Phil's married to."

"I've already done that. I'm waiting to hear what they come up with, and if it's the usual nothing...well...

"Oh. Okay, then, I'll come to you and we'll look into it together. Be just like the old days."

"No!"

"Yes! I'm just what you need."

"Aren't you busy setting up the new shop?"

"Not this time. I'm up here ostensibly to hunt for a condo or apartment, probably in Cambridge. Doesn't that sound posh?"

"But what are you really doing?"

"*Later*, dear witch-in-law. I'll be there tomorrow morning—by then you should know *something*. I'll be driving a company Buick, ugh. "

"No stopping you?"

"As if!"

"Okay, see you then. Lovely."

෮๑

To think it was only the second day of missing Joe. Feeling at loose ends that afternoon, I'd taken a cup of rejuvenating red raspberry tea outdoors to contemplate my spring plans for the herb gardens. After dusting off an Adirondack chair, I relaxed in comfortable meditation. Scruffy dozed at my feet while Raffles chased an indignant robin. The gardens were not very much different than they'd been in Grandma Shipton's day, but every year I tried to introduce a few "fresh" varieties, some of them heirlooms newly discovered but probably well known to our Shipton foremothers, who'd handed down herbal recipes from generation to generation. In a half-doze, I could sense the light and loving presence of those wise women around me as I meditated on our cherished garden with its aromatic plantings and neat brick walks.

But that feeling of unease about Sylvie disturbed the peaceful scene. My hand was on my cell to call Phillipa when she rang me.

"The Kingston police have been to the pub and questioned the proprietor, who is indeed Nick Deere's father," Phillipa reported. "Apparently, Nick lives in a rundown trailer in the woods over near Blackadder Pond in Kingston. Spruce Road. The officers checked it out and found young Deere working on his Harley. One of the cops asked for a drink of water so they could eyeball the residence, which wasn't any modern RV, just an ordinary old trailer with a shed on one side for the motorcycle. Appeared to be hooked up to water and, I suppose, some kind of septic system. In other words, not much to see, and they came away fairly convinced that the missing girl is not there."

"Did they search all through the trailer," I demanded.

"No, they felt they'd seen enough."

"And what do you think, Phil?"

Phillipa sighed. "As I told Stone, I wish they'd been more thorough. Anything could be going on in that Goddess-forsaken place. The officers really took the young man's word for it that he hadn't seen Sylvie since they split up."

"So what is Stone going to do?"

"There's absolutely no evidence for a warrant, you know that Cass."

"That's what Stone always says. I know it's not his fault, but these legal niceties are what drive a clairvoyant nuts."

"Possess your soul in patience, Cass. Ha ha, as if you ever would. Stone is looking into priors, things like that.

Nick's been tapped for some minor drug offenses, assault and batteries, a couple of domestics called in by an earlier girlfriend," Phillipa said.

"And what happened to her?"

Phillipa was silent for a moment. "Pauline Pelletier. She disappeared. Parents filed a Missing Persons. But no one knows where she went. Deere claims she caught a ride with some bikers heading toward New Jersey."

"Ceres save us! She's probably buried in those woods."

"That's my unpleasant notion, too," Phillipa said. "Maybe it's prescience. Or maybe it's the curse of a vivid imagination. The investigating officers said young Nick was a pleasant, friendly guy. He made such a good impression, I don't think we can count on their going back there to harass him further about Sylvie. Deere explained that they'd broken up months ago, and he hasn't seen Sylvie since, doesn't even know where she's been living, and doesn't care."

"Can't Stone do *anything*?"

"Listen, Cass, I'm on it. Stone's *promised* me he would find cause to go over there himself. So don't do anything crazy in the meantime. It will be so much better if the law intervenes in whatever kind of domestic crisis this turns out to be, *especially* if there is violence involved. We have enough on our minds with this arson business. Good Goddess, we haven't even done our Hoist spell yet. And I'm really looking forward to that."

"Hey, no, I'm cool," I lied. "I'm just hanging out in yard, making plans for my herb gardens. And I'm expecting Freddie tomorrow morning. She's been in Boston this week looking for housing. You know Iconomics is opening a branch here." For Freddie's sake, I was being somewhat misleading. "We'll have a good visit, and if Stone hasn't turned anything up by Monday, maybe the circle will get into this."

"In some perfectly legal way, of course."

"Of course."

Sometimes I wished Phillipa had not married a detective and gone all law-abiding, even if it was an outstanding love match. I wondered if there would ever be a time when Phillipa, too, would be tempted to take the law into her own hands. With that thought, some intuition flickered through my subconscious but never really made it into the light. All I knew for certain was that, underneath that wifely demeanor, Phillipa was still the wild, wise-cracking gal she'd always been.

⧬

Freddie breezed in at ten like a small spring whirlwind. She was wearing a tailored black leather jacket, a pair of glove-fitting jeans, a navy turtleneck sweater, and snakeskin boots. Her pixie hair, back to its natural soft wavy brown, was tucked behind her ears. Only one earring, a tiny winged goddess swinging from her right lobe. When she took off the over-sized dark glasses, her amber eyes were accented in the usual sooty fashion.

We embraced warmly, both dogs jumping excitedly between us. *It's the hamburger girl! I love her.* Scruffy never forgot a friend and her handouts.

"So this is the new little guy, what a darling," Freddie said, giving delightful scratches in the sensitive tail area to both ecstatic animals. "Talk about a chip off the old block. Bet he's great company for the Scruff."

If you like pushy pups hogging all the treats and attention. Scruffy tried his best to shove Raffles away from his favorite girl, but the pup was almost as big as his sire now, and stood sturdily where he could get the most pats and praise.

"Yes, Scruffy's teaching Raffles how to be a superior canine like the old man."

Yeah, sure, Toots. Don't hold your breath...

"How can Raffles help but learn when you set him such a excellent example?"

"You're talking to Scruffy now, right?"

"I was, but now I'm talking to you. Wow, let me look at you—love that casual chic. Perfect for Harvard Square."

"This is me incognito as a Harvard coed," Freddie said. "What do you think?"

"I think you should never try for incognito, my dear. You're wired with psychic energy, and you have that star quality that attracts all eyes—like an actress making her entrance. Unless you want to take low-profile glamour lessons from Fiona, it's a lost cause."

"Hmmm," Freddie said. "I just might do that."

"Come on, let's have brunch and you can tell me what you're doing here. I can see that you're busting with news, and I'm all attention."

Soon we had our heads together over French toast and mugs of coffee. Freddie actually whispered as she said, "I'm here for the *other* Company this trip. Doing some computer work of the monkey-wrench variety, you know what I'm saying? And I found out some things about your poet that might interest you." She toyed with the teaspoon she was holding.

"How in the world did you penetrate Lazaro's files?"

"Don't ask. But I'll just give you a hint. I was playing around with the Company's own security and found a wormhole. One that I'm not going to write up in my report, by the way, following that good old Wiccan rule: To know, to will, to dare, to keep silent. *Especially* to keep silent."

"Not to worry. I don't need to know the details of your illegal operations. I get enough of those on my own. So, Lazaro...don't tell me he works for them!"

"*Worked*, past tense. While our hero was in Cuba, until things got *too explosive* for him there, if you know what I'm saying. So his escape was *arranged*, and the homemade boat story was just that, a story. With no survivors and therefore no witnesses. Oops!" Freddie looked down at the teaspoon. It had folded over in her hand. "I hope this wasn't your best setting."

"I know better than to let you handle Grandma's sterling. Too explosive? Engaged in some anti-Castro activities, then, and coming to Miami was his payback. But was demolition or arson involved?"

"Maybe. Hard to tell from the official jargon. But I thought you'd like to know his, like, roots. Oh, and the usual background garbage. Mother a prostitute who got lucky and moved in with a highly-placed government official, along with her son, who was twelve at the time. A perfect age to get permanently warped. Maybe developed a dislike for Mom's lover that extended to Castro's regime. So, what think you? Is it him?"

"I'm beginning to hope so. Because Becky has got herself involved with my other chief suspect." I took our dishes to the sink and poured more coffee.

"Mother of God," exclaimed my daughter-in-law, whose years with the nuns had left their mark on her. "Have you got anything this damning on...whatshisname...Brand?"

"Abusive father was accidentally incinerated in his favorite easy chair."

"I guess both Lazaro and Brand are, like, *hot*, and having no problem wrapping women around their little pinkies."

"Yes, well Lazaro has the local poetry club swooning over his Latino good looks, Brand has already charmed Maeve Kelliher, Sylvie, and my own daughter—and those are only the gals I know about," I said.

"Speaking of manipulative guys, fill me in on what you think happened to your new protégé Sylvie with her ex."

I explained the situation, from my first indication that there was a troublesome boyfriend to yesterday's conversation with Phillipa.

"Well, look, this guy doesn't know me from Eve, if you know what I'm saying. I could, like, drop in and have a look around."

"No you could not! This place is desolate, my dear. How could you explain your presence on his doorstep? But then, maybe the two of us could coast by in your Buick, and if the Harley's not there..." I was thinking out this escapade as I talked. "Nick Deere doesn't know me, either. Even if he comes back unexpectedly, we could claim car trouble, looking for a phone, you know."

"Sounds like a plan to me." Freddie was already shrugging into her jacket and jingling her car keys.

"Yes, but wait a minute. I want to try one thing first. I concocted an herbal mix for a psychic vision dream pillow, but it proved too powerful to sell so I changed the formula. But I still have the prototype. I've hated the damned thing ever since...well, Will's passing, you know. I had a glimpse but I couldn't prevent the tragedy. In this case, though, I guess I owe it to Sylvie to at least try. Maybe I'll get an inkling..." I was unsure how to explain myself, but explanations were not needed with Freddie.

"Yeah, wasn't that a heartbreaker. I wrote to Dee, of course, but words are so lame. How's she doing?"

"Oh, you know. We're keeping tabs on her."

"I bet you are. And not just tabs either, but more like prayers, spells, healing vibes, white lights, blue lights. Okay, I tell you what. Why don't I take the dynamic duo here for a walk on the beach while you have that little séance with yourself. See what you come up with, then we'll go for it."

A walk! A walk! Let's all go pee in new places... Scruffy, who loved the beach above all canine playgrounds for its varied smells and endless opportunities to leave his mark, was sitting by the kitchen door in a flash, nosing his leash where it hung on its hook. Raffles looked from Freddie to his sire with a hopeful expression. Something fun was definitely in the offing.

After the threesome banged out the door amid joyful barks, I went in search of wherever I had stashed the psychic visions pillow, somewhere deep in the recesses of the new closet Joe had built for me. I found the pillow behind my winter boots, looking a little worse for wear but still with that clear, bracing scent, the fragrance of prophetic herbs I'd mixed together in a mad moment of inspiration.

Blue-bordered print sprigged with lavender. I smoothed it out. If the visions it brought me were as tragic as before, I hoped that this time I could do something about the bad news. Fiddle with fate. Rework the future. Amend karma.

Lying down on the bed, I leaned my cheek against the pillow's cool surface, and closed my eyes. I breathed in deeply and let my thoughts go away.

I found myself on a deserted woodland road. Up ahead I could see a shabby trailer parked near a shed. A young man came out of the shed dragging a dark plastic rubbish bag and carrying a shovel. He hoisted the bag over his shoulder and strode into the woods. At first I thought the bag moved against his back, but then it lay perfectly still.

The vision faded fast. My eyes flew open, and I screamed aloud, just as I had the first time I had lain against that pillow. But this time, I didn't break a family heirloom, and Joe didn't come running in to see what had happened to me. I was alone in the house.

The trouble was, I had no idea if this vision was something that had happened in the far past, the near past, was happening now, or would happen—always the clairvoyant's enigma. The only thing I was certain about—there was a body in that bag, the slim body of a girl, easy to carry on one's shoulder. And in my vision, she had been either dead or nearly so. Was it Sylvie? Or the other missing girlfriend? I would have to get Freddie to drive me over to that trailer immediately.

CHAPTER TWENTY-FOUR

Danger disintegrates satiety;
There's Basis there
Begets an awe
That searches Human Nature's creases
As clean as Fire

—Emily Dickinson

Freddie never needed much urging to join in a madcap scheme. Soon she and I were hurtling north on Plymouth's back roads toward Nick Deere's trailer in Kingston. When we neared Blackadder Pond, she slowed the Buick to a moderate speed; we rode through undeveloped woodland areas peering at street signs. On Spruce Road at last, we encountered a small cottage with two rusting cars in front and then nothing for nearly a half mile.

"There it is," Freddie said as we eased around a bend in the road. The shabby trailer was a faded mint green and black. The gray-shingled shed beside it had a closed double door. Freddie stopped fifty yards or so beyond Nick Deere's little homestead. We got out of the car and walked back toward the shed.

Freddie rattled the shed's padlock. "Locked," she said.

I knocked on the trailer door. No answer. I tried the handle. "Locked," I echoed.

Freddie was peering in the shed's one grimy window. "The shed is, like, totally empty, except for the guy's Harley," she said. "So where's Deere?"

"Maybe he's gone off with a buddy. I can't get into the trailer," I said.

"But what do you *feel?*"

I closed my eyes. It was far from the ideal setting for a vision, but I did get the tiniest glimmer. "Wherever Sylvie is, she's unable to call for help," I said, rattling the door handle. "And to think I swore I wouldn't break into anyone else's place again ever."

"This is different. It's called exigent circumstances or something like that," Freddie said. "I can help you. Just give me a few seconds to do something here." She was still peering into the shed intently. It seemed a long time before she came to join me at the trailer, but it was probably only a minute.

Freddie put her hand on the handle, closed her eyes, and hummed. The aluminum door seemed to bend and bow open a bit. After that, Freddie pulled it open quite easily. I looked back toward the road. As far as I could see in both directions, the surroundings were empty and quiet except for the usual woodland scurrying sounds and bird twitterings.

My companion in crime was already inside, poking around through cupboards and closets. I followed closely. "Whew," she said, holding her nose with two fuchsia-tipped fingers. "I've seen worse, but not by much. Doesn't this guy ever wash a dish?"

I peered into the sink, looking for signs of a second person, but it was impossible to tell in that mess.

Ten minutes later we were nearly through the trailer's living quarters, one bedroom, and two closets. Nothing. Still, I couldn't get over the feeling that Sylvie was *somewhere* nearby.

"Is there anywhere else we can search?" I was thoroughly perplexed. On the face of it, there was nowhere else to hide a grown young woman.

"Not that I can see," Freddie said. "Maybe we'd better have a look in that shed. Could be a closet or something I didn't see through the window. I don't think that padlock will give me too much trouble. Anyway, we'd better get out of this place. Wouldn't want to be caught like two rats in a you-know-what."

Once out the door, we tried to make it look as normal as possible despite the noticeable warp.

"Shhh. Listen," Freddie said.

We both heard the sound of someone tramping out of the woods. In a nanosecond, we were sprinting for the Buick.

"What the fuck..." a voice snarled. "Son of a bitch!" Footsteps came running toward us, but we'd had a good head start.

Without slowing, I looked back for a moment. The lithe, muscular young man with dark hair, and, if I actually saw auras I would have said, *a dangerous aura*, was racing toward the shed not us. "He's going for his motorcycle. He's going to follow us," I managed to gasp out as we ran.

"Not to worry," Freddie yelled back. "I doubt that Harley is going anywhere for a while."

We jumped into the car and Freddie revved the motor, taking off in a splat of gravel. "Oh, good girl. You zapped it."

Freddie merely smiled, racing along the rutty roads toward safety. But the crisis was not really averted. I still had to find out what happened to Sylvie. Freddie offered to stay for another go, but I dissuaded her.

"Let me see if I can get Tip to read the place," I said. "If Sylvie's been there, he'll know."

"Well, you have to tell me *everything*," Freddie said. "And if you need me again, just give a holler. It's a good thing Adam and I will be moving here soon—you never know when you'll need a Bad Girl Friday."

"Especially with your talents," I said.

ᐤᓚ

I called Tip in Wiscasset that evening. It was an imposition and a long shot, but I sensed the matter had become too serious for other considerations. "We've got a lost girl here," I explained. "I have a good idea where she is, but it seems an impossible place to hide someone. If you could manage to help me out without jeopardizing any of your schoolwork, I sure could use an expert tracker."

"It's Friday. I've got the whole weekend, Mz. Shipton."

"It's time you called me Cass, Tip."

"Okay. How about Aunt Cass, then? I'll take a ride down there early tomorrow. Good chance to give Uncle John's old cycle a trial run."

My heart was warmed by the "Aunt." Why not? I counted the boy as one of my spiritual family. "All that way on a motorcycle? You'll be careful? And wear a helmet?"

Tip chuckled in that dry, half-cough way of his. "Uncle John never wears his. I guess I could borrow it then. See you around noon."

"Oh, there's one little problem though. This place we're going to search. We have to get rid of the guy that lives there first. But don't worry. I'll think of something."

I'd better bring Fiona, too, I thought, although I hardly knew why. Like deliberately rolling a loose cannon onto the deck.

⌒〜⌒

"Patrick Deere? This is Kingston Police Headquarters," Fiona said crisply into her cell phone. "Officer Killgore asked me to call. He's trying to locate your son Nick. Yes. Nothing to worry about, just a few questions. He's where? Can he be reached? I see. Well, when you do talk to your son, please have him stop by our headquarters on Main Street." Fiona punched End, and turned to me with a satisfied smile. "Patrick Deere says Nick is at some local garage, he doesn't know which one, repairing his Harley. Looks to be a long job, some tricky little part in the motor has suffered a meltdown."

"That Freddie!" I said appreciatively.

"Is Freddie here?" Tip asked, brightening. He'd always been one of her ardent admirers, although royally ignored as being much younger and beneath her notice.

"She was. We got into the trailer while Deere was absent and looked around. *Nada.* Yet I had the strongest feeling..."

"So he caught you at it, did he?" Fiona asked cannily. A crochet hook and one pencil were stuck in her coronet of braids, looking like antennae. She was wearing her crystal pendant over a MacDonald tartan jacket and carried her green reticule with who-knew-what unexpected supplies. With her colorful striped skirt, perhaps she would blend with the dappled spring woodlands. And then again, perhaps not, since her silver bangles jingled with every motion. But one thing was for sure, Fiona was a force of nature and good to have on one's side.

"Okay, let's go then," I sidestepped the question, wondering if there wasn't some kind of negative karma working against my becoming a break-in artist. "At least he hasn't ever seen my new Jeep." I'd replaced the old Wagoneer with a year-old Liberty model, steel blue.

Twenty minutes later we were at the beat-up trailer on Spruce Road. Fiona sprang out lightly from the Jeep as if she'd never been crippled with arthritis. Whipping the pendant off her neck, she prepared to dowse.

"Wait. Don't move!" Tip ordered in an imperative tone I'd never heard him use. He crouched down and examined the ground around the trailer door inch by inch. Every dry broken leaf and grain of sand had a story to tell Tip. "Let me read what's here before you disturb the sign."

Fiona and I stood frozen in place, she holding her pendant in mid-air, like a game of Statues, watching the boy work. He kept up a running commentary. "See here...this is him. Nick Deere, you said? Then this is you on the side where his print didn't obliterate yours—I recognize those beat-up sneaks—and Freddie's over there. She must have given that door quite a pull—that classy boot really ground into the earth." Tip stood for a minute, his eyes moving toward the shed. "See this? Someone got pulled toward that shack over there. Could be your girl, small feet. Her toes are dragging."

"Let's try to get into that shed," I said. "There's a padlock, though."

"Oh, I can take care of that," Fiona said, reaching into her reticule. I knew what she was after—her lock picks. And I was glad of it.

My friend was positively cackling as she chose one pick and fiddled around with the padlock. A moment later, the lock had sprung open. "There you are, my dears. Nothing to it. Learned that trick back in the Sixties."

Tip opened the shed door gingerly and looked into the gloomy interior. The only light was from one dirty window and our slowly opening door. "Looks empty," he said.

"Good, let's go in then," Fiona said, sallying forth past the cautious boy. Soon we were all inside, looking at decrepit walls, a work bench of sorts, some automotive supplies and tools, a stained floor with a small pool of oil near the center of it. I found myself staring at that oil slick; the light from the door gave it a rainbow effect. In a moment, I felt as if I was falling into the blackness of that puddle. Then suddenly, I could *see*. Under the work bench, beneath the floor.

"Hey, are you all right, Aunt Cass?" I became aware that I was doubled over as if I'd been punched in the stomach, although I felt no pain. Tip had his hands under my arms, trying to raise me.

"It's the sight," Fiona said. "Just give her a moment to recover. This time wasn't too bad—at least she didn't pass out."

Suddenly I was tugging at the work bench like a mad fool. "Help me move this," I ordered my two companions.

There's something like a trap door here. I'm sensing Sylvie. She's in there!" That last I nearly screamed, so great was my distress.

Tip had grown up to be a wiry, strong young man, and he had little difficulty in pulling the work bench away from the wall. Underneath was a wooden crate with a rope attached and a piece of faded, spotted, worn carpet. We pulled the rug off and found the crack of the trap door with a small pipe sticking up on one side. Neither Tip nor I could budge the door. "Get a tool off the bench," I screamed. "Isn't there anything?"

"Not much but a few rachets and a Philips screwdriver," Tip said. He picked up the screwdriver, preparing to use it as a lever.

"Wait a sec," said Fiona, rummaging in her reticule. "Use this."

Who could have believed that Fiona would carry a crowbar in that extraordinary bag! A very small crowbar, in truth, but nevertheless made of cast iron and the perfect instrument to pry open a trap door. Tip lost no time in putting it to work.

As the heavy trap door was eased up, we began to hear muffled sounds in the cavernous blackness below. I thought about the flashlight back in my Jeep, but I didn't want to take the time to run back there.

"Here's a light," Fiona said, bringing forth a penlight with a clear penetrating beam.

What it showed below was a shock but not a surprise to me. A square hole the size of a small room or a large closet, about eight feet deep, had been dug in the earth and loosely strapped with wooden slats. There was another dirty piece of rug on the floor. Lying on the rug, bound hand and foot with duct tape over her mouth, was Sylvie, blinking piteously in the stabbing beam of light. It was clear from the smell that she had wet herself.

"Oh, Christ," said Tip, jumping down into the hole, already whipping out of its sheath the hunting knife strapped to his belt. It was the work of a few seconds to cut her free, another to tear the tape from her mouth.

Sylvie screamed. It was a small scream but filled with days of anguish.

"The poor baby," Fiona crooned.

"Hand her up to me gently," I said, and Tip did his best to hoist the sodden, miserable bundle toward our waiting arms. It took Fiona and me together to lift her up out of that grave-like prison. She was sobbing softly. Fiona held her fast.

"Let's get her out of here," Fiona said. I had my cell phone in hand and was dialing 911 to report what we had found. We needed the police here, and we needed them quickly.

I held out my hand to Tip, prepared to heave him out of the deep earthen room, but he said, "Drop the crate down here. I can stand on that." I did, and he heaved himself up while holding onto the rope so he could pull the crate up after him.

"So that's how he got himself up from the hole," I said.

"But I don't know what he used to pry up the trapdoor," Tip said.

"He probably carries tools in the Harley. I'm taking this child to the car," Fiona said. "We've got to get her cleaned up and feeling human."

"Is he gone? Is he gone?" Sylvie was moaning.

"Listen," Tip said urgently.

There was a roar as Nick Deere on his Harley burst into view around the bend and splattered to a stop. He was between us and the Jeep.

I kept dialing, got the dispatcher, and hastily described our predicament. "Spruce Road," I screamed into the cell. "A green and black trailer. We've just rescued a kidnapped girl. The guy who kidnapped her is here and is threatening us."

Tip stepped in front of Fiona and Sylvie. "Are you the bastard who did this? The cops are on their way. They'll be here any minute."

When the dark young man laughed, his mouth twisted in a sardonic way that foolish girls often found so attractive. "I'm just going to talk to this little bitch for a minute," he said, trying to reach around Tip and grab Sylvie away from Fiona. I didn't believe Tip would be much of a match for him. I stepped forward, too, to block Deere's access to Sylvie.

Fiona backed away, murmuring to me, "I'm taking her into the woods. Stop him if you can." I could hear Sylvie whimpering, but I kept my gaze fastened on Deere.

Deere tried to push past us, but we dodged around to block his way. In a fury of fists and feet, Deere flew at us. His shoulder crashed into me, knocking me right off my feet. A hard punch to Tip's jaw made the boy stagger backwards. Deere grabbed a wicked knife out of his boot and lunged, but Tip turned his body just in time and took a graze to his arm. I could see him reaching for his own knife. I feared this would end badly. I stuck my two little fingers straight out toward our enemy in an ancient banishing gesture, which even to me seemed rather feeble in confronting two enraged knife-wielding opponents.

But suddenly, Deere was off and running after Sylvie. He disappeared into the woods. I heard Fiona cry out as I scrambled toward her voice to help. Tip sheathed his own hunting knife. Holding one hand pressed against his bleeding arm, Tip ran after me. We found Fiona sitting against a tree looking dazed.

"Wow!" she said. "I hardly knew what hit me, but it must have been that young fiend."

"Hear the sirens?" Tip asked. "The cops are coming."

"Finally. Thank the Goddess. But where's Sylvie? If he finds her..."

Even in her dazed state, Fiona could chuckle. "She's right over there. I pushed her between those sapling pines. Deere ran right past her."

Deere had heard the sirens, too. When we half-carried Sylvie back to Spruce Road, the Harley was long gone. Fiona bundled the girl into my car.

Tip gazed at the ground as if it were a book he could read—and it was. "Deere drove into the woods right over there," he said. "Probably knows a trail in there. A cruiser could never follow."

Speaking of which, the police arrived, two cruisers, flashing and screaming their sirens. In my experience, they always showed up after the villain had fled the scene, and this time was no different.

Then it took much too long to explain what had happened before the officers understood there was a criminal to pursue. I'd had to show them the cut on Tip's arm, the earthen room, let them hear a few incoherent words from Sylvie. We declined an ambulance in favor of my driving my charges to

Jordan immediately, which Tip felt would be quicker, and he was probably right.

"Nick Deere," said Officer Killgore. "We was out here before. We looked around, seemed okay at the time. Straightforward kid—we know his da."

"Yes, and you screwed this one up, officers. The girl could have died. That's what happens when you only rely on your five senses," Fiona said. "Come on, Cass, let's go."

CHAPTER TWENTY-FIVE

All identities that have every existed, or may exist, on this globe, or any globe,
All lives and deaths—all of the past, present, future;
This vast similitude spans them, and has always spann'd,
and shall forever span them...

−Walt Whitman

"I have to admit I'm glad you bypassed the legal system this time," Phillipa said. All of us, even Deidre looking sad-eyed but calm, had gathered in the Sterns' living room in a kind of Wiccan debriefing session. "Stone might not be able to admit it, but he's glad, too, because the important thing is that Sylvie's been saved thanks to your visioning, Cass, and Tonto here with her medicine bag. The girl's okay now, isn't she?"

"Sylvie needed only a little guidance from me to rev up her self-healing mode." Fiona held out her cup for more coffee. "And she's writing positive reams of channeled messages with the Sharpie and notebook that I found in my bag while I was with her in the hospital. Sometimes the words run right off the pad of paper onto the sheets. I don't know what Dr. Blitz and the nursing staff will make of her. Well, one of the nurses pinned a crucifix to her bedpost, which just goes to show you."

The rest of us shook our heads as if we had a strange buzzing in our ears. "That miraculous reticule! Talk about Mary Poppins," Phillipa whispered to me as she made the rounds with the coffee carafe. "She'll be zooming about with her umbrella next."

"A broom would be more traditional," I whispered back.

"You've never seen bruises fade so quickly. But her spirit, that's another matter," Fiona continued. "It will take longer to come to terms with the fear, terror, and humiliation she endured from that monster. And there was rape, too. The ultimate male domination. I'm also working with her on the emotional trauma. And so, apparently, are some of the saints."

"Saints?" Deidre and Heather chorused.

"Sylvie's channeling saints now. St. Brigid of Ireland. She's a principal healer, and has quite a lot of comforting suggestions. And interestingly enough, St. Nicetas of Romania. You remember that Sylvie's mother was of gypsy stock out of Romania? Of course, it wasn't Romania at the end of the 4th century when St. Nice was composing the Te Deum."

"Whatever that is," Phillipa said.

"Catholic hymn. 'Te Deum laudamus, We praise You, God...Holy, holy, holy,' et cetera," Deidre said.

"Yes, the girl has been running off at the pen with holies," Fiona agreed.

"So Sylvie will probably be released from Jordan by tomorrow?" Deidre asked. "She won't want to stay alone at the Kellihers'. How about my house? There's a cot in the workroom." She followed Phillipa around, passing a plate of chocolate-filled danish that were to die for. How satisfying it was to eat chocolate again without fear, after last year's plague of poisonings had been solved and resolved.

"Actually, she's getting out later this afternoon. That's a lovely offer, Dee," I said. "But strangely enough, Sylvie *does* want to go back to Kellihers' as soon as possible. She worried about the feline menagerie."

"Our neighbor Brand has been looking after the kitties, bless his heart," Heather said. "He's so kind and conscientious that I'm hard pressed to imagine him as an arsonist who targets animals."

"You can't judge by good works. That could be part of his perversity, a depth of twisted needs that ordinary people like us cannot fathom," I said.

"Yeah, sure, just your ordinary tarot-reading, candle-burning, psychic-visioning, poppet-making, pendulum-swinging suburban witches like us," Phillipa said. "What do we know about depravity? Other than ferreting out the odd serial killer, occasional mad bomber, deadly angel nurse, or sociopath poisoner in our own hometown."

"Okay, okay. Point taken," I said. "Anyway, Sylvie will be back at her house-sit today. I bummed a ride with Fiona expressly to loan Tip my Jeep. He'll wait until Sylvie's discharged and shepherd her home. He's offered to stay with her for the rest of the week, but I won't let him skip that many classes. Sylvie does seem reassured by his company, though, and of course, she's devoted to him after her rescue. It was he whose arms lifted her out of that hell-hole where Deere imprisoned her. Although I've never said a word to Tip about my dryad image of Sylvie, he said that she reminds him of a shy woodland creature. That boy is so sensitive! But I'm insisting that he get back to Wicasset by Tuesday."

"Perfect match for a Native American. How old is Sylvie?" Deidre mused.

"Oh, cut that out, Dee. She's two years older than Tip. At their age, that's a century," I said.

"We live the closest," Heather said. "After Tip leaves, I could send Captain Jack over to keep an eye on Sylvie. He's a tough old guy and very protective. I think he'd welcome a bodyguard gig. Of course, we don't know how that wild bunch of cats will react to Ishmael—especially if that green terror sings 'Yo, Ho, Ho, and a Bottle of Rum'. Oh, if only Deere gets slammed into jail soon, we could all relax again."

"Relax? I doubt it. Putting away Deere will only be 'out of the frying pan, into the fire,' since we still have an arsonist to deal with," I said. "We haven't even had a chance to work on our Hoist spell yet."

"There's no time like the eternal present," Fiona said.

Like so many of Fiona's offhand remarks, that was true enough and we all saw the sense of it. After we cleared away the coffee things, our informal gathering became an impromptu session in spellcraft. Phillipa got her athame and cast a circle in which we could work between the worlds.

Hoist by His Own Petard was one of Hazel's most intricate spells, which we had all carefully studied in her Book of Household Recipes, that wonderful source of arcane magical wisdom. Before I'd got immersed in Sylvie's disappearance, I'd followed the recipe for pressed incense and burned it as required for nine nights in preparation for working the Hoist enchantment. And there were words, in old English that

Fiona had been pleased to translate. Not surprisingly, she was carrying the text in her reticule.

"Shit!" Heather exclaimed. "I have some very powerful blue candles I wanted to use for the Hoist thing, but they're at home."

"Don't you remember my telling you that this spell is *similar* to the Dispelling Demons recipe but *without* the blue candles?" Fiona reminded her.

"Yes, but I wanted to use my candles anyway," Heather whined. "I've imbedded a little sparkle powder in the blue-veined wax. Sealed it into little paper twists. I got the stuff out of some old firecrackers especially to use in these candles. To represent the 'petard,' you know."

"Just as well we're not lighting them, then," Phillipa said. "Good-bye eyebrows! Isn't it a bit early for fireworks?"

"I bought out the neighborhood convenience store last June. Wanted to make sure no juvenile delinquent set them off near my place and frightened the dogs."

"You'd better get rid of the stuff. I'll ask Stone if there's a legal way to dump fireworks," Phillipa said.

"Don't you worry. I've already taken good care of the fireworks," Heather said.

I lit the remnants of the nine-days incense so that we could all experience its essence. The heavy odor wafted richly through the room. "Powerful stuff, isn't it?"

"It won't make us hallucinate, will it?" Heather asked with a cautious sniff.

"Hallucinatory incense is not to be sneezed at," Fiona said. "When I was studying with the Navaho shaman..."

"Now, let me see that incantation we're supposed to chant," Phillipa interrupted. She took the page from Fiona's hand and read aloud:

Let the sinner now desist
For if in evil, he persist,
By his actions he will be
Hoisted unto eternity.

"Well, that sounds straightforward enough," Deidre said with grim satisfaction. "As far as I'm concerned, this guy was responsible for Will's passing, and you can't hoist him far and fast enough to suit me." She began to chant the verse Phillipa had read, beating softly in time on one of Phillipa's Moroccan brass tables. As the rhythm was established, we all joined in, clapping or banging on whatever was handy. Fiona took a Navaho gourd rattle out of her reticule and shook it to accompany the drumming, silver bangles tinkling. Soon we all felt an upsurge of power, a lifting of our energy into the cosmic energy. At that point, Deidre gave an especially loud drum roll, and as if it had been rehearsed, we all released the spell together.

Silence in the room was profound until Phillipa's plump black cat flew into the room with a shrill scream and climbed up the drape, hissing.

"Oh dear," Phillipa chuckled "I think we spooked Zelda."

"How long has it been, anyway, since we've had an arson? Maybe the rampage is over," Heather said.

"Not a chance!" Deidre exclaimed.

"You know what you have to do, don't you, Cass," Fiona said.

I dreaded the thought. Still, it had helped find Sylvie.

"Okay, okay. I'll try the psychic visions pillow one more time. If I can find where I hid it."

"How do you hide something from yourself?" Phillipa asked.

"Oh, you just stuff it somewhere while you're bemused," I said.

"Try praying to Saint Anthony," Deidre said. "Always works for me when I lose something."

"Will Saint Anthony help a Wiccan to find her psychic visions pillow?" Heather asked.

"Yes, of course," said Deidre. "Once those blessed miracle-workers are translated into Spirit, do you think they give a damn about your religious credentials when you pray?"

"A nice point," I said. "But I think I'm getting a glimpse. It might be upstairs in the rose guest room where I stored the winter coats. I sure hope this time won't be as traumatic as before."

"Traumatic but true. You saw the truth," Fiona said. "What matters now is foiling the arsonist before there are more deaths, animal or human. Because maybe he's feeling the need to up the ante, catch a bigger thrill."

"Okay, I'll do it. I suppose the God and Goddess gave me this gift to use, not to stuff into a closet."

☙

Fiona dropped me off at home around noon. After taking the dogs for a walk, I had a quick mug of soup and went to look for the blue, lavender-sprigged pillow, which I found on the floor of the rose guest room closet in a strew of my natural moth repellent sachets. With a deep sigh, I lay down on one of the twin beds with my cheek against the pillow.

Scruffy nosed in the door with Raffles close behind him. "Go away now," I said. "Scruffy, you show Raffles the room where Tip sleeps when he stays here. You two can have a nice nap while I rest for a few minutes."

The floor's plenty good enough for pups. Scruffy grumped and gave Raffles a little shove out of the doorway.

"Now, now. There are two beds, so don't be a dog in the manger."

Muttering, Scuffy trotted off for a snooze, his offspring following with innocent hopefulness.

Despite all the caffeine I'd consumed at Phillipa's, when I inhaled the deep mysterious scent of those herbs I had inadvertently combined into a psychic whammy, my mind quieted into a receptive alpha brain-wave state. After a few moments, I drifted even deeper into the theta brain waves at the edge of sleep, a timeless and bodiless sensation. Teetering on that theta precipice without actually falling into slumber is the place where waking dreams happen.

Becoming aware of a penetrating damp chill, I opened my eyes in that almost dream. The rose wallpaper had faded away and become gray stone. Was this some kind of prison?

A white-robed priest entered the room, his head bowed in prayer; in his hands was a scroll of parchment. He was followed by two soldiers in some kind of antique uniforms. As the priest read aloud in Latin from the parchment, I began to understand the words as if they were English. I was being formally charged with heresy. The priest concluded this reading by coldly intoning a prayer. "I pray to our Savior that the flames consuming your sinful body will purify your soul." But underneath that icy exterior, I sense a fillip of sensual pleasure. My agony would be his sexual release. I knew this priest—a bishop, actually. "Your familiars will be destroyed in the fire with you," he said. He looked at me with a penetrating, hungry gaze. He reveled in the anticipation of my death, and the death of innocent animals as well. A choking scream would not leave my throat. *I can't endure those flames again,* I thought. As soon as that denial formed in my mind, I became like a mist and floated upward into the clouds.

After a timeless interval, probably only a minute of two, I revived, overcome with nausea, remembering the face in my vision. Hadn't I always known who it would be?

But the visioning wasn't finished. I glided away from consciousness again and came awake somewhere in Plymouth in the present day. It was a balmy spring night. I heard fire sirens. I smelled smoke. What street was this? Dogs were barking frantically. Heather was running across the street screaming. Animal Lovers Sanctuary was on fire!

With that realization, I was jolted back to the present, screaming and sick. Again, my first instinct was to throw the pillow as far away from me as possible. Unfortunately, it collided with Scruffy who, having heard my blood-curdling shriek, was dashing in the door at the same moment.

Hey, Toots! What's with you? Don't you know a canine hero when he's rushing to your rescue?

The flurry of apologies and pats that followed helped to dispel my feelings of revulsion. At the same time I was aware of an iron resolve not to let this vision become reality as it had with Will. This horror could and would be prevented.

I had seen and recognized the face of my enemy as if in another life. Had I really lived that life, or was I merging with the stream of all lives and touching the one with the most to teach me? In either case, the face I had seen of the cruel bishop in his white robes was very much like the face of the poet Roaul Lazaro.

CHAPTER TWENTY-SIX

I will shutter the windows from light,
I will place in their sockets the four
Tall candles and set them aflame
In the grey light of the dawn...

–Adelaide Crapsey

What had taken me so long to realize that Lazaro was our local psychopathic firebug? The suspicions I'd felt about Brand—the fierce passion in his handshake, the elemental nature I'd detected at our first meeting—now I could see these things were due to his being an artist not an arsonist. Clairvoyants make mistakes, not in what they see and feel, but in how they interpret their visions. And then there was Brand's questionable past, his presence at the Shawmutt fire, coincidences that had confused me.

Before I told Heather of my vision that Animal Lovers would be Lazaro's next target and sent her off into hysterical death threats against him, I thought I'd better talk to Phillipa, although she was going to be terribly angry, too, for a different reason. No one likes to discover that she's been flirting with a fiend.

This was not a good day on the clairvoyant scene.

Maybe Phillipa would still be in doubt that I had targeted the right person. For that matter, I often had doubts myself, but anytime I didn't believe in the message of a genuine vision or hesitated to act, I was always sorry later. Years of experience had taught me to pay attention to every cosmic nudge.

I decided against delivering this evil news by phone, but I was without my Jeep until Tip showed up. The plan was for him to see that Sylvie was comfortable and safe before returning the car to me. Then I'd drive him back to stay at the Kellihers' so that he could watch over Sylvie until Captain Jack took over on Tuesday.

Okay. I'd have to get Phillipa over here, although I'd just spent the morning at her place. I called. "Listen, Phil, I still don't have my car. But something's come up that's really important, and we need to talk. Can you possibly drop over for a few minutes?"

"I'm in the middle of a very delicate custard sauce," she wailed. "Can't you tell me what's up right now on the phone?"

"Believe me, what I have to say will curdle your custard for good. Come over when you're finished. We'll have tea. Something calming."

When Phillipa showed up at my door an hour later, I brought a pot of camomile and lemon balm tea out onto the porch. It had turned out to be a glorious April day, only a little on the cool side. Little furls of leaves in the maple and birch trees were getting ready to open the moment we turned our calendars to the May page. At last the ocean was more blue than gray-green, dotted with a few brave sailboats. An enchantment not to be missed, the afternoon almost dispelled the vision's hangover. But not quite.

"All right, girlfriend," Phillipa said, putting her feet up on the wicker footstool and settling in with her tea cup. "Out with it."

"Sorry. There's no way to soften this, Phil. Lazaro definitely is the arsonist, and his next target will probably be Animal Lovers Sanctuary."

Down from the footstool slammed her feet as Phillipa sprang out of the chair, spilling her tea, planting a fist on each hip. "Are you *out of your mind*, Cass? Honestly, I think you've *wanted* it to be Raoul from the beginning. If you had any appreciation of poetry, you'd know that he has too much fine, deep feeling..."

"Oh, balls, Phil. I know now that it's Lazaro. Under that poetic genius pose, he's cold and perverted. And you have to believe me or we'll all be in danger."

"Well, I don't, and we're not," she insisted.

Our debate quickly descended into a tirade of abuse from my friend and a surly defense from me.

"Well, you must really have the hots for this guy if you refuse to see the truth when it's biting you in the ass," I yelled.

"Oh, you think you're so smart with your paranoid visions. And that's probably the worst mixed metaphor I've ever heard." Phillipa stormed out of the porch, slamming the porch door.

Looking out the porch window, I could see that she had her cell phone to her ear. *"Ceres save us,"* I prayed. *Let it be Stone she's calling and not Lazaro.* A few moments later, she raced out of my driveway in a NASCAR spurt of speed.

The dogs were under the kitchen table with their paws over their ears. Well, practically. Canine sensitivity can't deal with a screaming quarrel, and I felt pretty rotten about it myself. If Phillipa warned Lazaro and Heather's sanctuary got burned out as a result, it would be the end of our circle.

How to save us? There was only one hope.

Fiona, of course.

 ∾

"Look, Fiona, you've got to help me. I just don't know what to do. I had this vision that convinced me our arsonist is Lazaro, and I told Phil. She absolutely flipped out, and we said a lot of nasty words to one another. When she ran out of here, I saw her in the BMW talking urgently into her cell phone. What if she told Lazaro of my suspicions?"

"Suspicions? You realize, of course, that Lazaro has been the centerpiece of my Black Hill Library Branch revival and poetry program?"

"Fiona, I *know* it's Lazaro. I had this, like, unpleasant past life flashback to the burning times. And there he was. A bishop denouncing me for heresy. Getting a sexual buzz from the mere thought of torching me and my animals. You believe me, don't you?"

"Put like that, of course I do. When it comes right down to murder and mayhem, you're our Delphic oracle, Cass. But I must say, this makes me terribly cross," Fiona said in a dangerous tone I'd hadn't heard her use since Laura Belle had been kidnapped with Deidre's children. "I shall have to be very careful not to accidentally hex the son- of-a-bitch. To think I didn't catch on to his true nature myself! And that I urged the Erato Poetry Club to make him president. *All those poor innocent animals*. Well, it certainly won't be good if Phil has warned him that you've got his number."

"That's the understatement of the century," I said.

"Now, now, dear. I can and will help you."

"But wait, there's more." I sounded like a TV salesman touting miracle products.

"A fire? Yes, I'm expecting that. Do you know where?"

"Animal Lovers."

"Goddess save us! Now we'll have to deal with Heather's hysterics as well."

"You remember who has been urging me to work with that blasted psychic vision pillow?"

"And I stand by it. Would you want to have what occurred at the Shawmutt Pound happen at Animal Lovers, too? This Lazaro has brought his dark-side influence into our very midst, and for that I'll never forgive him. Now, it may leave our circle a bit unsettled for a time, but everyone must be informed, including Stone. You pass the word, and I'll do whatever I can to pacify Phil and keep Heather from going off the deep end."

"When?"

"When what?"

"When are you going to talk to Phil? She's the one I'm worried about right now."

"As soon as I can get a sitter for my little one, I'll go right over there and have a good talk with Phil. Her mind has strayed into a mundane direction, but I'll bring her back to our true path."

I sighed. "Okay. It would also be nice if she speaks to me again someday."

"Yes, if only people were more like animals. *To err is human—to forgive, canine,* that's what I say. I take comfort in remembering that we have that Hoist spell in place. Soon this devil is going to light one too many matches and blow himself to kingdom come. Oh dear, oh dear. Now I'm going to have to give myself a good shake to get rid of this negativity."

"Swell idea. Exactly how will you do that? You mean, shake it off your hands and feet like we usually do?"

"The way I feel, it's going to take a lot more shaking than that. I'm going to grab my broom and sweep Lazaro out of my house. Then I'm going outdoors to drum and dance until I'm clear-headed again and ready to proceed in a white magic way. Something I learned from the Navaho. Restores harmony with the earth, you know. Doesn't mean we won't drive a stake through Lazaro's heart, so to speak. But we'll do it in a calm and dignified manner."

I could just picture Fiona's neighbors peeking out their windows into her little backyard while she danced up a storm to the beat of that buffalo-hide drum.

"You bet we will, Fiona," I agreed.

⁐

Shortly after I appealed to Fiona for help and got her all wrought up (which reassured me no end), Tip appeared with my Jeep. Making up to the dogs for having to witness a screaming fight between humans, I took them with me as I drove Tip back to Kellihers'.

"I could stay the week, you know. Not a problem to make up my schoolwork later," Tip said. "Bad enough what that bastard did to her, but then she had to put up with the detectives and other stuff at the hospital—you know."

He meant Sylvie's interview with the rape team and having to submit to the required indignities.

"It's okay, Tip. We won't let her stay alone while Deere's still running loose. Heather Devlin's houseman is going to watch out for Sylvie after you leave. Which you are going to do on Tuesday morning. I insist."

"Okay. Maybe I'll come back next weekend though. Spell the old guy for a couple of days."

"You like Sylvie."

"Yeah. She's like someone out of a magical story, you know what I mean? One of those myths the old men tell, about the deer hunter and the white corn maiden, or the girl who married a merman."

"I know what you mean."

"Did you ever really look at the color of her hair, Aunt Cass?"

"The silvery green sheen, you mean."

"Yeah. Her hair's light brown all right but like she's standing under a birch tree when the sun shines through the leaves."

"Right. So okay, I guess it would be good if you spelled Captain Jack next weekend. Heather will miss his cooking while he's over at Kellihers'"

"Mrs. Devlin is a swell person but she's not much into cooking, huh?"

"Let's put it this way—it's a good thing that Dick Devlin is so fond of that elaborate grill. But Heather does make terrific deviled eggs and her cheese trays are legendary."

When I drove into Kellihers' circular driveway—very gingerly to avoid any free-roaming cats—Sylvie was waiting for Tip outside. She smiled and waved at me.

Geeze, this place is crawling with mean-looking cats. I wouldn't let the boy stay here, if I were you. He's sure to pick up something itchy-awful from those hair balls. Someone ought to call the Public Health Department about this place. Scruffy stuck his head out the car window and surveyed the Kellihers' front yard with disgust. Raffles looked out, too, whimpering with excitement at the scene before us. Cats were poised gracefully on the benches, sitting upright on the fence, and lolling on the patio. One fluffy-furred beauty was hanging over the goldfish pond with a paw at the ready.

"Sylvie needs Tip to guard her," I explained to the dogs.

"She sure does," Tip agreed.

"But Sylvie's not an entirely helpless heroine," I reminded Tip. "She's a girl who stood up to a couple of coyotes and won."

"Better to face a predatory animal than a degenerate like Deere," Tip said. "I'll hitch a ride over to your place and get my bike Tuesday morning then."

"No, no—I'll come and get you," I yelled after him as he ran off happily to where the sun was glinting on Sylvie. I was amazed at how fast the bruises on her face had healed.

I sure wish the boy wouldn't go there. We ought to take him home with us. Scruffy leaned out the window and watched his departing friend with a soulful expression.

"We'll see him soon. Right now I have to stop over at the Devlins' to speak to Heather for a few minutes. Who knows?—maybe Honeycomb will give you a rec. Then I'll take you and Raffles back home for your dinners."

Sounds like a plan, Toots!

༄

Heather was in the butler's pantry making candles. One whole glass-fronted cabinet had been pressed into service to hold her curious supplies, while the others were filled more appropriately with Limoge serving pieces and crystal stemware, items rarely used since Captain Jack had taken over the kitchen, or "galley" as he like to call it.

I shooed Scruffy and Raffles out into the so-called "dog yard," a lavish acre of lawn with a few welcoming shade trees. Honeycomb stood under one of them, eyeing the new arrivals with disinterest. Scruffy's nose-to-nose greeting was not rejected outright, however, which put a little spring into his step. Raffles assumed a hopeful play posture with Mom and Dad as I closed the French doors to the conservatory and hurried back to the pantry.

Heather was pouring hot wax. Not a time to jar her concentration. I waited patiently while she chatted on. "Now you see these candles are black, but don't let that worry you like I'm going over to the dark side with Darth Vader. I just want to have a few on hand, *in case*. Like Fiona keeps that old pistol in her glove compartment—a little insurance policy you might say. There! That's done. I put a little mandrake root in this batch—I wonder how that will work. Just in case I ever light these things. So, Cass—what's on your mind? Care for a glass of sherry to take the edge off?

"The edge of what?"

"Whatever's got you scowling like that..."

Maybe that would be a good idea, for both of us. I waited until Heather led the way to her cozy book-lined study and poured the usual liberal potion.

"I tried the psychic visions pillow again. It worked, all right," I said.

"And?"

"Your neighbor Brand is exonerated, my dear. The culprit is absolutely and positively Lazaro."

"*That bastard*—we'll kill him. I *knew* Pieter was okay, just a bit eccentric from being an artist—I told you so. You should have listened to me."

"But there was another part to the vision."

"Yes? What's that?"

"I believe Lazaro will get away free long enough to target another place, one dear to our hearts."

"Which is?"

"Now keep calm....don't get hysterical. Fiona will be over here soon to counsel you..."

"You mean...*Animal Lovers?*"

"I'm so sorry to be the bearer of ill tidings...but...yes. According to Stone, Wendy Windsong let Lazaro know that you and I had been skulking around his place, thus making us prime objects of his malevolence. And besides, I *saw* it."

I expected Heather to scream, but she seemed to turn to stone instead. After a while, she said, "Just you wait until that wax hardens..."

I would have to hope that Fiona would be able to reach Heather and swerve her away from those black candles.

CHAPTER TWENTY-SEVEN

Day of wrath, that day of burning,
Seer and Sibyl speak concerning,
All the world to ashes turning.
Oh, what fear shall it engender...

—Abraham Coles

When the phone rang at dinner time, I shuddered, thinking I was in for another harangue from Phillipa. What a relief to hear Joe's deep sexy voice that always warmed me right to my second chakra. "Hey, sweetheart—did you think I'd forgotten our Beltane date?"

Now there was something I hadn't even had time to think about for days, what with Sylvie's problems and the Hoist spell and now the revelation that Lazaro was our villain and another tragedy in the making at the sanctuary.

"Oh, I will be so glad to see you! When...when...when?"

"Wow, that was heartfelt! Much as I would like to believe you've missed me a lot, there's a bit of an edge to that exclamation of relief. Could it be that you're in trouble? What is it? Crime wave upsurge? Septic system overflow?"

"Trouble is putting it mildly. Just come home as fast as you can, and I'll tell you all about it."

"I'll be there tonight about nine, how's that for quick?"

"Thank the good Goddess! And, honey...?"

"Yes?"

"Our Beltane date is still on, no matter what."

◌◠◌

It was still a bit chilly, and I began to think how nice it would be to have a cozy fire on the hearth, always so dear to the pagan heart, for Joe's homecoming. "You guys stay in the house now. It's getting dark and I don't want to have to worry about your running into a skunk," I told my two disappointed companions.

We never get to have any fun. My superior senses might be needed to keep you out of danger, you know. Canines see in the dark much better than humans. Just one more skill inherited from our predatory ancestors. And our noses detect the smallest whiff of trouble.

"Yeah, yeah, like the last time I had to use a whole quart of vanilla to deodorize your superior self." I put on my old green lumber jacket that hangs by the back door and set out with my wood basket, closing the door firmly on the two eager snouts.

I hate it when the dog is right.

Laying the basket beside the stack of wood, I began to fill it with the small dry logs that would give me a fast, brisk fire. As I barely recollected later, I was bending over the pile pulling out a fragrant apple wood log when I heard the dogs on the window seat indoors barking wildly. Before I could straighten up to see what was going on, the stalker who had crept up silently behind me delivered a black-out blow to the back of my head. And that's all I knew for quite a while.

When I came to, I was catapulted into one of the nightmares that had so frightened me at the beginning of our arson troubles. I became aware that I couldn't move and I was in pain. A thin strong nylon rope bound me to a sturdy maple tree, biting into my wrists and ankles cruelly.

At the edge of my consciousness, I remembered this little clearing. I knew my surroundings intimately from hundreds of pleasant foraging walks. I had been dragged into Jenkins Woods. Duct tape across my mouth prevented me from screaming. Worst of all, I could smell the acrid odor of pine needles on fire.

Looking down at my bound feet, I saw that they were surrounded by a pile of leaves and dry twigs. A knife of fear stabbed at my gut, and I went cold with terror all over my body.

Jolted fully awake by panic and adrenaline, I took in the whole scene in one sweeping gaze—especially the ominous dark figure watching me from between the trees. He had a hank of rope over his shoulder and some kind of satchel on the ground beside him. I couldn't see his features in the dark; there seemed to be a hood over his head—the balaclava! But I recognized that figure, leaning just the way he had leaned on the wall in his book jacket photo. And I could sense his intense excitement.

In the pines a few yards away, fallen brown needles were burning in a small bright blaze. Looking down with horror, I could see that a moist line of some pungent liquid had traced a path from the fire to my legs. Although the spring woods were still damp, the fire burned steadily down this easy route.

A bursting headache made it almost impossible to think...or to pray.

Why wasn't he being hoisted to eternity? Where was my protective white light when I needed it?

Raw danger is not an easy time to pray anyway. My mind was fully occupied by visions of smoldering wood and burning flesh, my flesh, the worst anguish I could imagine. At the rate that line of flame was traveling, it would reach the pile of twigs and leaves around my feet in less than a minute. Still, I summoned with all my strength the spirit forces that I knew surrounded me. Unable to make a sound, I called for help with all my being.

Lazaro sensed what I was doing. He laughed softly.

A moment later I saw him listening tensely.

And what I heard, with a wild upswing of hope, was a mad barking at the edge of the woods moving in my direction. The tormenter watching my struggles slipped away in the shadows of the woods and was soon gone from sight.

Scruffy burst into the clearing in a frenzy of barking! He was closely followed by Raffles, and, thank the good Goddess, my beloved Joe. Never had I been more thrilled to see him! With one swift glance at the terrible scene—me tied to a tree and fire approaching—he immediately began to stamp out the flames in a wild frenetic dance.

"*Jesu Christos*, sweetheart, who did this to you? What if I hadn't grabbed that earlier flight? Okay, okay...just give me a minute to put this blasted thing out, and I'll get you free."

It wasn't easy. Whatever accelerant had been trailed across the ground toward me seemed to be intractable. When one place was stamped into smoke, another popped up a few inches away.

The dogs continued to bark, running toward the place where Lazaro had disappeared. I was afraid they would follow him and come to harm, but instead they ran distractedly from the edge of the clearing and back again to where I was still bound to the tree all the while Joe was beating out the fire.

Finally, when Joe was satisfied that he was in control, he strode over and pulled the tape off my mouth in one swift motion.

"Ouch, dammit! Oh, am I glad to see you. I thought I was going to be burned at the stake out here. I've never been so terrified in my life. Well, hardly ever." I realized while I was sobbing out my relief that this wasn't the first time I'd been in scary situations. And the thought flashed through my mind that perhaps I ought to change my life style to something a bit more mundane.

Joe had taken out his Swiss army knife and was cutting me free of the ropes. When he got to my feet, I sort of fell into his arms in a Victorian swoon. There was no strength in my legs to stand up.

"It was Lazaro. I found out he's the arsonist, and he found out I found out," I gasped, dimly realizing that I was babbling. "And don't you try to follow him. That's a job for the police, not us."

"It's nice to know that you've got that straight at last," Joe scolded, but his touch was infinitely tender as he helped me to walk back toward the house. He tucked me up on the sofa under Grandma's afghan and insisted I take a rather fiery grappa from his cache in the parson's cupboard. "Brandy is the drink for heroes, so Samuel Johnson said. Although I don't know whether to call you fearless or foolhardy. In any case, I'm staying right here with you until this bastard in behind bars. I'll take leave. I'm due anyway. We sailed into a helluva situation this trip."

"Tell me about it," I said faintly.

Scruffy, who hadn't left my side since Joe brought me home, was resting his head on my stomach. *Sure tires me out, saving your life, Toots.* He's a big dog, and the head was heavy. I stirred a little to shift the weight of it and took another sip of grappa. Raffles lay as closely as possible, relegated to the outside position as always. Omega pup.

"Plenty of time for relating my exploits after we get your attacker locked up. Where's Stone's number?"

"Could be any one of three, but the surest is his cell, which is almost always on." I recited the number from memory. When one's life has been in danger, it's really nice to have a detective more or less "on call."

While Joe called Stone, I stroked Scruffy, with many whispered words of praise, and kept on sipping the grappa. I began to feel quite relaxed and light-headed.

"It's you. You're my white light," I murmured when Joe returned to hold my hand and surreptitiously check my pulse.

"I got Stone. He sends his love and wants you to know that his partner Billy Mann will be here shortly to take your statement. I told him that would be okay—I thought you'd be up to it. Stone's taking a SWAT team to arrest Lazaro without delay. So...you mean white knight?"

"White *light*," I murmured. "It's a mystical thing."

"Mythical? You mean like King Arthur?"

"Explain later, honey." Under the loyal dog's doggie breath and the love-knitted afghan, I drifted away from the nightmare I had just endured. I hardly cared about the imminent arrest of my tormenter. I just wanted to sleep.

But Joe wanted to talk. "You'll never believe this," he said. "That earlier flight I caught was by the grace of God—it was fully booked but someone cancelled. Got me into Logan at six, and for once my rental was a breeze. So I was home by seven-thirty, thinking, *great*, I'll have a whole lovely evening with my girl. I had my key out ready to unlock the door, but I found that it was unlocked. Your car was still here, so I figured you hadn't gone far. The dogs were barking like crazy, not their usual reserved greeting at all, and clamoring around my legs. Now here's the most curious thing—I almost thought I 'heard' Scruffy saying that a man had attacked you in the yard. The words just came into my head, but spoken aloud. Yet I couldn't have really heard what I heard because Scruff never quit barking. When I let the dogs out onto the porch, Scruffy was out that pet door as if he'd been shot from a cannon. Absolutely purposeful. Raffles, of course, lumbered after him. Somehow I knew I'd better follow Scruffy, because something really was wrong. In fact, I could swear I heard him say, 'Follow me, furry-faced guy.'"

I smiled weakly. "Yes. That's how it is." I handed him the empty brandy snifter. "See you."

And I knew no more until Phillipa sailed into the living room some time later, all flags flying, Fiona in her wake.

❧

"Oh, my good Goddess, I am *so* sorry," Phillipa wailed, crouching down to where we were eye to eye. Her dark eyes were even blacker than usual, full of rage and sorrow, her black eyebrows winged together into a scowl of regret.

I sat up carefully, as if I was checking for broken bones. "It's okay. This was one way to know for sure. Much easier to arrest a guy who tries to torch someone than a guy merely suspected by the local witch."

"I called Raoul before...before this happened...you know."

"Yes."

"I said you had a bee in your pointed hat about him, but I would protect him."

"Tch, tch, we must never tattle on each other," Fiona clucked. "One for all, and all for one."

"The Five Witchateers," Phillipa murmured with a hint of her usual acerbity. "Well, don't you worry. Stone isn't letting any moss grow under his feet on this one."

"I just don't understand why Lazaro didn't hoist," I whined.

"He will," Fiona said. "One match too many—any day now."

"Well, he'd better blow himself up soon, because I am going to kill him," Phillipa said with intense passion. Hell hath no fury like a witch who's been charmed and deluded.

But then everyone was hugging everyone and crying and vowing eternal friendship.

Joe stood in the doorway watching us, his expression inscrutable, but since I am a clairvoyant, I knew he was thinking, "I married a nutcase who hangs around with a bunch of nutcases." Scruffy appeared to share that opinion and stalked off in disgust to the peace and quiet of the blue bedroom upstairs, followed by his devoted pup.

Later, when Phillipa began making a nourishing soup to rally everyone's strength, they followed their noses right back to the kitchen. The way she could take a few ingredients out of my refrigerator—a couple of leftover lamb chops, some carrots, onions, and barley—and produce such a savory aroma was true magic.

"Ah, Scotch broth," Fiona said approvingly. "Food of Highland champions."

∽

After the Scotch broth had been consumed and everyone had left, I persuaded Joe to tell me about his troubled trip. I assured him it would take my mind off Lazaro and the real life version of a nightmare that had haunted me for months.

Actually that was a good thing. Although Joe was a guy who hardly ever complained unless he had a cold, and then he was impossible. But he needed to gripe about this particular disaster.

"I'm not unduly superstitious, but I have to admit I took a dim view of having that albatross on board," he began. "And the few guys in the crew who were real seamen threatened to quit right then and there. Captain Hartog, who has the intrepid gene of some early explorer, talked them out of it somehow."

"An albatross! Shades of the Ancient Mariner. And what were you doing with an albatross anyway?"

"Captain had agreed to transport some birds to a zoo in Finland. And one of them was a goony bird, an albatross."

Joe wiped his hand across his forehead as if brushing away a cloud of evil presentments.

"Okay. Already you were in fabulous trouble. So then what happened? You didn't sink the ship, did you?"

"First there was a short circuit in the electrical panel, which could have sparked a fire. If I hadn't been able to sort that out, we'd have had to head for land. Then as soon as that danger was averted, we ran into a iceberg and began taking on water."

"Good Goddess, just like the Titanic. How did that happen? Was Captain Intrepid hitting the grog?"

"Hartog. Captain Dirck Hartog. I love your sense of the dramatic, but it was a very small iceberg, not much bigger than a house—a growler—and the hole it tore could be mended. We had to clear all our supplies out of that part of the hold and close it off, though, another mess. And if that weren't enough, one of the volunteers slipped on the deck in a rain squall and went over the side. Water temp's so frigid there, we only had a minute to pull Marty out before it would be too late."

"Hypothermia, yes. So...did you get him out in time? What happened?"

"Standard procedure for man overboard. I threw a life ring to Marty and shouted to the others for help. Captain cut the motor, and Marty managed to grab hold, I don't know how. Hitting water that cold shocks the air right out of a person's lungs. I was fixing to haul Marty up, but the rope attached to the life ring got tangled in a steel ladder. I had to climb down to free it. Soon as that was clear, the other guys fished Marty out of the water, just about in time.

"Over the side? In a rain squall? Freezing water?" I asked suspiciously.

He had the grace to blush. "It's a short steel ladder that hooks over the railing for boarding inflatable rafts. I never got into the water. Wouldn't do to have *two* men overboard."

"After promising me *on your gold cross* that you'd stay on the ship and let the younger guys do all the dangerous stuff with the banners?"

"Sometimes experience is more important than youthful zeal." He winked at me suggestively. "And as I recall that particular vow, I promised to stay out of small boats going in harm's way. That didn't include hanging over the side to give a buddy a hand."

"Oh, nice point. I'll remember to watch out for those loopholes next time."

"You have to realize, Cass, that I was the only one who witnessed the accident. I threw the life ring that got fouled. Once I gave the alarm, everyone came running but I was the closest—it was my responsibility. I knew the others would pull us back on board. Besides, if our positions were reversed, Marty would have done the same for me."

"Oh, I see. Camaraderie. Sea-going brothers. *A man's got to do what a man's got to do?*"

"You might say that. Something like your circle?"

"Touché."

❧

It was a frustrated SWAT team that busted into Lazaro's apartment above the *Footloose and Fancy Free Travel Agency* while being screamed at by Wendy Windsong, who owned the property.

"He's not here, I tell you, dammit," Wendy cried. "Can't you see that the Jaguar is gone, you cretins? And just who the hell is going to pay for that splintered door? I *knew* there would be trouble here ever since I caught that Devlin woman sneaking around Raoul's apartment with her crony, the shifty Shipton herb lady. If you ask me, the two of them have imbibed one herb too many. You can bet I told Lazaro about that incident. But he's such a darling, he just said not to worry, he'd take care of the matter himself."

This interesting monolog by the irate landlady was reported by Stone to Phillipa, and by Phillipa to everyone in the circle. Heather said, "Well, see if I book our cruise with that mouthy Windsong dame!"

"What cruise?" I knew I was still feeling dazed, but had we really decided to take a cruise?

"Oh, you know...to the Bermuda Triangle. Sometime. After things settle down to normal."

"Twelfth of Never?"

Stone had done his best to calm Wendy Windsong in order to glean a few more details. She said that she'd seen the Jag tear into the driveway shortly after seven-thirty. Lazaro ran upstairs to his apartment and came down a few minutes later to throw a few possessions into his car. A satchel of clothes, a box of old books, and what worried her most, his computer.

"I asked him where he was going in such a rush. He'd promised to read me his latest poem that evening. I was going to open a delectable Muscatel," Wendy said wistfully. "He said that true friends are never really apart, that he'd be in touch with me real soon, and not to believe any rumors

I heard about him because they would not be true. So I thought, since he was paid up for the next three months and all, I shouldn't worry. He'll be back, like he said."

Thinking that flashy car would be a cinch to spot, Stone put out an immediate APB on the salsa Jaguar. They found the vehicle all right, in the Massasoit Mall parking lot—empty. Obviously, Lazaro had a back-up plan. Probably stashed some anonymous wheels at the Mall just in case he needed to get out of Dodge in a hurry.

Later, I thought about the CIA link and called Freddie. As soon as I mentioned Lazaro's escape, she stopped me in mid-word. "Say no more. I'll get back to you later," she said.

And so she did. But as a precaution, she called Heather's cell instead of mine, asking her to give me a message. "Tell Cass that our friend has asked for help from his favorite Uncle," she said. "I don't think the local law can move fast enough to catch up with him this time. The plan is to get the guy out of the country by the end of the week."

"Where?" Heather had asked.

"Somewhere beyond the reach of prosecution for his crimes. In the right location, he'll still be a useful source of information to his benefactor. Possibly even continue to enjoy his literary career as well. But tell Cass not to quote me to your favorite detective and mine. This is strictly *Sub Rosa*, you know what I mean?"

Before Lazaro got his free ride out of local jurisdiction, however, he found time for another parting shot, besides burning me up in Jenkins Park.

The first encounter was my own fault. I'd confided Freddie's news to Joe, and we'd agreed that I would stick close to home and let him protect me until we were positive, according to the same *Sub Rosa* source, that Lazaro was gone from our lives and even our country. I had every intention of keeping this promise—until that cute little note came in the morning mail.

Normally, I would never think of reading Joe's mail, or anyone's for that matter. But then a square, pink, scented-with-roses envelope arrived, which he opened, read with a smile, then tossed carelessly on his bureau without offering to share. So later when he was out in the garage workroom repairing a tipsy tier table, I couldn't help myself. I picked it up just to look over the envelope. The return address read: Martha Beauregard, Pleasant Hill, Lynchburg, Virginia. At the sight of that name, something clicked in my brain— *finally*. Who ever said that a clairvoyant can't be fooled?

I owed it to myself to see how far wrong I had gone, I rationalized. So I removed the note card from the envelope. On its cover was a drawing of a restored ante-bellum mansion named, of course, "Pleasant Hill Plantation." I flipped it open and read:

Dear Wonderful Joe. My heart needs to thank you for your brave rush to rescue me on our last sailing. No one else had seen me slip overboard—it's to you and you alone to whom I owe my life. You put your own life in danger to save mine. Keep that in mind if you ever want anything—anything at all—that I can give you. I adore you.

Love, Marty

P.S. Regards to Cass.

Rats and mice! Joe hadn't once corrected me when I had assumed Marty was a guy. He'd even used the phrase, "man overboard." Sure I knew several of the volunteers on every Greenpeace voyage were young women—tanned, gorgeous, spirited young women who looked as if they had just stepped out of an ivy-league college. But I'd just never imagined one of them would be mooning over my own husband—a damned southern belle who dabbled in Greenpeace between fancy dress cotillions and reenactments of Appomattox.

"Regards to Cass," indeed! The letter had been written in a beautiful first-grade-teacher script, but the P.S. was printed in teeny, tiny letters.

Before I made a truly big fuss over this, I thought it would be a good idea to talk to someone with a cooler head. And that would be Phillipa. I grabbed my keys off the hook by the door, jumped into the Jeep, and raced away out of the driveway, fully aware that shaking off his body-guarding prowess would make Joe pretty cross. Good enough for him!

CHAPTER TWENTY-EIGHT

For 'tis the sport to have the enginer
Hoist with his own petar; and 't shall go hard
But I will delve one yard below their mines
And blow them at the moon...

—William Shakespeare

Lazaro got another chance to reveal his vengeful, psychopathic nature, thanks to my fit of pique. Apparently he'd been watching the house, just waiting for this opportunity to finish what he'd begun. He must have followed me to Phillipa's in his new anonymous wheels. If it weren't for the state-of-the-art security system that Stone had insisted on installing at their house, Lazaro would have slipped into the cellar incognito. And then, who knows what? But when he opened the cellar door with whatever James-Bond equipment the CIA had given him for just such forays, the security alarm shrilled worse than a smoke alarm run amok.

Phillipa dashed to the window just in time to see and recognize Lazaro, spooked by the racket, sprinting for the pines that surrounded her backyard. Without hesitation, she strode over to the wall and punched in the code, canceling the alarm.

"What did you do *that* for?" I demanded. "We *want* the police to arrive with sirens blasting. We want them to go after Lazaro, and catch him. *Don't we?*"

I had to say all this on the run, because Phillipa was racing upstairs to the master bedroom. "With the alarm off, Raoul may come back. If he thinks the coast is clear. And then I'm going to kill him," she said, as calmly as a person can speak who has just climbed stairs two at a time while planning an impromptu execution. "He *used* me and his devoted poetry harem as cover while he was sneaking around town burning buildings and killing animals. He tried to torture and kill my dearest friend. He's got to know that he's gone too far..."

"What are you doing now? What's that thing you've got," I cried. Phillipa was taking a metal box out of the closet's top shelf. She hefted the box, giggled maniacally, and hugged it. Had the stress of leaking information to Lazaro and almost turning me into burnt toast finally caused my friend to have a bona-fide nervous breakdown?

"I'm calling 911," I said with what I thought was masterful calm. I reached for the bedside phone.

"No, you're not!" With one swift motion, Phillipa pulled the cord out of the phone jack. "Stone didn't take his weapon to work today, and I know the combination to this gun safe. Just give me a chance to kill that son-of-a-bitch, and then you can call."

"Phil, this is crazy," I screamed at her. Ignoring me, she began to punch in the code for the gun box. Seeing her demented expression, I dashed downstairs to grab the cell phone in my purse. The dispatcher listened calmly while I tried to explain that a wanted felon had tried to break in to the Sterns' house, had been scared off by the alarm, and would probably give it another try now that the alarm had been aborted.

"I don't see any alert from the security office. If someone was breaking in, why did you turn off the alarm?" she asked in a doubtful tone.

"Long story. Is this Bunny? But let me clue you, Bunny— if you don't get in touch with Stone Stern *right now* and have the nearest patrol car sent to this address *immediately*, I guarantee you're going to be in *big* trouble. Trust me on this. Sorry. Got to go now..."

"Leave the line open..." was the last thing I heard her say. I tucked the phone into my slacks pocket and ran back upstairs.

"Fuck...fuck...fuck," Phillipa was yelling. "I know that code. I had it memorized."

The gun box was speaking!

"Entry not authorized! Enter correct code!" a computerized voice declaimed loudly and officiously.

"Quiet," I said to Phillipa and the box. "Do you hear something downstairs?"

It was a cracking sound in the kitchen. A window pane? The house alarm began to shriek again. Phillipa ran downstairs carrying the gun safe, and I followed her as fast as I could. We got to the kitchen just in time to see a hand tossing a burning bundle of some kind through a broken pane of glass. It landed in the copper planter filled with fresh green herbs under the double window.

"Get that, Cass," Phillipa cried, "and I'll get him." She pulled open the door and with a mighty heave, threw the gun safe at Lazaro's retreating back. Years of kneading breads and hand-beating sauces had given her a strong, sinewy arm.

Apparently she conked him on the head, because I saw him stagger before he stumbled off out of sight.

Meanwhile, I'd grabbed a sauté pan off its hook and scooped up what I assumed was an incendiary device. I could smell lighter fluid. Dropping the thing in the sink, I ran water over it full blast, hoping it wasn't the kind of stuff that water would spread. But no, the flames were quenched at once, I could see what I was dealing with—a rum bottle about two-thirds full, stopped with a tightly rolled white cloth, a man's handkerchief perhaps. Tied around the bottle's neck were the remains of a paisley cravat that had been drenched in lighter fluid and set afire. Had it not landed it the moist loam of the planter, the bottle would have broken and the alcohol in the rum could have set the kitchen ablaze.

The patrol car arrived, closely followed by Stone, whose face was ashen. "What the hell happened to our security system," he demanded while he hugged Phillipa close. "What's that acrid smell? And what in Christ's name is my gun safe doing in the front yard?"

"It all happened so fast," Phillipa said faintly, one graceful hand held against her forehead. "I can't remember..."

She winked at me over his shoulder.

Then we each told our garbled stories and pointed to where we had last seen Lazaro. The whole law enforcement team rushed off, but other patrol cars were arriving, so we were never alone. Officers Barb Roberts and Ken Mattel, whom we'd first run into in the Manomet Manor affair, were among them, or *Barbie and Ken*, as we liked to call them. In Plymouth, crime is not exactly rampant, so when some serious offense occurs, the scene soon resembles a block party with cruisers.

But as we learned later, the posse gave chase too late. Lazaro had already driven off and disappeared without anyone even getting the make of his car or the license number. Phillipa and I had been no help at all in that department. I had thought the car was gray, a Chevy or maybe a Buick. Phillipa had declared it was grayish-blue and could have been a Ford.

The kitchen smelled like a burnt rum cake. "What is this thing?" Phillipa poked a finger at the strange sodden bottle in her impeccable double stainless-steel sink.

"Here," said Officer Barbie officiously. "You'd better leave that for the crime scene people. And the bomb squad."

"You called the bomb squad for this little thing?" Phillipa appeared incredulous.

"It's a billet doux from your Cuban Don Juan, Phil," I said. "Hot one."

"Oh, shut up, Cass."

"Maybe you two ladies ought to depart the premises until the bomb squad gets that unknown item out of here," Officer Ken insisted strongly.

Phillipa had begun picking glass splinters out of her herb planter, but I dragged her away to the back yard. "Listen, if Lazaro is bent on revenge... Well, I have it on good authority that he's going to be given a get-out-of-jail-free pass by the end of the week..." Phillipa's slim black eyebrows rose in disbelief, but I continued without explaining the CIA connection. "...so what's the next stop on his agenda?"

"*Animal Lovers!*" we both spoke in unison.

❧

Leaving Barbie, Ken, and the bomb squad to sort things out in Phillipa's kitchen, we jumped in my Jeep and took off hell-bent for Animal Lovers.

I handed Phillipa my cell phone. "Here, call Joe, will you? Tell him I'm perfectly safe, and we've gone shopping. It's an emergency shopping trip." I was still too flummoxed about Marty—Martha Beauregard!—to ask him for protection.

She did as I asked and, after a few monosyllabic replies to Joe, ended the call, which was a surprise to me. I thought Joe would have made more of a rebut. I have to admit I was rather surprised that he swallowed the usual excuse.

"What did he say?" I asked.

"He said he had been going to explain about Marty, whatever that means."

"Yeah? Is that all?"

"No, he said to tell you, 'shop with extreme care.' Meanwhile he is going to listen to the scanner and see what we're up to, because he knows something's going down."

"Good Goddess, I think my cover is blown."

"Well, of course, dear. Joe's no fool, you know. If he was easy, you'd never have married him. Now, *will* you explain what that thing in the sink was, Cass?" Phillipa asked as we rattled along Route 3. "I do hope you didn't ruin the nonstick finish on my sauté pan. That was my best one, by the way."

"I didn't pause to evaluate your cookware, Phil. Looked to me like a Molotov cocktail improvised with a few things Lazaro might have had with him. You're lucky you don't have a smoking ruin where you used to have a Viking range and Sub-Zero refrigerator."

"Well, I have to say I think we're a terrific team in the quick-action department. That Japanese guy who wrote *The Art of War* would have been proud of us."

"Sun Tzu," I murmured. "Speaking of which, I was surprised you didn't skewer Lazaro with that Samurai sword you use to cleave Hubbard squash. Now, *that's* a weapon!"

"Action without reflection is the Samurai idea. A gun box in the hand, so to speak. I mean, even though I couldn't get the damned gun out of it. And I must say, your immersing that fire thing in water seemed to do the trick. To think Raoul would include me in his revenge! I'm really hurt about this."

"You were aiming to shoot him," I reminded her.

"That's different. He made a fool of me, and he almost made a shish kebab of you."

We drove the rest of the way in reflective silence.

"Oh, look...it seems quiet enough, doesn't it?" I said.

I parked down the street where the shadows of trees would obscure my car; we sat there studying the shelter, a rambling farmhouse caught in a semi-business zone among a roller skating rink, a bowling alley, and a truck stop diner. Having no residential value in that rundown location, it had been purchased by Heather to use as a sanctuary for the overflow of homeless dogs from her own home. With the Morgan name and a cousin in City Hall, it was not a great problem to get a kennel license. But then, of course, needy dogs by the dozens, and cats, too, were soon clamoring for a safe haven, and the farmhouse had to be constantly refurbished and extended, rather like the Winchester mansion in San Jose, but without the stairways to nowhere. Instead of campaigning against the mushrooming sanctuary, however, the townspeople actually seemed proud of its good work, and no real protest was ever mounted against Animal Lovers. The music from the roller skating rink was loud enough to drown out its noisy four-footed neighbors, and Heather's state-of-the-art solid waste management prevented the odor from becoming a problem like Pryde's Pig Farm. The smell of diesel fuel at the truck stop often was worse.

Not counting the occasional flurry of barking that rippled through the compound, nothing seemed to be amiss as we watched. I studied the windows. Grace Hulke was lumbering around her apartment upstairs. Downstairs in the farmhouse proper, where Heather keeps her office, a dim light shone, the shade was drawn, and I could see the outline of a figure.

"That's not Heather," Phil remarked.

"You think she's got that figure rigged?"

"Yep. Have you ever known Heather to sit that still for five minutes?"

"Only when she was doing the black candle thingie."

"Say, Cass, would you mind if I call Dee and Fiona?"

"Won't that kind of ruin our stealthy commando operation here?" I said.

"Well, think about it. Dee really has the right to be involved, with what happened to Will at that convent fire, and Fiona's always good for protection.

"Oh, I get it. You want to get your hands on Fiona's pistol," I said. "Still, I take your point about Dee."

Phillipa was already punching in Dee's number on speed dial. I glanced at my watch. Soon it would be just dark enough for a skulking intruder to strike.

"Dee, Cass and I are at Animal Lovers, and we thought you might want to join us. We've identified the arsonist.

It's Raoul...yes, to my chagrin. Oh, Fiona's already told you? She's there now? Look, can you leave the kids with Betti and meet us here? In case the police haven't picked him up, we're expecting that bastard to try something incendiary at the shelter as a parting shot. Yes, that possibility came up in Cass's vision, you remember. But we don't want to scare Raoul away, so just coast up quietly and park in the shadows behind Cass. Tell Fiona to bring you-know-what. Yes, it's me talking. Stone would want us to be protected, I'm sure. After all, he did get Fiona that permit."

We waited quietly for a half hour, during which I found out that I don't have the temperament or the bladder for a stake-out. I really wanted to run into the building and find Heather, her black candles, and a bathroom, not necessarily in that order.

Phillipa was preternaturally quiet. I didn't like that brooding aura. But I thought about those abandoned animals housed in the shelter. Anything in their defense would be defensible.

"Should we call Stone and tell him our suspicions?" I mused aloud.

"Raoul isn't going to fall for our trap if the entire Plymouth Police Force careens into this street. And it was you who said he's got a chance to get away free. So it may be we catch him tonight or never," Phillipa reasoned.

There was a tap on my back window that gave us both a terrible start. Heather's face was pressed against the glass. I rolled down the window. "What in Hades are you two doing here?" she whispered.

"Get in, girl," Phillipa said. "Waiting for Raoul—what do you think, that we'd leave you to deal with this by yourself? And where's Dick?"

"We're splitting up the watch. He's coming in at midnight to six."

"Here's Dee and Fiona now," Phillipa said as the station wagon slid to a stop behind us.

"Hail, hail..." Heather said.

"Shhhhh," I said. "Did you hear something?"

Several of the dogs began to bark. "Could be something or nothing," Heather said. "They like to exercise their lungs from time to time."

We waited. And waited. Another three-quarters of an hour went by.

"I'll go back and talk to Dee and Fiona," I volunteered. "Let them know what's not happening."

"Can't you sit still!" Phillipa complained.

"Nope. I'll be careful though." I crept out of the car to the station wagon.

Dee rolled down her window. "Come and join us, Cass. Fiona's doing this little humming thing to bring Lazaro out into the open."

Fiona was indeed sitting in the back seat with her hands in yoga position, humming with complete concentration. It was a hum that went up and down like a wave, very hypnotic. I would have to ask her about this later.

Before joining them, however, I glanced down the street. Perhaps I had time to pop into the diner and use the john.

"Wait a minute. Did I see a shadow move near the back entrance?" Deidre exclaimed.

What happened next was sheer pandemonium. Like a scene from a war movie, the old-fashioned kind, "rockets bright glare" arcing through the darkness. And between explosions, every animal in Animal Lovers had begun either to bark or to howl.

"Holy Hecate!" I said. "Looks like the fourth of July. Are those fireworks?"

Heather was already running across the street toward her sanctuary screaming curses, just as she had in my vision. Phillipa followed, another vengeful valkyrie.

Deidre punched in 911 on her cell phone, hollering for the fire department and the police. Fiona just kept on humming.

I jumped out of Deidre's car to follow Heather, too. A deafening spray of Roman candles zoomed into the air, each one leaving a trail of sparkling stars. I hadn't seen anything like this since I was a kid and my father had accidentally touched off his entire Fourth of July cache that had been intended to entertain the neighborhood for an hour. People were running out the bowling alley and the rink to watch the display. Some of the truck drivers had climbed up on their rigs and were breaking out cans of beer to enjoy with the show. Sirens wailed in the distance.

Heather and Phillipa were pulling out Lazaro, none too gently, from the back entry where he had thrown himself for shelter. He was covered with soot, and it appeared that both his hands had been injured. Screaming in pain, he attempted to crawl away, but Phillipa hung onto his feet and Deidre had rushed forward to clap one diminutive boot firmly on his back.

"So you're the son of a bitch who torched the convent," she leaned over and hissed in his ear. "Put a lot of good men at risk and killed my Will. Guess you messed with the wrong gals this time."

"What in Hades happened here?" I gasped.

"Must have been one of those fireworks I bought last summer," Heather said. "I thought I'd got rid of them all."

"Hoisted!" Phillipa exclaimed in triumph.

Lazaro kept crying until an ambulance took him away with two officers in attendance. There was little for the fire department to do except clean up the fireworks that hadn't gone up into the sky. Lazaro had been attempting to start the fire in a trash barrel outside the back door with the help of a can of turpentine. The first burst of flame had touched off a cardboard box of fireworks that had been left beside the trash. The resulting explosions had blown in the back door of the sanctuary, lifting the arsonist into the air as well.

Mick Finn was shaking his head. "It's a miracle that man is alive. But thank God we've got him in custody. So now, Ms. Devlin, would you please tell me what were you doing with a carton of Roman candles?"

Heather explained how she had purchased the entire stock of fireworks at her local convenience store so that youngsters in the neighborhood would not set them off and spook her animals. She'd donated the fireworks to the town for its Fourth of July celebration. Dick and Captain Jack had stored the containers at Animal Lovers, and a few days later they were picked up by the Parks Department and used as part of last summer's display. But now it appeared that one carton of Roman candles had been overlooked. It remained unnoticed in the back pantry until recently when Fred Crippen, needing more room to store special diets canned food, had put the dusty carton outdoors with the trash. He'd meant to ask Mrs. Devlin if that was okay.

"Don't you blame Fred, Mick. This was a blessing in disguise," Heather said. "Look, I've got to go and give Grace a hand pacifying those distraught animals."

"Wait, I'll help," I said. "Where's Fiona? She might like to say a few calming words to the cats."

"Still in my car humming I guess," Deidre said.

"It's just as well," I said, thinking that if Fiona were here, either Phillip or Deidre might have availed themselves of her pistol. I wanted to see Lazaro arraigned before either of my ruthless friends got herself in trouble.

Fiona strolled over calmly, reticule in hand, as if arriving at a picnic. "That Hazel really knew her spellwork!" she said admiringly. "I never would have thought of fireworks, would you?"

"Come on, Fiona," Heather said. "I have a wing full of distraught cats needing a soothing influence."

Fiona reached into her old green bag and took out a small plastic baggie of dried herbs. "Perhaps a pinch of catnip," she murmured. "Take their mind off things, you know."

"Listen, Fiona, put that stuff away," said Heather, already regretting her plea for help. "Those felines are riled up enough without making them drunk on that stuff. We never allow catnip at Animal Lovers."

Fiona drew herself up into her glamour without deigning to reply and sailed toward the sound of caterwauling in the Cat Wing.

"*Jesu Christos*, what happened here?" I heard the voice of my beloved on the run from his Rent-a-Wreck to the scene of near-disaster. "I could hear explosions all the way down Route 3. Were those fireworks I saw in the sky? The scanner reported an attempted arson at Phil's place. I rushed over

there, but you'd already left. Then, a second attempted arson
was reported, so I turned around and raced over here, found
myself following an ambulance. Was that your arsonist they
carried away? I'm just thankful to find you in one piece. Hasn't
anyone ever told you not to travel faster than your guardian
angel can fly?" he scolded, while wrapping me securely in his
arms.

"I'm sorry," I said, pressing my face into his reassuring
warmth. He smelled of summer herbs and the sea. "I just
wanted to have a chat with Phillipa. I never thought that
Lazaro would follow me. Then when he threw that thing at
us and got away, I thought we'd better keep an eye on Animal
Lovers. It was something I saw in a vision."

"Why the hell didn't you tell me that instead of having
Phil hand me that shopping crap?"

"Sure, like you tell me everything. What about that last
trip of yours? Didn't you sort of neglect to mention that the
'man overboard' wasn't a man at all? Some smarmy girl who
now is writing you billet-doux!"

"It was just a thank-you letter, for heaven's sake."

"If that's what you think... Never mind, let's go talk to
the animals. Heather needs some help here."

"Don't you ever scare me like that again," he demanded,
still holding me.

"Okay, okay," I said. "I need to get inside for a minute...
and freshen up. I promise I'll let you ride shotgun next time."
I was thinking that might be better than having my friends
shooting up the place.

"I'm holding you to that promise," Joe said sternly.

I supposed I owed him that. After all, he'd saved my life more than once. And might again, who knows? "A good man is hard to find," as the song goes.

We strolled off hand-in-hand into the cacophony of worried canines.

CHAPTER TWENTY-NINE

The Spring is here,
And would you weep for winter's tempest wild?
Sigh not for love,--the ways of love are dark!

–Helen Hay

In the time-honored way of married squabbles, Joe and I "made up" in bed much later that night. I never could resist the delicious scent of him and the electrifying touch of his slightly-roughened hands on my naked skin. We knew each other's body so completely now, and understood our fantasies as well—it was easy to give and receive pleasure.

"All's well that ends well," he murmured sleepily into my shoulder.

"Much ado about nothing," I agreed. I realized it was silly of me to fuss about Marty. It had just been the sheer annoyance of that "I adore you!" and the afterthought, "P.S. Regards to Cass" that had got me riled. But it wasn't as if she and I knew each other. No reason for her to consider what my reaction might be to her girlish enthusiasm for her savior.

We drifted off in complete accord, an atmosphere of loving well-being that hung around us all the next day like a rosy cloud. I thought nothing could puncture that mood.

But it seems that Creative Force of the Universe does not intend for us to wallow in green pastures for long stretches of time. After any idyllic interlude, life is always waiting to pull us up short.

Such were my philosophical ruminations when Tip called me that afternoon. It was Sunday, so I was making pizza for supper. I'd just put the dough in an oiled bowl to do its magic thing when the kitchen phone rang.

"Hey, you guys got that arsonist. Geeze, and him a poet and refugee. I guess that never fooled you, though—right, Aunt Cass?"

"It was Stone's collar, Tip. Where are you?"

"Like I told you, it's the weekend so I'm at Kelliher's watching out for Sylvie. Giving Captain Jack a break. And Ish, too. Those cats are giving him a nervous breakdown. Losing feathers and all. Cursing a blue streak, or maybe I should say green streak."

Although Heather hadn't complained, I imagined that she must be missing her houseman now turned weekday bodyguard. This situation wasn't good for anyone.

"It must be hard for you to drive down here every weekend."

"Nah, it's all right. So I saw it on the local news this morning, they were dragging this Lazaro away to the hospital. Is everything okay now at AL? I used to work there, you remember, in case Mrs. Devlin needs a hand with anything."

"Nice idea, Tip, but what we want you to concentrate on right now is getting back to school and working for those top grades so that you can go on to college later." The adult party line, so easy to slip into with teen-agers. Thinking of fragile Sylvie, I sighed. "I've been so mixed up with this arson business, I feel I've been neglecting Sylvie."

"Well, the thing is, Sylvie's not really well, you know. Being held prisoner that way spooked her plenty, and it seems she won't relax until she knows she's safe. I don't think she's sleeping very much, or eating either. And she'll never feel safe with Deere on the loose. So I was thinking, now that you medicine women have wrapped up the arsonists, do you think you could do something about Deere?"

I may have groaned because Tip added, "Or if you could see where he's at in a vision, I'd go out after him."

"Not on your life," I said. "Let me see what we can see. You're going back to Wiscasset today?"

"Yeah, I suppose. Please promise to let me know if you get any leads on Deere, will you, Aunt Cass?"

"Yes, I promise. Tell Sylvie that I'm going to come over to see her tomorrow afternoon. I'll bring some calming teas to help her sleep. And you—drive carefully, and study hard."

"See you next weekend maybe?"

"You're bringing your homework, I trust?"

"You worry about me too much, Aunt Cass."

"You're worth worrying about, hon."

❧

"No rest for the weary witch," I said to Joe later, as we set our fragrant pizza on tray tables in front of the TV. I supposed it would be the Discovery Channel again, some far-flung adventure. I checked the TV guide for romantic old movies, in case. I was really in the mood for Bogart. Joe had loaded his pizza with crushed red pepper, but I was saving my crusts, sans hot stuff, for the two salivating dogs at our feet.

"You're going after Deere now, aren't you? I've been expecting that," Joe said, reaching over to fill my glass with Chianti Classico. He took a scorching bite of pizza. "Mmm. This is really good. I'm still on leave, so you're not taking off without me this time. You've been wildly foolhardy, all of you, even for gals as pixilated as yourselves. So plan on my watching out for you until that animal is in custody."

Scruffy made a dismissive grumpy sound. Dogs find some human talk too dumb for comment.

But I knew what he meant. "Call Deere a monster, not an animal," I said. "No self-respecting animal would behave as sadistically as he did. Of course, I'll welcome having a bodyguard. But actually we can't do anything yet because we don't know anything. No idea where he is. He's got a passport, Stone says, but he hasn't used it. I had the notion he might head for Ireland, but I guess not."

"Don't be too sure. He didn't necessarily use his own passport."

"That's a thought," I said. "I'm visiting Sylvie tomorrow. Maybe she has some ideas. And checking with Fiona, naturally. So how do you feel about Bogart and Bacall?"

"Neutral. How do you feel about On the Trail of Genghis Kahn in Mongolia?"

"Men are from Mongolia, women are from Casablanca." Nevertheless, I let him have camping in yurts on the Gobi Desert while I divided crusts between Scruffy and Raffles.

Hey, what about the sausage, Toots?

"No sausage tonight." I said sternly. "Be happy with mushrooms and peppers."

"Who's complaining?" Joe asked.

"Oh, not you. That was for Scruffy."

We munched on pizza, watching the nomads and the Banana-Republic types riding over the steppes or sharing goat stew around the campfire. The voiceover droned on about icy sandstorms, snow leopards, and cashmere wool. My eyes glazed over. Suddenly, it was as if the channel had changed. I was watching Nick Deere swaggering around *Rick's Cafe Americain* in a Nazi uniform, chatting up a French gal.

"Round up the usual suspects," I murmured.

"What's that?" Joe asked absently. "Look, sweetheart. That's where they discovered dinosaur eggs."

"Shades of Jurrasic Park."

"Oh, I don't think they were still viable. What's that about suspects."

I came to and sat bolt upright with a start. "The pub. We have to start at the Erin Go Bragh. Nick's father might know that I had something to do with exposing his son's evil doings, but he won't know Dee, and better yet, she's Irish."

"You're not going to send her in there alone to ask questions!" Joe demanded, his attention momentarily diverted from the flora and fauna of the Gobi.

"We'll be just outside. No, she won't be asking questions. She'll be getting the feel of the place, maybe leaving a charm of some kind. That's her specialty."

Joe sighed. "How about gargoyle carrying a Celtic cross?"

"I suppose you think that's funny," I giggled. The sun was sinking slowly in the west as the Discovery Channel bid a fond farewell to Lower Mongolia. I slipped a CD into the TV. Maybe Rick's Cafe would give me some other ideas.

❧

The next day I did manage to convince Joe that it was safe to allow me out of his sight long enough to drop off some herbal tea for Sylvie, providing I promised to take no detours, concoct no spells, and chase no criminals. I knew that he really wanted to work on my front door anyway, the one so rarely used, it was practically unusable. And it had a bullet hole in it, too, that had never been repaired. I had painted over it—cranberry red. A nice New England color, and a good cover for bloodstains, too. Although its primary use through the generations had been for visiting clergy or departing coffins, I hoped the old door would still be on its hinges when I returned home.

When I arrived at the Kellihers' place, Captain Jack was outdoors feeding the cats. He scrutinized my car and me, and when we passed muster, waved me in jauntily with his cap. A crowd of cats were swirling around his legs. It looked to me like they were getting some fresh bluefish with their regular kibble.

I found Sylvie at the desk, perusing some of her automatic writing, while Ishmael on his perch on the corner was muttering, "Blast the bastards, I say...awk, awk."

After we had exchanged greetings and hugs, I said, "I brought you some tea that will help you sleep. My special herbal blend, Serene Dreams." I took a long look at her. "Good Goddess, you're more than slender, Sylvie. You're starting to disappear when you turn sideways."

Sylvie gave a small, tired giggle. "I thought you said I'd only disappear when I was among trees."

"Don't quibble. I know what a great cook the captain is—aren't you afraid of hurting his feelings when you don't eat properly?"

Sylvie blushed. "I'm lucky to have so many caring friends. The captain seems to know how to cook every fish that ever swam. Soups, too. And Tip cooks on weekends. He's a whiz with eggs and fry bread. It's so good of Tip to watch out for me, but I keep telling him, it's too much to keep traveling all that distance. I know I should eat more, at least to show my gratitude for their dear efforts. But you know, I keep remembering what happened. It was so awful. I felt as if I was already dead and buried in that hole, that no one knew I was there. If Nick was prevented from returning, or chose not to ...well. I couldn't believe that I'd been missed, that you were looking for me." She shuddered, and a tear ran down her pale cheek.

My wilting dryad. I felt like someone who had forgotten to tend a lovely plant that now drooped near extinction. "Don't you fret anymore, Sylvie. We *are* going to find Deere. The arson matter is cleared up now, and I'm going to make your welfare and peace of mind my personal business. Do you remember any place that Deere mentioned, or a friend he might seek out?"

Sylvie shrugged. "I don't think he had any friends. I've got something here in my latest writings, though." She handed me the untidy sheaf of papers on the desk, great looping letters darkly drawn with her Sharpie, no spaces between words.

Seeing me try to puzzle out the text, she took it back and read the pages to me. The spirit she was channeling now seemed to be a benign familiar dispensing generic advice in rhyme. Mostly about protecting herself with prayers and visions of shielding light, but between these exhortations there was one startling line. "You've naught to fear from Nicolas Deere. He's away to the Isle for a while."

I wondered what that meant. "What Isle?"

"Must be the Isle of Man," Sylvie interpreted.

"The Isle of Man! If that's true, Deere *is* traveling on a false passport, or someone else's passport. Why on earth would he go there?" I exclaimed.

"It's the motorcycle races," Sylvie said. "The place is famous for its spring motorcycle races. Nick has always talked about going there again. His da took him once when he was ten. They didn't get along so well after that, though. Did you know that Nick's mother died of a fall downstairs?"

"No, I know nothing about his background, but I'm not a great believer in excusing sadistic behavior because of childhood trauma."

"Nick says his ma was a slut but his da shouldn't have thrown her downstairs. He'd cry about that when he got drunk or stoned, then he'd start ranting about all women being sluts, and that's when I'd have to hide out somewhere."

"Even if they didn't get along, his father may have helped him to get out of the country. In fact, I had a sort of flash that the first place we ought to investigate is the Erin Go Bragh Pub. Anyway, your writing clue is an outstanding one, and I'm going to follow-up on it. You let me know now if you get any more hints from this new angelic spirit you're channeling. Nice change from the fire fiend."

Sylvie smiled, a full smile this time. "Yes, I'm glad to get rid of that scary stuff, but at least the fire writer brought me to your circle through Mrs. Peacedale, and that's been such a blessing."

I could have cried at such simple gratitude, but instead I gave the girl a warm hug and lots of motherly advice about eating right and sleeping well.

∽

"What we need to leave at the Erin Go Bragh is a bug not a poppet or gargoyle," Deidre declared.

She and I were having a conference of war in her living room, with Fiona acting as a Wiccan consigliere. Bobby and little Annie were being fed a mid-morning snack in the kitchen by Betti. The older children, including Laura Belle, were still in school. What bedlam would ensue when school let out for the summer, I shuddered to contemplate. I realized that I actually preferred barking dogs to screaming children, wondering if that was some terrible character flaw.

"*Charms 'r us*," I said, shaking my hands to rid myself of those negative thoughts. "Bugs 'r *not* us. Leave bugs to the CIA, the NSA, and other groups sworn to protect our freedoms. Give me good old-fashioned spellcraft any day. So what do you think, Fiona?"

"What exactly are we trying to accomplish—that's the question to ask ourselves before we start sticking pins in poppets," Fiona said.

"Please, Fiona. My poppets are pin-free," Deidre declared, her busy hands stuffing soft cotton into flesh-colored cloth dollies as we talked. "Anyone care for another arrowroot cookie? More coffee? A drop of the Irish?"

"No, thanks," Fiona and I chorused, although I had to admit that whiskey did wonders for Deidre's weak brew.

I wouldn't want to reek of whiskey when I got home, though.

"So how exactly do they work, your magical dollies?" I asked. I remembered the little red-eyed gargoyle Deidre had brought into the hospital when I was recovering from a poisoned brownie. Possibly meant to scare off bad vibes?

"It's hard to describe...an elfin presence to shift reality a bit. I used to use trolls, but you never can tell what *they'll* do. There's no good control with trolls, although the gift of a troll bride doll is a surefire spell for getting a gal married." Deidre sighed and seemed to lose her thought for a moment. Then she shrugged her shoulders and continued. "But in consideration of Fiona's question, we want a way to lure Deere into a police trap so that he can be sent to jail and Sylvie can breathe easy again. How sure are you that he's—where?—the Isle of Man? At the motorcycle races—Holy Mother! What a jerk!"

"If you don't believe in spiritual evidence, what in the world do you believe?" asked Fiona. "Sylvie's new spirit guide has put Deere on the Isle, and my pendulum agrees. That's good enough for me, Dee."

"Well...wherever he is...why don't we just do our regular Bringing Home thing from Hazel's Book, only I'll tie the effigy of him somewhere in the pub, because we sure don't want him anywhere near us or Sylvie," Deidre said.

"That could work," I agreed. "Stone said the cops would be keeping an eye on the pub, although the Plymouth force doesn't have enough manpower for a real stake-out like on TV. But if Deere is caught out, that's it for him. They'll arrest him on the spot."

"Okay, but I'll need another little charm to stick Deere at the pub until he's picked up. Stick, sticky, glue stuff.

I'll do a Gertie Glue-pot Gargoyle!" Deidre exclaimed. "Perfect!"

I took out the magical reminders notebook I keep in my handbag, and turned the page on which I had jotted down a list of Herbs for Lust, exposing a fresh page. "Okay, to sum up," I said, "our plan of action is...one Bringing Home spell complete with poppet to shake Deere loose from the motorcycle races and one Gertie Gargoyle to hold him at the pub until the cops can arrest him for kidnapping and aggravated rape. Whoever said the Craft is easy! This business sure is more than a wiggle of the nose and a pull on the ear."

"Unlike fictional magic, it's not infallible either," Deidre said. "You never really know how spells are going to work. And sometimes the Universe of Infinite Solutions simply says a flat 'no' to your hopes and prayers." She looked so suddenly downcast, we knew she was sinking into her grief again. There was no way around grieving, only through, but at least we could keep her too busy for a classic depression. There's something about being forced into action that gets one's serotonin perking.

"We must believe the Universe knows what is best for all," Fiona said, patting Deidre's hand with her many-ringed fingers. "Even when that personal 'no' hurts like hell. It's the way of the Universe that eventually each of us loses those we love best or they lose us. Thus we are tried and refined to cherish the moment."

"You're right about the hurting like hell part," Deidre said.

"But now, the Bringing Home..." Fiona got back on track. "We ought to have the entire circle for that. We'll ask

Heather to contribute some of her onion-skin yellow candles. Cass, you'll assemble the herbs...what were they now?"

I was busily jotting them down as the ingredients of the spell surfaced into my consciousness. "Heartsease—Genus *Viola Tricolor*—folded into the paper on which we write Deere's full name. Fiona, you check that out in case there's a middle name as well, all the better," I said. "Cinnamon oil to anoint the name before burning. A woven rope of sweet grass to hang Deere's poppet from the rafters or whatever. And for that we'll need a likeness of Deere."

"I'll see if I can hang that poppet somewhere inconspicuous right in the pub. And tuck little Gertie Glue nearby. We'll have Phil get a mugshot of Deere—surely she can wheedle something like that from Stone," Deidre said. "Phil being married to the Law, so ironic and useful, isn't it?"

"Yes, yes," Fiona said. "And we must *strike while the ironies are hot*. Phil will think of something. Let's get together again here tomorrow night. That way Dee and I won't have to worry about getting a sitter. 'Never fails,' Hazel wrote about this spell, 'if you do it aright.'"

"Oh, sure," Deidre said. "That's the loophole line." She was looking a whole lot cheerier, though, as she stuffed the last dolly and dropped it into her workbasket. Searching through her handiwork, she chose one of the blank-faced figures and held it up for inspection. "This one, I think. Slightly irregular, as they say."

"Lovely, Dee," Fiona said. "You simply have a feel for that sort of thing, and whatever you choose will be just what the sorcerer ordered."

Deidre snapped the poppet in the belly with her fingernails. "You are about to be screwed, dear Deere." There was something eerie about her expression. Something not entirely on the white side, maybe straying into the off-white or ghoulish gray.

But just then Annie began to howl. The strange Deidre vanished, and the concerned mother returned. She rushed into the kitchen.

"Don't worry so much, Cass," Fiona said. "We are all multiple personalities. Even dimpled Deidre has a dark side—don't we all?"

"Not you, Fiona," I said.

"Well, I'm older, dear. Age is the great homogenizer."

CHAPTER THIRTY

When shall we three meet again?
In thunder, lightning, or in rain,
When the hurly-burly's done,
When the battle's lost and won...

–William Shakespeare

"So what are you up to now?" Joe asked, watching me pack up my covered pie-basket with heartsease, sweet grass, cinnamon oil, a bottle of ink I'd blessed and sanctified for the occasion, and an old-fashioned pen. In a moment of inspiration, I added shamrock clover that had been growing in a pot on my windowsill since March. It was a New England April night, meaning chilly, and this was a formal ceremony, so I decided to wear the forest green wool cloak with pewter clasps that Joe had given me during our courtship days. With the pie basket over my arm, I patted the two dogs sitting at attention and kissed Joe.

"Ah, Little Green Riding Hood," Joe said, grinning wickedly. "Will you be safe from wolves tonight?"

"Perfectly. We are not up to any dangerous encounters. In fact, as I told you, we suspect that Deere is out of the country, possibly on the Isle of Man. This is just a little herbal meditation tonight."

"Yes, sweetheart, but you have to admit we're talking magical guesswork here." He softened the judgment by drawing me into his arms and pushing my hair back so that he could lay his cheek against mine. "A little automatic writing, a little dowsing by Fiona, and a lot of wild speculation. For all you know, that bastard might be right around the corner."

"But he's a wanted man now, for charges that will put him away for thirty or forty years, if not for life. I doubt he's going to hang around to be picked up loitering, don't you? So I think it's safe for you to let me go to Dee's for a couple of hours. I have my cell phone, it's charged, and you'll be my first call if there's a hint of trouble."

"Okay, I guess." After a soft bite on my neck, Joe let me go, contenting himself with an affectionate pat on the rear end as I hurried to get away before he could change his mind and insist on accompanying me. *Goddess forbid!*

༄

"Don't ask me what I went through to get *this*," Phillipa said, flourishing a miniature likeness of Deere in front of Deidre. "My darling husband has been slightly suspicious of my requests since the incident of the gun safe. Stone says he's afraid that, had I known the combination, I might actually have shot Raoul. Well, little does he realize that I do indeed know the combination but in the heat of the moment, I kept transposing two digits."

"Maybe you really didn't want to kill Lazaro," I said. "Deep down. Foiled by your inner goodness."

"Inner goddess, you mean," Fiona corrected me. "Divine alignment. Each of us has a guiding spirit, you know. She who strengthens us on the journey of self-discovery. Athena with her wise old owl guides me."

"Isis, queen of abundance, lady of love and magic, diviner of secrets." I hardly knew I was going to say that, but it slipped out of my mouth without passing through my brain.

"Hecate," Heather said smugly. "Never says no to a yen for revenge."

"Danu, the Celtic all-mother," Deidre said. "And you, Phil?"

"Brigit, of course, if you don't mind sharing the Celts. Goddess of poetry and all good crafts. Now can we get on with this Bringing thing?"

Deidre snipped away the little face of Deere and pasted it on her poppet. I handed her the slim braid of sweet grass, which she stitched around the poppet's middle.

"I hope no one in the pub notices you hanging this thing with Nick Deere's face on it. Not so easy to explain."

"Those are the chances we have to take," Deidre said calmly, biting off a thread. "But don't you worry about me. I have a plan..."

"So...share it," Phillipa demanded.

"Wait..." With the sanctified ink, on a square of rich ivory paper, Deidre was lettering *Nicolas Damian Deere* in her best calligraphy, an art she had practiced in her "spare time." She sprinkled the name with white sand, then blew the sand off the page. "By this ink, be you writ...by this crystal, be you fixed," she chanted, handing the page to me.

I folded it around a sprig of dried heartsease and shamrock clover "By this heartsease, be you drawn...by this clover, be you called." Last of all, I anointed it with cinnamon oil. "By this oil, be signed and sealed."

Heather lit the fat yellow candle, dyed with onion skins and imbedded with honeycomb and bees.

"By earth, by water, by air, and by flame," Phillipa recited. "Nicolas Damian Deere must come home again."

Fiona took the folded paper from me and very dexterously burned most of it in the candle flame, dropping the last bit into a small black cauldron. The scent of cinnamon wafted around us and rose into the air.

"There, that's that," Fiona said, clapping her ringed fingers together, her bangles jingling softly. "Now who's going to go pub-crawling with Dee?"

"It will have to be me," Phillipa said. "Sophia protect us!" She held up a hand to prevent my next plea. "No, Cass, we can't take the chance of you being seen and recognized as the person who saved Sylvie. You either, Fiona. And before you say a word, don't worry, I'll call you on my cell as soon as we're clear away."

"What about me?" Heather asked in a hurt tone.

"Oh, all right," Phillipa said ungraciously. "If you promise not to order anything memorable, like, say, a magnum of Vive Clicquot."

"I can drink beer as well as the next witch. What about you, Phil? Draped in black from head to foot. All you need is a pointed hat, my dear. And I suppose you think *you* blend?"

"Girls, girls," Fiona said. "Let Dee order for you, Heather. And Phil, do you think you might lighten it up this time? Possibly deep purple?"

∽

"Dee was amazing," Phil said approvingly. Her cheeks were flushed an attractive rose, and her dark eyes sparkled. I made a mental note to get Phil out in the field more often in future. Always worried about what her detective husband would say, she'd been loathe to commit herself even to actions she herself suggested. Now we were debriefing the Erin Go Bragh team in Fiona's living room. I had really wished to join in this operation myself, but I had already compromised myself with the Deere family. Still, I could feel a little impulse to jealousy that I had to quash with maturity and common sense.

"Shit! I'm *so* jealous of you three!" The words just spilled out of their own accord. I clapped my hand over my wayward mouth.

"Oh, come on, Cass. It was my turn, don't you think. Every magic mission can't be about *you, you, you*," Phillipa said. "Anyway, Dee ordered us a pitcher of beer and a basket of fried potato skins—pretty good ones, too. Did you know that Julia Child's favorite fries were MacDonald's?"

"Never mind the food, Phil," I said testily. "What happened?"

"There was a Celtic band there, practicing for that evening performance. Not too many people in the pub at two in the afternoon, and that might have been a problem. But Dee managed to sneak away without anyone noticing her."

"Well, how about me," Heather said. "Didn't I provide the distraction?"

"I was just getting to that." Phillipa resumed her narrative. "Heather fainted."

"Heather *fainted*!" I exclaimed.

"Would you like to see how I did it? Might come in useful someday." Heather stood up. The bronze braid falling down her back suddenly swung in the air as Heather swirled around twice in a blur of mauve suede. Then, bending her knees, she collapsed gracefully onto Fiona's braided rug. Her breath expelled in a sigh and her eyes fluttered closed. She almost seemed to pale. "Learned this at Vassar," she whispered.

"Wow!" I said. "You do that elegantly. But I'm afraid if I tried it, I'd fall into an ungainly heap. So then, what happened? Everyone rushed to your aid?"

"You bet. No one even noticed Dee slipping into the back room. You'd better tell the rest, Dee."

Deidre took up the story. "In the back of the pub are the rest rooms, Pat Deere's office, a storeroom for cases of booze, and a closet for cleaning supplies. That's where I hung Nick Deere. Way back on a dark shelf behind a box of Bartender's Friend brass polish. From what I saw out front, they don't waste much time polishing brass at the Erin Go Bragh."

"And Gertie Glue-pot?" Fiona asked.

"The girl gargoyle is sitting right beside Deere, a nice bit of company to keep him from wandering." Deidre grinned and looked, for a moment, like her old impish self, without the deep little line of worry and sadness that had appeared between her brows during this year of troubles.

"By the time anyone took notice of us, Dee was back at our table," Phil went on. "We hung around Heather solicitously, of course, which was somewhat foiled by her ordering shots of Irish to accompany the beer. Goddess help us! It was a good thing that I was driving," Phillipa said with smug satisfaction. I noted that she was indeed wearing a lighter color, more deep navy than black, and a blue scarf with silver moon and stars around her neck. And a silver pentagram. *A pentagram!*

"Phil! You didn't wear that pentagram into the pub, did you?" I demanded.

"Under the scarf, Cass, under the scarf. No one even noticed, I'm sure."

But when we went outside to ride home in Phillipa's BMW, there was a scrawled note lettered in red on a torn page from the phone book and fixed under her windshield wiper. It read, "You fucking witches stay the hell out of our pub, or else."

"Holy Mother! So much for our being undercover," Deidre said. "You'd better show that one to Stone the minute you get home."

"Are you out of your mind," Phillipa snapped. "I told him we were going to Patty Peacedale's for a prayer-and-paganism tea."

"Well, if he believed that, I think I'll try to sell him Jenkins Park," I said.

ᏽ

We never really know whether our spells are working or things we want to materialize in the world of form simply happen of their own accord. Or if our spells give fate a little push in the direction of our desire, which is what I believe. But it seemed to me that our circle was becoming stronger in spirit with every Esbat and Sabbat, more in touch with the powers of the unseen world. And our magic was especially strong whenever we adapted one of Hazel's spells—such had been the case with Hoisting Lazaro, and such was the case with Bringing Home Nick Deere.

Only the reality didn't play out as we had envisioned. When Deere got home from the Isle, on whatever false passport he had borrowed or manufactured, he did not stay "glued" to the pub. He'd won a sum of money on the motorcycle races, and he'd come back secretly, so he believed, to settle a few scores and buy himself a complete new identity from a reliable source. Then he would disappear where no rap sheet could ever follow him. He would be a different man.

If our circle had known what day he arrived or the cops in their spasmodic surveillance had discovered his return, all would have been well. Even if we had known when he left the premises to pursue his latest schemes, we would have been one up on the situation.

Most dangerous of all, what we didn't know was that Deere had discovered the little poppet bearing his face behind the case of Bartender's Friend. Why Nick Deere was poking in the shadows of the cleaning closet was something we were never to learn. Perhaps some Celtic sixth sense. As soon as Deere's father took one look at the poppet, he was able to put two-and-two together, and got five, the five of us.

None of us, not even Deidre, realized that Will, restless and angry at being benched for medical reasons, had taken to dropping in the Erin Go Bragh often enough to be fairly well known there. Then when Pat Deere had attended Will Ryan's spectacular funeral, he'd seen the pretty blond widow and her children at the graveside. He knew who she was and identified the young woman who had slipped into the back of the pub when her friend fainted as Deidre Ryan.

CHAPTER THIRTY-ONE

There is no wrath in the stars,
They do not rage in the sky;
I look from the evil wood
And find myself wondering why.

Why do they not scream out
And grapple star against star,
Seeking for blood in the wood
As all things round me are?

–Lord Dunsany

Nick Deere studied the neat garrison colonial with the bright swing set in the fenced back yard. How many brats did this broad have, anyway? They were in and out of that yard like a swarm of gnats, dumped by their ma on that creepy dwarf woman. And those two stupid poodles. Nick had always hated dogs. Once he had thrown a poodle into the North River, just to have a moving target to shoot at with his BB gun. But some jerk kid had waded in and pulled the mutt out, so he had shot the kid instead. Took a chunk out of the kid's ear, too. Bled like an axed chicken.

Nick lit another cigarette and swung his lean, muscular body into the Buick he'd borrowed from his da. It was an anonymous old scow with several sets of license plates that could be changed as necessary and a roomy trunk that his uncles used to transport illegal guns to customers in Boston. He'd parked in a good spot, right behind a landscaping outfit doing a spring clean-up; looked as if he was part of the crew. Slinking down in the seat, he watched the garrison through the rear view and side mirrors.

After he'd hung around for an hour or so, he saw a Jeep drive up and park in front of the house. A hippy broad with long sandy hair got out. Viciously Nick stabbed out his cigarette in the over-flowing ashtray. Jesus Christ! The driver was one of the cunts who had found that slut Syl! Big mess he'd been in then and all the fault of those interfering bitches. Probably he would have let Syl out pretty soon once she'd learned her lesson. But then those ball-busters got the cops involved and he'd had to split.

It hadn't been like that with Pauline, who'd gone and died on him in the hole in only a couple of days, weak stupid little broad. But Pauly was safely buried where she would never cause him a problem again. No trouble with Pauly, but Syl was a different story. She kept popping up to cause him grief, something he would have to pay her back for before he got out of town.

But right now, he had his eye on the little blonde momma who had hung that voodoo doll in Da's place. "Thou shalt not suffer a witch to live." Nick Deere knew that was a commandment or something in the Bible. "Your day of reckoning has arrived, cunt," he whispered to himself, lighting another cigarette. "I'm going to send you straight to hell." There was another place no one knew about where he could keep the blonde until he got tired of playing with her.

∽

When Deidre went missing, all of us knew about it within the hour. This abduction wasn't like Sylvie's, who'd been all alone in a houseful of cats, only one neighbor dropping in from day to day. Sylvie had been missing much longer before the alarm had gone out to us. But Deidre, mistress of time, was the soul of punctuality in her habits. Having hired an assistant to keep Faeryland open during extended Mall hours, Deidre left the shop promptly at five-thirty every evening, and at noon on Sundays. She never failed to be home by twelve-thirty on Sunday to relieve Betti, who then scooted away on her Moped to her own little cottage. So when it got to be one-thirty, Betti called the store. The assistant told the au pair that Deidre had taken off at the usual time; Betti knew something was terribly wrong. So Betti called me.

"It could be an accident. Can you find out if Mrs. Ryan got into an accident? She's never, never late, you see. I'm just *so* worried," Betti wailed.

"Stay right there, Betti, and mind the children. That's the important thing. You did right to let me know. I'll call you as soon as I have news," I said. Already I was shaking inside.

I called Phil, tasking her with investigating the accident theory. But I really knew differently. The shaking got worse. "I have an awful feeling in my third chakra that our spell worked," I said. "Nick Deere came home. Now something's happened to Deidre, and I feel it has to do with that unbalanced creep. We have to find Deidre and we have to do it immediately." Suddenly I felt Deidre's fear out there somewhere, and I screamed.

Joe was beside me in a nano-second. "What happened to you, Sweetheart?" The dogs ran downstairs from their after-lunch nap in the blue bedroom, whining and trying to wheedle themselves between us, to be comforted for whatever madness had me in its grip.

"It's something I *know, absolutely know.* You have to believe me," I said to both him and Phillipa who was still on the phone. "Nick Deere has Deidre, and it's going to be ugly if we don't stop him."

"Why Deidre? Why not Sylvie?" Phillipa asked.

"I don't know," I wailed. "I just know that Deidre's missing, and Deere is responsible. It's like a gut feeling, only it's more than my gut."

"Yeah, well...I've been acquainted with your gut feelings. They're almost always on the money. I'll alert Stone to this one—he'll check the pub and the hospitals—and I'll be right over to your place," Phil said. "We'll all be there. Meantime, *you* try to figure out where to look, okay? Go put your head on that damned pillow and *see* what you have to see, like Fiona has always told you that you can."

I let the phone drop and threw myself into Joe's arms. "I can't stand it if anything's happened to Dee. I just can't stand it. She's been through so much..."

"Shhh, shhhh," he crooned, pushing the hair back from my ear, and softly rubbing my neck. I sobbed on his shoulder, an absolute sodden mess of irresolution. "If there's something you can do to find Deidre, you have to do it now, sweetheart.

Is it that pillow you stuffed in the closet? Do you want me to get it for you?"

"I'll get it," I blubbered. "Phil, Heather, and Fiona will be here very soon. Honey, I want you to get a map of Plymouth out of the Jeep and have it ready for Fiona, in case I can't... But I've got to...I've got to..." I pulled myself away from all that warmth and security, ran into our bedroom. Scruffy was there ahead of me and got himself closed in the bedroom when I slammed the door.

Need a buddy, Toots? I'm here.

It was the work of a moment to unearth the dreaded psychic visions pillow, but it took several more minutes to pull myself together, to get centered, and to trust my ability to meet this crisis. I lay down on the bed with my face against the herb-patterned cloth. Scruffy hopped up beside me and just lay there watchfully. Somehow that was comforting. I shut my eyes.

In a whoosh I was out of myself and into a wooded area that I thought was near Deere's trailer. "He wouldn't dare come back here," I was thinking, just as an old blue Buick came chugging into view and turned into an overgrown dirt road. As if borne by the currents of air, I drifted in its wake. When the road petered out, the Buick stopped. Deere jumped out and looked around. He smiled and lit a cigarette. Then he strode off between the trees, humming to himself.

I drifted closer. I could hear some faint sounds coming from the Buick. There was a bundle in the trunk. *A struggling bundle. Deidre is in there.* She was bound and gagged, stuck into a rubbish bag! I tried to move forward, to open the trunk lid, to free her, but I was stuck in dream mode, like wading in mud.

Where is Deere? As soon as I thought that, I found myself following his quickly-moving form through the trees. He strode purposefully, knowing just where he was going. I floated after him. Once he looked back as if checking that no one was following, saw nothing, and shook his head to shake off the demons. Stamped out his cigarette. Finally he reached the place he'd been looking for.

With his boot, Deere pushed away a concealing layer of leaves and other spring debris, exposing wet wooden planks. They must have been in place there all winter; it took some jiggling to pull them up. Deere swore as he ripped a fingernail, but his words were soundless. Only the furious expression on his face defined the ugly phrases. Finally, the empty hole under the planks was exposed. In her vision, Cass saw that it was deep enough for a coffin but bigger than a grave, being square in shape.

He was going to bury Deidre in there!

In another instant, the scene vanished. I threw out my hands as if trying to grasp more of it, which tossed the pillow onto the floor and spooked Scruffy. Moaning, I sat up on the bed in my own bedroom, meeting with surprise the dog's expression of concern. Coming back to myself with a deep sigh, I touched him briefly on the head, "Thanks for the company, Sport." Then I swung my feet onto the floor and rushed into the kitchen.

"Come on," I said to Joe. "I can find this place, and we have to hurry. He's going to bury Deidre alive." Even as I spoke, I was running for the Jeep.

We were already outside when Phil roared into the driveway in her BMW, rolled down the window, and shouted. "Hey, where are you going?"

I stopped at her window while Joe drove the Jeep out of the garage. "To rescue Deidre. Follow me, and clear a phone line through to Stone. Tell him, Deere's got Deidre in the woods somewhere near his trailer. And I think it would be better if the cops came in quietly, without sirens. Otherwise... Deere might panic, you know. Like, he might do something." I couldn't bring myself to say any more.

It's a good thing I had Joe to drive, because reason was slipping away from me. I was on the steep edge of hysteria. I even forgot the most obvious thing, but Joe remembered. "If this is a woods thing, we'd better call Kellihers' and see if Tip is still there," he suggested as we squealed up onto the main road.

"Oh yes, brilliant! I don't even know where we're going, except that Deere's driving an old blue Buick and he turned into an unused dirt road somewhere near his trailer. In my vision, Deidre was in the car—in the trunk—and Deere went off into the woods to find a dug-out place concealed by planks. Do you think Tip can track the Buick?"

"I think Tip can track anything, but you don't really know the time frame, do you? You've always told me that time is the thing that escapes you gals with the second sight. The thing is—now don't go all crazy—Deere may have already gone back to the Buick to pick up Deidre. We need Tip to track the car *and* Deere's movement through the woods.

"Oh, good Goddess protect her," I moaned.

Joe was never big on talking on the cell phone while driving, but he rightly guessed that I was hardly coherent. After getting Kellihers' number from me, he punched it in as he drove, a major feat of dexterity, but then he was a man of many skills.

In a very short time, an ill-assorted posse had assembled near Deere's trailer. Three cruisers spilled out officers, including two with rifles and in SWAT outfits. Heather and Fiona arrived in the Mercedes; accompanying Heather was her elderly bloodhound Trilby, a tracker whom only Heather believed to be reliable. Joe and I were there with Phil who had followed us in her BMW. And wonder of wonders, Tip drove in on his motorcycle, noisy but most needed.

Into the center of this milling crowd strode Stone Stern, holding up his hand for quiet, warning everyone to stay back until Tip had a chance to study the scene. Meanwhile, two of the officers broke into the shed where the Harley was still garaged, abandoned by Deere in his flight, and another searched the trailer. I wondered why Heather followed him until she came out carrying a man's sweatshirt which she thrust under Trilby's nose.

I was leaning on the Jeep with Joe's arm around me, when Tip came over to me. "Detective Stern said we're looking for a dirt road. Which way is it, Aunt Cass?"

"I don't...I don't know." I was on the verge of sobbing again, and there was no time for that now.

"Yes, you do," Tip insisted. "Close your eyes and go back there. What time was it? Where was the sun?"

"That's no good. It must have been noon when he snatched her out of the Mall parking lot. The sun would have been overhead." But I did as Tip asked, closed my eyes and looked around at the scene as I remembered it. Hadn't there been a telephone pole with some kind of poster on it near the road?

"Land for sale!" I cried out triumphantly. "With a telephone number. The road is near a pole with that sign pasted on it."

"I think the cruiser passed that," Tip said. "Come on, Joe. Let's go back and see."

The three of us piled into the Jeep, and everyone followed. Less than a mile away we found the telephone pole and the road we were looking for. Tip jumped out of the Jeep and crouched down, studying the road. "An old car did drive in here recently," he said. "But it came back out again, see here?"

"Oh, what about Deidre then?" I cried out.

"She may be...he may have left her there," Joe said, holding me tightly around the shoulders. "Let's see what Tip can tell us. Tip, you go, man." But Tip was already sprinting down the dirt road, checking the tire marks as he went.

Joe waited to speak to Stone. "Tip says he's been and gone. We've got to see if he left Deidre in the woods. Maybe in a hole like Sylvie Waldes."

Stone spoke to some of the officers, and two of the cruisers took off down the street, one in each direction in pursuit of the Buick. The SWAT team stayed and followed Tip. In only a matter of minutes, we found where the dirt road petered out in the woods. The oil-leaking Buick had stopped for a while, then turned around and sped away again. Nothing else was to be seen. At least not by most of us. Listening quietly and intently, we heard only the chirrup of birds and small scattering sounds of squirrels and chipmunks going about their business.

Meanwhile, Heather again held out Deere's sweatshirt for Trilby to scent. After several deep snuffles, Trilby began to strain at the leash.

"Give Tip ten minutes to get ahead of that hound," Joe suggested. "Don't want Trilby destroying the sign, do we?"

"Okay, ten minutes," said Heather, checking her watch. It was her camouflage watch to match the camouflage suit she was wearing. I could see the camouflage cell phone peeking out of its pocket. Good thing this wasn't hunting season, that girl and her hound would have been too invisible among the leaves. Fiona would be safe, though. Standing beside Heather, she was wearing her coat sweater of many colors and a multi-striped skirt, reticule in hand. Probably carrying. What a team! For one hysterical moment, I thought I would laugh and lose it.

Pulling myself together, I followed Joe, the SWAT team, and Stone who were all following Tip, as quietly as they could, which was not very. Exactly ten minutes later, Heather gave Trilby her head, and the old dog took off like a vigorous one-year-old on her first run, her nose shoveling leaves and grass along the ground, hauling Heather after her willy-nilly in ever widening circles. Trilby had her own ideas about pursuing scent in the woods; she pulled Heather through tangles of bushes without regard to life and limb. Fiona walked beside me, brisk but sedate, and Phillipa strode along with Stone.

Tip continued to duck-walk on the barest kind of path, the sort that's made by occasional walkers seeking the easiest footing. He found a ground-up cigarette butt and silently held it up in the air like a trophy. At one point, he stood up and motioned Stone forward for a conference. Ignoring protocol, I pushed myself forward after Stone, and Joe followed me. "He carried a heavy bundle this way," Tip pointed to a footprint in the wet leaves. "And he came back without it. See over here, a much lighter step returning to the car."

"Oh, hurry, please hurry, Tip," I gasped. I could hear Stone moving to one side to call for an ambulance on his cell. Fiona began some humming spell of her own devising, and even in my half-hysterical state, I noted that her hand reached into her reticule.

"Cool it, Fiona," I muttered. "We have enough guns here already."

Tip had crouched down again, following the trail intently, motioning all of us to stay back. A few yards later, he made a sudden right-angled turn, pushing through some scrubby pines in a new direction.

The ground was carpeted by wet brown needles. "Here... and here," Tip was muttering to himself, checking one side and then the other.

Suddenly, ahead of us, there was a triumphant howl. Trilby had found a strong cache of the scent she was following. Tip, too, began to rush forward. All of us seemed to arrive at the same time to the place where a small clearing was half-hidden between a young growth of pines and a stand of sapling maples, disturbing several ominous crows who were poking the remains of something nasty on the wet ground.

Trilby towed Heather forward so that she could scratch away debris with her paws. Seeing what she was about, Tip began dragging leaves away from the earth with his bare hands. The SWAT team joined him, using the butt of their rifles and their boots. "Lift the planks! Lift the planks!" I screamed.

Now that Deere had loosened them, the planks came up easily in Stone's hands. From the edge of the crowd, I saw Joe leap into the pit and pull up a woman's form, bound and gagged as Sylvie had been, but no longer enclosed in the plastic bag, which was still down in the hole. Mud and dirt splattered Deidre from head to bare feet. *Where are her shoes?* I wondered incongruously.

"She's breathing," Phillipa called back to the rest of us. With quick strong fingers, she ripped the duct tape off Deidre's mouth. Tip unsheathed a hunting knife clipped to his belt and set to work carefully cutting her free. An ambulance siren whined in the distance, racing our way.

"Oh, my poor babies," Deidre moaned. "What would become of them?" Then she simply crumpled into a small heap, fainting dead away. Fiona pushed through and took Deidre into her warm capable arms, reaching in her reticule for smelling salts that she waved under Deidre's nose.

She whimpered and opened her eyes. "We're doing something wrong," she said, looking directly at me. "Too many enemies."

"I know," I said, meaning I knew what she meant and I knew how she felt tied up and terrified.

"At Beltane," Heather said.

"Right on," Phillipa agreed.

"Purification," Fiona said. "Rededication to peaceful paths."

Joe, who had been giving me a disbelieving look, abruptly said, "Shhh. Listen." We were quiet then and could hear officers crashing through the brush bringing paramedics with a stretcher. "Hey, over here!" Joe yelled in a relieved tone. Then to me, he muttered, "'Too many enemies' is exactly the problem, Cass. You gals have to get out of the crime-fighting business for real this time. Leave it to the law officers. I'm going to have to insist."

"You're right of course, honey," I said. "But right now, let's just take care of Deidre. And get Deere out of circulation for good and all. Just that, and then maybe..."

"No *maybe* about it," Joe asserted. I'd never heard him use such an inflexible tone to me before. I didn't know whether to feel relieved or insulted, but soon I was fully occupied with watching Deidre being lifted carefully onto the stretcher. One paramedic checked her vital signs. The other paramedic and one of the uniformed officers picked up the stretcher handles and made ready to cart Deidre out to the street and the waiting ambulance. Joe assigned himself the task of lifting branches out of their way.

Phillipa was holding Deidre's hand and Heather on the other side was patting her shoulder and uttering encouragement that sounded mighty like calming a nervous dog. "Stay now, stay now, atta girl. You're doing fine."

Fiona sidled over to me. "Men have to lay down the law from time to time," she whispered. "It's the testosterone talking."

"Yeah? Doesn't estrogen have any rebuttal."

"Estrogen smiles, nods, and does as it damned well pleases."

"I think I knew that," I said.

CHAPTER THIRTY-TWO

On the way to the grove you'll pass the Fates,
Shadow-eyed, bent over their weaving.
Stop for a moment...you see
The thread of revenge leap out of the shuttle...

—Edgar Lee Masters

Although mothering was not her favorite role, Phillipa, who had cared for and enjoyed the Ryan children before, volunteered to stay at the house so that Betti could motor home for a little rest. Fiona eased the burden somewhat by taking Laura Belle home to their cottage. Joe went back to our place to let Scruffy and Raffles have a run and some dinner while Heather and I drove to the hospital to be with Deidre. By the time we arrived, we found Deidre had been installed in a private room and was in conference with a rape counselor. She would not allow us to enter Deidre's room until a resident had come in to draw the privacy curtain and take his samples, and the nurse had followed to clean up our dirt-caked friend. The counselor was prepared to stay longer, but Deidre insisted that her friends waiting outside the door would be all the comfort and companionship she needed.

"Yes," she said to our two concerned expressions. Amazingly, she looked stronger and feistier than anyone would have expected. "The dirty bastard, may his balls rot and fall off. Did it when he got me in the woods, trussed up like a damned turkey hen. Mostly spilled himself all over me—ugh!—but just in case I've requested a morning-after pill, and Dr. Blitz has okayed it. You know how easily, I ...well. Ladies, I feel like shit. I want a real shower. A long hot shower. And where the hell was my inner goddess when I needed her?"

I hugged her. "You are she. You are Danu. That's why you survived that vile treatment, why we found you in that goddess-forsaken place."

"Well, have they caught the sonofabitch yet?" Deidre demanded.

"Ah, not that we know of," Heather said soothingly. "Phil will call the minute..."

"And what about my children? What do they think happened?"

"Don't worry, Phil is staying so Betti could go home for a while. Fiona talked to Jenny. Told her that you'd encountered a bad man, but you were fine, just resting in the hospital until tomorrow."

That seemed to tip Deidre over the edge, for she began to howl and sob. We held her and murmured all the good words we could think of, only moving aside for the nurse to accomplish her routine. I'd met that particular nurse with the protruding eyes and fine brown hair falling out of its coil before when I was having my stomach pumped out; her name was Brenda.

"I'll see if **Dr.** Blitz will prescribe a sedative," Nurse Brenda offered.

"Now what about a cup of hot sweet kava tea? Do you have a Navaho drum on the premises?" Fiona asked.

Nurse Brenda looked at Fiona as if she had just wandered in from the psychiatric ward.

Deidre had reached the gulping and retching phase of a good cry. Maybe Joe was right, I thought. Maybe there was something to be said for our getting out of the crime-solving business.

"It's better this way," Nurse Brenda whispered to Heather, handing her a box of those tiny tissues hospitals favor. "The stiff-upper-lip victims have more trouble later. Your friend was not too badly injured, just a few superficial bruises. She'll probably be going home tomorrow."

"I'll sleep here," Heather whispered to me. "I'll just go out the front entry so I can use my cell phone to call Dick. Then in a while, you go home. Get some rest and take over in the morning. Maybe you'd like to drive Deidre home."

"Sounds like a plan," I whispered back. Brenda finished her check-up and Heather went to make her call. Deidre had quieted, and was just hiccuping from time to time. I held her hand and sent her my best healing vibes.

This relatively calm moment was short-lived. Patty Peacedale came rushing into the room with Father Dan Lyons from St. Peter's whom she'd waylaid in the hallway.

"It's okay, Cass," Deidre muttered to me. "Get yourself a cup of coffee, and one for me, too—something with real caffeine." She smiled faintly at her two visitors. "Ah, Father Dan. So good to see you, always a friendly face in troubled times."

"I'm so sorry to find you here, Deidre." The priest's concerned expression reflected what we all felt, that too many burdens had been heaped on Deidre's slight shoulders.

"And Patty, how did you...?"

"Oh, my dear, dear girl. This is Plymouth, after all. I was at this Personal Concerns Committee Meeting—we drive old folks to their doctors' appointments and you know, whatever—and one of the committee members...her son drove the ambulance that brought you here. Small world, isn't it? Now how are you bearing up? I won't offer to pray with you, because I'm sure you'll want Father Dan for that. Even though you're Wiccan and all, I'm sure you still enjoy the comfort of your roots. But if there's *anything* I can do... anything at all..."

I tiptoed out of the room, hoping that Nurse Brenda would not show up with the morning-after pill until Father Dad had departed.

◌◍

Deere didn't get far this time. In the end, most criminals do the stupid thing that gets them caught. Loitering in Plymouth, possibly in hopes of another spot of sadistic revenge, had been his undoing. And I like to think our finding skills helped, too. Heather stayed with Deidre; Phillipa and I got together at Fiona's to give her whatever support we could. While Fiona was dowsing the maps, Phillipa kept flipping tarot cards out of the deck, keeping one hand ready to dial Stone on her cell phone.

"Ah ha!" she said. "Six of swords." The card showed two heavily-cloaked passengers being ferried across the water.

"I'm finding him at Logan airport," Fiona murmured. "But the detectives are expecting that, aren't they?"

"It's that damned false passport he's using. If he's disguised himself at all... What we really need is the *name*." And then I had a brainstorm, *Sylvie!*

"I wonder if Sylvie..." I began.

"Why don't you bring her here, then," Fiona said.

I found Sylvie in the Kellihers' garden, raking old leaves out of the flower bed. She was more than willing to help, and twenty minutes later we arrived back at Fiona's.

"Whew! After that rush across town, it may take me a bit to quiet and center," Sylvie said. I handed her a clipboard of Fiona's. She took the Sharpie out of her bag.

Fiona put an arm around the girl's slight frame. "Think of the trees, dear. How peaceful they are, leaves whispering in a breeze that has come for a thousand miles to bring news of other lands...." And more in that vein, reassuring murmurs that would have put anyone into a light hypnotic state. Listening, Sylvie's breathing became deeper and surer. She gazed out the window at Fiona's backyard where maple trees had just uncurled their earliest pale green leaves. The pen began to move.

"*Thou art a priest forever, thou art a priest forever, thou art a priest....*" the Sharpie wrote over and over again.

Phillipa called Stone. "He's at Logan Airport disguised as a priest," she whispered. "No, I don't know the name... wait...."

As we three continued to watch the girl's hand avidly, the words being scrawled on the clipboard changed, growing more angular and darker.

"Father, oh Father Raymond, oh Father Raymond Flint Dominican Dublin Dominican Dublin Dominican Dublin..."

"I think we do have the bastard. He may be going by the name Father Raymond Flint. Or his contact is Flint. Dominican order, Dublin."

Sylvie finally dropped her pen to the floor, and nearly folded up there herself. Fiona rushed to make her a strong cup of sweet tea. Phillipa and I held her between us on the sofa. "Bravo! That was grand," Phillipa said.

Sylvie picked up the pages she'd written and studied them without recognition.

"What's this, then?"

"This, my dear," I said, "may very likely be the identity that Nick Deere is using to get out of the country. You simply pulled the name right out of his brain. Now *that's* what I call a useful skill in channeling."

"I almost wish he'd go to Ireland and never come back," Sylvie said.

"No, you don't," Fiona assured her, coming in with a tray of tea things. "Then you'd never feel safe for a moment, wondering if he were going to return and find you. No, my dear, prison is the place for Nick Deere. The longer the sentence, the better."

"Some eternal circle in Hell would be nice," Phillipa said.

༄

Fortunately for Sylvie and Deidre, there would never be a need to testify at trial. Faced with the witnesses and evidence against him, Deere agreed to plead guilty and offered the district attorney a tempting deal, evidence against his two arms-dealing uncles, in return for a reduced sentence.

At his allocution, the jaunty Irish lad looked somewhat worse for wear. Apparently he'd been knocked around while awaiting his day in court. Beyond complaining that a dentist visit to save some loose teeth had been denied him, however, Deere refused to blame anyone for his pitiable condition, perhaps fearing worse consequences. Will Ryan's many friends on the force had not taken insult and injury to his little widow Deidre with equanimity.

Judge Lax imposed the agreed-upon sentence for rape, kidnapping, and assault, 15 to 18 years at MCI-Cedar Junction state prison at Walpole. Sylvie took a full deep breath at last.

Deidre said darkly, "I doubt he'll live out that sentence." I didn't even ask our mistress of poppets what she meant. I preferred to imagine it was precognition not voo-doo. Admittedly, narrow escapes from menacing psychopaths did invite one's principles to stray a bit from the white side of magic.

౭ง

The news about Lazaro was hardly as reassuring. And we might never have known the real story if it hadn't been for Freddie letting her fingers do the walking through CIA computer documents. While her mentors were training my daughter-in-law to use her notable talents for penetrating other systems, sometimes to freeze them and sometimes to extract information, she was learning more than they bargained for.

Freddie was too careful, however—thank the good Goddess—to impart information about Lazaro over the phone. Meanwhile, as plans had moved ahead for Iconomics' new Boston branch, Freddie had found an apartment in Cambridge she liked and invited me to have a look and a lunch.

The second floor apartment was lovely, with long windows that filled the sizeable front room with light, two bedrooms, and oh luxury! two and a half bathrooms. There was a miniscule office and a retro green and white kitchen overlooking a tiny back garden maintained by the owner and landlord, who lived on the first floor. I congratulated Freddie on such a wonderful find in the heart of Cambridge.

"And so much more spacious than the usual studio or *pied à terre*," I rejoiced.

"Oh, I'm sure we'll expand to fill the space available," Freddie said vaguely.

The weather smiled on us with balmy breezes and blue skies, belying the notion that April is the cruelest month. Freddie had packed a hamper with gourmet goodies of the Harvard Square variety, and we picnicked on the banks of the Charles.

"Wow, this is heaven," I said, sighing over the sunshine, the chardonnay, and the excellent cheese and bread.

"As the poet said, 'a loaf of bread, a jug of wine,' and whatever else he was ranting about." Freddie, who clearly was not a Fine Arts Major, leaned over and continued *sotto voce*, "And speaking of ranting poets, your friend, the fiery you-know-who, will not see another day of jail in the U.S. of

A. He's been whisked away to South America where he has miraculously attained full citizenship in Argentina, the late great home of escaping Nazis."

"Well, if there's a little good in all this, it's that he won't ever dare come back. I wonder how the Argentinean authorities will deal with his future arson exploits. And if his books of poetry will continue to sell in this country."

"I am not the clairvoyant, you are," Freddie pointed out, refilling my glass with wine and offering me another slice of veal pate. *Heather will never know*, I told myself, holding out my plate. I noted that Freddie was sipping Perrier with lime, and then, like tumblers in a lock, all the bits and pieces clicked into place.

It was like being hit with a thunderbolt, but I restrained myself. At least I would have time to prepare a proper face for the formal announcement. Some newly pregnant gals don't want to push their luck by caroling about it too soon.

Eyeing me over her glass, Freddie said, "I figured you'd guess. And to think that I haven't even told Adam yet."

"He'll be thrilled. It's a boy, I'm guessing."

"Oh sure, my mother-in-law the great guesser," Freddie laughed. "What I want to know is why you never play the lottery."

"Because it doesn't work in a mundane material way. And failure dilutes one's sensibility. Great guessing ought to be saved for really, really important stuff, like this."

Then we embraced and cried, empowered by the beauty and fecundity of spring. Later, I would try to sort out my feelings about being a grandmother, and what sort of grandson would emerge from the genetic whammy of talents he'd receive from his mom and my son.

BELTANE, MAY DAY
CHAPTER THIRTY-THREE

Tra la! It's May! The lusty month of May!
The darling month when everyone throws
Self-control away.
It's time to do a wretched thing or two,
And try to make each precious day
One you'll always rue.

—Alan Jan Lerner

Beltane! Surely the loveliest of Sabbats. (Okay, okay, that's what I say at every holiday.) After the tragic and terrifying events of the past months, we five had many reasons to celebrate our emergence from winter, although our joy was inevitably tempered with sadness over Deidre's loss of Will and her dangerous encounter with Deere. With her innate courage and strength, however, Deidre had been moving steadily from anger and depression toward acceptance, and even hope, that blessed light that shines, often unexpectedly, in the darkest closet of ourselves.

At the exact opposite of the year's wheel from Samhain, Beltane is the beginning of summer and a time to rejoice in life, the abundant fertility of the earth. It's a casting off of winter's deprivations and monochromatic depression. Beltane colors are bright and sassy, predominantly red and white, laced with of vivid splashes of green. And, of course, anything else you fancy. At Beltane there are always fires (Beltane translated literally is "fire of Bel") sometimes constructed of the seven sacred woods. And as we had decided to hold our ceremony at Heather's, she had gone to some trouble to construct the fire at the center of the wide stone circle on her ample acreage with apple, ash, beech, blackberry, hawthorn, hazel, and maple splits of wood.

"I hope she isn't expecting us to leap over that thing on a broom," Phillipa whispered to me.

"Oh, you won't need a broom to leap, dear," Fiona averred. "And it will be a very small fire, after all."

We'd decided to begin at dawn, not only to observe the Pleiades star cluster rising at sunrise as it did every Beltane, but also to wash our faces in dew, a nice old custom said to give a youthful aura to the skin. Well, maybe that was promising a lot, but so did those ads for anti-aging lotions at many dollars a half-ounce. *Dew at Dawn* was, at least, a free gift available to all.

Beltane is the one Sabbat that has never been Christianized, but then all that emphasis on fertility and fire might be difficult to sublimate. Like Samhain, Beltane is the other "no time" of the year, when the veils between the seen and unseen worlds are thinnest, psychic intuition (of which I had had my fill this year!) is keenest, and the world of faery is nearest. As priestess of this event, Heather cast our circle, blessing the sacred space with garlands of flowers. Wearing a tipsy circlet of mayflowers in her hair, Fiona lit the May fire, and it was, indeed a small one well contained among rocks.

Phillipa invoked the four directions and welcomed all the good influences they would bestow upon our lives.

Beltane hopes are meant to bud, leaf out, and fruit, so we wrote our wishes on slips of paper and tied them to the branches of Heather's three apple trees. My wishes had been for Freddie and the health and happiness of the boy who would be born next winter, and for Deidre, healing and hope.

Led by Fiona, who could, at times, be mighty fleet-footed for a supposedly arthritic senior, we leaped over the fire in our different styles, Heather gracefully, Deidre lightly, and Phillipa and I with fearful determination. Then we danced... and chanted...and danced...and raised a cone of power we could all feel coursing through our bodies. At a signal from Heather, we threw up our hands and released the energy of our desires into the Universe of Infinite Solutions.

Deidre and I did an improvised ceremony with purified salt water and incense to rid our aura of the frightening events we had endured and to protect us in the future. Would it work? Would we never be tempted to play the Justice card again? In the tarot, that would be a queen with an upraised two-edged sword in one hand and a golden balancing scale in the other.

"Cakes and ale" on this occasion was translated into a superb May Day breakfast served by Captain Jack on the Morgan mansion's huge patio, with traditional bannocks and many pots of his amazing boiled coffee.

"By the way, Cass," Fiona said to me casually as we sipped our mugs of steaming brew. "I *am* calling an owl to be my familiar. It was your idea, and an excellent one. Perhaps you will help me with your potent good thoughts?"

"With all my heart and soul," I said. "I believe, in some other life, your companion was a commanding, glittering owl. I mean, actually I saw it. And how could I see scenes of other lives, unless they are true?"

"Because, as Yeats has said, our memories are part of one great memory. Isn't that fantastic enough?"

∽

At home later I surveyed my burgeoning herb gardens with pleasure. Everything was coming into fragrant life, a joy to behold. Didn't I sense the spirit of my grandma, perhaps I even saw her pluck a sprig of mint and breathe in its freshness with a smile.

But there was yet one more divine tradition of May Day. The weather blessed us with a warm evening. Joe and I took blankets and wine down to the beach, closing the insulted dogs into the house, and in the time-honored way of this sacred time, did our sensual best to assure the fertility of the earth. Hidden in a nest of blankets, we made love at first reverently and then with abandon as the music of the rushing waves mingled with our own wild heartbeats and cries of pleasure. Under the spell of Beltane, we belonged to each other more deeply than ever.

And did the earth move? Ah, yes! Even a few stars fell through the sky leaving in their wake dazzling trails to wish on.

∽

When we got back to the house, sandy, bedraggled, and a little drunk with wine and sex, the two dogs looked us over and smelled our clothes with disgust.

At least you could have taken us along for a good run on the beach, Toots!

"Okay, Scruffy. We'll take you out now for a few minutes if you promise to go straight to the beach with no detours to trail skunks."

Me, too. Me, too. I held my breath. Was that? Yes it was Raffles, who looked at me with hopeful eyes and one of those heartbreaking canine smiles, and spoke to me for the first time.

Joe groaned. "Scruffy really didn't ask us to go back down to the beach, did he?"

"Yes. Actually, they both did. Come on, honey. We'll take that nice jasmine bath I promised you as soon as we come home."

"Both of them? Raffles, too? Listen, promise me you'll never take another dog into this family. I wouldn't want to be outnumbered."

"Don't worry. I think I'm going to be way too busy this year."

"Yeah, with what? I put my foot down on the crime-solving spree, didn't I?" The Aegean blue eyes looked at me sternly.

"Not to worry," I said. "I'm concentrating on being a grandma, as good as my own. Oh!"

"What? What is it?" Joe's gaze followed mine, looking out the windows opaque with night shadows.

"Never mind. I just thought I saw something. Let's take the dogs for that walk I promised them." I wanted to get back outside right away to see if I could glimpse again that delightful faery face I had just seen at my kitchen window. Was that my grandchild waiting in spirit to be born into the world?

૭∿૭

The Circle

Cassandra Shipton, an herbalist and reluctant clairvoyant. The bane of evil-doers who cross her path.

Phillipa Stern (nee Gold), a cookbook author and poet. Reads the tarot with unnerving accuracy.

Heather Devlin (nee Morgan), an heiress and animal rescuer. Creates magical candles with occasionally weird results. Benefactor of Animal Lovers Pet Sanctuary in Plymouth.

Deidre Ryan, prolific doll and amulet maker, energetic young mother of four.

Fiona MacDonald Ritchie, a librarian and wise woman who can find almost anything by dowsing with her crystal pendulum. Envied mistress of The Glamour.

The Circle's Family, Extended Family, and Pets

Cass's husband **Joe Ulysses,** a Greenpeace engineer and Greek hunk.

Phillipa's husband **Stone Stern,** Plymouth County detective, handy to have in the family.

Heather's husband **Dick Devlin,** a holistic veternarian and a real teddy bear.

Deidre's husband, **Will Ryan,** Deputy Fire Chief of Plymouth

Cass's grown children
Rebecca "Becky" Lowell, the sensible older child, a family lawyer, divorced.

Adam Hauser, a computer genius, vice president at Iconomics, Inc., married to **Winifred "Freddie" McGarrity**

an irrepressible gal with light-fingered psychokinetic abilities.

Cathy Hauser, who lives with her partner **Irene Adler,** both actresses, mostly unemployed.

Thunder Pony "Tip" Thomas, Cass's Native American teen-age friend, almost family, whose tracking skills are often in demand.

Fiona is sometimes the guardian of her grandniece **Laura Belle MacDonald,** a.k.a. **Tinker-Belle.**

Deidre's family
Jenny, Willy Jr., Bobby, and **Baby Anne**
Mary Margaret Ryan, a.k.a. **M & Ms,** mother-in-law and devoted gamer.
Betty Kinsey, a diminutive au pair, a.k.a **Bettikins.**

The Circle's Animal Companions
Cass's family includes two irrepressible canines who often make their opinions known, **Scruffy,** part French Briard and part mutt, and **Raffles,** his offspring from an unsanctioned union.

Fiona's supercilious cat is **Omar Khayyám,** a Persian aristocrat.

Phillipa's **Zelda,** a plump black cat, was once a waif rescued from a dumpster by Fiona.

Heather's family of rescued canines is constantly changing, and far too numerous to mention, except for **Honeycomb,** a golden retriever and so-called Therapy Dog who is Raffles' mother.

Cass's Banana Surprise Breads

4 large ripe bananas, pureed in food processor (2 1/2 cups pureed bananas; can add a little non-fat yogurt to make up measure)
4 cups all-purpose flour
2 teaspoons baking soda
2 teaspoons baking powder
1 teaspoon salt
1 cup (2 sticks) butter, softened
2 cups sugar
4 eggs at room temperature, beaten
1 cup coarsely chopped walnuts (optional)
1 (10-ounce) jar maraschino cherries, drained, halved
1 cup chocolate chips

Preheat the oven to 350 degrees F. Butter 2 standard loaf pans and line the bottoms with thin plain paper or wax paper. Butter the paper also.

Prepare the bananas. Sift together the flour, baking soda, and salt.

By hand or with an electric mixer, cream the butter until light. Gradually add the sugar, beating well. Beat in the eggs, then the banana puree. Stir in the dry ingredients. Fold in the nuts, cherries, and chocolate chips.

Divide the batter between the pans. Bake on the middle shelf for 60 to 65 minutes, until a cake tester inserted in the center comes out clean and dry. Cool 5 minutes in the pans on a rack. Loosen the breads on the sides, and turn them out onto the rack. Peel off the paper, turn them right side up, and cool completely.

Makes 2 breads. They will keep a week wrapped in foil and refrigerated, or they may be frozen for longer storage.

LaVergne, TN USA
18 August 2010
193798LV00006B/113/P